ELDER BORN

THE BEING OF DREAMS BOOK 3

CATHERINE M WALKER

❀ Created with Vellum

ALSO BY CATHERINE M WALKER

THE BEING OF DREAMS

Shattering Dreams

Path Of The Broken

Elder Born

EMERGENCE (Available late 2021)

Unwanted (Coming)

Sacrifice (Coming)

Defiance (Coming)

NEWSLETTER

If you'd like updates of my progress, promotions and advance notice of when the next book comes out drop by my website and join my newsletter.

You'll receive a copy of the character chart that I created while I was writing the Shattering Dreams and a few other extras as well.

Visit my website to get started!

Catherine M Walker

1

LOST

Feeling the other slip into slumber, Amelia sobbed, pressing her hand to her mouth to muffle the noise. She didn't want to risk waking her other self; these moments free of torment were rare enough.

Even though she was aware that she only continued to exist in that small corner of her mind, her surroundings seemed so real to her.

Here she'd constructed a bare cell-like room with two small barred windows. The rough stone floors bit into her bare feet. Her now filthy and ripped linen shift afforded no protection at all against the damp air. Amelia pushed her matted hair from her face, looking up at the windows. She shivered. Sometimes, when she grew brave enough, she would peer out the windows and see the world that her body—that the *other*—was walking through. Amelia liked to think the other was insane, that it wasn't her committing all those horrible acts.

That she hadn't killed her king.

Those moments were rare. Even here there were other moments where she revelled in the power she possessed. The power her master had woken in her. In those moments she could see so clearly that she'd been a possession, a thing. She'd been the perfect lady, spent her life perfecting being the kind of possession that would appeal to people with power. It was what she'd been trained for, what *all* those of her birth and rank were trained for.

Oh, women like Jess existed—controlling who they were, forging their own path and destiny in life. They were exceedingly rare in her social circles. Yet even Jessalan, for all intents and purposes, was a kept woman. Everyone knew that the crown prince, William, favoured her. While he was looking her way, no one else would dare. That of course explained her favoured position within the court, why she had been allowed to get away with the behaviour she had. None but the king could gainsay the crown prince's will.

Amelia stilled, her eyes widening in horror. She didn't believe that about Jess. She hadn't really hated Jess, even if many of the other ladies in court had. Jess had been kind to her. The *other* hated Jessalan. Amelia felt a tear tracking down her cheek and beat the side of her head with her fists. Whispering to herself in an internal litany.

Remember who you are.

The Lady Amelia Strafford had always had her eyes firmly on Prince Alexander, the Fourth, as most young and some not-so-young ladies of the court had. She had known from her father that the crown prince was not for her, nor likely any of the peerage of the realm. She took her father's council seriously since, as Lord Strafford, he was a close friend to the king and the highest in rank of all the other lords. Or she *thought* she'd accepted his advice. Until now.

Amelia whimpered, pressing her fist against her lips to stifle the noise, even though she knew she really wasn't doing any such thing. Her body slept soundly, under the control of another. She felt uncontrollable tremors start, sweeping through her body as her fear, loss and despair rose up to overwhelm her once more. As reason fled, she screamed, flinging her torment out into the world.

The scream choked in her throat as Amelia froze.

There it was again. The noise was faint but distinct: a sucking noise as if air was being expelled or displaced, a clatter of chains, the deep metallic clunk of a key turning in a lock echoing around this cell of her own imagination.

A steady rhythmic thump, exceedingly loud in the confines in her own mind—a sound she was all too familiar with. Booted feet in a measured tread walking towards her. Amelia cowered, scrambling backwards, a part of her mind aware that the rock wall that had been at her back receded as she crab-walked away from the approaching intruder. The cell with the windows she'd imagined receded, fading from her sight to be replaced with encroaching darkness.

A scream ripped from her mouth as she felt a force wrap around her, halting her retreat.

THE WORLD DARKENED, power cracking down from the sky, bolt after bolt raining down in counterpoint to the deep rumbling that rolled above. William could feel the reverberations through his bones, his breath catching in fear. Colour faded away as if a thin grey lace curtain hung between him and the world around him.

He stiffened as the screams started, faces of lords he recognised calling out in fear and pain as they died. They died to protect him. William looked, across the heads of the milling terrified lords to see the king, his father, on the dais, under attack.

William grappled with his sword, trying to push his way forward only to feel hands grab him desperately. He looked down, struggling and cursing the lords that prevented him from going to his father's aid.

Father!

William screamed the word as he saw the splash of red spray from his father's throat, a stark contrast to the grey world around him.

Everything shifted, and the hands grappling with him, pulling him back, all of them turned grey too, except for the red — the red of blood spreading from the throats and hearts of the owners of the hands, as they died around him, a shield of flesh. Others' cries rang in his head as their hands pulled him back.

No, you must live, Your Highness!

You are our king now!

His father's body hit the ground and the dark figure of his assassin turned, and William screamed at the pain lancing through him. As the darkness rushed towards him he saw it cut down all that stood in its way. The bodies crumpled as the darkness passed them by, all disintegrating as they fell.

As the screaming rose in tempo, the grey swirled, a deep rhythmic thrum sounded and there was the sudden rustle of feathers as the giant eagles rose from the grey ash all around him. William watched as the people and palace around him flaked away to ash, swirling in the wind. The screams mingled and became the mournful cries of the giant birds of prey as they flew in every direction, the beat of their wings taking them away from the centre of the madness. Their cries rang out, spreading the word across the realm— the king was dead.

2

REGENT

Elizabeth knew at some point she would stop, and allow herself to grieve over the death of her father. Directly after his death she couldn't afford the luxury of locking herself away to mourn privately away from public eyes. Healers had surrounded William in those terrible days after the attack, always with him. They'd forced him into a healer-induced slumber, to allow his mind to heal. That had been the first decision of many to require her approval as Regent. It had only taken a few moments at her twin's bedside, seeing him writhing in pain, to be convinced the healers were correct.

With the king dead and William hurt and unconscious, the burden of running Vallantia fell to her. Elizabeth hoped that William continued to improve; despite being next in line for the throne, she had no desire to sit on it permanently.

Elizabeth smiled. Of course she wasn't alone in carrying this burden. William had assured her in the weeks leading up to this tragedy that their little brother had grown up a great deal. Then again, William always did have a soft spot for Alex. As it turned out, she should not have doubted his assessment. Alex had surprised her the most, stepping up in his role of

Fourth and lifting a great deal of the burden from her shoulders.

Kyle, despite the tragedy surrounding the corruption and betrayal of his own sister by the Order, shared the responsibility. She shouldn't have been surprised. Lord Kyle Strafford had been in William's confidence for years and despite the party boy image he'd maintained, he was well aware of the affairs of state. He was his father's son, after all. A great deal of his time was spent standing not only at Alex's shoulder in his position as a Companion of the Fourth—the Fourth's Blade, to be precise—but he stood at her shoulder as well to offer advice. His take on the internal family politics and scrambling for position among the peerage of the realm had proven invaluable on more than one occasion.

Of course it didn't help that rumours were running wild throughout the realm faster than the heralds and scholars could spread word. It always amazed her how fast rumour could fly. It seemed the more tragic the news, the faster it ran. The king's death and the circumstances surrounding it had plunged the whole country into mourning.

On the back of the terrible tragedy, the news of William being hurt as well nearly brought on a panic. Reports indicated most believed he was either mortally injured or already dead and the news was being kept from the people. No number of proclamations seemed to assure the bulk of the population that while he was badly hurt, William would be fine. She doubted they would believe it until her brother was well enough to make an appearance and shoulder the burden of the crown publicly.

Elizabeth shifted in her seat, impatiently pushing a lock of her long brown hair behind her ear after it escaped the pins meant to hold her hair up in its intricate design on top of her head. The conversation around the table was going around in circles, and she resisted the urge to look up at Kyle and roll her eyes.

"I understand that protocol dictates that the new monarch be crowned directly after the interment of the previous one, Lord Kastlemain." Elizabeth kept the impatience out of her tone only with great effort.

The lord was new to his seat on the council, elevated on the death of his father, although he wouldn't officially be acknowledged as the lord of his family line until William ascended the throne and conceded him the rank. Elizabeth and her brothers hadn't been the only ones to lose people in that fateful court session.

He looked at her, startled by the interruption. "Yes, Your Highness, but perhaps we could crown him in absentia. It would reassure the people."

"I doubt it. If we did that, it would add more fuel to the flames and convince them that we are hiding his death." Kyle's tone was acerbic. Elizabeth felt her lips twitch in response. Kyle could and did break the polite boundaries to slap down the councillors when he deemed it necessary.

Lady Cain frowned. "He will, of course, have to get married promptly as well. We should give thought to a suitable queen."

Elizabeth tried not to groan watching the lady preen. She was also young and newly risen to take her house's name on the death of her parents. It was too obvious she fancied herself as the perfect match for William. If Elizabeth knew one thing about her twin's taste in women, she was certain that Lady Cain was not in the running, even if he'd had the option.

Elizabeth had been appalled when Kyle informed her that his father, the Lord Strafford, had negotiated a contract on behalf of her father, before his death, to accept the Imperial Princess of Sylanna as William's consort. That had prompted her to send a hasty message to the Empire requesting they hold off on their intended journey to court.

Elizabeth was saved from replying to Lady Cain's comment due to a commotion. Horns sounded outside the walls, and booted feet thundered down the corridors. She could hear doors slamming and yelling echoed in the hallways outside. Her eyes widened as the doors to the council chamber burst open.

Kyle was in front of her, his sword already drawn, only to relax his stance marginally at seeing the Elite. Elizabeth realised she hadn't even seen him move, nor been aware that she'd also stood.

"Your Highness, it's Crown Prince William. He's missing from his bed."

Kyle swore and the room stilled as he put up his hand, a dire look of concentration on his face indicating he was using his powers. Elizabeth bit her lip as the colour started to drain from Kyle's face before he suddenly chuckled.

"It's all right. Stand down the guards, Alex has found him. William will be fine." Kyle refrained from saying any more.

There was only one way that Elizabeth could see how William could have gone missing from his rooms without anyone knowing where he was, particularly given how many guards surrounded his suite. The lords and ladies at this particular council didn't need to know the finer details—that their future king now numbered amongst the Kin. Not at this point in time, anyway.

Elizabeth let out the breath she hadn't been aware she'd been holding. She nodded, resuming her seat. Running to her brother's empty room would not achieve anything at all. She waved the council members back to their own seats, determined to ignore Lady Cain's rather poor attempt to raise her own status further. After all, the woman was destined to be disappointed since William was promised to another. Elizabeth smiled to herself and relaxed, Lady Cain and her advances were her brother's problem to sort out. Not hers.

~

When the phantom screams filling William's head finally ceased, he sank to his knees, whimpering in relief at the blessed silence. A familiar voice spoke to him out of the grey fog that surrounded him.

It's all right William, I'm sorry we left you. You burnt off Aaron's sleeping draught faster than expected.

Arms pulled him into an embrace and William felt himself tremble as relief washed over him; he rested his head, unresisting, on his brother's shoulder, accepting the shelter and comfort for what it was. He laughed suddenly, remembering all the times he'd comforted Alex when he had been a boy. Now it seemed the tables had turned. He opened his eyes and watched in awe as the bleak nothingness that had surrounded him was replaced in a wave rippling out from Alex. His nightmare—the giant birds of prey, the blood and the spectres of those who'd fallen to protect him—banished, being replaced by a peaceful glade. Tall trees, rushing water from a river, the sweet songs of birds, dappled light filtering through the trees and a soft warm breeze wafting through.

Where are we?

William was perplexed. As lovely as this place was he didn't recognise it at all.

You transported yourself into the veil. It brought your nightmare to life around you. We're still in the veil but I thought you might find this place a little better. It's a recreation of a glade in the deep forest near that inn that you tracked me to.

William felt himself relax, he pulled away from Alex and found he was suddenly leaning against a log that he could've sworn hadn't been there a moment before. He shrugged, guessing that if Alex could spin this whole glade from the veil, he could create a convenient log to lean on. They sat in silence.

William took a deep breath and felt muscles he hadn't realised were tense slowly relax.

Is it wrong to wish I could stay forever? Hide from the duty birth compels?

William heard the almost wistful tone in his voice and smiled at himself.

Alex turned to look at him.

No. You won't though, you just need time to heal. Your survival instinct kicked in, ripping a part of your mind that you didn't use wide open all at once. It's a lot to take in as suddenly as this has all happened.

William grimaced.

You seemed to cope through all of this.

Alex chuckled. *Oh, don't worry, I wallowed in self-pity enough for the both of us growing up.*

You had reason to rebel, Alex.

William tilted his head to one side, looking at his little brother who seemed to have grown up, leaving behind his youthful reckless behaviour. He appeared calmer, more self-assured, the image of the man he was always destined to be shining through—the man William had never doubted Alex would be.

Alex snorted. *I've been an arse.*

Perhaps just a little. William couldn't help but laugh at Alex's newfound self-deprecation.

Honestly, William, you are doing well. Unlike you I don't remember a time when I couldn't hear everyone talking in my head. Alex looked at him soberly.

William felt his eyes widen with the implication of Alex's calm statement. He closed his eyes, remembering Alex screaming in terror as a child, awake or asleep, night or day. He'd thought... They *all* had thought that it was due to witnessing their mother's death. It had never occurred to him or anyone that Alex heard the tormented cries of the others with the Taint, the Sundered Ones. William shuddered; he was an adult and knew what was happening, yet it was enough to drive him to madness. To imagine a child having to face this... William felt horror wash over him. He'd thought he knew what his brother had been going through. Now he realised that he'd had no idea at all.

I'm sorry, Alex. I didn't understand.

Mother used to maintain a shield on me, before she died. Or left. I think I learned to block them out instinctively after that for self-preservation. Alex shuddered, a pained expression flicking across his face. *Aaron also did his best, but I think I broke through his efforts even as a kid.*

William closed his eyes and took a deep breath, then pushed himself up, looking around.

I never wanted to be this. I still don't.

Alex looked at him apologetically and stood up, slapping him on the back. *Then you'll be relieved to know, you're still not. You have all the pain and confusion, with few of the benefits.*

William turned his gaze back to Alex, looking for any sign he was lying to him.

I won't turn into you?

William nearly held his breath as he realised how rude and petulant that had sounded even in his own head. He relaxed, ducking his head and grinning sheepishly as Alex laughed.

No William, Aaron says you have a little more power than you did; you'll heal a little better, enough to make you Kin but not that much more. I'm surprised you had enough power to even get into the veil. Please don't do this again.

William grinned, then looked around, perplexed. *Don't worry, I don't know how I got here in the first place. I should probably get back.*

Your dramatic disappearance caused a major stir. Horns were blowing, guards were slamming through the palace room by room and thundering out the gates. Kyle and Jess have convinced them all you are fine for now, but I think you are right. It is best you get back before we try their patience too far.

William felt Alex's power envelop him, and he shuddered at the sudden cold as they moved through the veil, nothing but a grey blur of motion before they appeared back in his room. He realised in that stillness that Alex was shielding his mind, yet upon stepping out of the veil he found he was the focus of many outraged eyes glaring at him.

The commotion that ensued wasn't the type of voices that Alex could block from his mind, however, and he had to endure it patiently. William traded a rueful glance with Alex and contemplated asking his brother to take him back to the sanctuary before deciding against it. The others would only get more agitated and at least two of them were quite capable of tracking them down in the veil. He would have to face the music sometime, and it might as well be now.

ELIZABETH NODDED AT THE PROPOSAL, one of the few sensible ones and the only one that could be implemented forthwith.

"Yes, Lord Stanton, we can at least move forward with planning for the coronation. If you could look up the protocols and get back to us all?" Elizabeth smiled her thanks at the lord for the breath of sanity he conveyed.

Elizabeth looked up expectantly as her servant appeared at her elbow.

"Your Highness, Crown Prince William is back in his rooms."

Elizabeth nodded her thanks and stood, Kyle but a moment behind her as the councillors followed suit, flustered at being caught flatfooted.

"Thank you for your input, my lords and ladies. That will

be all for today." Elizabeth turned and left the stunned councillors with Kyle on her elbow and the Elite following.

She nearly groaned thinking about the absolute panic that had ensued when William had disappeared from his bed. Even though it had only lasted for a few minutes, it would not help. Nothing could be more certain than yet another rumour spreading about the prince's disappearance.

She didn't have far to walk down the wide opulent stone corridors, since the meeting room she'd been in was just off the Royal Wing. She ignored the framed paintings on the walls, and the cool breeze that wafted through the large windows showing the manicured gardens of the palace beyond them. It was normally restful. Today she was intent on getting to William.

The Elite on duty outside his rooms snapped to attention and the attendants pushed open the doors for her, allowing her to breeze into William's rooms unhindered. She halted just inside the doors to see her twin being berated by Jess and the healer, much to Alex's obvious amusement. She gathered her little brother was enjoying the fact that for once it wasn't him getting yelled at for being irresponsible.

Elizabeth realised, seeing them standing there side by side, how much alike they looked with the same dark brown hair, piercing blue eyes, tanned olive skin that showed off their well-honed muscular bodies. That had been one of the few differences between them: William had always had a little more flesh on him than Alex. It seemed with his recent illness the extra flesh had dropped off William's frame, making the resemblance between the brothers unmistakable.

"William, sit down before you fall down." Elizabeth hadn't raised her voice, yet it was enough to command the attention of those in the room. In the silence that fell, William smiled apologetically and sat down with a sigh.

Alex waved Aaron off as he approached with what looked like one of his sleeping draughts.

"William's fine for now Aaron, I have him. Be assured I will let you know if his pain levels increase. William just burned off your last potion and without a mind barrier in place, well, between his nightmares, pain and newfound powers, the confusion that creates is enough to make anyone flee into the veil." Alex settled into one of the chairs near William, still grinning.

"William, I know you didn't mean to, but please try not to do that again. The guards were in an uproar." Scolding him might have been more effective if she hadn't been grinning in relief to see her twin alive and well.

"Sorry, honestly everyone. I have no idea what I did or how I got there. If Alex didn't show up to rescue me I'd probably still be sitting there not knowing how to get home." William at least had the grace to look contrite.

Jess shook her head and placed her hand on his shoulder as she took a seat on the armrest of his chair.

"As soon as the rawness in your mind recedes, we'll teach you how to shield." The anger had drained from Jess as soon as she'd realised that William was fine.

Elizabeth walked over to William and kissed him on the cheek.

"Take all the time you need and get better, William. We can manage until the healers clear you. Please at least *try* to follow their instructions." Elizabeth smiled at him, and then with a nod to the others turned to leave, with Kyle but a step behind.

3

MADNESS

Shhhh... don't despair, my girl, I am still with you.

Amelia tried to scramble back yet felt herself held in a firm hand, her head twisting around desperately looking for the source of that voice. The person remained invisible to her yet the voice was oddly familiar. She paused, her eyes widening at that thought.

She did know it wasn't Kevin. His voice was one she was overly familiar with. Tremors ran through her, though she doubted her body actually reacted, but her mind was convinced that she was trembling. Amelia squeezed her eyes shut, trying to push her fear aside.

Who are you?

You know me, child, I have always looked over you. There was amusement and a hint of kindness in the man's voice.

It was a man, of that she was certain. He was also correct; she did recognise his voice although she suspected he was not someone that she had ever met in person.

If my master discovers you talking to me, he'll punish me. He'll hurt you as well.

The voice chuckled with amusement. *Never fear, Amelia. That one does not know you are still present.*

Startled, Amelia felt her eyes pop open, even though she knew her body still slept on the cot in the room she'd been assigned, unaware and undisturbed by this nocturnal visitor.

He... he, doesn't?

No. His voice was emphatic.

I thought he left me here to torment me.

A shimmering started in the blackness and a man stepped out of the darkness, walking towards her confidently. Amelia froze, looking up into the dark eyes of a man who appeared to be only a little older than herself, yet somehow she felt certain that he was much older. He knelt near her and she felt the sensation of being gathered into his strong arms. She stiffened as she felt a hand stroke her hair.

No. I'm sorry, I should have spoken to you sooner. My name is Aiden. I created this safe haven for you. Kevin does not know you have survived.

Fear thrilled through her as Amelia felt his power caress her, roll over her. Somehow she knew: This man didn't want to help her. He wanted to possess her, to take this small part of herself that she had left and twist it to his own ends.

No!

She surged up, thrusting out with her powers, pushing that spark that was the other one away from her, slamming the door to her cell shut, large bolts clunking into place. She scrambled to her feet and ran, the long, dark, cold stone hallway of her mind stretching out before her as she fled.

4

TREATMENT

Darkness.

His world was narrowed to darkness.

Sometimes a roof; he would be aware of it. The healers would coax him to feed during these times, then the moment he feared. They would give him that liquid, fire and pain would run through him causing him to convulse, lose control. He didn't even scream anymore.

I will kill your son.

A whispering mind voice in the dark, causing a woman unbearable torment. At times he would realise the cruel voice causing heartbreak and driving the other to madness was his own. It was his own voice, yet it wasn't. Another ordered him, controlled him. Despair crashed in on him every time he became aware of what he was doing, but he was unable to stop or fight what they did with him.

They.

The nebulous 'they'.

He didn't know who they were, yet the enemy, *his* enemy, used him to kill. Or he had killed under the direction of that evil once. Images would flash in his mind that caused him no end of torment when he realised what had been done.

What *he* had done.

Still the enemy didn't know what the boy had done to him either.

This small spark of himself that woke again, in the back of his mind. The boy's own mind voice ordered, begged him not to kill. That injunction still existed in his mind, compelling him. The child even then had been stronger than the evil that tried to use him.

He remembered, the images showed him they had tried to take him out to kill others, to compel him to kill again. They had power—he could feel the compulsion racing through his mind. Yet the boy's voice, echoing in his mind over the ages, overrode theirs, always. He would stand there merely looking at his prey, until they compelled him to return.

The other, the one that would cause him to shrink away and shudder if he could, appeared in his head, seemingly delighted.

Ah, Brian, you can be of use yet. I cannot touch her, she is too well guarded. You can, though. You can plague her dreams both waking and sleeping with nightmares. The dark cruel eyes and the laughter had burnt into his mind.

He'd been used to torment her since, and little did she know he was incapable of following through on the threats they made him issue.

Brian's eyes flashed open, as they did sometimes, yet his keepers paid him no attention even if they noticed.

Something had changed. He had the distinct feeling he was more aware than he used to be, although his keepers still hadn't worked out the spark of self-awareness the little prince had granted him. He was no longer chained and shackled, groggy from medication, yet he still could not leave this place. They had ordered him not to.

The boy had grown, the child's voice that still echoed in his head, ordering him not to kill. The eyes, those bright blue, intense eyes way older than they should be in such a child, still burnt into his mind. That child was no longer a child; he'd grown, and there were times Brian heard whispers of the man the boy had become. He'd come into his own. He was looking for his enemy. Brian wasn't sure how he knew, only that in that moment, when his intended victim had turned him from his purpose, a link had been established, and he was able to sense him still, that old order compelling him to kill the child coming up against the order for him not to kill.

Brian looked blankly up at the ceiling. A small part of his mind willed the child, now a man, to find him. To find them. He settled down to wait. In a small act of defiance, he sent his own words out to the woman he tormented.

Find me.

Kill me.

Brian knew the madness he suffered from was still there, but now it was as if it was held back by another. He'd become aware by degrees, with the female healer's face swimming into his vision. At first her face had seemed friendly. She'd had a sweet smile. Time had taught him better. He remembered her voice and words promising to help him, pushing back the blackness of his despair, at least for a very brief moment in time.

Time had taught him better.

"I'm your new healer, Brian. I've changed your medication, and it's why you are more aware. I'm sorry, it is better for you to be conscious for this part of your treatment." Her voice faded before continuing in his head.

Let me in, Brian. I'm here to help you get better.

Brian contemplated what she meant by letting her in. He couldn't stop her; he hadn't been able to stop any of them since this nightmare had begun all those years ago. Her face faded as her eyes seemed to grow larger and burn into his mind. He gasped, back arching from the cot, as dagger-sharp pain lanced through him. Brian felt the strong hands of others restraining his arms. Her hands grasped his head, he could feel each of her fingers gripping his skull, forcing him to keep his eyes on her own, forcing him to endure her torment.

Session after agonising session his world narrowed to her eyes boring into his own, his body convulsing as fire burned through his mind and every fibre of his being. She didn't even allow him the release of screaming. He had no way to tell how long the sessions went on for. When her face swam into his vision and her hands clamped onto his head, her cruel voice insisting he look to her, a small part of him retreated, whimpering like he was a small hurt child, shivering in fear and pain in that tiny sanctuary the boy had created for him. It terrified him even more that she would find his hiding place and pull down those mental walls before the one who had once been his Queen, now reduced to a mad woman, or her son the young prince found him to end his miserable existence.

5

CULTIVATION

Elizabeth sighed with relief as she walked into her own private domain. It had been a long day and while she did not begrudge William the time to heal, she wished the process was faster. Hearing a throat clear behind her, she turned to see Abby.

"I'm sorry, Your Highness, but Lord Kastler is here to see you." Abby gestured into the public-facing sitting room.

Elizabeth stifled a groan. Of all the lords to seek an audience. There were times she felt like the man was mentally undressing her. He was a tedious, grubby lord of a once great house who'd lost its relevance generations ago. Successive scions had squandered their fortune, and now they wallowed in their past glory without facing their current reality. She also strongly suspected their moral compass to be well off track.

"Thank you, Abby." Elizabeth plastered a pleasant smile on her face and walked into the sitting room.

Lord Kastler looked up as she entered, his eyes tracking down her from head to toe. Elizabeth suppressed her irritation. She knew very well the man had pressed her father to make her his consort a time or two since she'd come of age, a request that her father had denied on every occasion. All talks of consorts were off the table with her father's death, but she doubted William would have a different position on that score. She fully expected that once the current situation died down, her brother as king would endorse the contract between her and the son of the Speaker for the Heights Protectorate.

Elizabeth ignored the lord's hungry eye and took a seat opposite him.

"Please sit. What is so pressing that it could not wait or have been said in council, Lord Kastler?" Elizabeth almost winced as some of what she was thinking was reflected in her tone.

"Your Highness, it's a delicate matter that I thought best to bring to your attention privately." Lord Kastler sat down, his eyes darting around the room.

Elizabeth gazed at the man, instantly on guard. Something about the lord's manner made her wish that Alex, Kyle or Jess were present. As diffident as the man seemed to be, there was just something about him she did not trust. He made her skin crawl.

Of course, it was probably nothing. Still, she'd spent enough time training under the weapons master's tender mercies and felt the flat of Jess's blade in training often enough that she was confident she could defend herself against him should he get inappropriate. That and she knew very well her guards were just on the other side of the doors. Her thoughts about having to defend herself against him gave her pause, unaccountably causing a shiver to run down her spine.

"Go on, my lord." At least her tone was a little smoother this time.

"It's about Prince William. It is such a shame he was so badly injured in the fight that killed our king." Lord Kastler licked his lips, his eyes darting over to her before looking away again.

"Indeed, Lord Kastler." Elizabeth wished the man would get

to the point. Although at this odious little man mentioning her brother's name, the skin on the back of her neck crawled, and a sharp protective instinct rose in her.

"Perhaps it is time to admit he is not suited to ascend the throne, Your Highness." He hastily held his hands up. "It is far from his fault, but I think I speak for many of us in saying you would be a better candidate for the throne. I would support you as the Queen of Vallantia."

Elizabeth felt her back stiffen in response to the lord's suggestion and took a moment to throttle down her anger.

"What you suggest amounts to treason, my lord. I will never usurp my brother's throne. You have my permission to withdraw. I'd suggest you retire to your estates for a time." Elizabeth stood, turning her back on the flustered lord and swept back into her private domain, fuming at the man's cheek.

LORD KASTLER PAUSED with his glass halfway to his mouth and looked up as the door to the sitting room opened. He took a sip and waved in Scholar Clements and Master Healer Kevin over to join him.

"Please, my friends, join me." He gestured to his servants and smiled warmly at the men. It was a sad thing, the state of Vallantia, where the so-called leaders of the realm ignored a plague spreading and destroying lives. He'd known the royal family was removed from the concerns of the regular people, but he hadn't known by how far. Even with a noble prince of the realm slaughtered by filth, his own father and his brother paid no mind. Of course they had never admitted that Prince Daniel had been killed by a Sundered, but word had spread about the brutality of his murder.

Of course, the fact that the royal line had allowed itself to be contaminated and had refused to deal with the youngest son spoke volumes. He'd waited patiently, but it had proven that even the second most powerful family, the Straffords, could not be relied on to do their duty in the king's stead when necessary. It came down to him. His own family could be traced as far back as the Rathadon and Strafford lines. There were times when one of noble birth had to stand up and do their duty. Now was that time. He was only sorry his father and his father before him had not seen the clear duty that had fallen to them, as Vallantia had regressed to a state where the commoner suffered under the depravity of those born with the Taint.

Kastler straightened in his chair, filled with pride. At least he was going to bring greatness to his family line. It was time for the Rathadons to be disposed of and a new royal line to be put in its place.

The leader of the ancient Killiam Order sat down, with his second in command but a moment behind him. Clements smiled at the servant who handed him a drink, taking a moment to savour it before nodding.

"I admire your loyalty and willingness to stand up for the people, Lord Kastler." The elderly scholar raised his glass in salute.

Kastler tried to adopt a modest expression, such as one a future king would adopt. Arrogance would be the unravelling of the Rathadon monarchy. That was not an example he chose to follow.

"It is my clear responsibility, Scholar. Someone has to stand up for the people of Vallantia when those in power blatantly ignore their duty." Alfred held out his drink to the servant for it to be topped up. The man bowed his head, dropping some of the rapidly melting ice into his glass and then topping it up from the glass decanter with the smooth amber liquid. It was a new acquisition he'd tasted at the palace. He'd sent his people to find out what it was and obtain a shipment for him.

"It is so rare to see one amongst the peers of the realm put the people before themselves." The healer, Kevin, leaned back and sipped his drink as he regarded him.

Alfred smiled, accepting the praise. It was his due, after all, and when he was king, these two would be rewarded, as would all the members of the Order for their sacrifice. His mind turned to symbols. He licked his lips and looked back at his guests.

"Lady Amelia couldn't attend with you this evening?"

The lady was tainted goods and accused of heinous crimes, including killing the old king, yet she was still a symbol of an old family line. The Strafford family went back to the founding of Vallantia, much as his own did. He hadn't broached the subject yet but he thought it would be well to take her as a consort. That was if their cause couldn't take Princess Elizabeth alive; *she* would represent the old family line even better than Lady Amelia.

Kevin looked up at him, his mouth turning down.

"Lady Amelia is resting right now. The weight of all these events rests on her. I'm sure you understand, my lord."

Alfred held up his hands, distressed that the lady would feel so badly. After all, it was not her fault her own brother and her Consort Elect had proven to be numbered among the most vile monsters in the world. That she had been forced into action to defend her own life and the Order against the perfidy of the king and court must be causing her unimaginable heartbreak.

"Of course, it must be terrible for her. If there is anything I can do..." Alfred trailed off, not wanting to be too transparent with his intent.

"Of course, my lord, I am certain it will comfort Lady Amelia that you are concerned for her welfare. I'm sure you understand she remains in my care for now."

Kevin's face showed compassion for his patient, which was something Kastler could perfectly understand in a healer, even if it did stand in the way of his own plans. After all, the girl didn't have to be sound of mind to produce an heir for him. When it came to it, she could just be a figurehead and he could get an heir on one of his serving girls. It was a simple thing to claim the child when it was born and dispatch the mother.

"I completely understand, the current situation must be traumatic for her."

"How did Princess Elizabeth take your proposal?" The old scholar's tone was almost absent, glancing at him as he sipped his own drink.

Alfred felt himself stiffen. "She was most unreasonable. She rejected me out of hand, thus my return here early. I thought it better to give her anger time to cool."

"Ah, that's too bad." The old scholar's face crumpled in sympathy.

Alfred had to remember the old man had been a tutor to the royal children at one point before the king had chased him from the palace, for trying to warn everyone about the plague that the Tainted represented as they swept the realm. It had to be heart-breaking for the old man to see the depths of depravity the children had fallen to once he'd been forced to leave them to fend for themselves. Alfred nodded, vowing to himself that the old man would have a place of honour on his council when he was king.

Kevin smiled at him. "It's probably for the best. You don't want the princess to send you away permanently. You provide vital information for the Order with your position in the palace."

Alfred returned the smile, relieved. "Well, she can't entirely. That would take the monarch, since she refuses to take the crown in her brother's place." Alfred shrugged. "That reminds me..."

Clements looked at him. "Reminds you of what, dear boy?"

"My man in the King's Guard? He has information for us." Alfred bowed his head at the two men.

Both of them had praised him when they found out about Commander Janson being uniquely placed to give them information. They'd been most insistent that he let them set up another way for Eric to contact them, so now when his nephew wanted to contact him, the special bottle of liquor he kept in his permanent day rooms at the palace was turned around, so its label faced the window.

Except it wasn't he that would go to meet Eric in town, it was one of the Order's other men. Kevin would send someone into town and meet up with his nephew. It was a shame that he couldn't go himself anymore. He'd found the clandestine meetings to be thrilling. It made him feel as if he was really contributing to their cause, like a real rebel. Kevin and Clements had stressed to him that he was too important to risk. That thought made him sigh. It was something he would have to get used to as the future king.

Kevin smiled, stood, and clapped him on the shoulder. "Well done, Lord Kastler. I'll send someone to go meet with him."

Alfred smiled with pleasure at the praise. He did like to be useful. He waved his permission as both men requested to be excused and raised his glass to be topped up once more.

KEVIN WAITED until they were down the hallway and out of earshot before he turned to Clements. He raised his eyebrow at the man who'd been the closest thing to a friend he'd ever had in all the years he'd been alive.

"You do realise, Clements, that vile little fool truly does believe he will be king?"

A wolfish smile spread on the Scholar's lips as he chuckled.

"Ah yes, I know. I cultivated him when he was a child."

Kevin's eyes narrowed. "At the same time as Daniel?"

The loss of Daniel had been a blow to the Order. Kevin had been slow on the uptake during those years and had missed the prince's conversion into a loyal follower of the Order. Still, he understood Simon's dilemma as the Skull Lord. When Alex had gone after him, if he'd been in Simon's place he would have thrown Baine and not so coincidentally Daniel himself to Alex's blade as well.

After all, as far as Simon was concerned the man deserved it for coming up with the scheme to direct the blame for the kidnap attempt on the League of Skulls. Not so coincidentally it pointed the blame squarely at Simon, since he was the Lord of Skulls. That had prompted the damn Rathadon prince to come after Simon and clean out the bulk of his den of carefully cultivated talented killers. His friend didn't have his own desire to rule, but he didn't take kindly to someone trying to take what was his.

The League of Skulls had been a small group but each and every one of them had no compunction at all in doing what Simon asked, particularly when it was the wealthy they were targeting. Unlike his Sundered, Simon's people had the brains to follow through on instructions without being carefully controlled. Simon and his people had been extremely useful. Kevin was sure they would have proven even more so if Alex hadn't cut through the bulk of them. Now, thanks to Alex, Simon only had a few handfuls of them left. Still, Simon had placed some of those that were left to guard the approaches of their current base. That had been of great benefit to Kevin, keeping their current position right under the nose of the king a secret.

"Of course. I didn't want to leave anything to chance." Clements's eyes glittered.

Kevin frowned, and then he laughed as understanding dawned on him. The old man was extremely crafty.

"You cultivated followers in the Rathadon, Strafford and Kastler families!"

"Well, the Kastlers were the fallback. They are hardly the most powerful of families but they are one of the older ones that can trace their line back to the founding of Vallantia." Clements shrugged, dismissing the death of his most strategic convert.

Kevin paused outside the door to his own rooms and had to grudgingly admit he admired the old man.

"I'll send one of my people to see what it is that the good commander has for us. Given who his uncle is, the man is surprisingly competent." Kevin's eyes narrowed at the thought.

It was a shame Janson would have to die. After all, how could a man who'd ultimately turned his back on his sworn duty be trusted?

He caught Clements's nod of approval, watching him as he walked further down the hallway to his own rooms before retiring himself.

6

DUTY

Kyle looked up to see one of the house staff enter his rooms.

"My Lord Kyle, your father Lord Strafford is here to see you as you requested. He's in the guest lounge waiting your convenience." The man bowed and retreated as Kyle nodded his acknowledgment.

He looked at Bennett as he assisted in strapping on the last of his weapons; dark brown eyes much like his own stared back at him as he caught his long-term servant's eye in the mirror.

"Well, this could be an interesting conversation." Kyle wished he had a better idea of how his father was going to respond.

Bennett held out his hand to one of the other staff for the jacket, then helped Kyle into it with a practiced ease.

"Yes, my lord. Maybe he just needs this prompt." Bennett's face and tone showed no indication of what he was actually thinking.

"Perhaps. I guess I'll find out soon enough."

Kyle tugged at one of the sleeves of his formal jacket. He hadn't worn his less formal attire since the death of the king.

That awful night and the failure they all felt keenly was something his mind shied away from. He'd stepped up in his role of Companion of the Fourth, taking turns with the others in guarding William while he recovered. Kyle shuddered. That they had nearly lost William as well didn't bear thinking about. When he hadn't been standing guard over William, he'd been on Elizabeth's shoulder as she took up the burden of ruling as regent while her twin brother and soon-to-be king recovered.

Kyle shook his head as he gave his appearance one final check in the mirror. It surprised him, really. He felt, given everything that had happened to him, that a wizened, old grey-haired man would be staring out at him. Instead, his black hair showed no sign at all of age, no more than the rest of him did. He still looked fit and healthy. The man that looked back out at him was lean and well-muscled, with no signs of the excesses and strain he'd put on his body in recent times. Of course his appearance was aided by the power of the veil that flowed through him and a body that would heal most things—except his head being parted from his body or a dagger in the heart. Kyle smiled tightly.

Realising he was delaying, Kyle straightened his shoulders and turned resolutely towards the doors of his suite. Bennett was a step ahead of him, well used to his mannerisms. The doors swept open in front of him without him having to ask and Kyle stepped out into a living room area, ignoring the comfortable, inviting lounging chairs. This room was private, shared by himself, Alex and Jess with doors from their individual suites all leading into it. Visitors to their private domain in the Complex of the Fourth were never brought in here unless one of them gave permission.

His measured pace soon took him into the wide corridor leaving the palatial, private lounge with its throw rugs and wide windows looking out into the garden courtyard behind him. He walked the short distance down the corridor, and lights flared to life ahead of him as he walked. Kyle grinned. It was a habit he'd picked up from Alex and with such a small use of power he wasn't even aware he was doing it half the time. He was absolutely certain Alex never notice he was doing it or that it left some in the court a little wide-eyed in panic.

A servant on the doors opened them on his approach and he passed through, leaving the private areas of the Complex for the more public side. Kyle noted the presence of the Elite, always around since the assassination of the king, and gestured for them to withdraw before turning his attention to his father. As his father began to rise on his arrival, Kyle grimaced and waved him back into his seat.

"Please, we are in private and you are my father."

"Even so, you are dressed for court and as Fourth's Blade you do outrank me." His father smiled at him but complied, relaxing back into the leather chair.

Kyle shook his head. "I have enough people bowing and scraping to me, seeking favours. I may be dressed for a formal court session but until I'm out of the Complex there is no need for formality."

As he spoke Kyle assessed his father. It saddened him that he seemed to have aged so much in the last year. Recent events had weighed heavily on him. As much as Kyle didn't want to add to his father's burden, Kyle knew it was past time for Lord Strafford to step back up into public life.

"Well, you did summon me here, Kyle, and in your official capacity I take it, not as my son." There was not even a hint of resentment in his father's tone.

"I did. Father, I understand your grief, but Elizabeth needs you." Kyle almost sighed as he saw his father's face crumple a little before he caught it and his expression smoothed.

"I failed Michael."

Kyle made sure to hide his impatience. "We all failed our king that bloody night in the court, Father."

"The mess with your sister, the things I said to Alex, to Michael."

"Yes, he was your king, but he was also a parent himself and your friend, Father. He understood your pain and grief over what happened to Amelia. He didn't blame you."

"I should have been there, at his side..."

"Then you'd be dead too." Kyle smiled grimly as his father looked up at him, shock written all over his face.

"I might have been able to save him."

"Amelia knew full well you served as the King's Blade. She would have killed you." Kyle knew he was being blunt, but sometimes a little bluntness was needed to cut through wallowing.

His father winced. His mouth opened then closed abruptly although Kyle was relieved to see he was at least thinking things through.

"What do you need from me?"

"Elizabeth needs you. Where you lead, the others will follow. At least start to appear in court again and on the council sessions. Either Alex, Jess or myself will stand at her shoulder, but the older councillors will be less inclined to argue with her if you are seen to be supporting her."

"They are being difficult?" His father looked at him, frowning.

Kyle's eyes narrowed. "Lord Kastler suggested Elizabeth usurp the throne and take him as her consort."

It had been a close call when he'd found out. His first instinct had been to place a blade in the man's heart and ending his miserable existence. The lord had no idea the only reason he was still alive was because Elizabeth had ordered Kyle not to kill him where he stood. She'd said there had been enough death and Vallantia didn't need to add yet another member of the peerage to the death count right now.

"He did *what*?"

Kyle smiled grimly at the outrage that shook his father's voice. He'd known that little piece of information would get to him.

"Without you being there as Lord Strafford, he's been puffing his chest out and seems to think his family can rise in influence."

His father laughed. "He has none, but I take your point. I will start resuming my duties again. I've spent enough time mired in self-pity."

Kyle stood and placed his hand on his father's shoulder, squeezing it.

"Elizabeth understands your grief, Father. If I could let you withdraw from official duty I would, but we've lost too many and the realm needs your leadership right now."

"I'll do what I can and return to council duties from tomorrow." His father ducked his head, then stood. "Son, about Amelia..."

Kyle nearly sighed, he'd hoped this was the one time they wouldn't have this conversation. "Father, we've discussed this."

"Please Kyle. Alex never gave up on you when you were in trouble and Amelia is your sister." Kyle could hear the ragged edge in his father's voice.

"I know and I would have been lost more than once if it weren't for Alex, Jess and William." Kyle stared at his father with seeming calm; his father didn't need to see that the topic hurt him as much as it did him.

"Then at least try to help her. Please. She's my little girl, I can't just forget her no matter what she's done. Damn it Kyle, even if she's lost as you say, she wouldn't want to live as what they've turned her into!"

As grief clouded his father's face, Kyle felt like he'd been hit over the head as he realised what his father was asking of him. To actively track down Amelia, and if he couldn't save her, to kill her. While it was his job since she had killed the king, it didn't mean he liked to think about it. Of course, as soon as William healed and they could start looking for the Order, it was likely that was exactly the position he'd be forced into.

"Right now my duty is clear, Father, but rest assured I will look for Amelia."

Kyle didn't apprise his father that there was nothing left of Amelia to save. It was an argument they'd had before. He'd come to the conclusion that if it helped his father to think that he could save Amelia then for now the lie could stand and serve its purpose. Kyle let the relief he felt show that the cloud of grief that had been dogging his father since Amelia's capture had finally lifted. His father left the room with his head up and purpose in his stride once more.

7

RECALL

Healer Chelsie Kattaline ran her finger lightly over the finely crafted metal implements, accounting for all of them—the scalpel, scissors and clamps. Not that she was expecting any of them to be gone, it had just been a long time since she'd actually checked them. Her fingers lingered on the scalpel, being careful not to cut her finger on the fine blade. They had belonged to her father before her and she didn't want to risk losing any of them, particularly now. Rolling up the leather bundle, she walked across to her pack sitting on the wooden chair at the table and placed the small bundle of implements securely in the side pocket. As a real healer with talent, she didn't need or use the old implements much, but on occasion they came in handy, especially if she expended a great deal of energy healing others. Looking around the small sparse stone cottage, she felt a twinge of regret. It had been a good home while she had been here with her assigned villages.

Healers throughout the realm had been given a recall order, no matter the consequences to the local communities they served. Word of the disgusting attack on the Healers' Guild had spread through their own channels, and in light of that attack she could understand why the recall had been issued. It was better this way.

Chelsie flipped the cover of the pack closed, doing up the buckle with practiced ease. She picked up the saddle bags and looked around what had been her home one last time. She had left her home many times in the past—it is what a journeyman healer did. This time, unlike the previous times, she knew that it was unlikely she would be back. Sighing, she turned her back on the orderly cottage, walking out and closing the door quietly behind her.

CHELSIE SWUNG her leg over the saddle and slid off her horse, tying the reins to the rail in the front yard of the property on the outskirts of the village. It was early, so she knew Ronald and his wife would still be home. Neither of them worked the land; the farmers around them used it. Instead they worked in the village. They had their reasons to want some privacy without neighbours being on top of them and watching everything they did.

Chelsie approached the door, knocking on it with three sharp raps. She heard the creak of the floorboards approaching the door, which cracked open a little. Ronald's eyes peered out at her, a look of relief flooding his face as he saw her.

"Healer, it's good to see you. The boys are ready." Ronald opened the door and Chelsie saw both boys sitting at the table in the small kitchen, dressed and ready for travel.

"Good morning, Tyson, Jimmy. It's good to see you are ready. Say your goodbyes to your parents. Quick now, we have some distance to travel today." Chelsie smiled at them both, hoping to cover her impatience.

Constance ushered both boys towards her, looking at her earnestly with tears welling in her eyes.

"You will look after them, Healer?"

"Of course, Constance. This new treatment they are going for is doing wonders for those who bear the Taint." Chelsie placed her hand on the woman's shoulder, pulling her in for a hug.

Ronald had gone around the corner of the house and led an old horse that looked like it had seen better days to the front. It was already laden with saddle bags that Chelsie guessed held some possessions for the boys. Constance ushered the boys out and both parents hugged them before helping them mount.

"We could only afford the one horse but Jimmy hasn't gone through his growth and Tyson hasn't reached his full stature yet either." Ronald looked at her, wringing his hands.

"It will be fine, Ronald. You are doing the right thing by your boys. I'll ensure they receive the best treatment." Chelsie hugged them both one more time, with Ronald pressing a small coin purse into her hand as she drew away. She smiled her thanks and, mounting her own horse, she led the way off the property out onto the road that led out of town. She wanted to be well under way before there was much other movement on the road. Hopefully they'd run less chance of encountering anyone that recognised either her or the boys.

CHELSIE PULLED her horse into a crop of trees with a sigh of relief. The early start had been beneficial and as she had predicted they had met no one on the road that knew them. Not that it would matter that much, just the fewer people who knew which direction she headed or where she'd disappeared, the better. Walking her horse to the clearing, she dismounted, pulling her saddlebags from her horse. With concise instructions she ordered the boys to do the same. Tyson looked a little confused since they hadn't gone far, but complied without asking any questions. His little brother was a few years younger and didn't know enough about what was going on to show any hesitation at all.

Chelsie extracted a bottle of the medication she used on the Tainted. This was the new distillation they'd all been instructed to use. From what she could see, already it was having better results. She poured a measure and looked over to see Jimmy not far away.

"Come here, Jimmy," she said quietly.

The boy looked up from where he lay on the ground corralling in a beetle he'd found with sticks. Climbing to his feet he complied, and at seeing the measure in her hand he opened his mouth without comment, swallowed the liquid without complaint. Having done as requested, he went back to playing with his bug.

Tyson looked at her calmly and walked over to her. Taking the stopper out he paused with the bottle halfway to his mouth, glancing up towards the sun which wasn't anywhere near the middle of the day. "I did have my tonic this morning, Mother made sure of it."

Chelsie smiled lightly, touching his hand and pushing it towards his mouth. "Of course you did. We have a long way to go today, this extra dose will see you both out until we make camp tonight."

She saw the flicker of hesitation on Tyson's face and tried not to grind her teeth; he was of that age where he'd started to question everything. Then he shrugged and swallowed the medication.

Chelsie watched him closely while keeping the unconcerned smile on her face; it had been a double dose of the medication. Tyson looked down, confused as his hands started shaking a little and the bottle fell from his fingers, landing with a dull thud. His knees buckled and he sank to the ground, his whole body trembling. She side-stepped adroitly as he slumped forward onto the ground, shudders sweeping in reaction to the drug in his system. His mind was open to her own and she'd been forging the ties between them that would bind him and his powers for months now in preparation.

Help me.

His voice whispered in her mind, still not understanding she had overdosed him on purpose as she compelled him to sleep.

Trust me, Tyson, this is for the best. I'll save you.

Chelsie stood up as soon as she was assured Tyson was asleep. She felt it would be easier with Tyson asleep when they were taken to the enclave. Turning, she noticed that Jimmy lay curled up on the ground where he'd been playing with his beetle. The lad was much easier to deal with, but she didn't need him wailing all the way back to the Order. She had considered leaving him behind when Master Healer Kevin had issued her recall; he was certainly too young to be useful right now. Then she had reconsidered. He was young now, but he already showed signs of being strong in the taint when he grew. Potentially as strong as his brother.

Tyson was Tainted and strong, but that wasn't such a deterrent with the new medications and what she'd been told could be achieved. She had no doubt her master would be pleased with her offerings. He had after all ordered her to bring any of the Tainted she was treating with her.

Chelsie smiled, satisfied.

8

CONNECTIONS

Amelia picked her way through the rapidly expanding tent enclave that spread out across the open grounds outside Lord Kastler's estate. The Order's followers now called this place home. Their numbers had increased as Lord Kastler called in the minor lords that looked to him and their personal estate guards. At least now they had trained fighters, although she doubted they could stand long against the King's Guard, let alone if the combined ranks of the Elite fell on them. Still, they would provide a welcome distraction when they were discovered.

Amelia had no doubt the king would learn about their location eventually. Or he would when he recovered and took the throne. Amelia did not know William as well as her brother Kyle did, but she had no doubt about his reaction when he found out. William would not take the rebellion of one of his lords lightly. It would be better if they had found elsewhere to be, but her master insisted they stay put, that they were safe enough at least for now.

She had been keeping an eye out for any sign of movement from Jess and in particular her brother, expecting they would commence searching for the Order's new location. Yet she had detected no movement from them at all. That gave her hope that William's condition was far worse than she'd thought. At least if she kept a lookout, she could warn her master that it was time to move unless they were ready to take up the fight.

While the consensus was that the death of the old king had been a massive blow, it had become more than apparent that William had survived his shock transition. At least that is the word they were receiving from the palace. It remained to be seen if he'd done so with his mind intact.

None here, not the other members of the Order nor any of Lord Kastler's people, knew who or what her master was.

Her eyes narrowed, and a smile curved on her lips. They would be right to fear if only they knew the truth. She had no doubt they would run in horror seeking the king's forgiveness and protection if ever they found out.

A group of men clustered around one of their camp fires turned to watch her as she walked past. The men laughed, all trading glances with each other. She gathered she was the subject of their conversation. One of the men stepped out in front of her as she went to go past them.

She smelt the alcohol on his breath and seeping out of his skin as he leered down at her. "So what do you say about you and me having some sport to relieve the boredom of sitting here?"

A rank unwashed smell assaulted her as he stepped in closer, pressing his body up against her. Amelia didn't flinch away from him, she simply stared up at him coldly. He looked over his shoulder at his companions and laughed, one of his hands attempting to grope her to pull her into his tent.

Amelia contented herself with snatching his arm, twisting it as she stepped back. He squealed as she pressed his wrist at an angle just short of breaking it. He thumped into the ground.

She glared at the man's friends who'd gone to take a step

towards her, and wrenched the struggling man's wrist back further so he squealed again, halting their progress. Amelia dropped the guard's arm and strode away, aware that every eye was on her as she passed through the camp.

~

ONE THING about being free from the constraints of the Lady Amelia Strafford persona was that dressing didn't take anywhere near the amount of time it used to. In her old life she'd looked down on Jess, who wore her hunting and training clothes whenever she could get away with it. Many of the ladies of the court had gossiped snidely about her normal state of dress. It hadn't helped that Jess looked good no matter what she wore; that was what really stung for many of the ladies. Now that Amelia didn't have to pretend to be something she wasn't, life was so much simpler.

Amelia slid the last of her blades into its sheath and turned, smiling coldly. Now it was time to pay a little visit to the poor excuse of a man who'd laid hands on her. Killing him in front of his friends would have been educational for them all, but her master preferred her to be a little more discreet.

Concentrating, she pulled herself to that other place. Her room receded and she shuddered as the coolness washed over her. She could see her room still but it was like a thin grey veil hung between her and the room she'd been standing in moments before. Under her master's guidance her understanding and abilities had progressed rapidly, the knowledge he'd gained over the years overlaying and replacing her own ignorance. Pushing herself further away from her room, she moved the short distance outside the castle walls. With the encampment spread out below her, she paused to look down at the glowing fires of those who couldn't fit within the confines of the estate walls.

Amelia saw the small cluster of tents where she knew her quarry was located. Keeping the thinnest of veil between her and the real world, she stalked around those still around the camp fire. A wolfish grin lit her face—he wasn't one of the ones still at the fire. Eyes narrowing, she walked over to the tents. She passed by the ones with the flaps open; she could see they were empty. Only two of the tents in this cluster had their flaps secured. Amelia walked carefully around the back of the first one. Pulling in more power, she inched forward, shuddering as she felt the fabric of the tent wall slide past. It was an unnerving feeling, one her master assured her she would outgrow as she became more powerful. A sigh of relief escaped her lips when she found herself standing inside the tent.

Looking over to the man inside, she saw he'd only just retired for the night as he was disrobing. Her eyes glinted.

Success.

The foul man who'd accosted her today had peeled off his shirt and was now fumbling at the belt of his trousers. Amelia closed the distance between them, and she observed him shudder as she stood at his back, her knife drawn. Her grin widened. He had a touch of the talent.

As he unbuttoned his trousers and started to pull them down, Amelia leaned forward.

You will pay for what you have done.

He started and straightened, holding his pants with one hand as he looked around, his eyes wide in sudden fear.

You will never harm another woman again.

Die!

He gasped and swung around wildly. Amelia let go of the veil as he swung to face her. He dropped his hold on his pants, stumbling as he tried to back off in horror, falling back onto his cot, his legs tangled in his trousers. Amelia fell on him, her blade flaring with a life of its own and flashing, plunging into his chest. His hands clawed weakly at her arm as she grabbed what passed for a pillow and clamped it over his face, muffling his gurgling. As his eyes bulged in terror, she took delight at the last twitches of fear rolling through the man just before the light died from his eyes.

Amelia rolled off the beast, her eyes half lidded, taking the moment to enjoy the pleasure that swept through her as the body of her kill cooled beside her.

KEVIN LOOKED over as Amelia arrived, smiling at the success he'd had with her. It had taken years of work and trialling many combinations of the toxin, constantly refining it. The numbers who had died in the process over the years didn't bear thinking about. That refined toxin in combination with his tame journeymen having strong mind control gifts had proven the essential key he'd been searching for all these years.

Amelia was firmly under his control now to the point where he didn't have to constantly order her around. Once she had been broken to his will—mind control restraints in place with the assistance of the toxin to help break down her natural resistance—she was his. Now, she followed his direction without him having to consciously control her. Humans with weak minds and abilities were easy to break, particularly once he had infiltrated the Healers' Guild and learned their methods. Normal humans had proven to be so fragile.

"You're late."

"Yes, Master. There was a matter I had to deal with."

Kevin saw her eyes glow, her lips parting. He knew she had killed. His Amelia loved to kill. Not that he cared whose life she extinguished. The shell that had been Lady Amelia had been shattered, falling from her in a million pieces, scattering, lost. Having been trained in the healers' ways he knew very well there was no redemption for her. Controlled from childhood, she belonged to the Order. Smiling, he patted the seat next to him.

"Anything to report from your patrol?" Kevin couldn't help the proprietary feeling he had for Amelia.

He'd known of the rumoured long-term problems of taking another Kin as a thrall. If one or the other was subject to madness, then both could spiral down. That wasn't something he'd wished to court. He wanted power, he just needed the right tools—and he finally had them. He'd noted in himself the benefit of his method of control was that while he definitely felt possessive of Amelia, she was undoubtedly his. That ownership, her enslavement, wasn't causing him to spiral into madness. Of course, now that he was certain her treatment was complete, he was careful not to be in her mind all the time. Amelia was also stable. He felt that was the key to holding madness at bay himself.

"I could find no indications of anyone around our base, Master. Jess and my brother are nowhere close." Amelia rarely showed any emotion, but right now he sensed satisfaction.

"Good. What about your former consort-to-be?"

Kevin felt his irritation rise as it tended to do any time he thought about the Rathadon prince. Any of them. They were all so infernally lucky and yet showed no ambition to really rule as they should.

"Alex is still at the palace, where he has remained since the death of the king. He killed the last Sundered dispatched to the palace, I saw that much before its life was extinguished. At a guess, he is at his brother's side a great deal of the time." Amelia's eyes grew cold as she thought about her former lover. "I don't believe he has discovered our connection, Master."

Kevin contemplated her, surprised; a hint of emotion had entered her tone as she spoke of her former Consort Elect. He would have thought by now Alex or his friends would have discovered the connection. Granted, the bonds between his slave and Alex weren't useful for much other than plaguing her former lover with dreams. He couldn't be compelled by them and was immune to the toxin. It had been useful to nudge the prince into believing he was in love with Amelia, but she still had to work at it, as distance between them when Alex had fled the palace and the confusion caused by transition had shown. That damn Rathadon luck had run true yet again. Still, Amelia had managed to surprise him on more than one occasion.

"What use do you think you can make of them, besides unsettling his sleep?"

"I think I can make him come to me, Master."

Kevin sat up straighter, suddenly intrigued. "Why would he do that?"

Amelia's smile turned predatory. "Alex still believes the feelings he has for me are genuine."

Kevin thought about her observation, looking at her steadily.

"So you think he will be driven to come to you?"

"I know I can get him into bed with me. He'll believe he really does love me."

"Then what?"

"Then I can bring him to you, of his own free will." Amelia's eyes lit with anticipation.

Kevin chuckled at the thought of a Rathadon prince submitting to another's will. Still, he had nothing to lose from allowing Amelia to try, and potentially a lot to gain. At worse Alex would have some sleepless nights plagued by nightmares.

"All right. I'm not certain it will work. The Rathadon princes, with a few exceptions in their history, tend to have a well-ingrained sense of honour and duty. In my interactions with Alex I haven't seen any sign that he lacks those family traits." Kevin nodded his approval for her scheme. "You will look to your own safety at all times. I will not risk you. If you met up with him, take one of the others with you as backup should Alex try anything."

Amelia frowned at the last. "I'm sure if I can get Alex into my bed I can control him. If Alex senses anyone else, he will retreat."

"Very well, Amelia. I will teach you both how to shield appropriately so not even Alex will know anyone is watching over you."

Kevin stood and led her out of the room. It wouldn't do for him to give her lessons here. Anyone might walk in, which could lead to questions he wasn't ready to answer right now.

9

LEARNING

Alex realised he had never sat in on one of his brother's training sessions before, especially since his brother was years older and trained predominantly with his own Elite, just as Alex normally trained with his own guards with the addition of Kyle and Jess.

"Hold!" Alex let the frustration he was feeling show.

He sprang up from the bench and strode towards his brother, ignoring the guards as all eyes swung to him, obviously shocked at the unexpected interruption.

"Alex, I—" William cut off abruptly as Alex drew his own weapon. He swallowed nervously.

"Damn it, William, you need to pay attention." Alex frowned at the Elite present. "You aren't doing your king any favours by encouraging sloppy sword work."

William grimaced. "I know, I'm sorry. I've had a lot on my mind of late."

Alex didn't soften his attitude. "You nearly died, William. Our father did die. The enemy we face can appear between you and your guards. You are not powerful enough to live if an assassin slices your throat open. You need to be good enough at blade work to stay alive long enough for us to all get to you."

William winced at his words, yet Alex steeled himself against showing any sympathy. Granted, William was only just recovering from a near-death experience, but that didn't mean he shouldn't train properly, particularly since Aaron had given him a full clearance to train. He knew very well the Master Healer would not have done that if William wasn't well enough. He himself had ignored the advice that he wasn't healed and should rest more often enough to know. Eyeing his brother's protective training gear, Alex smiled grimly. Just as well he was wearing it. For the first time in what was likely years, his brother was going to need it.

"I know Alex. I've just always been busy. There's always been other things that were more pressing." William looked down and, sighing, he raised his own weapon, flipping it in salute, indicating he was ready.

"Your life is a priority, William." Alex flipped his own sword and launched into an attack without hesitation.

He forced William to respond, going through the techniques he'd just tried to perform, although badly. Every time William showed poor, sloppy form, Alex lunged, slapping him with the flat of his blade in reprimand—something his brother's people obviously hadn't done for the longest time. Finally, as William's responses became slower with fatigue setting in, he called a halt to their session.

Alex smiled at seeing his brother wilting as he flipped his sword, ending the bout just as they'd begun it.

"Better. Much better." Alex sheathed his own sword, almost grinning at his brother's evident relief that the practice session was over.

"Thank you, Alex. I think." William shook his head, fumbling slightly as he put away his own sword. He was clearly exhausted.

"Open yourself to the veil, just a little. Draw it in and let it replenish your energy, you should be strong enough for that." Alex modelled what he wanted William to do, opening himself up and drawing in energy from around him. He smiled as his brother blundered slightly but then managed to copy the technique. One of the things he'd learned in training William: he was exceptional at copying things he'd seen being performed. That talent certainly made getting him up to speed on his new powers a lot easier.

"Oh..." The relief in William's face showed quite clearly that he'd managed to do as he'd been instructed.

"It won't last, but it does help. Let's go eat." Alex closed the distance between them and helped unbuckle his brother's training gear, handing the pieces off to the hovering guards.

Clapping his brother on the shoulder, he led him back towards William's rooms and the food he knew would be waiting there. He'd learned the hard way that while the veil could replenished energy levels rapidly, it was a false energy. The Kin had to stop and eat eventually or face the very real consequence of collapse. He'd gone through it enough himself before he'd learnt that very important lesson.

While it might have been mildly entertaining to see his brother learn that one the hard way, he resisted the urge to allow it to play out. The drama that would unfold if William collapsed again would be a nightmare to manage.

KYLE WALKED through the outer public areas of the king's suite. Not that any area of the king's private quarters could be really called public, but these were the only areas anyone outside of the immediate family or closest advisors ever saw. Now these were William's, although he was yet to be crowned. Still, they had moved him while he was insensible as soon as they could.

While William's old suite had been secure, these were even more so. Even William, the crown prince, had been regarded as a line of defence for the king before their father had died. Alex, with input from both Jess and himself, had determined it would be easier to protect William here.

Kyle smiled. Alex had stepped up and assumed a great deal of responsibility, and as Fourth had overruled objections to the breach in protocol. Some of the older surviving lords had been rather insistent that William not be moved into the king's suite until he was crowned. Given that the attack that had killed the king and a great many prominent lords had been at the hands of Amelia and the Sundered, at the hands of those utilising the veil, it clearly fell under the Fourth's responsibility. It helped that Elizabeth, as regent, had backed Alex up fully and reinforced to all that responsibility for the safety of the realm fell to the Fourth and his Companions when the realm was threatened by those with talent.

Kyle thanked the guards who stepped aside on his approach, one of them pulling the doors open for him, and walked into the inner sanctum. He smiled as Alex looked up from where he sat chatting with William.

"That time already?" Alex stood and stretched.

"You know it. Go, get some rest." Kyle walked over and paused, frowning at Alex's obvious fatigue.

Are you all right, Alex?

I'm fine, just trouble sleeping of late. Alex looked at him and shrugged, clapping him on the shoulder as he walked past.

Kyle watched his friend leave. He wished he could take more of Alex's burden from him, but suspected it wasn't the extra workload that was causing his sleepless nights. Alex had grown up plagued with nightmares of his mother's death. Kyle sighed and wondered if those nightmares had been replaced with those of his father's death and the feeling of failure—a failure that he knew they all felt keenly.

Shaking himself, he assumed position on the couch previously occupied by Alex.

The three of them had been pulling duty on William with Ed, Kat and Cal relieving them on occasion. Thankfully William was on the mend and wasn't confined to his bed anymore.

William sighed and pushed away the reports he'd been reading.

"You know I'm well enough that I can call you if something goes wrong?" William looked faintly embarrassed.

"Once we're happy with your ability to maintain your shield and keep others' random thoughts out of your head we'll consider it. I'll be happier once we've dealt with Amelia." Kyle's eyes narrowed.

William stood and walked from his desk to the couches. "You recovered from being drugged and controlled."

Kyle shook his head. "They didn't have full control of me before I realised something was wrong and broke away. That isn't the case with Amelia."

"You don't believe the healers could help? You seem to have recovered from what Joanna did to you." William looked at him intently.

"They have had their hooks in Amelia since she was a little girl. She has ceased to be the person we thought she was. She is their creature." Kyle returned William's look sombrely.

William sighed, looking over to the large garden windows. "I'll have to declare her a traitor for assassinating Father. It would be preferable if we were absolutely certain she can't be helped before I have to order her death."

"You've been speaking with my father." Kyle understood William's hesitation, yet knowing what he did about the Order's methods, he didn't have the same reservations.

William turned and nodded. "You can't blame him and he is

correct. She is under the Order's control; her actions aren't her fault. If we can save her, then we owe it to her to try."

Kyle sighed. "It's not as easy as all that, but you have my word. If the opportunity arises I'll do my best. The declaration still needs to stand; it can always be rescinded if, against my best judgement, it is proven she can be saved."

He'd had the same conversation with his parents and with Elizabeth. It had taken some persuasion on his part to get Elizabeth to include the information about Amelia in the early dispatches. What finally convinced her was the reports that flooded in from all over the realm. They all told of how unsettled their people were, as rumour flew on the wind from the palace, of the death of the king and the way of it.

She'd agreed and the scholars, under the protection and escort of the guard, had gone out to spread the word that the Killiam Order had been behind the assassination of the king, along with the tragic news that Lady Amelia and others born with the power of the veil had fallen under their control. It assured people that those with the power of the veil were just as much victims as those that had been killed; that the deaths, all of them, had been at the hands of the Killiam Order. They also reassured the people that their crown prince had survived the attack and the Fourth and Companions were working to safeguard them all.

All that was needed was for William, on ascending the throne and taking the crown, to officially decree the Killiam Order and all those who joined the Order or sheltered their members, guilty of treason.

"From that moment she will be stripped of all rank and status." William shook his head, clearly struggling with the decision despite the circumstances.

"She cannot remain as a lady of the realm or the Consort Elect of the Fourth. You know that, William." Kyle looked at William steadily.

William nodded. "I know. It is still a difficult thing to come to terms with."

"It means you are getting better, since you are able to think through problems and issues. How's your head today?" In all that had been occurring, at least it was good news that William was up and sane.

William ducked his head. "Much better. I have a new appreciation of what you three felt like when you nearly burned your minds out."

Kyle chuckled. "Actually I think what happened to you was way worse. We have been dealing with the veil and its effects our whole lives. Your mind was blasted wide open, making you Kin abruptly, like Joanna."

William shuddered. "Without Alex, you, Jess, and the healers' care it *would* have driven me mad."

"Enjoy this respite from the tender mercies of the court. Until Alex lifts his restrictions, no one but the healers and us are getting near you." Kyle looked at him solemnly.

William turned to look at him, his eyes wide. "Alex is in control? Even the healers are acceding to his will?"

Kyle nodded. "Alex has stepped up as Fourth. Elizabeth has made it clear he is the one in control of all matters involving the power. Aaron has say over your medical condition, Alex over matters concerning your transition. Until he agrees, no one else is getting near you."

William opened his mouth, then shut it again, clearly thinking things through.

"So my little brother is growing up?"

Kyle grinned and shrugged. He had to admit it was a side of Alex that he'd never seen.

Now, since we have some time, let's work on your shields, both mental and physical.

Kyle chuckled as William covered his face and groaned.

You know I never wanted this.

Kyle smiled a little sadly at William's plaintive tone. It was rare for him to wallow in his own misery, or at least to share it. William's current mental state and his need to get used to being Kin was another reason both Aaron and Alex had insisted he get the time he needed, or at least as much as they could give him.

I know, William. If I could take this burden from you, I would.

William shuddered. *How do you all stand it?*

We were born this way, William. Alex, Jess and I know no different in our lives.

You all sheltered my mind, stopped me from going insane like Joanna.

Kyle nodded. *Yes, we did. Us and the healers. You must learn, William.*

It would have been easier if you'd all let me die. William's eyes were shadowed in pain, glancing away from him.

Give yourself time, William. Good or ill, you are Kin, and soon you will be crowned our king. Take heart, you still have barely enough power to light a candle if that helps.

Still more human than Kin? William glanced up at him.

I'm afraid so. You can speak mind-to-mind better, heal better than a human. That's about it.

Kyle watched carefully as William considered his options, almost sighing with relief as his friend and future king shook himself, straightening in his chair and nodded, indicating he was ready.

10

DESIRE

Amelia lay down on her bed. Unlike many in the Order, she'd been given her own room in the estate house. It was a small closet of a room but a room nevertheless. Lord Kastler had recognised her immediately. There had been no way to hide her identity unless she stayed away entirely. That was not a situation her master was willing to embrace. It meant she had to suffer through the lord's attention on occasion. Unfortunately she had been ordered not to kill the snivelling fool.

A smile spread on her lips as she contemplated her night. She may be forbidden the sport of killing Lord Kastler, but her master had given her permission to torment Alex. It puzzled her that her former Consort Elect still had no idea she had a connection to him. She knew he hadn't found out, since if he had then the little bond she'd forged between them would have been cut. Amelia was certain she would have felt it if the bond had been broken.

It was a small, subtle thing.

Under the circumstances it had to be, otherwise the Master Healer might have discovered it—or worse, Alex himself.

Although she'd been unaware of what she was doing, at the time she'd used that connection to foster feelings in Alex towards her. It had worked remarkably well at the time. Alex had turn from the party boy prince to falling in love with her. Or at least he believed he had due to the feelings, emotions and images she'd prompted in his mind. He'd started to think of nothing but her and believed it was all his own emotions.

Now she would use the attachment with him to stoke those fires again. She knew Alex and had a way to get to him. He would feel that passion once more, along with a healthy dose of guilt. Thankfully she had plenty of her own nightmares she could share. After all, it was only fair; she'd lived through that nightmare because her master had wanted Alex.

Amelia pondered her thoughts about that time for a moment, albeit a brief one. She knew her master had taken her. He'd tortured her and warped her mind, turned her into the killer she'd never been, inflicting pain and his depraved touch until she'd begged his mercy. It wasn't just that her mind shied away from rebellion. When she'd given herself to Kevin, the constraints he'd burnt into her made it impossible for her to conceive of betraying him. She knew what they'd done to her, but she belonged to her master now. A part of her ached, worried that she wasn't good enough for him, that she was the secondary prize. He wanted Alex more than anything.

What her master wanted she would do her damnedest to ensure he got.

A smile forming on her lips, Amelia closed her eyes and began to dream.

ALEX MOANED, his sheets twisted about him in testament to his unsettled sleep. A part of him was aware that he was dreaming and wished he would wake from this latest nightmare.

Yet another part of him couldn't bear to pull away from this torment that in the back of his mind he knew he deserved. Images, thoughts and feelings clearly not his own assaulted him. He knew this, since they all showed him what Amelia had suffered at the hands of Kevin. What she'd suffered because of him.

Feeling Kevin's hand as it slipped under her shift, her scream ringing in his skull as she pleaded with her tormentor to stop. Then her sobbing mind voice begging Alex to save her.

Alex! Find me, save me. Please.

Alex woke, sitting bolt upright in his bed. Heart in his throat as he tried to calm his own panic, spurred on by the nightmare he'd been having for weeks.

"Amelia, I'm sorry I failed you." Alex slumped back down, rolling onto his side and sinking down into his pillows.

As tired as he was from the constant nightmares, he couldn't bring himself to sleep. If he did, he knew that he would return to that nightmare that was playing on repeat in his mind, showing him Amelia's capture and the torture she'd been subject to at Kevin's hands.

Alex squeezed his eyes shut, body tensing as he wrestled with himself. With a groan he hauled himself out of bed. He shook as he went to his closet. He knew this wasn't a good idea, but if he didn't do something it was going to drive him insane.

He pulled on a set of his unadorned clothing that he normally wore for training, or for when he was out on the town. Not that he'd had much time for his own pursuits of late. He'd confined himself to the palace since his father's assassination. With Jess on duty with William tonight, Alex was intent on prowling.

After one last check on his weapons, he pulled himself into the veil with a sigh. It had been too long since he'd left the palace grounds, and it was a relief to be on his own, even if he knew the freedom wouldn't last for long—particularly if the others knew what his intent was, for whom he was searching. He was certain that they all thought he was going on his own sweep to try to locate signs of the Order.

Alex shook his head; he hadn't admitted to any of them that his dreams had been plagued with nightmares about Amelia. Her capture and torture. Her screams pleading with him to save her. It had been driving him to distraction, guilt assailing him only to be replaced with longing for her when he woke.

There was only one solution he could think of.

After putting enough distance between himself and the palace, with only a cursory glance he moved from the veil to the darkened cobblestone path in the middle of a small sleepy village not far from the Winter Palace. With a final glance around, he called out to her.

Amelia?

Alex tensed as the cold of an arrival through the veil washed over him and stared at Amelia as she appeared in front of him. He was unable to help the longing that welled up in him just at the sight of her. It confused him since during transition he'd barely thought of her. During that time, whenever he'd thought of any woman it had been Isabella, and he had only thought of Amelia out of guilt. He knew he should hate her—she had killed his father—yet somehow his mind was filled with thoughts and images of their time together.

Amelia took one slow step after the other, closing the distance between them, sheathing her swords. Her eyes smouldered with a hungry possessive light. Alex could see the coldness behind that fire. As much as he knew he should not be here, that Amelia was dangerous, he sheathed his own blade. She laughed, the sound low as her hands divested him of his shirt. Alex closed his eyes, groaning as the memory of that moment they'd shared on the couch at her brother's bedside flashed up in his mind.

I know you still desire me, Alex.

Alex swallowed. As her voice filled his head and she uttered the word *desire*, he trembled in reaction. He opened his eyes to look into hers, and pushing consequence aside, he pulled her close and kissed her. Alex pulled them through the veil to his rooms at the Winter Palace. He knew she was too dangerous to allow anywhere near his brother. A little sense asserted itself, if not much. A cursory glance and search with his mind told him no one was nearby, not even the maintenance staff left behind to take care of the palace and grounds until the royal court migrated back at the end of summer.

She was a traitor, assassinating his father on behalf of the Order, and she'd tried to kill his brother. He had no doubt she would do so again. William would declare her to be a traitor and order the breaking of her position as his Consort Elect. If the others found out he was meeting up with her, still sleeping with the enemy, they would be horrified. Despite all of that, he admitted even if it was only between the two of them that she was right. He did still desire her; unaccountably he still loved her.

Pushing his own doubts and consequences aside Alex stripped Amelia of her clothing as she made short work of his own. She placed her arms around his neck, wrapping her legs around his waist as he backed them both up to the bed.

You're right, I want you. Always.

Alex could hear the hunger in his own mind tone. Her only response was a breathy chuckle as he fell on her, giving in to his very real desire.

11

TRAINING

Ryan stumbled and fell back, hitting the ground hard as he heard the weapons master call an exasperated halt. He covered his face, unable to stifle his laughter. While it was true, he was getting better with his blade work. How could he not, being singled out for personal training sessions, and the rest of the time being drilled and put through his paces by the Fourth's Elite? Regardless, he still ended up on the losing end more often than not. He usually trained with Matthew under the guidance of the weapons master. Still, all the men and women here had been training in sword work since they were old enough to hold a blade, many by their own family members who were also in the guard. He'd been a little awed to discover that most of them had the single-minded ambition to be exactly where they were from very young. It was a level of dedication and purpose he couldn't ever remember having. Until now.

Matthew shook his head at Ryan and held out one hand to help him up off the ground. Ryan just ginned in return. Hearing caustic laughter, he looked over to see the younger courtiers had been let into the training grounds for their own lessons.

"Ah, orphan boy. So you can't even manage to stay on your feet? Such a shame! Don't worry, you won't be here long before my father gets you kicked out of the palace." Branton sneered at him as his friends laughed.

Ryan looked back at Matthew, who looked ready to explode.

"Ignore them, Matthew. It's fine." Ryan sheathed his blade.

It was one of his new ones with the sigil of the Cohort etched onto it. Any who got a close enough look at it would have recognised it instantly. Lord Kyle had taken a hand in his outfitting and as a result he also had some nondescript clothing without insignia to train in. He hadn't appeared in his formal clothing yet, feeling a little uncomfortable and not really sure he'd earned them yet. Kyle had insisted he train with his new blades, though, and Matthew had laughed, advising him not to worry when he'd expressed the concern he might hurt his training partner. So unlike his formal uniforms, which stayed in his closet, he carried the blades.

"Carson, who let that lot in here?" The weapons master's bellow was enough to cause stillness to settle on the training grounds.

"Sorry, Weapons Master, I think they might have just let themselves in." Carson looked over toward the younger men and women, all of them the children of the courtiers.

"Sir Ryan's training takes precedence over that lot by order of the Fourth. In future, have someone on the entrance so we aren't disturbed until his sessions are finished." The weapons master turned his back on them, clearly dismissing them from his attention.

Ryan felt his eyes widen at the use of the title. While he knew that being a member of the Cohort conferred rank, even if not the lands to go with it, no one called him 'Sir' anything.

He was just Ryan to one and all. He doubted the weapons master had slipped up; he didn't tend to make those kinds of mistakes.

"Now, let's try that again. This time use your augmented fighting style. Don't worry about Matthew, he's faced off against Lord Kyle often enough and managed to survive." The weapons master grinned at his startled expression.

Ryan gathered the weapons master wanted a display, although he guessed he wasn't the recipient of this particular lesson. While Matthew was a much better swordsman and on track to be declared a Master Bladesman, in the use of power, Ryan was much stronger, even with the head start Matthew and the rest of the Elite had over him. In this one area he excelled. With Alex, Kyle and Jess around to help train him, he was progressing in that area in leaps and bounds. The first session he'd shared with the king had been a little off-putting. To think how much his life had changed from running on the streets, homeless. Now he found himself training with the preeminent members of the kingdom.

Ryan stepped back into the training ring, drawing his blade and saluting Matthew, who returned the salute in kind although his own added a twist of the blade to signal to his opponent that he was a master. Concentrating, he drew in the energy he could sense all around him, as much as he could manage. He knew that doing so would give him a blinding headache. The healers advised him he should limit his use of the veil as much as he could. The more frequently he drew power, the more it would course through his brain and body, pushing him inevitably towards transition. Ryan steadfastly ignored them, taking a tonic to ease his headaches when he needed to, which with his training schedule was most days. He knew Alex, Kyle and Jess could use all the help they could get. The assassination of the old king had made the coming fight inevitable.

Elemental flame sprung into being along his blade and he took a deep breath as the euphoric feeling rushed through him with the inrush of power through his body. It was a feeling that was becoming addictive. He grinned as Matthew called his own power and wondered if his eyes glowed with power as Matthew's did. Matthew was one of the stronger members of the Fourth's Elite.

Without warning Matthew launched a dual volley of blows at him with his blade and power. The power cracked on his own shield as he met Matthew's blade with his own. Grinning with confidence, he hurled his own power at Matthew, his eyes narrowing as this time the combination of his sword and power had Matthew backing up under the onslaught. Matthew was trained to utilise his own power in concert with his fellow squad members. Ryan, however, was not only learning their defensive style but also how to take the lead in a battle of power, with the Elite protecting and backing him up.

Ryan's world narrowed to his current fight, as it so often did when he used the energy of the veil. The young courtiers lining the wall in hushed silence along with the handful of the guard were only on the periphery of his awareness, although he knew that a couple of the other guards had thrown up a shield to protect the young courtiers. The power levels they were both using had the ability to seriously hurt each other should either of them lose concentration. The splash of their excess power could also have hurt those watching without the ability to shield themselves. The protective padding used to protect them while practicing sword skill would do nothing against the combative power they both used.

Ryan grunted and winced as the flare of fire flashed on his shields, only just catching Matthew's flicking blade as he used the distraction to push back. He lunged to one side as his opponent's blade whistled past his ear. Ryan grinned in appreciation of the move and, drawing yet more power, thrust it at Matthew, following through with his own blade as the force of the physical blow caused Matthew to lose his footing.

"Hold!" The bellow filled the practice ground.

Ryan's blade stopped just on Matthew's neck. He withdrew, releasing his hold on the veil with effort, and this time it was his turn to reach down and help his training partner to his feet.

Matthew accepted his hand and hauled himself up from the ground, grinning at him, not at all embarrassed that their roles had been reversed.

"Well done, Ryan, you are getting stronger every day. I take it those extra lessons with His Highness are paying off?" Matthew sheathed his blade and they both turned, seeing the dismissal from the weapons master, who had a satisfied expression on his face. That satisfaction dropped off as he turned to face the young courtiers and bellowed at them to get the protective gear on.

"Mmm, although in those sessions it's me ending up on the ground. Alex is incredibly strong. Seeing what the three of them can do, particularly together, is astonishing." Ryan didn't add that they were making up their training as they went along. He didn't think that would have been terribly helpful.

Ryan was getting an education and more often than not others joined in on the sessions to add their own combat knowledge to the collective group. While the Elite kept training journals on the effective use of power with standard fighting techniques, the previous Fourth had not.

Of course, the fact that Prince Edward was still alive helped fill some of those training gaps, although Ryan had the distinct feeling that Alex was stronger than Edward. It was an observation that he mostly kept to himself. He wasn't sure that it would have been particularly helpful to voice it. Still, as easy-going as not only Edward but Cal and Kat were, he doubted any of them would have minded. He was reminded though that Alex, Jess and Kyle were only recently through their own transition and were still settling into their increased power.

Walking out of the training grounds, Ryan grimaced and stumbled a little as fatigue hit him. He hoped no one noticed. Then, right on cue, his head started throbbing. It was expected, but he knew he should get back to his rooms to rest before he fell over and ended up in the disapproving hands of the healers.

"Thank you for your time, Matthew. As always it was educational. I might even be getting marginally better with my use of the sword." Ryan grinned at the older boy, who was fast becoming a friend despite the couple of years' difference in their age.

Matthew clouted him on the shoulder. "You've improved more than a little. Now come on, I'll make sure you get to your rooms to rest before the healers get a look at you. I don't want you collapsing halfway there." The look Matthew threw at him left him in no doubt at all that Matthew knew full well he'd drawn more power than he should.

Ryan didn't even try to deny that he needed to rest after their session. He knew that there was no point, Matthew seemed to be able to see straight through him with an ease that he found astonishing.

Matthew, true to his word, escorted him back to his rooms in the Cohort's wing of the Complex of the Fourth. With a groan Ryan collapsed onto his bed, cradling his head in his hands, not feeling any need at all to hide the fact that he was in pain. Matthew glanced around and, spying the tonic the healers had given Ryan for his headaches, poured out a measure.

Sitting on the side of the bed, he handed the medication to Ryan and watched as he took it, swallowing it all without complaint. Taking the measure when he was finished, Matthew placed it on the bedside table near the bottle of tonic. He helped Ryan pull off his boots, placing them to one side, then carefully pulled up the blanket as Ryan turned over onto his side, muscles relaxing, slipping into a sleep aided by the healers' medication.

12

GUILT

Jess curled up in the chair by the windows in what had become her usual spot when she pulled guard duty on William. She pressed the heel of her palm against her forehead as she watched William sleep.

"Fool." The words were barely a whisper from her lips.

She had no intention of falling into William's bed again. It had been easy enough to refuse him while he'd been sick, even though he'd begged her on more than one occasion. That had caused a few wide-eyed stares and embarrassment from some of the healers.

Now he was insistent he was well and truly healed enough for bed sport. He was a little harder to resist now and she wasn't immune to his charms; she never had been. Like it or not, William's future consort in the shape of an Imperial Princess would show up at court sooner or later. Regardless of her disposition and the political nature of their impending union, Jess doubted the woman would appreciate William having a mistress already installed prior to her arrival.

She knew William had been trying to steadfastly ignore the issue, but ignoring the fact he'd already been promised to another wouldn't make it go away. He wasn't above using his forced transition and his confusion over it to try to play on her sympathies either.

The thought had the effect of irritating her as she realised William had almost regressed to a wilful, bratty child, except he'd never been that way as a child. The more she said no to him the more he seemed determined to pursue her. Of course, falling in bed with her wouldn't solve any of his issues. It would only add one more to the seemingly growing list.

Hearing the door open, Jess wiped a tear from her cheek, then relaxed and smiled as Kyle crossed the room and came up beside her. Jess knew that, after being friends for so many years, he could see right through her. She was almost relieved that Alex was too occupied in his own world right now to be aware of periphery things. He had enough to worry about without her adding to it. Besides, it was a minor thing that she didn't need to make a production over. It would sort itself out. Or at least that is what she kept telling herself.

"Do you want me to speak to him?" Kyle looked across to William's sleeping form.

"You've noticed." Jess kept her voice soft. She lay her head against Kyle's forearm as he squeezed her shoulder.

Kyle frowned as he glanced from her back towards their sleeping charge. "He's still recovering and dealing with all of this, but that is no excuse."

"He's being so stubborn."

"Now that he's mostly recovered he's also not above using all of his current pain as a means to get you to feel sympathy and not so coincidently back into his bed." Kyle slid into the chair next to her, wrapping an arm around her.

Jess leaned into his shoulder. At least with Kyle, unlike with William, it was nothing but the support offered by a concerned friend. Without other eyes on her, that was support she could take without it starting a rumour that would run through the palace like wildfire. Not that either of them would truly care what others thought, but right now she didn't want to hear them.

"He's lost and hurting, he's never behaved like this before." Jess closed her eyes.

"That doesn't mean he should start now."

They sat in silence for a moment before Jess looked up at Kyle. "Did you know he just found out from his father that night?"

"About what?" Kyle looked at her, confusion on his face.

"He didn't know about the negotiations for his consort."

"Ah." Kyle shook his head.

"Then moments later the king died. He was angry. It's why he wasn't on the dais with his father as he normally would have been."

Kyle groaned. "Powers. So he's feeling guilty. He'd be dead too if he'd been up there."

Jess nodded. "I'll be fine, Kyle."

Kyle looked at her and leaned in and kissed her gently on the forehead.

"I know you will be, but it doesn't mean his pressuring you doesn't hurt. I'll speak with him." He pressed his fingers against her lips when she went to object. "Enough, go and get some sleep before he wakes up."

"No Kyle leave it, I'll handle it. If he doesn't see sense when he's up on his feet and fully healed, well, I'll beat him into it."

Jess sighed as she looked at Kyle, realising this was an argument she was not going to win. Also with Kyle knowing, it meant Alex would know soon enough, which would cause him to worry as well. Still, between the both of them they might be able to knock some sense into William, get him to understand it wasn't his fault his father was dead, and while they were at him get his head out of the sand about his future consort.

13

SERVICE

Matthew walked down the hallway of the Elite barracks, turning into officer quarters. James looked up from the couch, dressed in his ceremonial uniform, with his formal jacket hanging on a hook on the wall. He waved and jerked his head towards the office. Matthew knew there was a formal ball tonight, and Alex was obviously going to be in attendance. That meant others were currently on duty surrounding Alex until Marcus and James arrived. It was one of the few times that particular duty went to others. Of course, given the hour, Alex was probably in his own rooms getting ready. James hauled himself out of the chair and walked with him to the office. He looked at James and raised his eyebrow. Being summoned to attend Marcus's office was unusual, and having James join in the conversation as well made him wonder if he should be nervous.

"Don't worry, it's nothing bad. You may look back with longing after this meeting to the time where you had a life." James grinned at him and after a perfunctory knock opened the door.

Matthew followed in James's wake and entered the office,

seeing Megan sitting in one of the chairs, booted feet up on the edge of the desk. She smiled a greeting as they entered and Marcus waved them both into chairs. All of them were ready for their evening duty. Matthew wondered how they did it, pulling more hours of duty than any other in the guard bearing the primary responsibility for the safety of the Fourth and his Companions. Originally the three of them had performed the primary guard duty on Alex. Then with Lord Kyle and Lady Jessalan being elevated to the rank of Companions of the Fourth, they had been stretched. The rest of the Fourth's Elite filled the gaps, yet the greater burden still fell on the three of them—the best swordsmen and the strongest of the Elite in the use of the veil.

He'd come to realise that while the rest of the Elite were good, they weren't *that* good. It was a realisation that scared him, given the current environment. There just weren't enough of them. He knew there were some even in the Elite who would have been annoyed to run duty for the three of them, fulfilling basic tasks for them that they just couldn't get to. When he understood how stretched they were, he found he didn't mind at all and wished they would lean on him more.

"How's the boy?" Marcus leaned back in his own chair, casual and relaxed.

"Pushing himself. He has an insane sense of duty. An obligation to Alex for saving his life." Matthew relaxed in his own chair. He was learning from the three of them that when in the Elite, particularly the Fourth's Elite you rested when the opportunity presented itself.

"Well, he'll fit right in with the three of them." Megan's tone was dry.

Both Marcus and James snorted in amusement, clearly agreeing with her assessment.

"I take it you all felt the power he used in today's training session?" Matthew looked at his superiors as they nodded their acknowledgment. "He's good, despite being new to this style of training. He's resting right now, sleeping off a veil-induced headache."

Marcus frowned. "You think he's trying to bring on transition earlier?"

Matthew shrugged. "Yes, and I don't just think so, he admitted it. Biggest mistake the healers made was sitting him down and explaining the possible consequences of him continually using the veil at high levels."

"The healers know what he's doing?" James straightened, trading glances with Marcus and Megan.

"They know. Aaron knows their disapproval won't stop him, so he gave him some tonic to help him sleep off his headaches. I made sure he got back to his rooms and took some. He should be fine within an hour." As interested as the three seemed to be in the discussion, Matthew knew this current conversation wasn't why he'd been called into conference with them.

"You are young for the post but we all agree, as does the weapons master and the Commander of the Elite. Will you accept a position in the ranks of Personal Service to the Fourth?" Marcus's gaze on him was steady.

Matthew felt like someone had hit him; if he hadn't been sitting his legs would have buckled under him in complete shock. In times gone past, those in Personal Service were the elite of the Elite. They were in the inner circle of Elite, personal protection detail to the Fourth and his Companions. They were also leaders within the ranks of the Elite, leading their own efforts in combination with the Fourth, his Companions and the Cohort in the fight against those with talent who would harm the realm. Right now there were only three of them—the three he was sitting in the same room with now—and he was being asked to join their number.

"If you accept, you can kiss goodbye any kind of personal life." James shared a smile with both Marcus and Megan.

"It isn't for everyone and it will be understood if you do not wish to step up." Megan grinned. "On the plus side, our barracks is better and a little more comfortable than the general barracks. Better food than the regular Elite, due to our irregular hours the house staff fetch us food from the kitchens."

"You'll be pulled off general duty around the Complex of the Fourth. However, you will share the lead of the personal protection detail of His Highness, Lord Kyle and Lady Jessalan with us. Ryan will be presented officially at the court as a member of the Companion's Cohort and conferred the title of Sir by the king, which will add him to their number." Marcus settled back, clearly giving him time to think about his options.

"Of course, when they go out, more often than not Alex, Jess and Kyle are together, which makes it easier than it sounds. They tend to go off on their own pursuits using the veiled paths. It's a habit we haven't been able to break them of." James grimaced at the last.

Matthew couldn't help but grin. "I'd be honoured to join your ranks."

All three of them grinned at him and James reached across and clapped him on the back.

"Take the rest of the day and tomorrow off to get settled. Pick a set of rooms in our barracks, there are plenty so don't feel shy about checking out a few. You'll need to alert our house staff and they'll clean it up for you." Marcus paused, handing Matthew a list written in his neat concise handwriting. "Go to the quartermaster, you'll need to be outfitted with new uniforms. I will expect you on duty the day after tomorrow. Kicking off the day with the training session, I'll expect you to be there." Marcus stood, indicating the interview was over.

Considering the time, Matthew guessed it was getting close to the time the three were due on duty.

"Our days always start with the training session, it's later in the morning. Thankfully Alex, Kyle and Jess are predisposed to sleeping in late. Of course, that makes up for being up late. You'll need to adjust your sleeping patterns. I hope you can get used to being up half the night." Megan grinned at his startled reaction.

Of course she was right. When Marcus had said he'd be expected at training, he'd automatically thought of the regular training session the Elite attended. He'd forgotten the three of them had their own session later in the morning, usually prior to Alex, Jess and Kyle having theirs. They rarely attended the regular session and when they did it was never all three of them at the same time. He wondered if they took that duty in turn. Matthew ducked his head, unable to wipe the smile from his face.

James led the way out of the office and grabbed his formal jacket off the hook, glancing at him and gesturing to the hallway that led to their private barracks.

"If you go look at rooms now, the house staff will have your choice cleaned out by the time you finish with the quartermaster. Then you can enjoy your day off settling in." James waved him off as the three of them headed off towards the corridor that led directly to the Complex of the Fourth.

Matthew stood there stunned, watching as they left. He'd worked hard to get right where he found himself now. Yet there was a part of him that hadn't believed that someone like him would make it into the rarefied ranks of Personal Service to the Fourth. Matthew turned to walk into what would be his new life, a smile on his face.

14

CORRONATION

William looked at Elizabeth earnestly. "Eliza, seriously, I think you should take the crown. I'm not certain our people are ready for a king who is also numbered amongst the Kin."

Elizabeth laughed. "Oh no you don't, brother. By the end of this day you will be king."

Not getting any sympathy from his twin, William looked over to Alex, hopeful that he'd get an out there. A slow grin spread on his brother's face and dashed his hopes.

Alex chuckled. "Oh don't look at me, I agree with Eliza."

William sighed and tugged on his ceremonial robes of state. He'd thought his ceremonial clothing, in particular the vest, had been bad as the crown prince. These were worse. They were highly ornate and heavy. It wasn't his imagination; the weight of the robes hit him as soon as his servants swarmed around him to help him get ready. It had been a mad house behind the scenes to get everything crafted for his ascension to the throne, although thankfully he'd missed most of it.

Even though he'd known this moment would come and he'd been trained for it from birth, he was unaccountably nervous. Of course there was a part of him that was still sad —like any child, he'd held the forlorn hope his father would never die. It was certainly a shock for it to have occurred this soon.

It didn't help he'd mostly been insensible himself during those early days and his father's interment in the Royal Catacomb. The memory of the burning, aching pain, nightmares, voices whispering in his head that weren't his own, pleading for death for everyone to let him go, caused him to shudder. Alex had accompanied him to the Royal Catacomb, without all the fuss and ceremony, so he could say his goodbyes.

Elizabeth looked at him sternly. "This whole mess was started over a few disaffected people being afraid of those with the gift. I think you are exactly what we need to move forward."

William sighed. Shaking his head, he looked over to Alex again, who still didn't look like he was sympathetic to the idea either.

"You will be our king, William, don't even think of abdicating." Alex's lips twitched as if he was restraining laughter.

Kyle cleared his throat. "I'm going to check out the security of the Great Hall once more. I'll see you all in there."

"I'll join you." Jess turned to follow Kyle.

William tried to grab her hand as she walked past him.

"Can't you stay, just until it's time?" He looked down at her, realising there was a note of pleading in his voice.

Jess's face shut down. "No, William. You know the protocol as well as I."

Kyle threw him an exasperated look as Jess joined him and they both left the room.

As the door closed, the smile slipped off William's face to be replaced by a frown as he contemplated the closed door the pair had retreated through. He turned from the mirrors, waving off the fussing servants to look at Alex, who sat on the windowsill, as was his custom.

"Is she all right?"

Alex tilted his head. "What do you mean?"

William shrugged. "Jess seems a little... remote."

"I hadn't noticed but we've all been a little preoccupied." Elizabeth smiled at him.

"Brother, we've talked about this. You are about to be king. Stop trying to pressure Jess." Alex had an absent look on his face.

William opened his mouth, then closed it again. He ducked his head to hide the struggle with that little part of himself that didn't want to give up this one last thing. Both Alex and Kyle had sat him down and given him a dressing down. He was a little ashamed that they'd thought it was necessary and that he kept backsliding to the state of a sulky child. William shook himself as he realised he'd done it again. He owed Jess an apology.

William now recognised the absent look on his brother's face as a sign he was talking with someone else. Not that Alex wasn't perfectly capable of carrying on a secret conversation and maintaining appearances. His brother just showed less inclination to hide the double talk now.

He guessed that Alex was checking in with Kyle and Jess about the security of the hall prior to their arrival. William knew the Elite and palace guards were crawling all over today. He doubted anyone would be able to step a foot out of place without being investigated, or arbitrarily thrown in the deepest cells in the palace. The security, *his* security, had been increased dramatically since the assassination of his father. He knew both his sister and brother had been at the heart of everything and had borne the brunt of the pressure and decision-making since their father's death, with him being out of commission.

"Thank you. Both of you." William looked between his twin and brother. He didn't have to explain; both of them seemed to understand.

Alex shook his head. "You would have done the same for either of us. For me you have, multiple times."

He knew well the burden they'd carried while he'd been insensible, the petty complaints and power plays they'd defused between them while he'd been convalescing.

A part of him was amused at the power plays being exhibited by the courtiers. All of them knew that with the change in king a shake-up was coming, and sensed the potential to further their own families' positions. The scramble to attempt to place their daughters in front of him was also escalating. They would find out that those efforts were in vain soon enough. Families with more experience, like the Straffords, were already in positions of power and more secure, which of course made them look even better since they held themselves above the mad rush.

A wave of sadness crashed over William as he thought of Amelia and one of the first actions he would have to take as king.

Alex suddenly swung his head back to focus on him and William felt reassurance wash over him.

William ducked his head. "I'm sorry, Alex."

"I've already spoken to Lord Strafford." Alex spoke quietly with an undertone of pain in his voice, as there was whenever ever he spoke about Amelia.

Elizabeth placed her hand on his shoulder. "Kyle knows as well."

Alex shrugged uncomfortably. "Kyle has been advocating for me to break protocol and put her aside since Father was killed."

"I spoke with Kyle and his father yesterday. Kyle understands first hand what it is to be under another's control." William pulled himself together, pushing aside his own sadness at the tragic circumstances surrounding Amelia.

He knew that Kyle's opinions on the subject of his sister

were much stronger than Alex's. Kyle had disabused him of the notion that there would be anything left of his sister to save by drawing him into his own memories. The absolute control both Alyssa and Joanna could enforce on him was truly frightening.

"If it didn't need your consent, I would have put her aside already to spare you this burden." Alex looked up as the doors opened to see Joshua standing in the doorway.

He slipped off the windowsill and endured the fussing of the servants as they clustered around him. He was adorned with his own ceremonial cloak, and the circlet of the Fourth on his brow, finishing off his full formal attire. In a rare concession to the occasion, he'd forsaken his normal plain training leathers. Instead Alex's vest was almost as fully adorned as William's own in a deep royal blue, denoting the Rathadon line, the same as his own and the colouring in Elizabeth's dress—the difference being his sister's and brother's clothing was threaded with gold and silver, while his own was only gold. William noted that Alex had obviously had some input into the formal gear since it was more practical than his own. He had no doubt at all that none of Alex's ceremonial clothing would hinder his ability to fight in the slightest. His weapons were on display, as were Kyle's own in his deadly role as the Fourth's Blade.

"Ready, brother?" Alex closed the distance between them and clapped his hand on his shoulder.

William took a breath and nodded to both Alex and Elizabeth, who took their places in front of him as the trumpets blared, the double doors sweeping open. As the children of the late king, they would all enter together, presenting themselves to the peers of the realm.

A hush fell over the assembled lords and ladies congregated in the hall under the heraldic banners of all the prominent families. A quick glance told William there was no one missing, or at least no one important. That was a relief since if there was, one of his first duties after ascending the throne would be to send his guards to deal with the families that thought they could go it alone. He'd been advised representatives of all the major and minor families had been arriving all week with the stragglers coming in the gates this morning. It was still a relief to see all of the banners on display.

No one bowed as they passed them. In this moment they walked between their peers as equals. Elizabeth and Alex mounted the steps approaching the preeminent families lined up on the dais. Peeling aside, they took their own places to either side of the throne facing him.

William approached the dais and knelt on the padded stool placed there for that purpose and bowed his head. It was the last time he would kneel before anyone.

The old Lore Keeper rapped his staff of office on the floors, the sound echoing off the walls and ceiling.

"Who approaches as supplicant to lead Vallantia?" The old man's voice carried throughout the great hall easily.

"I, William Michael Rathadon." William kept his gaze down and voice steady.

"By what right do you make such a claim to those here assembled?"

"The right of birth, being the eldest child of the late king." The words had changed over the years, yet their intent had not.

"Is there anyone here who believes they have a greater right to the throne?" As the old man's voice intoned the formal words, William felt the skin on the back of his neck crawl and his stomach drop.

Hearing the scrape of swords and feeling Alex, Kyle and Jess draw their powers, William looked up startled as he was suddenly surrounded by the Elite, their weapons bristling outward in a defensive cordon around him. As shimmering bodies materialised in the court, those assembled started to scream.

William felt another surge of power that he identified as Ryan, who strode into position to one side of the Elite and threw up his shield, adding his own strength to the one already between him and whoever had decided to intervene. Embarrassed not to have thought of it sooner, William added his own personal shield to the mix. His hope that no one noticed his delayed response to putting up his own defensive shield were dashed as Ryan gave him an approving nod.

JESS'S HEAD snapped up as she felt the incoming surge from other Kin that she didn't recognise. While she was half expecting an attack, it still shocked her that they would make the attempt now. She felt Alex push his own power between William and the incoming threat along with Kyle and Ryan.

Jess drew her own power, seeing the woman materialise only a few paces from William's back, her arm blurring even as she materialised, with a glint of silver spinning from her. Pulling the veil to her, Jess surged forward, blurring past William. She had enough time for her eyes to widen in shock as the projectile sliced through her shields before she felt the instant of sharp pain then the burn as the dagger, glowing with power and tainted with a poison intended for William's back, plunged into her own shoulder. Jess diverted some of her own energy internally to battle the poison, breathing a sigh of relief that it wasn't the debilitating toxin the Order used. Ignoring her injured shoulder, Jess pulled one of her blades from its sheath with her good arm and launched herself at the attacker.

The woman tried to flee, already slipping halfway into the veiled world. Jess snarled, then felt Alex's power surge. She saw energy shoot past her, the cold blast of power causing her to shiver. She watched in fascination as Alex's own power intervened. The veil under Alex's control swirled around the enemy, wrapping around her. Then without ceremony she was yanked back into the real world. Jess didn't waste any time wondering how Alex had performed that particular feat. She wrapped her own power around her sword. Blue and red flames licked up the blade, flaring and crackling, seeking its target as she swung her arm up. The woman, flung back by Alex, was impaled on her weapon, and Jess channelled even more of her power through her blade into the woman. The enemy stiffened for a moment, her mouth open in a soundless scream as both Jess's sword and power rushed through her.

Power bled from her eyes and her mouth. Pinpricks of light started to glitter all over her as the veil burst from her and she disintegrated, life fleeing her body as she burned from the inside due to energy she couldn't contain being thrust into her body. Jess looked from Alex to Kyle and saw her friends' eyes glow with their own power and wondered if hers did the same. She restrained her sudden mirth. Having all three of them thrust their power through the woman had clearly been overkill.

As quickly as the attack commenced, it was over. If it hadn't been so serious, William would have laughed as Alex, Kyle and Jess all glared at each other, battling between irritation and amusement. Amusement clearly won out for the three of them as they grinned at each other.

The Lore Keeper stepped forward and rapped his staff on the floor, calling for order and for people to take their places. William noted with concern that Jess winced, pulling the dagger that had been meant for his back out of her shoulder and passing it to one of the Elite with a quiet caution that the blade was poisoned. She waved off the assistance of one of the servants, although it was clear she was injured. Even though he knew she would heal, he hated that Jess had taken a dagger for him.

William waved off the guards, who retreated to their assigned places, before returning to his own place kneeling before the Lore Keeper and assembled high lords.

The ceremony continued, being as long and tedious as he'd thought it would be, with each of the high lords accepting his claim for the Rathadon throne. Finally it was Alex's turn, as the Fourth, the last of those assembled to acknowledge him.

"William Michael Rathadon, I accept you as my king and will faithfully serve you and our people as Fourth in the Realm, placing myself between the realm and those who seek to abuse their gifts." Alex turned and signed the scrolls that bore witness to his pledge, and then returned to his position.

At a gesture from the Lore Keeper, Shaun stepped forward bearing the Rathadon Crown on an ornate blue pillow with gold trim. The Lore Keeper passed his rod of office off to one of his assistants and, grabbing the crown with both hands, raised it high for all to see. It sparkled as the sun shining through the ornate windows surrounding the hall gleamed off the jewels inset in the old crown. Everything had been timed and planned, even to that small detail.

"By the consent of all the lords representing the high families in the realm, I declare in front of all witnesses that William Michael Rathadon is the King of Vallantia." William felt the weight of the crown settle onto his head and came to his feet.

As he did so, the assembled lords, led by Alex, all took a knee in front of him, heads bowed much as his had been just moments before. Trumpets blared, announcing to all that Vallantia had a new king. Even through the thick castle walls William could hear the cheering from the amassed locals who'd made the journey to the palace to fill the grounds for his coronation, just so they could tell people in the years to come that they had been here when the king had been crowned.

William reflected that the crown was as heavy as his father had complained about. As long as the day had seemed already, it would be hours yet before he could take the thing off, with a presentation to the people congregated outside, then the feast and grand ball to follow.

William waited patiently as the servants swarmed all around him, divesting him of his formal attire. He carefully removed the Rathadon Crown, placing it on the cushioned stand. Shaun replaced it with his new woven gold band around his forehead. As irritated as he was to have to wear it, at least it was lighter than the full crown. Walking from his inner rooms, he eyed Alex, Kyle, Jess and Elizabeth, who all waited on him. The conversation they'd been having suddenly cut off as he entered the sitting room. He frowned as he noticed Aaron had just finished affixing a dressing on Jess's shoulder.

"Thanks, Aaron." Jess stood calmly as a servant helped slip the shoulder of her dress back up and do up the buttons on the back.

"That shoulder hasn't healed yet?"

"It will. I'd almost forgotten about it but I think one of the guards must have told on me." Jess shrugged, then winced.

"I can't reveal my sources, my lady. The bloody hole ripped in the shoulder of your gown was also a giveaway." Aaron smiled, then bowed to William and packed up his things before leaving the room.

"The combination of energy and blade hinders the healing process, even the healers' gifts. It's one of the reasons we all sheath our blades in power if we are fighting Kin." Alex looked unconcerned as he explained the principle. William decided to file that away for future knowledge.

"You were shielding?" William was almost certain Jess had had her shields up.

"I did, but they were mostly covering you. Power fights power. The power on the blade sliced through the shield. Stopping the blade with my body was inelegant but effective. I'll be fine. Stop fretting." Jess waved off his concern.

"I want you to take it easy until you can clear the rest of that poison from your system my lady." Aaron's tone was stern as he pinned Jess with his gaze.

William's eyes widened. "Poison? Are you sure you are alright?"

Jess threw the healer an exasperated look. "I'm fine William, the poison was meant for you remember? Not me. It's not one I've encountered before but my own abilities to heal are holding it off."

Carl bustled over and handed him a goblet as he sat eyeing the four of them suspiciously.

"Why is it I get the distinct impression you all knew that attack was going to happen?"

"William, please, you had other things to concern yourself with." Elizabeth held up her hand.

"All right, spit it out. Now." William knew they were hiding something from him. He could see it in the guilt written on their faces.

"We didn't *know*, William, it was just an educated guess." Kyle swallowed a mouthful of his own drink, his tone calm.

William swung his head over to Alex as he spoke up.

"They've been dumping Sundered and Kin on us periodically since Father was assassinated." Alex's tone was blunt, obviously dumping the party line that everything was fine.

"Ah, I wondered why the three of you were constantly at my side." William frowned. He'd missed a great many things during his own recovery from the attack that had taken his Father's life.

Kyle shook his head. "We also needed to help shield and contain you, William. Unlike ours, your transition was unexpected and sudden."

"You also wanted to make sure I didn't go mad like Mother from the shock and agony." William felt his lips twitch, amused despite the circumstances.

"Yes. That too." Alex looked at him blandly.

Jess's expression was calm. "You didn't have your whole life to get used to the idea, William."

"Oh, because having all that foreknowledge helped the three of you?" William raised his eyebrows at the three.

Alex laughed unexpectedly. "No, it didn't, not really. But no offence, William, we all have access to a lot more power than you. You should be grateful for that."

William shuddered, thinking about having all of the power Alex had access to suddenly running through his body. He was grateful that his own powers were minimal right now, even if like his mother before him he never should have gone through transition at all. Of course, he would have been happier not to have his life turned upside down. He was never meant to be Kin. That was Alex's lot in life, always had been. William suddenly laughed, amused at his own reaction. All those years he'd spent counselling Alex, only to find it a struggle to accept himself.

William shook himself and regarded them solemnly.

"I take it you haven't had much of a chance to go looking for the Order?"

Alex shook his head. "No, it's been a little hectic here with Father's death, then the funeral. With your permission, now that you've recovered we'll start looking for them."

"Why didn't any of you just take one of those assassins they've been sending as prisoner? Or even the one today could have proven useful rather than just evaporating her. Then we could have found out where their base is." William turned and frowned at them all.

Alex threw him an exasperated look. "Exactly how do you propose we keep them William?"

William's eyes narrowed at the clear tone of sarcasm in his brother's voice. He opened his mouth only to be interrupted by Kyle.

"We'll give it thought, William. If the opportunity presents itself."

William could feel Kyle willing him to calm down and was about to take offence, then remembered their conversation about Amelia with Lord Strafford. Kyle had indicated he would try. If they had to capture one of the Sundered it might as well be Amelia.

Jess glanced between them, placing her hand on Alex's shoulder who still didn't look mollified at all. "Perhaps with our powers and the help of the healers we can come up with something. To be fair, William, we've been preoccupied with you."

"I asked the same question while you were sick; the logistics of imprisoning someone who can appear and disappear seemingly at will hadn't occurred to me." Elizabeth looked at him, a blush rising on her cheeks and she rolled her eyes.

William wanted to stay angry, but when his twin put her mind to it he struggled. Finally he nodded, dismissing the problem. He'd leave it to Kyle.

"Ah. I didn't think of that."

There was a silence for a moment, as if none of them knew how to continue.

Elizabeth grimaced. "We've been carefully monitoring all the incoming reports but there hasn't been anything suspicious."

Jess shrugged. "One of us will of course be staying here at all times."

"We'll take it in turns to play bodyguard and that way you can concentrate on that being-king thing." Kyle grinned at him.

"Now that is a role that is all yours, brother. I no more wish to be in your shoes than you wish to be in mine." Alex's eyes sparkled, indicating he had pushed aside his irritation.

William grinned in response. He'd had some very bad moments when he'd thought he might turn out like Alex. He'd been reassured he'd never possess the power to accidentally blow up the palace, like Alex did. He had a sneaking suspicion that Kyle and Jess could as well. He could shield his own mind now thanks to their training. Now it was time for him to not only be the king but hopefully follow in his father's footsteps to become a good king.

15

RECOGNITION

Kyle looked over as Ryan entered tugging on his vest, looking a little uncomfortable in the formal court gear. He traded glances with both Alex and Jess, who both grinned. That uncomfortable tugging at the vest was a habit they all recognised.

"Best get used to them, Ryan. Your days of being anonymous are over." Kyle chuckled as Ryan groaned.

"I don't really need formal recognition or rank. I helped shield the king during the coronation without it." Ryan looked at Kyle hopefully.

"Yes, you really do. Your actions at the coronation reminded William your position has to be formalised." Kyle showed no compassion at all and had to stop himself laughing outright at the woebegone expression on Ryan's face.

"Besides, Ryan, if you don't join us in the painful part, being the formal ball, you can hardly join us for our own private celebration after." Alex shook his head as the last seemed to spark Ryan's interest.

Jess grinned at him. "We might even take a run into town, although keep that to yourself."

"Be grateful, Ryan, the frippery of the Companion's Cohort formal gear is nowhere near what Alex has to put up with, let alone the king."

Kyle noted that while Ryan had gotten better around Jess, he still blushed every time she spoke with him. He had a feeling the boy was smitten with her and was bound to be terribly heartbroken when he found out she viewed him more like a little brother, let alone when he worked out the most recent fling she'd had was with William, who was now their king. Now that he was about to appear officially in the court, he had no doubt that gossip would reach the lad's ears.

Kyle gazed at Jess and filed that thought as a conversation they needed to have again. Jess had been withdrawn of late and he suspected it had to do with the impending arrival of William's future consort, the Imperial Princess from the Empire of Sylanna. It didn't matter how frequently she'd told herself that the relationship between her and William was a temporary fling, Kyle knew it was still difficult. The pair had been foolish to reignite their relationship and if they'd known about Her Imperial Highness, they probably wouldn't have. Still, sometimes there was what you knew the smart thing was, and then there was what actually happened.

Kyle did know how Jess must feel. His own situation with Elizabeth had been similar. Then the negotiations had started in earnest for the contract between her and a son of the Heights Protectorate. It had effectively ended their own relationship, particularly when Elizabeth's intended had shown up at court. It was the thing with their rank. For the most part they could do as they wished within certain boundaries, however they would all do their duty and enter into arrangements for the good of their families.

He knew William had been much better since he and Alex had sat him down and effectively told him to stop pressuring Jess. That didn't stop him from backsliding on occasion, although he and Alex were quick to intervene when they caught it. It was a fine line the two trod, moving from lovers back to friends. He knew that withdrawing wasn't the answer to that.

Kyle shook himself from his train of thought and back to the present as the door opened and Joshua appeared.

"Your Highness, it's time. I'm advised the king is almost ready." Joshua moved forward, taking the circlet from Alex and placing it expertly on his brow. Then he moved aside as all of them heaved a universal sigh and stood to head out the door.

Kyle laughed. So much for them all providing a good role model for Ryan. At least on this occasion it was Ryan that was likely to be the centre of attention. Not that the boy realised it yet. He was in for quite an education.

RYAN RESISTED the urge to tug on his formal tunic and looked again at the silver ring on his finger with the crossed swords of the Companion's Cohort—yet another thing he knew would take time to get used to. He'd never worn jewellery before either, yet now he was told he wasn't meant to take it off. Of course he'd noticed that Kyle, Jess and even Alex ignored that and quite regularly divested themselves of any sign of their ranks. Ryan decided that was another tip he'd take from them since he was modelling his behaviour on a mix of Alex and Kyle. He was taking his cues from them, although he wasn't sure he was doing it right and was certain everyone saw straight through him.

He was surrounded by some of the very people who had mocked him since he'd arrived at the palace. Although some looked dumbfounded at his elevation to the rank of lord, they all seemed to be doing their utmost to ignore that previously they'd treated him with disdain: the poor orphan boy who was beneath them. It had to smart that now he would possess a rank higher than their own.

Ryan glanced across the packed court and saw Alex was still at the king's side. Since the death of the old king, someone with the talent in the veil was always with him when he was holding court. No one was taking any risk with his safety.

How did you even know I'd reached my majority?

Ryan caught Kyle's amused smile at his exasperated tone, and both Alex and the king glanced in his direction. To his shock it was the king who answered.

The healers keep records of births they attend. Since we know who your parents were, I simply asked them to confirm the date for me.

Ryan digested that little piece of information, endeavouring to keep his irritation from showing on his face.

That's cheating, you know that, right? Ryan's eyes nearly popped out of his head at his own audacity to backchat the king.

There has to be some advantage to having this job, Ryan. The king's tone was clearly amused.

Don't worry, Ryan, you still have a couple of years before you will have to shoulder full responsibility as an adult.

Kyle grinned, although he wasn't looking at him, and Ryan nearly choked when he realised that one of the ladies surrounding Kyle thought the smile was for her and preened.

You are old enough to come and play without us getting in trouble.

Jess's eyes sparkled in amusement. William chuckled, not quite as good at hiding the fact he was having a conversation with them and not paying attention to those who surrounded him.

Since when has that stopped the three of you getting into trouble?

Ryan's interest was sparked as Alex looked at William, his gaze measuring before grinning.

I have a different kind of excursion planned for tonight. You did ask why I kept going back to The Last Stop. Why don't you come with us?

Jess looked across at Alex, startled at his offer. William didn't look at Alex, keeping his attention on those chattering at him, yet he looked intrigued.

The only time I disappeared, everyone panicked.

Kyle grinned. *Retire for the night. We'll tell your people you aren't to be disturbed, then pop you back into your bed before morning.*

Jess chuckled. *That might just work.*

How often in your entire life have you had the night off, William? Alex's mind voice held a clear note of cajoling.

William took a breath and excused himself, then turned to walk out of the private doors to retreat to his rooms. His mind voice floated back to them all.

If Elizabeth finds out about this, she is going to kill me.

16

REALISATION

William found himself unaccountably nervous. He knew the Summer and Winter Palaces and the towns along the route between them both, yet this was a new experience, entering a bar in a prosperous border town —or any of the towns in his kingdom. While he'd been to some of the establishments in Vallantia and Callenhain, those visits had been all carefully controlled and executed, and there had probably been more of his own people in those places than locals, all in the name of security, of course. Alex should never have been to the bars, taverns and brothels he'd attended either, but Alex had been a law unto himself. Oh, he listened politely enough to the security briefings that told him why he shouldn't do such things. He even agreed about the rating of most of the places he went. Then he'd turn around and, along with Jess and Kyle, go anyway.

William realised that this was probably why Alex attracted such a following amongst the commoners. While he himself had been the dutiful crown prince, listening to all that came before him for judgement, lord or commoner alike, it still took the average person without rank to make the effort to come to him. Alex had always been more accessible, at least to those without rank. He always had time for the guards, merchants, innkeepers and even homeless thieves, as long as they weren't in the process of trying to rob him.

William glanced at Ryan, and wondered if he would have seen the potential in the street urchin that Alex had. His brother had always proven to be an exceptional judge of character. His people adored him and would follow him anywhere. It had always been the case. Well, they did when they weren't being exasperated that he kept leaving them behind. Alex had a quality that he doubted even they could put their finger on. He could be stubborn, irritating and totally irresponsible, yet the reports he'd received indicated that even the innkeeper at this bar had nearly thrown the guard out on the street simply for asking about Alex.

One concession had been made, probably due to his own presence: Alex had brought Marcus, James, Megan and Matthew with them. The guards had looked astonished to be asked to come, or most of them had; Marcus had worn a look of suspicion on his face. Then their faces had shuttered, showing no emotion at all as soon as they realised that their king was coming along on this particular excursion. It had obviously dawned on them at that point exactly why his brother had chosen to bring them along. Alex showed no compunction about risking his own life, but he wasn't about to risk William's.

William held back as they entered the bar, smiling as the innkeeper, at seeing Alex, came from out behind the bar with a grin on his face.

"Ah, my boy! It's been some time since we've seen you here. I'd feared the worst." The innkeeper enveloped Alex in his bear-like grip, pounding him on the back in welcome.

William held back his own grin as Marcus, James, Megan and Matthew all tensed at the unexpected familiarity shown to

Alex, their hands straying to the hilts of their swords in what he expected was an automatic reaction.

"I'm fine, Ian, sorry, I should have sent word." Alex glanced back and drew William forward. "This is my brother, Will."

William could almost see the man's brain processing the information. The innkeeper knew very well who Alex was and William had no doubt that Ian knew who he was, yet Ian didn't show the slightest hesitation. His gaze flicked around them all before settling on him.

"Welcome to The Last Stop, Will." Ian glanced at the party and smiled, then looked back at Alex. "Your usual table is free, or I can set you all up in a private room, if you prefer?"

Alex waved off the suggestion and started toward a table at the back of the bar. Despite the late hour many seemed to recognise him and nodded greeting as their party passed. William noted that their guards split up, Marcus and James retiring to a position at the bar with a clear view of the whole common room and easy access to take out anyone who came through the door. Megan, subtly guiding Matthew, took over an empty table not far from their own.

William had barely settled on the bench when he noted that Alex, Jess and Kyle looked perfectly at home, and Ryan only marginally less so, glancing around at the other inhabitants of the bar. William realised with a start that this was Ryan's home village. He wondered whether Ryan recognised any of the men and women in the bar, or whether they recognised him as one of their own lost merchant brats.

The innkeeper came across with two of his bar staff carrying pitchers and platters of food, placing them all on the table. Kyle reached for his money pouch to pay the man, only to be waved off.

"No need. Alex is paid up well in advance, and even if he wasn't, it would be on the house. All of you relax and have a good evening." The innkeeper nodded, then withdrew, ushering his people before him. William noted that he sent pitchers of what seemed like water and platters of food to their guards as well.

Ryan grabbed a pitcher and poured them all a round.

William picked up his goblet and raised it, waiting a brief moment as they all raised their own, looking at him, waiting.

"Congratulations, Ryan." William wanted to say more but discretion stayed his tongue; he was too aware of those in the bar pretending not to listen.

Ryan ducked his head before looking back up with a self-conscious grin on his face, and took a careful sip of his drink. William's mouth twitched, noting his reaction. It was obviously not the first time that he'd had a drink even though he'd only just reached his majority. He guessed he shouldn't be surprised given the hard life Ryan had led before Alex found him and took him in.

Sighing, Alex leaned back against the rough rock wall behind him, looking more relaxed than William had seen him in a long time.

"You clearly like this place."

Alex shrugged. "Somehow I just seem to keep ending up here."

As the night passed, William began to relax. He looked around, perplexed. There was something he couldn't quite put a finger on about the place. After the first covert glances in their direction when they'd first shown up here, no one seemed to pay them much attention. William looked around. There were those who were clearly merchants, heads together engaged in serious conversations, although William doubted any real business was being done given the hour. Others were merely sitting around, enjoying each other's company after a long day. A bard's voice floated above the soothing sound of his instrument from where he crooned over in one corner.

Startled, William realised what it was that was different: for the first time since he'd been old enough to leave the nursery and attend the court as the crown prince, no one cared about his presence. Everyone—every single person outside of family and close friends that had surrounded him his whole life—had wanted something from him; wanted something from his father, the king, even if it was an attempt to gain further prestige for their own families by associating with him. That odd feeling came from the fact that there was no one pestering him for some material gain of their own.

No one here wanted anything from him.

He watched as the barman's lad used a small burst of power to heat a bowl of food before handing it to a customer, with no fear or furtiveness about his actions; he just did it. It was for people like this, so they could sit in a place with their friends and relax after their day's work, that the fight against the Order was important. People deserved to live without fear.

William and every one of his peers had thick castle walls to protect them when trouble reared its head. Folks like these had no one but themselves. Themselves and the belief that the Fourth and his people would leave the safety of their walls to come out and fight for them, just like they had in that ancient past, placing themselves between the common folk and those they could not hope to fight against.

Right now William was just a man, sitting in a bar with his friends. Alex's habit of mixing with commoners was well known. They trusted already that he, of all those they looked to, wouldn't cower behind the palace walls when trouble came knocking. Alex would be out here with them.

William looked across the table at Alex, and raised his glass in salute. For the first time, he understood why his brother spent so much time escaping the trappings of their birth.

17

DISCOVERY

Kyle paused in a crouch on the rooftop in the current village he was checking when he felt an incoming surge of energy that meant someone with power had arrived. He was up and running, making his way towards where he'd detected the arrival of the other, only using small low-level pulses of power in order to augment his own strength and hide his presence. To anyone else with power, the small amounts he used would be lost in the general hum of energy. Before he knew it he was lying down on a rooftop looking down to the street below. As he looked at the cloaked figure below, his eyes narrowed. There was something about the person that was nagging at the back of his mind.

Kyle started to push himself up from the roof to investigate further when he froze. Another distinct pattern within the veil heralded the arrival of another, a signature that he knew. As Alex appeared in the street below, Kyle looked on in shock. He carefully lowered himself back down on the roof. The other walked forward, a delicate hand reaching out from the depths of the cloak to curl around the back of Alex's head and pull him down for a kiss. Kyle found he was holding his breath as

Alex grabbed her around the waist, pulling her into his body. The woman's hood fell back as she tilted her head and Kyle felt as if someone had dumped him into an ice cold river in the middle of winter. Equal measure of shock and dread causing through him.

Amelia.

Kyle rolled over onto his back, staring up to the night sky. He pressed one hand against his face, squeezing his eyes shut, trying to block out that image.

Ah, my friend. What the hell are you doing?

Shaking himself, he rolled back to keep his eyes on the lovers. As much as he hated it, the body language of the pair below made it clear that is what they were. When he felt Alex draw his own power to retreat into the veil, Kyle was ready. He reinforced his own shields—he'd become remarkably good at them since he'd won his freedom back from Joanna. It was amazing what a motivator self-preservation was. Kyle eased his way into the veil and followed Alex. It wasn't that hard since his friend really wasn't trying to mask his presence. Then again, Kyle doubted that Alex suspected he was being followed. It was easy to grow lax about personal security over time. It didn't take Kyle long to work out the pair's destination. He breathed a sigh of relief. The Winter Palace. Alex may be behaving like a lovesick idiot, but he wasn't entirely stupid. It was better to conduct his secret affair here than in a run-down pub, or worse, at the Summer Palace. The fact that he'd brought Amelia here told him at least a part of Alex's brain was showing some caution, even if it wasn't much.

Kyle drew closer, carefully checking on Alex to confirm his suspicions before flinching back from the scene in Alex's bedroom. Definitely an affair with the enemy, since they had made short work of divesting themselves of their clothes and ending up in bed together. Kyle groaned and turned away from them. He could watch over Alex without having to watch his friend have sex with his sister.

Damn it, Alex.

Kyle stopped, casting around as he sensed another presence close by, not moving through as he would expect but loitering. Cautiously Kyle moved himself closer to the other presence. He couldn't think of any other reason why the other would be hanging around, except to watch Alex and Amelia. The male Kin was doing a remarkable job of trying to shield, but his control had slipped, allowing Kyle to catch his presence. Kyle felt cold as he realised this could be a trap for Alex.

The veil around him reacted as he drew his weapons and power. The energy sizzled around him, buzzing with his determination and anger yet focussed on the enemy. Whoever the male was, he was definitely watching Alex and Amelia. He started up as the veil vibrated around him, his eyes wide when he finally noticed that he had been spotted. He jumped aside as Kyle hurled a bolt of energy at him while closing the remaining distance between them.

Kyle saw a moment of indecision on the face of the other as he turned his attention back towards Amelia and Alex before drawing his own power and fleeing.

Another day, Fourth's Blade! The stranger's mind voice whispered in his head, taunting him as he disappeared.

Kyle was torn between following the Kin and not being drawn too far away to keep an effective eye out for Alex. The veil rumbled, rolling out from him as he cursed again and reined himself back in. Allowing the other to lead him too far off was stupid and now that he was concentrating, the other's barriers were obviously firmly in place since Kyle couldn't sense him at all. Still, he would recognise the Kin's signature in the veil in future, just as he knew Amelia's. If he felt either again, he'd know them for the threat they were.

While he didn't know the hostile Kin, it appeared that he

knew Kyle. He guessed that the man was connected to Amelia. That made Alex's affair with her even worse. Kyle paused in his assessment of the other being Kin. Not Kin, yet not Sundered either. That one was something between—his controlled madness was closer to what Kyle sensed in Amelia the few times he'd encountered her since she'd fallen to the Order.

Kyle closed his eyes, trying to think calmly. Given the activity Alex and Amelia were engaged in right now he didn't think his friend would do anything stupid. Kyle shook his head. Anything more stupid than what he was doing now. He was also certain that the disturbance in the veil would have impinged on the pair's awareness no matter how distracted they currently were. Or at least he hoped Alex had the common sense to still keep a part of his mind on the lookout for potential trouble.

ALEX PUSHED ASIDE his guilt at his continued relationship with Amelia. He had been trying to get the location of the Order out of her, or at least that is what he told himself. Unfortunately he didn't believe his own very thin excuse. Every time he left her bed, he told himself he would not be going back. He felt like he was alternately drowning, lost, only to rise up again with a semblance of sanity where he asked himself what the hell he was doing. Yet somehow he found himself falling into her arms again.

"I'm sorry I cannot be what you want me to be, Alex." Amelia rested in his arms after their lovemaking, her hand absently trailing up his chest.

"It isn't your fault, Amelia. There isn't any way you could have fought back as a child." Alex rolled over, leaning down for a lingering kiss.

"My master gives me a certain amount of freedom. The

drug he used on me is different from the one used on Kyle, but I can't go against his orders." Amelia shuddered as she talked about her master and the control he had on her.

Alex winced, the images of the torture she'd endured at Kevin's hands flashing in his mind.

"Come back with me, Amelia. Let the healers try to help you." Alex watched her face, his heart sinking. He already knew the answer.

"I can't, Alex. There is no hope for me. I belong to my master. He wants you, and I am the instrument he is using." Amelia was earnest, dragging his head down to kiss him again.

At the mention of the word *master* Alex caught the image of Scholar Clements. It flicked to another man he didn't recognise who bore the tag of *Aiden*, then back to Clements. He wondered why the old scholar had flicked into her mind when she thought of her master, rather than Kevin. Then the flash of a woman in a ripped shift, matted hair covering her face, grubby arms and hands with chipped fingernails reaching towards him.

Beware Aiden. Kill me...

Alex was diverted by Amelia's intentions for a moment, held in her spell, but then he frowned, withdrawing to look into her eyes.

"He knows about our continued liaison?" Alex found his mind whirling, trying to deny the answers that were adding up in his head—the very real possibility he'd been trying to ignore since he'd started sleeping with Amelia again.

Of course he knows, lover. As it so often did, all the previous warmth bled from her, leaving dark cold hard eyes staring at him.

Please, Amelia, I do love you but I can't keep doing this. Alex swallowed, guilt assailing him.

He was flung back onto the bed with Amelia straddling

him, her hands on either side of his head. Her eyes flickered with a cold dark flame.

I was taken, tortured and enslaved because of you, Alex, because my master really wants you. You will keep coming when I call. You owe me that! Amelia's mind voice hissed in anger.

Alex recoiled, gasping as sharp pain struck his side. His mind went numb as he realised Amelia had stabbed him with one of her small daggers. He reached up to her, trying to apologise, only to have her disappear into the veil, her voice echoing in his head.

You will come to me as I desire.

Alex shuddered with guilt, as images of her torture at the hands of Kevin assailed his mind, her screams for him to come and save her echoing in his head.

Amelia, I'm sorry, I didn't mean for you to be hurt because of me. Please forgive me. I'll come when you call.

He groaned, wondering not for the first time what he was doing and why he felt compelled to keep meeting up with her. She was dangerous, he knew that particularly well when she wasn't around. The stabbing thing was new and unexpected. As dangerous as he knew she was, he'd never believed she was capable of truly harming him.

A sardonic smile spread on his face. He knew it was a foolish belief. Her murder of his father should be enough to prove it. This Amelia was a very different person to the one he'd fallen in love with. She was harder, with a violent streak that didn't seem to have many controls. Amelia's tastes now also ran a little to the rough side. The sudden spurt of desire he'd felt just as she'd lashed out with her knife at him was telling.

Alex fell back against his pillows, hands pressed against his eyes, trying desperately to block the world out. The implications of what he was doing, how William would react when he found out—and he *would* find out—weighed down on him.

ALEX APPEARED BACK in his own rooms still languid after his encounter with Amelia. Thinking of her caused equal bursts of guilt and a desire to see her again. If he hadn't been thinking so much about Amelia, he probably would have noticed a hell of a lot sooner that Kyle was sitting on the couch waiting for him. As it was, when he did notice, he had the distinct feeling he looked as guilty as he felt. He went to take off his cloak only to have Kyle stand, stopping him with his hand on his shoulder.

"Come on, Alex, we need to go somewhere and have a chat." Kyle's expression was closed but Alex could tell his lifelong friend was extremely unhappy with him.

"Can't this wait, Kyle? I..." Alex's smile faltered.

"No. Let's get out of here." Kyle didn't wait for an answer, simply sweeping them both into the veil.

It didn't take Alex long to work out where they were going, since it was one of their old haunts.

The Barrel.

Alex didn't get a chance to object as Kyle had his hand on his shoulder, propelling him into the bar. It was getting late, and a number of booths were empty, although he had the sinking feeling Kyle would have cleaned out a booth for their use regardless. Kyle directed them both to one in the back corner.

Kyle gestured to the barman, who nodded and sent a pitcher to their table promptly and a platter of finger food from the kitchen following in short order. The proprietor knew exactly who they both were; they'd been hauled back to the palace by the Elite at dawn on more than one occasion over the years.

Kyle sat in silence until the servers had retreated from the table after setting down the food and pouring them each a drink.

"What the hell are you thinking, Alex?" Kyle hissed at him.

"What do you mean...?" Alex broke off as Kyle's eyes flashed in anger.

"Don't play games. You're still sleeping with my sister." Kyle's eyes bored into his own.

Swallowing, Alex picked up his drink to take a sip, his mind racing, trying to find a way to make what he'd been up to seem better. He knew there was no simple or good explanation for what he'd been doing.

Alex looked away from Kyle's penetrating stare. "I can't help it, Kyle. I still love her."

The silence stretched between them.

"Damn it, Alex, she is playing you! There is no way Kevin doesn't know what she is up to." Kyle shook his head in disgust.

Alex glanced away uncomfortably and Kyle groaned softly. His friend knew him far too well.

"She said as much." Alex turned his glass slowly on the tabletop, refusing to look up.

"Alex, damn it. She is a murderer and she has been declared a traitor. She killed your father!" Kyle hissed out the words.

Kyle motioned off the waitboy who'd noticed their goblets were empty. He picked up the decanter and poured them both another round.

"I know. I swear every time that I will break it off and tell William. I dream about her torture, what he did to her. It's my fault she was taken. Damn it Kyle she's not all bad, I know it. If we can somehow get her to Aaron he will be able to help her." Alex stopped playing with his glass and took a mouthful, swallowing it slowly before finally looking up at Kyle.

Alex could see his friend was wrestling with himself, torn between friendship and duty and now a measure of pity, but Kyle kept pushing.

"Alex, get your head together and break it off. You know

that isn't true, face it. Amelia is gone. What do you think William will do when he finds out?"

"I, I don't know." Alex shook his head. It was difficult to explain his own behaviour to his best friend when he didn't understand it himself.

"I thought you had something going with Isabella."

Alex went pale at the thought of Isabella and buried his face in his hands. "She's going to kill me."

His life was a mess. His continued liaison with his former consort confused him.

"You're right, Kyle, I... I don't know what I'm thinking. I won't do it again." Alex looked up from the table to glance at Kyle. He meant it, but he also couldn't help feeling miserable at the very thought of not seeing Amelia again.

Alex could feel Kyle's frustration and anger rolling over him. The look in his friend's eyes spoke his disgust as clearly.

As Kyle's lips thinned and his expression hardened Alex had the feeling that his friend saw straight through him. Even he wasn't so certain he would stick to his promise next time Amelia called him. He vowed that he'd find a way to stay away from her next time she called. Or he'd try.

"You are correct, you won't or I swear to you I will report this to William. As I should do now." Kyle's eyes flashed. "I will track her down and kill her. As I should have done well before now...." Kyle bit out each word then stopped suddenly, his eyes glinting as he smiled.

Alex swallowed. "What?"

"Next time you go on one of these little trysts with my sister..."

"Kyle, you just finished telling me not to." Alex had to admit he was confused by his sudden change.

"You will tell me. Then I can follow her back to her hideout, where I have no doubt the rest of the Order is hiding as well. Then we can finish this."

Alex drew his breath in sharply, conflicting emotions warring through him. He knew he should have tracked Amelia back to her base himself and he couldn't work out why he hadn't grasped the opportunity. The other half of him was terrified that Amelia would be hurt. That reaction confused him even more. Alex looked at Kyle and nodded acceptance for the plan despite the fact he seemed to be at war with himself over it.

18

BINDINGS

Brian felt the power pulse through him again. He didn't even scream anymore. It was an eternal torment. Knowing where you began, who you were, and being able to differentiate between yourself and another person should be such a basic thing. Images of people he'd killed flashed in his mind. There were times he recognised, where he revelled in the kill, the pain he could inflict on others. Other times, like now, brief times, he knew what he'd done and was consumed by guilt.

There was one death that flashed into his mind, and he grasped it, always holding onto the familiar face. Regardless of the pain that welled in him at her death, he knew he'd been responsible for it. Or at least his body had tried to kill her. Tried to kill her and been unsuccessful. That knowledge gave him some solace. That solace was always brief. His controllers used him to torment her still, to force her further down the path of madness—her punishment for not dying when they wished her to.

He remembered what he'd been before his captors had taken him, bent him to their will. Brian cried out in this moment of sanity, no matter how short-lived it might be, hoping that someone would hear him. Someone who was strong enough would track him down and kill him. Give him the ultimate release. At least then he could not be used to hurt her or anyone else again. Except he knew no one would come and save him. He would plunge back into darkness again.

Find me.

Kill me!

The plea he flung out wouldn't work. He knew they would use him again to kill and torment others.

AMELIA ACCOMPANIED Jenny through the foothills with the new Sundered One that she had been working on. Her master wasn't happy that Jenny was out here and potentially at risk; she was still useful to his purpose. Yet they insisted the test of this new one, Brian, was necessary.

Amelia looked at him, raking her eyes over this new addition to their fighting ranks. He was like many of the old ones they initiated the new treatment on. This Brian was half back, not totally consumed with madness as most of his kind were. There was something odd about him, but Amelia couldn't quite pinpoint what the oddness was that she sensed. It was clear to her Brian was nothing like herself. Still, he had apparently been a fighter in his day. Jenny had advised her it was why he was one of a handful the healers were trying the new treatments on—to assist Amelia and the others like her to push the Order's campaign across Vallantia.

Amelia smiled coldly. At least there were plenty of the old mad ones to burn through. They made very handy sacrifices. Indeed, their master Kevin had ordered them to throw the lives of these ones away rather than risk their own.

Amelia glanced around and moved in front of Healer Jenny,

her hand up in caution. The small encampment of regular humans had been located not far from their own base, and that was something the Order could not tolerate, particularly since it was walking distance. It was distinctly possible the small family could stumble upon them by accident. Besides, it was also clear that they didn't belong to one of the local farms or villages beholden to the Kastler estate, otherwise they wouldn't be camped out here.

"Mistress, there, down near the small pool of water." Amelia gestured, drawing her attention to the couple and their neat encampment.

Jenny's own eyes held not even a hint of emotion as she looked down on the man and woman. Amelia understood. She could feel their mutual master's mark on her stronger today than it had been. She knew that Kevin routinely strengthened his hold on her. She was strong as a healer, even she could sense Jenny's own powers working away trying to heal that which bound her to another, although she doubted the healer was aware it was happening. She turned to look up at Brian.

Go, Brian. Kill the couple below, they are a threat to our safety.

Amelia heard her order but since it wasn't directed at her, she wasn't compelled to assist. Not unless she chose to. Her eyes narrowed as Brian pulled the veil to himself, disappearing momentarily before appearing in the clearing. Brian was strong, stronger than many of the other mad ones.

The woman was the first to notice the new arrival to their camp and her high-pitched scream rang around the surrounding hills. The man spun at hearing her cry and yelled something inarticulate as he charged at the stranger.

Amelia watched shocked as Brian just stood there, looking down at the woman, not moving or making any attempt to obey Jenny's order. He seemed frozen. As the man reached them, he drew his sword and launched a wild strike at Brian.

~

As he walked calmly alongside Healer Jenny, Brian cringed on the inside. He knew she was going to try and make him kill again. Every time they did this he feared they would find out about him, then find a way to work their way around the boy's injunction. That they would turn him into a killer again. As he had been when they first took him.

He glanced at the Sundered one that walked with him and the healer. Amelia. She was one of the new ones. He knew she was what they were trying to turn him into. As he looked at her he suddenly saw two of her. One superimposed over the other, her form seeming to flicker back and forth between the two. Brian looked at Healer Jenny who walked on, unconcerned as if she hadn't a care. Or perhaps not perceptive enough to notice anything wrong.

Brian looked at Amelia again; there was the strong Sundered fighter who burned with bright power. Controlled with layer upon layer of compulsions. He could see them, similar to the web of power that lay on him and in his mind.

Then there was the other one. The young, mad woman in a white shift and matted dark hair.

As his own body walked on, following the directions of Healer Jenny, without the need of his input, he stared at the other one. The mad woman who, it seemed, against all odds was similar to him. Separate somehow from herself, yet still trapped and constrained.

Amelia? Brian whispered at her, watching, fascinated to see if she'd hear him.

While the strong, rather frightening Sundered walked calmly, the mad one jumped, spun around looking for the voice. Comprehension hit Brian: this other Amelia, the scared mad woman was what survived, or was cut away, when she was created into the killer she was now. The mad Amelia existed in a space in her own head, locked away from her body. The flickering he'd seen between the two was when she came closer to the surface of her mind. Possibly staring out of what had once been her own eyes.

Shhh.... Don't fear me little one...

Trusting his body would keep on doing as he'd been commanded to do Brian chased after the mad woman as she retreated in fear, further into her own mind.

Who... who are you? Amelia's voice trembled as she turned, her back to a wall staring at him.

I am Brian, the one that walks beside you in the real world.

Brian watched her carefully as she considered what he'd said.

What are you? She looked around as if wondering how to escape him.

I'm like you, there is a part of me that survived what the Order did.

No, my master left me here, locked up to punish me further. So I'd know what I've become. Her voice sobbed, the wall behind her starting to fade as she backed up, tears streaming down her face.

No little one, you locked yourself up. If your master knew you still existed, he would kill you.

Brian threw those last words at her as she fled, hiding in madness. Perhaps she would remember. Perhaps the words would sink through her madness and she could cling to them. Use them to drag herself back from the insanity that possessed her. To cause trouble for their masters.

Brian smiled. Another small victory, while he waited to die.

AMELIA SHOOK HER HEAD, certain for a moment that she'd heard another speaking to her. She looked around with her eyes and her mind but only saw those she expected to see.

Amelia! Help him!

Jenny's command burned into her brain, shaking her out of her momentary confusion. Amelia swung her attention back to Brian and jumped the short distance between them. She drew her own weapon, seeing blood spurt from Brian's side as the man's sword bit into his flesh.

Without pause she cut down the attacker, who hadn't even noticed her arrival, then lunged past Brian, running through the woman with her blade. The woman stiffened, her face going pale, slumping back as she jerked out her sword. She was still alive but Amelia dismissed her. She was only human and with that injury, unlike the Kin, who would heal, she would die soon enough without a healer.

Amelia looked up as her mistress rushed down the embankment into the makeshift camp. She ran straight past the woman moaning on the ground to Brian's side. Even though he was showing signs of healing already, she expended her own energy to hasten it along.

"Please, help me." The woman lay on the ground, her blood pooling around her.

Amelia looked at her, her eyes narrowed in disdain. She was so pitiful and weak, not even able to help herself to live. Amelia smiled. Their master was correct. Humans were too weak to live except as the most meaningless slaves to serve the Kin.

Her smile widened even further as Jenny looked down dispassionately at the dying woman before looking back at her.

Amelia, can you help get us both back to the healing compound, please? I need to check Brian's bonds again. Ignore that one. She will die on her own eventually.

Amelia nodded, and drawing her powers to her and gathering her mistress and Brian with her, they returned to their own camp, leaving the intruder in the clearing to die.

BLAKE WAITED until the Order's corrupted healer and her two pet Sundered Ones left the clearing. He waited fully shielded, tracing their path back to their encampment. He sighed, walking forward, dropping the barrier he'd maintained to hide not only his own presence but those of his two companions.

He looked down as the woman moaned.

"Please, help me..."

The woman's voice was weak, barely audible; it was obvious she would die by nightfall. Without a hint of expression, Blake stepped to the woman's side. He drew one of his blades with one hand and brushed her hair out of her eyes with the other.

"Shhh... the pain will be over soon." As she smiled weakly, gazing up at him, Blake struck with his dagger.

Blake stood and grimaced looking around at the bodies and evidence of the slaughter, shaking his head.

"Amateurs. All right, let's get this cleaned up."

"If they keep killing like this... well, eventually someone is going to notice." Lain grumbled at him but started to move around the makeshift camp to gather all of the gear.

"I know. Still, the Skull Lord's orders are for us to keep that lot from prying eyes as long as we can." Blake shook his head. Lain was correct.

As the numbers mounted, eventually people would start reporting those that went missing in this area. That was bound to provoke investigation. All he could do was report back to the Skull Lord. It was up to him how long they stayed here fulfilling this current task.

JENNY MOVED to the next patient in the large hall, packed with one stretcher next to the other. All of them had survived their initial treatment. Her personal theory that she hadn't shared with the master yet was that they survived the old treatment regimens because they *weren't* powerful. They were powerful enough compared to regular people who could light up a room or communicate in a limited fashion mind to mind. Regular people could use power that was external to themselves. Healers could use more of it, powerful in their own way, but the power was still external to themselves.

She sat on the edge of Brian's cot, her hands lightly touching his forehead, assessing his progress.

Then there were the poor souls like this man. The power wasn't just around him. It wasn't just a matter of stopping himself from channelling it. The power ran through him constantly, unless he was fully medicated. The Order had learned from trial and error that this inevitably led to death. Jenny pushed down the sadness it caused her to think of all the deaths their great endeavour to find a cure had caused. The thing that kept her going was knowing they were working for the greater good of all.

As strong as Brian was, compared to Amelia he was a small candle flame compared to a raging fire bringing down great tracts of forest land unchecked. Jenny shuddered, thankful that the Order had located and treated Amelia. She would have been extremely dangerous left to her own devices without the necessary control of the Order. A smile touched her lips; she admitted a little bit of pride at her own role in the refinement of the medication that had made it successful. While there was still some loss of life, particularly for those who came late to the treatment, the success rates were much higher now. Identifying the children early and beginning their treatment and mind control young was key, even though some believed their new treatment plan to be cruel.

Jenny's lips thinned in displeasure. It was necessary for those poor children. Their lives would be highly controlled, yet at least they would *have* a life. Normal people would also be safe from their excess. It was no different to how those like herself, normal children who could use some power, were identified by the Healers' Guild and had controls placed on them for the good of all. It was just that those constraints used by the Healers' Guild didn't work on even those like Brian at the very lower end of ability with the power, let alone those as powerful as Amelia.

Many of those under the Order's care, like Brian, were starting to respond quite well under the new treatment plan. It was a relief, healing hundreds of souls. Some had even graduated and become much more useful to the cause, going out in forays with Amelia. It saddened her that it had come to war to protect people but sometimes everyone had to make sacrifices for the greater good.

Brian had shown an initial improvement but had stalled. They had taken him out as they had on previous occasions to test his compliance. He was controlled enough that he didn't have to be shackled anymore. He would go where he was ordered and stay where he was told to. Her patient's reliance on the medication was now reduced. Shown a target and ordered to kill, he would not engage. It was a mystery.

Jenny froze for a moment as the image of the woman begging to be saved flashed in her mind. Her breathing became erratic as something she couldn't name battled inside her.

Hearing the doors open, Jenny looked up, broken from her spell, her frown clearing as Master Healer Kevin walked in. She removed her hands from the temples of her patient and stood, clasping her hands in front of her. She smiled and bowed her head in acknowledgement.

"Master, what brings you here today?" Jenny smiled in genuine welcome.

He didn't comment, simply placing his hands on her temples, and she felt the firm touch of his mind on hers. Her breath caught in her throat, fear thrilling through her mind as she stiffened. Pain raced through her brain, from her temples it ran like fire through her whole body and she felt herself trembling in reaction. If she could have screamed, she would have, but his firm hold on her prevented even that release. She could only feel and stare into his dark eyes that danced with a fire of their own.

You are mine. Your allegiance is to me. Never try to break these bonds or look to another. We do what we do for the greater good.

His words burned into her mind as the litany continued. A part of her mind was analysing it as he reinforced her bindings. They were more effective than the shackles they used on the Sundered. As her master, he was responsible for making sure she stayed on track. For that to work, she had to obey him, trust him completely. Eventually the pain receded, and she felt him retreat to a light presence in her mind. She sobbed and crumpled, trembling into his arms as he held and supported her while she recovered from her rebinding. It was excruciating every time, yet necessary. She knew that.

"Thank you, Master." She looked up at him, reactionary tremors still running through her as her binding settled on her once more like a firm, well-fitting glove. The image of the dying woman no longer burned in her mind or troubled her.

"I'm sorry for the pain, my pet, but you know it is necessary." His hand stroked the side of her face; she saw it tremble as he stroked her and he licked his lips, his voice low.

Jenny shivered as his hands traced a light pattern on her, and she could feel the power coming from him.

"Master." This time, instead of causing pain, it receded under his seeking fingers.

He grabbed her hand and led her toward the door.

"Come, Jenny, I have need of you. Leave Brian and do not worry about him, he serves another very valuable purpose."

There was power in his words and Jenny shuddered as his will settled on her.

They walked from the large underground cavern where they kept all the Sundered who were under treatment and into the tunnel that led to the estate house. Jenny sighed. She remembered her master had his own rooms in a quiet corner tower with easy access to the caverns. He'd taken her there a few times before. His rooms were much more comfortable than her cot in a small alcove off the healing cavern that she shared with her master's other bonded healers. As they should be. He was her master, after all.

Jenny frowned, vaguely remembering that she had been treating a patient, or so she'd thought. As he led her down the hallway to his rooms, she pushed aside her concerns. It couldn't have been important.

19

OBSESSION

Alex pulled on his tunic, hands shaking in his haste, not caring if it was one of his plain set or emblazoned with the crest of the Fourth. Running his fingers through his hair, he glanced around the room, spotting his boots off to one side, where he had no doubt Joshua had carefully put them. A stab of irritation hit him. He'd have to talk to his servant about that annoying habit. He walked across the room to pick them up, retreating with them to the seat. Fumbling and swearing softly, he finally managed to complete the normally easy task and get his boots on his feet.

He gathered the veil to him but habit made him pause. He should go armed. Swearing again, he stopped and walked back to his dressing room, straight to his weapons rack arrayed on one wall. Alex armed himself with an assortment of weapons, not paying any attention to the ones he was grabbing. He didn't really care except everyone would be angry with him if he went out unarmed. He snorted derisively.

Not that it made much difference now, he could kill just as easily with the power of the veil. Others might have the fear of encountering someone stronger than they were, but it wasn't something he was worried about since his transition. He swore again as he fumbled with one of his daggers and it dropped to the floor, landing with a dull thud. Sighing, he grabbed for the next one on the rack, paying no mind at all that it was one of his ceremonial daggers. A dagger was a dagger, and unlike some of the fools who had weapons constructed that were for ceremonial display only, all Alex's weapons were fully functional.

Alex started to transition into the veil with one thing on his mind, one thing driving him.

Amelia.

AMELIA SMILED as she heard and felt Alex respond to her call. It had worked and sooner than she'd thought it would. She could hear and feel the longing in him. She'd picked the image of them in the waterfall where they'd made love—it seemed like a lifetime ago—and gently insinuated it into his mind. To Alex she had no doubt it would seem as if he'd just remembered that moment.

Come to me, Alex.

Amelia carefully flamed his desire for her, manipulating him through those tiny little bonds they shared, the same ones she'd used to make him think he loved her in the first place.

You love me, only me.

Amelia smiled in satisfaction as she felt his almost frenzied response, his need to get to her.

ALEX HEARD a noise to one side as he was crossing to the veil and had his blade out before he realised what he was doing.

"Alex? What's wrong?"

Isabella stood in the doorway to his dressing room wrapped in his robe, a look of concern on her face as she rubbed her eyes.

Alex froze as her voice echoed in his head, allowing his hold on the power to drop away. All thoughts of Amelia blew away at the sound of her voice. His eyes wide, he looked back at her and swallowed.

"What am I doing?"

He licked his lips nervously, his breathing rate increasing as she walked forward slowly. She gently took the blade he was holding out of his hand and placed it back on the weapons rack. Alex shuddered and allowed Isabella to draw him in closer. Being this close to her caused his agitation to lower, caused what had been his very real desire to be with Amelia but a moment before to fade. He hadn't thought about Amelia, dreamed about her, until recently. He'd gone to bed every night, resolute since he'd promised Kyle that he would not go to Amelia again. He'd been confident he wouldn't when Isabella had shown up to join him for the night. Now he was about to rush off again and throw himself into his former Consort Elect's arms.

Alex felt his eyes widen and his breath catch as a horrible possibility hammered into him.

"Alex, what is it? Talk to me."

"Shield me. I... I don't trust my own will right now."

Alex nearly breathed a sigh of relief as he felt her shield widen to include him within her own protective bounds. She'd extended her mental shield to protect his mind and thrown up a shield against metaphysical attack from another without him having to clarify.

Alex pulled away and stripped off his weapons, leaving them in a pile on a bench to one side. Walking out, he called for a servant, grateful when one appeared promptly despite the hour.

"Get Lord Kyle, I need him. And send for Master Healer Aaron."

The startled servant bowed smartly and bolted out the door. Alex nearly groaned. He had no doubt word would spread throughout the palace at record speed that the healer had been called to the Fourth's Complex.

Unable to settle down, he began to pace, aware that Isabella watched him, obviously concerned yet waiting for him to finally say what was wrong. Alex jumped and spun around as the door opened behind him. He fell into a defensive posture, his hand groping reflexively for a weapon he no longer wore. Alex let his breath out and straightened as he saw it was Kyle who stood motionless, observing him for a moment.

Kyle glanced around the room, his eyes resting briefly on Isabella before he entered cautiously.

"Alex, what's wrong?"

"When Alyssa was in your head, forcing you to do things, what was it like?"

"When Alyssa..." Kyle stopped, his eyes widening.

Alex felt his friend's light touch in a wave over him, causing his skin to prickle as Kyle scanned him. He had no doubt his friend noticed that Isabella was maintaining a protective shield around him. Kyle's own shield expanded, and Alex felt its chill as it passed around him, leaving him on the inside of yet another layer of protection not his own.

"Did you find yourself doing things, then later wonder why?"

Alex allowed Kyle to guide him towards his lounge. He complied and sat down as Kyle nodded, noticing his own hands were shaking.

"Sometimes it felt like I was driven. I couldn't think of anything but her."

"Until recently, I haven't thought of Amelia, not really since well before the assassination, except for feeling a little guilty that I didn't miss her and kept ending up with Isabella." Alex glanced across at Isabella and smiled.

He swallowed again and saw Kyle glance from him to Isabella, both of their expressions grim. Alex had the feeling they shared a communication but didn't pry.

"All right. What happened tonight, Alex?"

Alex shuddered and leaned forward, burying his face in his hands.

"Not just tonight. Since just before the coronation I haven't been able to get Amelia out of my head."

Isabella stiffened, and Alex was about to apologise to her when he felt the ripples of her power brush over him as she reinforced her shields around him.

"You think Amelia is in your head?" Kyle kept his own voice level but Alex felt him follow Isabella's example and strengthen his own shields.

"Her capture, her torture at Kevin's hands... I keep seeing images I've never really seen. They could only have come from her." Alex sat up, taking a deep breath, trying to calm himself down.

Isabella walked across to him and sat down on the sidearm of the chair, her hand resting on his shoulder.

"Where were you going when I disturbed you, Alex?"

"To Amelia. I knew nothing but desire to be with her. I couldn't think of anything just then except my need to get to her. Then you spoke and it was like, like I woke up." Alex felt conflicting emotions running through him all tangled together, making it hard for him to think.

He was startled to see Aaron standing in the doorway. It was a sign of how agitated he was that he hadn't heard the healer come in.

20

CLEANSING

As Aaron approached, Alex went to get up only to have the healer wave him down.

"Relax, Your Highness. This will be easier for you if you do." Aaron waited until he rested back against the couch again and then walked around behind him.

Alex felt Aaron's hands on his temples.

Relax, Alex, this won't take me long to check now that I know what I'm looking for.

Alex felt himself going hot then cold as his emotions swung from fear to anger, then back to fear again, but he complied with the healer's orders as best he could. Alex knew the moment the old healer stiffened in response to something he'd found and felt himself tense with a thrill of fear in response.

Ah, Alex, this is going to hurt, I'm sorry I didn't notice this sooner.

At the healer's warning, Alex felt himself tense, his breath catching, but he concentrated on letting Aaron do his job. It was hard not to automatically raise his own shields and kick the healer out of his head. He felt Aaron's gentle probing and unbidden thoughts as images and feelings flashed into his brain. Alex recognised the whispering voice in his head, a voice that had whispered to him as he'd slept.

You love me, you can't live without me.

Amelia's eyes boring into his own. Her smile. Her voice whispering to him when they slept together, instructing him, using words that seemed to echo and repeat from deep in his own head.

As Aaron worked, Alex felt as if his time with Amelia was on replay. One incident after the other, every moment they'd spent together prompted by her voice in his head, a smile or a touch. The healer brought all of it painfully to the forefront of his mind. There was the stark contrast in his feelings for Amelia—he'd seen her as a little sister, but then she'd insinuated a small bond between them. He'd been so consumed by guilt over Kyle being sick, he hadn't noticed. It had prompted a reaction in him that he'd not felt for her previous to her suggestion, seeing her the way Amelia had wanted him to for that very first time.

Alex felt pain hammer into him as he realised that nothing he'd felt for her had ever been real. Right from the beginning she'd prompted him, subtly pushing him in the direction she'd wanted. Aaron pulled up his memories, each time highlighting the thoughts and patterns that weren't his own. Alex turned his eye inward as the healer flashed in his mind what he was seeing, and that small bond Amelia had forged between them, the bond so small and personal he hadn't known it was there. The bond she'd been using all along to change how he thought, how he felt. It hadn't been enough to alter his thoughts permanently, but fed into the back of his head drip by drip, it had been effective.

The healer paused, his question evident in Alex's mind, seeking his permission.

Do it, Healer. Get rid of it if you can.

Alex felt himself stiffen as Aaron's own healer's gift burned into his head, searing him with pain. He felt himself buck and then hands restraining him. Such a small little bond, yet extinguishing it burned.

A voice in his head—Aaron's—telling him it was nearly over.

Yet in the moment none of it mattered; he was mourning the loss of a love he knew now had never been real, the loss of that little piece of normal that he'd tried to create for himself, that Amelia had stolen from him. He knew exactly how he felt now.

Anger won over fear.

ALEX'S HEAD snapped back and he screamed. Isabella caught him as he slumped.

Kyle winced, remembering the feeling well. He imagined he could hear the echoing scream over the veil that he knew belonged to Amelia. He readied himself for the next blow, for what he knew now was multiple minds, pounding, grappling, trying to grab for Alex.

Alex felt the collective mind questing after not only himself, but Aaron and Isabella as well through their current connection to him, their intent clear.

"No."

Alex pushed the healer out of his mind and turned his attention inward, paying no attention as the healer sprawled to the ground. He shunted Isabella out of his mind as well, instinctively throwing a barrier around her to protect her. While Aaron had cleaned out the main bond, Alex knew there were more. Amelia had been busy building her own little bonds in him. He could feel it now like an insidious web throughout his body.

Now that he could feel the bonds, he poked and prodded at

his own mind and body until he found them. If he hadn't had experience with what Alyssa had done to Kyle, he would have overlooked it even now.

What they didn't have this time was their toxin blocking his ability to access the veil, since he was immune to its effects. That was how they stopped the Kin they took from healing and repairing the damage they inflicted. His face hardened and he gritted his teeth. Looking up to the glowing power above and around him, he opened himself up and drew it in. He could feel the power welling up and spilling over, yet he still drew in more. He felt the lines of malignant power light up in his internal eye. A feral grin spread across his face, his eyes lighting up with the glow of pure, raw power. He forced that energy down those thin, spiderweb bonds of evil that constrained him.

A thunderous crack of power sounded, echoed by an ominous rumbling from outside with the crack of lightning as the sheer power spilled from the veiled world into the real world. Thin red spiderweb lines of power glowed all over Alex's body, growing brighter, surrounding him, constraining him like a net. Then in a burst of bright burning silver light that seemed to swell from within him, it surged along the webbing. As the cleansing power passed, the glowing web stuttered and burst apart, spreading out from Alex like a red spray of blood intermixed with silver white, glittering in the air around him before disappearing.

Then Alex screamed once more and drew power in, and Kyle gasped as Alex threw his power out in a hammering blow, following down the signatures threaded through the veil. Peals of thunder rolled across the veil, spilling into the real world in response, vibrating the air around them. The outpouring of power shook the palace down to the very foundations and Kyle felt a number of the minds that had attacked them stutter and shut down.

The stillness across the veiled world was deafening as all heard the arrival of one who could only be of the Elder Born, now at last come into his own.

21

FAILURE

Amelia waited patiently on the cobbled street for Alex. She knew it wouldn't be long. She'd managed to drive him to a fever pitch in his desire for her. Right about now she knew he'd be reacting automatically to her promptings. It had taken some time, but she was finally learning how to best use her bonds to drive her former Consort Elect to her.

Amelia smiled. It wouldn't be long now before she could take Alex to her master. Under her constant whispering in the back of his head, his own will and control were eroding, becoming easier to overcome.

Almost humming to herself in anticipation, she listened absently to the background chatter she received from Alex —not full conversations or thoughts, just broken snatches, words, images, feelings. Just enough for her to know that Alex was coming to her.

Amelia stiffened as she felt a burst of horror just before that flow of communication from Alex suddenly ceased. In her experience it shouldn't have stopped like that, at least not right now, not even if he was shifting into the veil. She opened her mind further, concentrating on her bonds with Alex.

She followed the strings of emotion that bound them both, knowing they would lead her to Alex. Wherever no matter where he was and what stood between them. She'd almost sent her mind questing all the way back to the palace when she staggered as she felt something hit her. She staggered in reaction to the metaphysical blow that hit like a fist to the stomach. Pushing the pain that assaulted her aside, she looked around, confused, before reeling under the impact of more blows.

It took a few moments more before she understood. Her bonds to Alex had been discovered. They were being cut away with practiced precision, the remainder of the bond snapping back, sending the power recoiling into her. It had the distinct flavour of the meddling healer and the other woman who often stood between her and Alex.

No!

Amelia sharpened her focus on Alex, drawing on the minds of the Sundered with her. Gritting her teeth, she rallied, launching an attack on those that would keep Alex from her. Blow after blow that she rained down on them splashed off the barriers of multiple Kin. Among them was the distinct feel of her own brother.

Amelia screamed as pinprick points of pain ran along her body, as if all the bonds she'd wrought on Alex were being burned away.

She felt a tugging, a tapping, as if someone was trying to get her attention.

No, Amelia, come back!

She was barely aware of the voice of her master in her head, the note of panic in his mind voice, as she writhed in pain. She felt as if the veil stilled and held its collective voice before a crack of thunder rolled through it in her direction. She felt as if a giant fist slammed into her. The connection she'd maintained with the Sundered who'd augmented her power stuttered out. Her vision burst to shining ribbons dancing white in her vision before she felt the blackness take over.

22

ADMISSIONS

After his display of power Alex collapsed, slumping to the floor. Kyle scrambled over to check on him, relieved to discover that while he was unconscious, he was still alive. With the assistance of the staff, Kyle helped transfer Alex to his bed, moving aside so Aaron could check on his patient one more time.

Isabella maintained her shield around Alex's mind, preventing interference from outside influences, although she doubted after such a display their enemies would try that particular trick again.

She watched carefully as the healer reinforced Alex's exhausted slumber with a compulsion to keep him in that deep sleep he needed, for at this point Isabella had to concede it would be a kindness. It would take time, even for Alex, to heal, and sleep was the best remedy. Isabella placed her hands on Kyle's shoulder. He looked at her and moved aside.

"Not that I don't trust your skill, healer, but let me see." At his nod Isabella placed her own hands delicately on Alex's temples.

She paid the healer no mind as he watched carefully over

what she was doing. Not that she blamed the man. Isabella gasped and her eyes widened in shock.

"You did a remarkable job of keeping Alex sane all these years, Healer. You knew and you never told him." Her eyes narrowed on the last and she saw Kyle look from her to the healer, clearly confused.

Aaron didn't even try to pretend that he didn't understand what she was talking about.

"He was traumatised when I arrived at the palace all those years ago. His mind was raw. He was young to have sustained a forced transition, but the signs were all there." Aaron stared at her calmly. "I did my best to heal his mind and I shielded him as best I could for as long as I could, just like I do for my junior healer trainees. Alex was just significantly stronger."

Kyle frowned. "I'm lost, what are you talking about?"

Isabella looked from the healer over to Kyle. "Alex's mind broke and he wakened to being Kin when he was a small child, in the glade when the Sundered attacked. It is rare for one such as he to survive. The trauma is usually too much for a child to sustain." Isabella looked back at Aaron, considering his strength. He was strong for a human.

Aaron shrugged. "I did what I could. I didn't know at the time, but Edward shielded him a great deal as he was growing up as well. Healers don't learn as much as we should going through training about those who will be Kin."

"I'll take my leave. His own natural shield is back in place, he should sleep well under the healer's influence without my interference. Alex will need some space to come to terms with what she did to him. Call me if you have further need." Isabella looked at Kyle.

"If my sister comes after him again, I'll deal with her." Kyle's lips compressed, his eyes narrowed and shining with a glittering angry light.

ALEX WOKE, aware instantly that his brother was in his room. He had a brief moment of peace, wondering what he wanted, then he recalled the previous night's events. He groaned at his own stupidity and knew without a doubt he deserved the dressing down he was certain William was about to give him.

"I'm surprised you didn't make it here last night." Alex couldn't bring himself to open his eyes and look at his brother.

One bright point was that William was obviously getting very good at shielding his own thoughts. Alex doubted his brother was terribly happy with his behaviour. Hearing liquid pouring into a cup, Alex finally rolled over and opened his eyes to see William at the serving station. The coffee was obviously for him, though, since there was already a mug on the table indicating where his brother had been sitting the moment before. Taking stock of himself, Alex noticed he had a hangover, or at least what others described as a hangover. He didn't want to get up or face anyone right now, although with William he didn't have a choice.

William turned and walked back to the couches and placed the extra mug on the table. He didn't say a word, just stared at his brother calmly. Alex took the hint, wondering if he was facing his brother or his king. Biting back a sigh, he rolled out of bed and wrapped his robe around himself, the softness of the fabric bringing some comfort. He grabbed one of the pillows from his bed and walked across to prop himself up on the long couch facing his brother. He grabbed the mug that William had left for him. The steam that suddenly started curling up from the mug was a testament that his brother even heated it for him.

"I did. You were already sleeping it off, and Aaron requested I let you sleep." William spoke quietly, keeping his gaze on him.

Alex wished he could hide from reality for just a little bit longer.

"I didn't know, William. If Isabella hadn't stopped me, I would have gone to her." Alex closed his eyes against the pain and the rawness.

"Prompted by Amelia, sending thoughts and feelings not your own into your head." William continued to watch him carefully, no doubt assessing him and his responses.

Alex took a deep, shuddering breath. "She made me believe I loved her." Alex heard the catch in his own voice but didn't care.

"For you it was real." William's voice didn't hold even a hint of recrimination, though he had full right to be extremely angry with what Alex had done and concealed from them all.

"None of it was real, not from the very beginning." The admission hurt more than he wanted to admit, but the anger he'd felt last night at being tricked and used this way by Amelia and the Order returned.

"This is war, Alex. You were the target, as Kyle has been. And Father. I'm just grateful she didn't mess with you enough to get you into the Order before Kyle and Isabella realised something was wrong." William sipped the last of his coffee and placed his mug back on the coffee table.

"I should have believed Kyle sooner. He told me Amelia had never been the person we'd thought she was. It just felt so *real*." Alex sipped his coffee, turning his head to gaze back up at the ceiling.

"She was in your head, Alex. You felt and did what she wanted you to. The rest of us should have realised something was wrong a lot sooner."

Alex turned his head and looked at William, shocked to hear the undertone of apology in his brother's voice. "I should have realised it myself. I only ever thought of her like a little sister. I think I wanted to believe it was real."

Alex closed his eyes, searching his mind for any sign that Amelia remained in his head. Then again, given that he hadn't picked up on her interference all this time, he doubted he would now. He did trust Aaron, though. That and the emptiness, the lack of feelings other than anger when he thought about Amelia.

"Aaron, Kyle and Isabella all assure me you couldn't have known, Alex, so stop beating yourself up. Give yourself some time."

"Isabella helped to save me again, it's becoming a habit." Alex covered his face with one hand, groaning.

He realised he did like Isabella—more than just liked, if he was being honest with himself. He doubted after the mess he'd made she would want to have anything to do with him.

"There is a substantial line of people wanting to eradicate the Order for what they have done, Isabella among them." William's smile didn't reach his eyes.

"I betrayed you. I should have told you as soon as Amelia started reaching out to me. You should be yelling at me, angry, something. How can you possibly forgive what I've done?" The last was whispered.

Alex felt shame flood him, it seemed no matter how bad a mistake he made, his big brother always seemed to be there to support him.

"Go spend some time at your room at The Last Stop if you need, there is still a guard contingent and some of the Elite there. Get your head straightened out. Talk with Isabella. I promise you she will come if you call her and she seems able to get you to see sense when the rest of us fail. I need you back and functioning. I'll be fine, Kyle and Jess with Edward and the others are on call if needed."

"William, I'll be—"

"That wasn't a suggestion, Alex." William's voice hardened. The order was unmistakable this time.

Alex closed his eyes and took a deep breath, trying to settle his own mind. He didn't even know why he was trying to fight the order. Facing the court in his current state wasn't something he cared to do. No matter how much he was reassured he couldn't have done anything, more than anything he felt ashamed of himself and what he'd done. He couldn't help but feel he should have known somehow, been able to detect Amelia's influence and stop it. In a way he *had* known; he remembered the guilt that had assailed him every time he'd been with her. He remembered thinking he would cut ties with her, only to end up dreaming of her, seeking her out and falling into her arms again. He opened his eyes, turning his head to look at William.

"Yes, Your Majesty."

Alex watched as William put his empty mug aside and walked over to his side.

"Kyle is beating himself up for not noticing sooner, and so is Jess. I'm sorry that I failed you, brother. Keep to the Fourth's Complex if you choose. Retreat to The Last Stop. Whatever you need, just get your head sorted. I'll call if I need you." William squeezed his shoulder before straightening and heading to the door, letting himself out without saying another word and closing it quietly behind him.

Alex lay back, allowing the tension to drain out of him. He knew that if he stayed here in the palace, dramas would drag him back into the fray before he was ready. William was right, as usual. He would sort himself out sooner if he was away and he also acknowledged if he really was needed, they would call him. It wasn't like it would take him long to get back to the palace.

Besides that, his absence would allow William to settle into actually being king. One of the side effects of his brother being struck down for as long as he had been was that when Alex was around, some of the courtiers looked to *him* when William requested anything, almost as if they were afraid if his brother did too much too fast, he would collapse on them again.

Alex finished his coffee, placing the mug on the table when he was done. He crossed the room and, pulling open a small drawer on the side board, withdrew the key to his room at the inn. He did not even take the time to dress; he knew he still had a chest of clothes in his rooms. He pulled himself into the veil and retreated to his room at The Last Stop.

He had to get his head straight as his king and brother had ordered.

23

CHOICES

Simon stood at the window of one of his favourite premises looking out over the forest beyond the town walls. There were advantages to being almost immortal as long as you took care not to allow someone to stick a knife in your heart or cut your head off. One of them was acquiring wealth and comfortable places to live. Of course, it would be pleasant to have the kind of power to be able to spin whatever type of home he wanted out of the veil, but that was not a power level he possessed. Yet.

Simon scowled. Over the years his power had increased, but not enough to do what Alex Rathadon had been able to do almost from childhood. Even if he didn't realise, it should not have been possible. There were rules to wielding the power of the veil—or so he'd thought. As it turned out, it seems there were rules for people like him but they didn't apply to the Rathadon family; not those born with power, anyway. Still, being the Skull Lord had proven to be an advantage over the years, allowing him to possess places like this.

Chewing his lip over the reports from his men that he'd stationed on the access points around the Kastler estate, he shook his head. He dumped the concise report on the desk. He'd taken quiet steps to keep the presence of the Killian Order under wraps. If he'd been asked—not that he had—he'd have told Kevin it was foolish to camp out on an estate so close to the Summer Palace. While there were advantages to being right under your enemies' noses, there were also disadvantages. Like being discovered before you were ready.

Not that he cared for the Order, but Kevin had been someone he'd called friend for a very long time. He couldn't keep disposing of people who might stumble onto the Order's hiding place this way. Although his men had managed to divert many people to other roads, the kill count was already getting a little higher than he liked.

Even though he didn't quite know the full details of what the Order were planning, he thought this desperate move was a foolish one. Kevin and his friends had to act or move. Sooner or later the disappearances around the Kastler estate would come to notice and the newly installed king would be informed. As soon as that happened, Alex and his friends would turn their attentions to the Kastler estate. Then there would be nothing he could do to save the life of his friend.

Making a decision, Simon drew himself to the veiled paths. It was time he warned Kevin of the inevitable.

FINDING KEVIN within Lord Kastler's estate proved to be relatively easy. His friend's shielding, never really the best even in their Companion's Cohort days, was outright slapdash now. Strangely enough, it was as if over the years their roles had reversed. Kevin had always had slightly more power and ability than Simon to start with. Yet now, looking at his friend, he realised he was the one who not only had more power, relatively speaking, but he used it much more efficiently. Being in the heart of the Healers' Guild had not done his friend any favours in that regard. It had made him sloppy.

Simon let go of the veil and used the more mundane method of walking through the door that led to the room Kevin was sitting in. His friend would likely be startled but probably take it in his stride. Simon ignored the guards down the end of the hall, they were barely competent and at this moment were staring out the windows rather than protecting their master's door as they should have been.

Simon paused just in the entrance of the large sitting room, glancing around it. The furnishings had obviously seen better days. The Kastlers had fallen far indeed.

As the men inside noticed his entrance and it dawned on them that he wasn't a servant, their conversation stumbled to a halt. The portly man in a stuffy over-embellished surcoat that could only be Lord Kastler stood looking at him with a look of pure outrage.

"Who are you and how did you get in here? I'll have my people flogged!"

Simon flicked his eyes over to Kevin, who looked amused at his appearance and not at all concerned about Lord Kastler.

"I'm the one who has been helping to keep the presence of your guests from the attention of the king. Sit down, Lord Kastler." Simon allowed a little menace to creep into his tone, almost smiling as the easily cowed lord took a step back.

"Simon, it's good to see you, if a little unexpected." Kevin smiled and looked reassuringly at the lord, who swung his gaze at him.

"You know this man?"

"Indeed, Lord Kastler, Simon is a man of many talents. What brings you here, Simon?" Kevin's gaze left Lord Kastler, dismissing him.

"Whatever you are planning, I'd recommend you do it soon. That or move. You and your friends have been holed up here too long. I've done what I can, but the king will find out you are here. It is only a matter of time." Simon had been ignoring the others in the room, but now his gaze slid to the third man and the smile almost froze on his face.

Kevin, seeing his attention switch, gestured with one hand at his other companion.

"Simon, this is Scholar Clements, the leader of the Order."

The elderly scholar smiled, the corner of his eyes crinkling.

"A friend of Kevin's is a friend of mine and the Order. Welcome to our ranks, Simon." The man's voice was dripping with sincerity.

Yet there was something about the old man that made Simon uneasy. He certainly didn't trust the sincerity. As the Skull Lord, he'd developed a skill at picking out vipers. That seemingly sweet old man wasn't so sweet. Of course, the fact that his guild wished to replace the current ruling family of Vallantia was also at odds with his harmless old man routine.

"I wouldn't say I'm in the ranks of your Order, Scholar Clements. I have my own." Simon didn't see any point in pretending to be nice; he'd made peace a long time ago with the fact that he wasn't.

"Wh-what do you mean *helping*?"

Simon swung his gaze back to the stammering lord, who'd obviously just plucked up the courage to speak again, and allowed what he knew was a cold smile to touch his lips. He almost ruined the whole impression by laughing as the lord paled.

"I've had my men stationed at access points around your lands. When outsiders get too close and can't be persuaded to go elsewhere, well, let's just say they aren't left in any state to bother anyone with their tales of the current location of the Killiam Order."

"I, um, I don't understand. What do you do to them?"

Kevin looked at the lord, exasperated.

"His people kill the intruders, Lord Kastler."

Simon didn't think it was possible for the lord to go even paler that he was, but somehow he managed it. His head swung from Kevin to Clements, then back to look at him before his eyes flinched away.

"Who... who gave you the authority to do that? When I'm king, I'll not tolerate that kind of thing!"

If the fool's voice hadn't been quavering, Simon might have found the declaration a little more impressive. It was becoming increasingly clear how and why he'd been manipulated into committing treason against his king. He was a quivering fool.

Kevin's low mocking laughter caused the attention of the aspiring king to switch back to him.

"I should have mentioned Simon is the Skull Lord. I doubt he cares for a king's permission."

Simon bit back a curse. Kevin was a fool. That piece of information wasn't something he spread around. He traded by being in the shadows, by people not knowing his identity. His eyes narrowed as he contemplated Kevin.

"One other thing: tell your pets to leave my own people out of your recruitment efforts."

Simon didn't wait for Kevin to acknowledge his request. Turning, he nodded to Clements and, ignoring the wide-eyed lord, turned and left the room and estate the way he'd entered.

24

IDEAS

Matthew walked out to the general lounging area. He knew this is where the Elite working Personal Service congregated between bouts of duty, particularly when they knew that there would be a requirement for them in short order. The others were frustrated that their charges kept disappearing along the veiled paths, hunting for the location of the Order without them. While them disappearing into the veil wasn't a new thing, it wasn't any less frustrating for their guards, particularly since they knew the murderous intent of the Order. Alex's bland observation that there weren't enough of them and their talents were better off here to help defend the king should he come under attack didn't placate them at all. The fact that it was true was even more galling.

It filled all of them with a sense of dread that something would go wrong and they wouldn't be there to help. Lord Kyle had explained to him there was no way he could drag them with him everywhere he went. Matthew conceded the point given the lord's description of how he searched the villages, half in this world, half in the veil, using his powers to propel him silently from roof to roof like a thief, except much better than the regular kind since he was faster and unless an individual was Kin, they were unlikely to see him at it.

Still, Matthew felt he could take a few of them with him, even if Lord Kyle left them in the veil nearby while he went to search. Matthew knew he couldn't get to the veil himself. Yet. He'd been practicing, though, and observing the manoeuvre every chance he had. He was fairly confident that he could keep the other guards in place if Lord Kyle got them that far. It was an interesting problem that they had debated. If they were dragged into the veil by a Kin and left there, what would happen to them?

Would they just appear back in the real world?

Become lost in the veil, with no way to get themselves back home?

Die?

All of that was something they would need to practice and test if they were to win their argument to be taken on the excursions. The other thing they needed to solve was numbers. Prince Alexander was correct. The Elite was vastly diminished in number from the days of the Sundered War. In that day they had been a force to be reckoned with, and their numbers in combination with the Cohort rivalled the guard. They had been the fighting force the Fourth used, stretching out across the realm to protect the villages during the Sundered War.

In this current era, they had been reduced in number to the personal bodyguards for the king and his family. Now that the Fourth and his Companions were added to the mix, they were stretched even thinner. There was no way they could spread out to cover the villages, not even in a thin net with many holes in it.

He walked into the room to see James slumped in one of the chairs with his jacket thrown on a nearby hook on the wall. Marcus was sitting there for once rather than in his office. He looked up, breaking off their quiet conversation as Matthew walked over, carefully removing his own jacket and placing it on a hook before joining them on the lounges. The fact that both of them were here was testament to the fact that Alex was still away from the palace, although at least from the reports they'd received they knew he was in Amberbreak. It also meant the probability that Kyle was out hunting by himself again was extremely high.

"Ready for another fun-filled evening of sitting around waiting to hear if any of our charges have shown up today?" Marcus smiled, taking the sting out of the sharpness of his tone.

Matthew nodded. Marcus hated it when Alex went off by himself. He always had. It was a part of that extra mystery and legend that surrounded Marcus, that thing that was whispered: it wasn't his own exceptional ability with his blade all those years ago that had won him his position as Alex's primary shield. It was Alex himself, although a child and younger than Marcus by several years, who had made the choice and wouldn't accept any other. The young prince, with Kyle as the permanent fixture by his side as he'd become back then, had proven he could go where he wanted and the Elite couldn't do anything to prevent him. It was either Marcus, or nobody. That had been Alex's decree. Rumour had it that Alex had been remarkably good at taking Marcus—and then James, when he was added to the mix later on—with him when he disappeared. It was only in later years that he'd taken to disappearing without them. That was something that Marcus hated.

It was his primary duty to protect the prince, something that was a little hard to do when he kept running off, and even harder since Alex could disappear into the veil and none of them had the ability to follow under their own power. Alex would have to agree to take Marcus or any of them with him, something he didn't tend to do unless the king ordered him to.

It wasn't just Alex, though. The same could be said for both Jess and Kyle.

Kyle had confided that it didn't particularly please him when Alex left him behind either, since he'd been the unseen blade at Alex's shoulder most of his life, long before he was ever formally acknowledged as the Fourth's Blade. Of course it was a little easier for him since he could get to Alex in moments if necessary through the veil using his own powers, unlike the Elite.

"I have an idea that might be totally nuts but could be worth trying." Matthew noticed he had the instant attention of both men.

He paused as Megan walked into the room, which meant Lady Jessalan was off on her own tonight as well. There had been a period right after the death of the king where at least one of them was always present in the palace, at the king's side. They had since called in reinforcements to help with that duty. It had caused some consternation when the court had realised that the reinforcements were none other than Prince Edward, Lord Callum and Lady Leanna, or Kat as she was more commonly known. The fact that all of them were meant to be dead was taking some adjustment in beliefs and attitudes. The effect of having more of them that could guard William meant that it hadn't taken Alex, Jess or Kyle long to revert to running off by themselves. Even more concerning was the fact that unlike before he didn't think they were all together this time.

"Anything is worth a shot. Come on, spill, I promise not to laugh." Megan smiled and poured herself a glass of water from the pitcher on the table before leaning back in her chair and placing her feet up on the footstool.

"It's really an extension of what we were practicing with the King's Guard before the assault at the Healers' Guild." Matthew looked up at them, noticing he had the attention of all three. "We'd need to test it, but what if, say, Lord Kyle took me and a couple of the Elite and some of the guard with him when he goes hunting? Enough for the formations we had started practicing with him."

James frowned, shaking his head. "We've already suggested it. Lord Kyle has flat-out refused."

Matthew nodded. "I know. His main objection is that we can't do anything in the veil without him hauling us along. But what if he could take us with him when he goes to check a village, and then leave us there while he explored?" Matthew shrugged. "At least that way we are all kitted up and closer. If he needs us and something goes wrong, he can haul us in to help."

All of them looked from him to trade glances with each other before Marcus cleared his throat, rubbing his chin with one hand.

"Not ideal, but better than the current status. The problem is that Prince Alex, Lord Kyle and Lady Jess don't know what would happen to all of us if they take us into the veil and leave us there." Marcus watched him carefully.

"I think it is time we found out. I'll volunteer. Lord Kyle can drag me into the veil and leave me there." Matthew shook his head and smiled. "Hopefully he can then find me and draw me out again."

Megan chuckled. "I can't see that being a test Lord Kyle is going to like."

"I know, but I'm much stronger with the veil now. Not like the three of you or anywhere near Lord Kyle, but I've been practicing with shields." He ducked his head. "Healers tell me they believe I went through a sort of mini transition, although not like Prince Alex. They don't quite know what it will mean."

Marcus nodded. "I know, they briefed us. Welcome to the club."

James reached across and patted him on the shoulder.

"We have some records, I'll dig them out for you. Many of

the Elite were like us— strong enough to be useful but not necessarily enough to be truly dangerous." James looked at Marcus, then back at him. "So going back to your idea. Kyle dumps you in the veil, then goes back to get you. If you survive the experience, what then?"

"Then we get more volunteers. We've been practicing shields. I know I can extend mine to cover a small group. We all can. If the first stage works, then Lord Kyle dumps a small squad of us and I keep my shield around them and try to keep us all in position. If that works..." Matthew broke off, leaving it unsaid that it would hopefully kill off some of the objections.

Marcus raised his eyebrow. "Getting Lord Kyle to agree to this test might prove to be problematic."

James laughed. "Finding volunteers for the second part of the test could be interesting as well. Could be worth trying, though." James leaned forward. "I get the feeling they've all just been hauling us along with them. I haven't sensed them doing anything else."

Megan nodded. "I agree, it could be worth testing. Maybe if we can get the king on our side? Mention it at one of the training sessions when he is here with them?"

"We can see if we have the ability to move, supervised from a distance, so Lord Kyle can play catch. Sorry, I'm making this part up as we talk...." Matthew stumbled to a halt, embarrassed he'd rambled on.

Marcus shook his head. "Don't be, it's a good idea and worth trying. We need to keep up our sessions integrating with the guard anyhow. I'll see if we can bring this idea up sometime at the appropriate moment."

25

RECRUITING

Devon stepped out from the side street and stopped in the middle of the lane. The figure walking towards him stopped and looked at him, a smile on her lips that chilled him. Devon raised his hands he turned to walk back the way he'd come. He drew in his power as he heard the woman slowly follow him. He spun, drawing his own power only to see she'd gone. He walked backwards, his skin still prickling with alarm. He could feel the malevolence and violence emanating from her. As he stepped back he felt himself hit a body behind him, an arm wrap around his throat. Panic seized him.

"You really aren't very smart, are you?" a woman's voice whispered in his ear.

Devon licked his lips, fear thrilling through him as the woman dragged him into the veil. His eyes bulged as he saw another Kin waiting for them.

Now, Amelia, is that any way to treat our latest recruit? There was no need to frighten him. The other Kin, or perhaps Elder, Devon couldn't tell stared at him, smiling.

I'm sorry, Master, he ran before I could issue your invitation.

Devon could hear the insincerity in both her voice and the voice of the one she called master.

Recruit? Please, no, leave me out of all of this. Devon's mind voice shook and he was unable to stop the trembling that shook him.

As the man approached, Devon was unable to stop the trembling that shook him.

You think you haven't already chosen a side? The Fourth isn't likely to forgive that you attacked his mother. The man patted him on the cheek, grinning at him.

No, you have the wrong person. I haven't gone anywhere near the palace.

Oh, I know it was you. You've certainly lost your will to fight. Was it the shock of attacking a crazy woman at her estate and finding the Fourth's Blade at her side that did it? Or when the Fourth himself arrived? The one the woman called master laughed as Devon's eyes widened.

He stiffened as the woman who held him drew one of her daggers down his jawline. *My brother dearest and former intended may have seemed a little distracted at the time, but trust me, they will have marked your signature.*

Devon tried to struggle, screaming in pain as she sliced him open, her blade sheathed in blue flame. His mind shrieked in fear as they drew him through the veil and he wished he'd listened to his friends and hidden rather than scoffed at the stories of their kind going missing.

26

A PLAN

Kyle glanced up, breaking off from his conversation with Jess as the doors to the small council room opened. His eyebrow rose as he recognised Janson, Commander of the King's Guard. The man paused briefly to nod in his direction.

"With your permission, Fourth's Blade?"

Kyle frowned before nodding, noticing the large rolled parchment Janson was carrying with him. At his nod, the commander smiled tightly and walked up to the table, where he unceremoniously unrolled what proved to be a map of Vallantia.

"I take it there is a reason for this intrusion, Commander?" Jess watched the man, a guarded look in her eyes.

"Sorry for the intrusion, my lady, my lords. I thought perhaps the search for the rebels might go smoother with a little coordination." He glanced around those of them gathered in the room before settling his gaze back on Kyle.

Kyle sighed. "I guess it couldn't hurt. What did you have in mind?"

"A more systematic and ordered approach, my lord Blade. If you'll allow?"

Kyle assessed the man in front of him; something about the commander had always niggled at him, though Kyle suspected it was because Janson wasn't a member of their inner circle and had often seemed to be trying to insinuate himself into it. He glanced at Jess, who shrugged, then looked to Edward, Kat and Cal, all of whom settled back and nodded.

"Can't hurt to try, I guess." Jess's tone was cool and hard to decipher.

A flash of triumph flared in the man's eyes as he nodded and started explaining his plan, pointing to various locations on the map, assigning each of them to check them out. He smiled at them, informing them pins would be placed in the towns and villages as they searched and cleared them. They would work their way systematically across Vallantia.

Kyle observed the man through his reflection in the window. There was something about the overly helpful commander that was bothering him, and had been bothering him for some time, yet he couldn't quite put his finger on what it was.

COMMANDER JANSON SAT at the table in the run-down bar on the docks. He took a long swallow of the beer he'd ordered on arrival and grimaced. It wasn't to his tastes but it would look odd if he'd come into this place and just sat here waiting. Hearing the doors open, Janson nearly breathed a sigh of relief as his contact walked in.

Janson raised his hand in greeting as the cloaked figure made their way across the filthy bar. He could tell by the voice that the individual was female but that was about it, the deep hood of the cloak hid her identity. It was the simple pin on the cloak, a sliver circle with crossed swords on top of flame that identified her as his contact. She pulled out the remaining stool on the opposite side of the table and sat.

"What information do you have for us?"

Janson smiled. The woman was to the point. Keeping his voice low he passed the list he'd written across the table, trying to keep the move discreet.

"You're aware that Lord Kyle and Lady Jessalan search for your encampment every night?" Janson glanced around the room as he spoke but didn't notice anyone else paying particular attention to them. The other inhabitants of this place seemed too intent on their own drinks, which was just as well.

"Of course." She shrugged, placing the paper she'd been given in an inner pocket of her cloak.

"That list I gave you will guide you to which villages they will be at each night this week." Janson grinned in triumph.

"Well done. I'll pass this news back to your esteemed relative and the Order." The woman stood and nodded at him before turning and striding out of the bar without a backwards glance.

27

STALKING

Kyle prowled through another village, this one of medium size with a few decent-looking pubs and inns—not surprising, since it was on the trade route just down from what had become Alex's favourite haunt on the Tri-Border. Not many of the trade barges bothered to make their way here, preferring to stay in Amberbreak and unload their goods from there.

Keeping to the shadows of the nearby dockhouse, Kyle contemplated the barge moored at the dock. The trade families were a strange people that kept mostly to themselves, dealing only with their select agents. At least, they were like that here in Vallantia. Kyle wondered if they were a little more outgoing in the other countries. He suspected one of the reasons they kept to themselves was Vallantia's nasty habit of killing those who could use the veil. Sensing small surges in the veil indicating someone was using power was one of the reasons he'd decided to stop and check out this village.

That had led him here to the dock and barge, the main source of the energy use. It wasn't the same signature as the

Sundered, though, and he doubted the Order was hiding amidst the barge families. Still, it made him realise how little he knew about the places beyond their own borders. Vallantia had been fairly well isolated and shunned in recent generations. Other than official delegations arriving at the palace to consult with the king, outsiders tended to be traders who mostly stuck to the border towns, with a few exceptions of some hardy souls. Kyle smiled. At some point when he had a little more time and they weren't in the midst of an emergency, he vowed to explore the world beyond.

Dismissing the trader family, Kyle pushed himself off from the wall and turned to explore the village some more before moving on. He doubted the Order was here, but since *he* was, he could explore a little more and definitely strike it off the list. Kyle kept himself concealed, not feeling particularly sociable.

One of the benefits of his current task: he was certainly getting a better understanding of Vallantia, getting to see in person those places that previously had just been dots on the map. He'd already known the bigger and more important villages and towns, but hadn't really had cause to visit many of them. This place seemed pleasant enough, although Alex's haunt, Amberbreak, was much better. At least as far as he was concerned, this place was a little too small and sleepy for his tastes. Kyle snorted. It wasn't like he needed to check *that* place for the Order, though. He had a sneaking suspicion Alex would have stumbled upon them if they'd been there, or they would have fled elsewhere as soon as they realised he was practically a resident.

Feeling a sudden surge in the veil, Kyle halted, drawing in power himself and sheathing his blade in it. His eyes narrowed as he saw the Kin a short distance away from him down the road. She was concealed from normal view, the inhabitants streaming around her on the bustling street without even knowing she was there. The Kin pulled down the hood of her cloak to reveal her face and held up her hands, indicating she hadn't drawn a weapon. Not that she needed to; she was Kin, she was already holding power, and it didn't take a big twist to go from shielding herself to launching an attack.

What do you want, Kin?

The woman smiled at his bluntness, but didn't seem rattled at all. Then again, she had obviously sought him out so she had some purpose.

A warning. You seek the members of the Order.

Kyle frowned at her. It was hardly a secret since the king had issued a proclamation. He guessed that almost everyone in the realm should know by know that the Order was wanted for conspiring against the Crown.

That is hardly news, Kin. Do you know where they are?

Kyle saw a smile flicker on her lips as she shook her head.

No, although I do have information about them for you.

Kyle considered her, paying no attention at all to the locals around him any more than the strange Kin did. His attention was caught by a shop owner who paused outside his shop, watching the people walk past. The man rubbed his eyes and squinted in the woman's direction. He obviously had a touch of the gift, vaguely aware that someone who seemed like a ghost was standing in the street.

What do you know?

They are recruiting. She kept her hands where Kyle could see them and paced forward, stopping just out of range.

Recruiting? Kyle frowned, tilting his head to one side.

The master, Kevin, and his thralls. They seek to bring the Kin of Vallantia to their own side in the coming conflict.

Kyle's eyes narrowed. *What was your answer?*

The woman shook her head. *I value my freedom, and I'll not let him turn me into one of his slaves. Some have believed his lies and joined his ranks. They believe the falsehoods that drip off his tongue when he tells them of the great power they will possess over the normal humans after he has dispatched the king.*

Kyle smiled cynically. He knew full well that those who joined Kevin and the Order would find enslavement or death after he had what he wanted. It didn't surprise him at all that Kevin was recruiting, trying to grow his enslaved army. It did surprise him that this woman had seen through him and that Kevin had let her go.

Why would he let you go?

He didn't. His thralls are not the only ones who can shield. Some that I know have gone to his side. She shrugged. *I'll not go against the Fourth, neither against them, but I won't join them either.*

Kyle felt the strange Kin woman gather her power and he held out his hand.

Wait! The woman paused, looking at him impatiently. *You obviously know who I am and how to find me.*

The Kin's eyes danced. *Of course I know who you are, Lord Kyle Strafford, Companion of the Fourth, Fourth's Blade.*

I don't ask that you put yourself at risk, but if you find out information regarding where the Order and their Sundered are holed up, I'd appreciate you letting me know.

The woman eyed him, then nodded.

I can do that. The Kin paused and looked at him. *Is it true?*

Kyle frowned. *Is what true?*

The proclamation from the king, declaring that the Order are responsible for the rise of the Sundered? Poisoning those of us who are Kin?

Kyle looked down, anger burning deep within him as it did every time he thought about the atrocities the Order had committed for generations.

Yes, it's true. Investigate the old stronghold of the Killiam Order if you choose, there are mass graves behind where they've been dumping the bodies of our people for generations.

The Kin's eyes narrowed as she considered his words.

If I find out anything, I will let you know.

She dissipated and Kyle let her go, realising he didn't even know her name.

Olivia.

Kyle smiled as the woman's voice floated back to him.

28

TORTURE

Amelia walked down the damp underground tunnel that ran from the Kastler estate to the caverns where the ranks of the older Sundered and new arrivals were housed. She'd heard there was a new arrival with much potential—nothing like her, of course, but powerful—and she'd decided to check him out.

It was a fine line, she'd learned, when to progress from the medication regime through to full conversion. Through trial and error her master's healers had learned it made a world of difference in the state of the newly converted and controlled Sundered. Too late and they were closer to the old breed of Sundered Ones, in various states of madness. She had proven that even those ones could be useful in the assault on the palace when she'd killed the king. If, however, the timing was just right, the results were her own kind—controlled and much more useful to her master's plan.

The Sundered slaves, as she thought of them, were good as a disposable shield to stand in front of those like her. It was just as well they had so many of them; in real conflict against her former lover and his friends, they were cut down fast. Still, not everyone could be a leader, there needed to be followers as well. In the ranks of the Sundered, Amelia and the others that ranked amongst the new breed were the leaders, if they could be called such a thing. Among those few, she headed them all.

Amelia turned to the left as the tunnel forked and felt a faint breeze hit her cheek. This path led to a vast cavern, and beyond that was a separate tunnel and opening allowing those within to either make the trek through the underground tunnels to the estate or to take the tunnels on the opposite side that led out into the hills. The first of the Kastler line had been a paranoid man who'd thought he would constantly come under attack, so when he'd found these lands with its vast network of underground caverns and tunnels, he'd built his estate on top of it. This perfectly suited their purposes and she wondered how Clement's had known. Or perhaps it was just luck.

Humming to herself in anticipation of the work to come, Amelia strode into the cavern. This one was slightly smaller than the other and served as the reception room for the newly arrived healers and the Tainted they brought with them.

Amelia's eyes glittered in anticipation, her tongue darting out to lick her lips as she contemplated what would happen to the Tainted one next. It was her favourite part to witness the excruciating pain they suffered while undergoing their final treatment. Just as she had suffered.

Ignoring the healers that turned to stare at her entrance, she walked across the intake facility to one of the smaller caverns that they used as a treatment room. She saw two boys. Well, one boy and the other... she smiled in appreciation. The other was on the verge of manhood, his body showing the signs of the man he would be.

"Amelia, nice of you to join us. I think Tyson here is ready for his final treatment." Kevin glanced at her and smiled, his own anticipation evident.

He loved to inflict pain on others, but he also liked to watch as his creatures inflicted the torture that had been done on them on others. There was little that touched her since her own treatment. At first she'd been a little hesitant, watching her master and the others as they treated the other Tainted. It had been startling to feel that rush of delight when the others screamed in pain. Then when she'd learnt enough of the process, Kevin had invited her to participate in the final treatment of others. The pure rush of pleasure it gave her to hurt the other, to have them under her control, screaming her name and begging her to stop—it was similar to the feeling she had when killing and she revelled in it.

Amelia smiled. One of the more agreeable differences between this and killing was that this lasted longer.

She looked away from the fine specimen of her own kind standing before her to the younger man, and knelt in front of him. With her hand on his shoulder she probed his mind as she'd been taught, assessing him and his potential future strength.

"Jimmy, isn't it?"

The quiet young man regarded her and nodded.

Yes, Mistress.

Amelia smiled. The lad was perceptive and already knew that he would come under her command one day.

"Go with your healer, Chelsie. We have business with your brother."

Jimmy gave one final look to his brother before holding his hand out to Chelsie, who took it without comment and proceeded out of the smaller cavern, though Amelia noted that she looked faintly disappointed to learn she wouldn't be the one to finish Tyson's treatment.

Amelia stalked up to Tyson, who stood calmly as she ran her hand up his chest and checked the bonds forged in his body and mind. She smiled. He'd been under treatment most of his life from early childhood, much as she had.

She looked at Kevin, who indicated with a sharp nod that she was to proceed.

Amelia knew the power glowed from her eyes by Tyson's indrawn breath. He'd been calm up to that point. She insinuated herself into the well-worn paths of his mind. The ease at which she gained control of the man was a testament to Chelsie's efforts. Amelia smiled as she felt a thrill of anticipation rush through her. Tyson would be a delight to break.

Lie down, Tyson. You'll be one of us soon.

A sudden burst of fear thrilled through her connection and Amelia laughed in delight as the Tainted one complied. She closed her own eyes briefly, enjoying her victim's fear. She opened her eyes again and saw her master's eyes were glittering in anticipation of what was to come.

She knelt down and placed her hands on either side of Tyson's head, compelling him to look into her eyes. She knew what this would feel like, Tyson's world narrowing down to just the two of them. She fanned the flames of his fear and as they peaked, she shot a shaft of power into his mind and sent fire racing along his body. He stiffened at the pain and she allowed him the release of screaming. Amelia smiled; she liked to hear them scream. He would be calling her *mistress*, begging her forgiveness and for the pain to stop before too long.

She would take her time with this one.

AMELIA CRINGED against the wall of her cell, weeping in frustration as her other self tortured another young man with the Taint in an attempt to do to him what had been done to her.

Please, I'm sorry! Please, Mistress, stop.

His scream of pain echoed in her mind and Amelia cringed,

hands blocking her ears, trying to keep out the young man's screams. She started to rock back and forth, her fists hitting her own head, tears streaming down her face.

No, please no, Amelia begged, wishing for once the other would hear her and stop what they were doing.

She knew that she was deteriorating. This little part of herself was shrinking, her cell growing smaller. As the light faded, despair flooded her as she sat on the floor of her cell rocking back and forth, fear catching in her throat. She knew the other would sleep well this night after revelling in the pain, after breaking the other to her will, and given the burst of desire she'd felt, he would likely follow her willingly to her bed.

Amelia sobbed in horror as it occurred to her. He would come for her again tonight.

Aiden always came after her when the other slept.

29

CONFUSION

Kevin checked the latest report handed to him by one of his healers on the progress of the Sundered Ones the Order had in their ranks. All the survivors had previously been kept drugged to keep them under control until needed. They had simplified matters over the years and now, once the treatment took, they only needed one strong mind-speaker to keep them under control, particularly with a low maintenance dose of the medication being administered.

Now, since the success of the latest batch of the toxin, they were seeing how many of those who'd had the old batches could be brought back to some semblance of normal. Those like Amelia were much more useful to his cause. His journeymen were arriving from around the kingdom at his summons, many of them bringing with them at least one person they had already commenced treatment on. Those were housed separately and responding well to the new treatment plan.

His former position in the Healers' Guild had been handy for a number of reasons, one of them being the opportunity he'd had to convince the Guild that those born with true power were becoming less common. They only thought that because it is what his journeymen had reported. Through his journeymen healers, spread out throughout the realm, the Order had managed to drug and contain most of those with power, at least those that didn't die outright due to the medication. The Guild had no idea how many of the Sundered they had in Vallantia. How could they? That meant the king had no idea what he was facing either.

With their numbers swelling every day as his journeymen healers arrived with their slaves, the day grew closer where they would be ready to face the king and his people. The new treatment meant more and more of them were useful now, like Amelia. It was just as well once their initial treatment was completed it took fewer controllers to keep an eye on them. Indeed, Amelia and a few of the others could now be trusted to keep some of their own kind under control and make sure they receive their treatment.

Amelia in particular had shown a particular flair for taking and breaking the new ones, just as she had been broken. While he missed being able to inflict such torture on another, he at least got to experience the pleasure through his thrall. The healers may be compelled to do as he ordered them, but they didn't share Amelia's passion for inflicting pain on another Kin. Amelia was totally his now, the proper lady no longer. She knew what he'd done to her, yet it made no difference; she was his devoted servant.

Even the original Sundered in their ranks were showing signs of improvement, although nothing would really heal their minds. The original medication had broken their minds in such a way they would never truly heal. Not that it mattered. With Amelia, and a few more like her, they could each control a handful of Sundered Ones in battle. The initial test—with Amelia able to kill the king and survive—had been a marginal success.

Kevin's eyes narrowed as he considered his next move. His troops definitely needed more real training, preferably in a place without the Rathadons or their people getting in the way.

He looked up, broken from his train of thought as Clements walked into the chambers they were using as the official meeting place for the running of the Order, where the council met. There were a few more who voiced opinions on occasion, but in truth the running of the Order fell to Kevin and Clements. It was useful for now to let them think their opinions mattered. Kevin found he was greatly amused by their belief that they actually knew what the Order was and what it wanted to achieve. It had never been what many of them thought, not even back when Gail Killiam founded the organisation. Clements was one of the few who knew the original charter of the Order.

Despite his initial intention to kill the old man, he'd decided to let Clements live. As a figurehead, he was invaluable.

"How are our plans progressing, Kevin?" The old man relaxed into a chair opposite him. Unlike most people, the old man preferred the more straight-backed chairs.

"Going well; I think it's time we used the information given to us by Commander Janson to good effect." Kevin liked the fact he could discuss his actual plans with Clements.

"It is unfortunate that we haven't managed to capture or rid ourselves of Lord Kyle and Lady Jessalan." Nothing could be deciphered from Clements's tone at his comment. It was almost as if they were discussing something as innocuous as the weather.

The silence between them stretched while Kevin read the relevant pieces of information from the report. While Alex had killed off a great many of Simon's thieves, he hadn't taken out all of them. Simon could still gain useful information about the peers of the realm and what they were up to from the League of

Skulls, which of course Simon passed on to the Order. Infiltrating the palace might have been too difficult to achieve, but being in strategic locations where the peers of the realm congregated was not.

"I'm thinking of sending Amelia out with a handful of the Sundered under her control. She can go after Lady Jessalan first, she should be easier to either capture or kill now that we know where she'll be." Kevin frowned, glancing at his companion to see what he thought of the idea.

"Are we certain she was hit by that blade at the coronation?" The old man rubbed his chin with his hand.

"Simon confirms it." Kevin smiled and waved the report he'd been reading.

"Amelia knows Lady Jessalan, I take it that is why you've chosen her to spearhead this first attack, rather than one of the others?" Clements gazed at him, his eyes sparkling at the prospect. The old man was just as excited to see their plans coming to fruition as he was.

Kevin nodded. "If Amelia is successful with Lady Jessalan under control or dead then we can send a party to go after Lord Kyle. It will be good training with the potential of taking out Lord Kyle as well."

"Hmmm, what of the new ones your healers have been bringing in? Do any of them have as much potential?" Clements smiled as he looked out towards the window and beyond, his mind clearly racing ahead with their plans.

Kevin grinned in appreciation. "Yes, there are some very good candidates. It will take a little time to see how they respond to treatment. However, I believe with their addition to our ranks we will be very well-placed in this battle indeed."

A broad smile spread on Clements' lips. "This will shake our enemy to the core and rock the faith some of the common people still have for the Rathadons."

Kevin nodded agreement, glad that the old man agreed

with his assessment and with the plan for the Order to finally take the fight to the Rathadons. Better than the nuisance attacks they'd been performing, although he'd been rather proud of the coronation attack. It had set them up well for this one giving them the best chance to take Lady Jessalan. He brought over a large map he'd been studying earlier. The villages where they knew Lady Jessalan and Lord Kyle would be were clearly marked on it, and he pointed out to Clements where he proposed to launch the attack.

It was something they both agreed on: it was time for the Order to start making an impact.

30

AMBUSH

Jess's eyes narrowed as she pursued a distinct trail through the veil, one that she recognised. One that she would always recognise. Either she had become sloppy or Amelia wanted to be found. She had no doubt Kyle's sister, or rather the one who walked around in her friend's body, knew that she was behind her. Even though Amelia gave no indication at all of being aware of her, the fact only made Jess consider her purpose in allowing herself to be tracked. Divide and conquer. It would be much easier for their enemy to win this game they were playing if she wasn't going up against all of them. Jess grinned, though it held no real humour. Kevin must be cursing his luck every time he contemplated them all. With the exception of taking Amelia, he'd been thwarted at every turn throughout the ages. That must be galling for a man like Kevin.

Still, the man had done something right in being able to hide his true nature until recently. Jess still didn't quite understand what Kevin's ultimate goal was, but she wasn't likely to stop long enough if she encountered the man to ask him either. That would end up badly for them both.

Jess caught her quarry's sudden shift out of the veil in the middle of a village. Jess's eyes widened as she sensed the multiple incoming surges. Before she could move into the village, she felt the roar buffet her as a building from the village below burst into flame, the elemental fire rising from the village and flickering up in a column of flame even here in the veil. Jess stepped through the thin curtain of the veil, knowing full well it was a trap for her yet unable to stand by and let villagers die when she knew she was the target. Amelia knew her well.

Drawing her weapons, she reinforced her shields, dropping into the middle of the village where Amelia and her henchmen were making short work of the town and villagers. Smoke filled her lungs and the screams of panicked adults and children sounded all around. She tried to block out their plight, knowing—*hoping*—that she was correct. Amelia and her people would turn their attention to her.

She kept her shields firmly around herself, wondering how close she could get before she would be detected. She saw one of the Sundered aim a blow at a man clutching two screaming children in his arms as he tried to run for shelter. Jess swore and lashed out with her blade as she passed, the length of her sword lighting up as she sheathed it in power. Following through, she thrust a shaft of power into the Sundered's mouth, which opened in a shriek that rang across the veil. The energy that Jess had thrust into him streamed from his mouth as he screamed and crumpled, his body incapable of handling that level of energy. At the cry of one of their own, the Sundered all turned to face the new threat. She quickly dispatched the next one before he could even contemplate trying to fight back.

Jess smiled grimly. She knew there were too many of them; she would go down. Amelia had set her trap well. Still, she couldn't have stood by and let the woman kill the townspeople in her place. Amelia spun, her eyes lighting with an internal fire as she spotted her.

Jess thought about Kyle telling her his father's urging for him to try and help Amelia. Alex's insistence, his hope that some of Amelia still existed to be rescued. Jess chuckled, if she survived this encounter she guessed she could settle the issue firsthand. Although this situation would not have been the most ideal situation to resolve Kyle's fathers and Alex's doubts.

Jess gathered the power around her and surged forward. She jumped the distance between her and the shell that had once been her friends sister, only to have another of the Sundered Ones interpose himself between them. It forced her to stop and lunge to one side reflexively to avoid a wild strike, and she felt the blade score across her upper arm. She frowned, distracted momentarily as she felt the burn of poison again. They really did need to find a new trick.

She gritted her teeth, aware the others were drawing closer as she fought and that she was being surrounded. It was a losing battle. She was better with her blades and her use of the power than they were, but she was outnumbered and wouldn't be able to stand against the onslaught for long.

Jess glanced between the gathering attackers, spotting Amelia who was in control of the others. She saw that Amelia's eyes narrow as she watched her flunkies do her dirty work. Then, in a snap decision, Jess expanded her power rapidly, and seizing them all she hauled them out of the village and into the veil.

The move clearly startled Amelia. Jess jumped as two of the Sundered that surrounded her lunged, spinning up and around, and it came to her that the normal rules didn't apply in the veil as it did in the village. Oh, she could do a great deal in the real world, drawing the power to her through the veil. Here it surrounded her, ran through her. The veil *was* power, and here she was learning she was in her element with far more access to power than most, and without even the thinnest barrier between her and that power. She spun the veil around her as she jumped, increasing her speed and strength. She lashed out with blade and power at the confused Sundered who had been behind her moments before. They'd been too slow to track her movements. Jess's eyes narrowed as she recognised their fumbling, rudimentary attempts to draw power to themselves.

Even with the advantage she had here, Jess felt herself faltering under the effort of fighting off so many at once. She could see the other's feral grin, the one like Amelia, one of the new breed. As each of the mindless slaves fell to Jess's blade another took its place, pulled through the veil by Amelia.

Looking over at Amelia, who still hadn't engaged but instead backed up to put distance between them, Jess jumped. Using the power of the veil she propelled herself, blade slashing as she surged through the air towards her adversary.

Come, you wanted this fight.

Without waiting for an answer she launched herself at the woman who'd once been a friend. Amelia's sword rose to meet her own, a sardonic smile on her face.

Is this any way to treat your best friend's little sister?

Jess's eyes narrowed as she felt Amelia gather power.

My best friend's little sister died long ago!

Jess could feel fatigue settling on her and shook her head, she'd obviously used more power fighting off this attack than she'd thought.

Oh Jess, you wound me. Here I was thinking you were like my big sister.

Amelia's tone was mocking. Jess frowned, sensing she was keeping her distance, waiting, anticipating something that she thought was going to happen.

A dazzling splash of energy lit up the space in front of her eyes. Sensing that her opponent lunge towards her rather than seeing it, Jess parried her attack. Ducking to one side on pure instinct, Jess felt the movement of Amelia's blade past her ear. Confusion hit her as her lunge caused her to stagger and power deserted her.

Ah sweet Jess, you didn't think I'd fight fair, did you?

Amelia swum into focus as she stalked towards her, vision greying out and starting to fade.

What have you done? Jess desperately tried to grapple for power again, to fight, to flee but found she couldn't.

One poison does nothing when used by itself. Neither does the other. Combined they can neutralise the Tainted. Amelia's tone was mocking as her eyes drew closer into focus in Jess's vision.

That poisoned blade at the coronation was never intended for William.

Amelia's laughter rang in her head as she suddenly understood.

Oh well done, dear Jess! Don't worry, my men and I will kill all those below in the town before we take you to our master. Rest easy knowing your noble efforts to save them are in vain.

An explosion made a counterpoint to her announcement, killing any hope she had that Amelia wasn't going to follow through with that threat. As her world darkened Jess struggled to stay conscious yet felt despair wash over her as oblivion won.

31

THE DELEGATE

Kyle walked through the private entrance at the back of the dais, nodding at the Elite on duty as he passed by, aware he was a little late. He walked up behind Ryan who stood at attention by William's side as he held court, and he touched him gently on the shoulder. Ryan had pulled morning duty with the king, which is why he hadn't been too worried about his tardiness. He only needed to relieve Ryan so he could go and attend some of his training session. As trusted as Ryan was, it was either Alex, Jess or himself that pulled duty regardless when important matters of state were occurring. With Ed, Kat and Cal taking turns as well now that they had moved back into the palace, this duty was a little easier. Ryan acknowledged his presence before retreating and disappearing out the back using the same private entrance.

One of the merchants was droning on to William, trying to get more concessions for the members of his guild. He guessed this happened every time the monarch changed since everyone hastened to improve their own standing. Kyle had no notion of how William put up with it.

Kyle scanned the packed court. There were minor talents

present, all with lesser ability that didn't concern him in the slightest, and certainly no Kin that he could sense. Not that it would automatically mean trouble if a Kin did attend the court; it would just mean that he would be showing extra caution.

Kyle looked up sharply, drawn suddenly from his thoughts. William glanced at him as he felt the increase in the strength of the shield Kyle maintained between him and the court. While William maintained his own personal shield around his own mind now, it was Kyle that was holding a combative shield. Anyone who attempted to run at him or throw a weapon, either physical or metaphysical, would find it stopped dead at the foot of the dais—unless they really knew what to look for and what they were doing, and even then it should slow things down enough for him to react.

Amongst those approaching is at least one who is Kin.

Kyle shot his warning at William, who nodded subtly at him.

As the doors opened, the herald announced the arrival of a delegation from Sylanna. Kyle felt irritation stab at him, although this time it was not his own. He urged calmness on William and was rewarded by the slight curve of his lips. He knew full well Elizabeth had put off the Sylanna delegation, indicating that now was not a good time for them to visit. It seemed that they had decided to ignore that advice and attend the court anyway. Kyle could see their point: there was a new king on the throne of Vallantia and they wanted to make sure the contracts they'd negotiated with the old king were honoured.

Kyle looked appraisingly at the petite, graceful woman in the lead of the delegation. Her flawless olive skin was offset by colourful flowing robes in hues of red and cream. Kyle found herself intrigued by the design despite himself. Seemingly made of strips of silk, the bottom of the skirt whispered as the woman glided over the ground. The fabric was all gathered at the waist and the bodice fitted her like a glove. Kyle found himself staring into the almost black eyes of the woman he had no doubt was the Imperial Princess of Sylanna and William's future consort.

While it was nice that some of their neighbours paid them a visit, it would have been preferable if they could have waited. Kyle was well aware that there was a wide world beyond filled with vast lands and people. Vallantia only had interaction with a few of them. It remained a mystery to him as to why the Emperor had sought a union between Vallantia's crown prince and his daughter. They were regarded as a backwards realm by most outside their borders.

Merchant clans bartered with the outside world and agreed to bring trade goods into and out of Vallantia. They charged a hefty commission for the trouble using the threat of the Sundered as the reason for the price tag. Representatives from the Heights Protectorate were amongst the few who dared to come here, along with trade delegations from Sylanna. Of course, since both countries shared the tri-border with them, it probably wasn't that surprising.

The merchant who'd been speaking looked over his shoulder at the interruption and sighed, moving aside without the palace staff having to prompt him.

The envoy for the Sylanna moved two paces forward from her party and curtseyed adroitly to William. She straightened promptly.

"I bring you greetings, Your Majesty, from the Emperor of Sylanna." The woman wore more practical clothes than her mistress. Although they were long and flowing and made of similar fabrics, rather than a skirt they formed loose-fitting trousers with a long coat coming down to her mid-thigh.

Kyle smiled dryly. The envoy was new. He doubted very much that it was happenstance that the Sylanna envoy was suddenly a woman now that news undoubtedly flew beyond their borders that Alex was free to be pursued. What better coup for Sylanna to have the Imperial Princess as William's consort and the envoy Alex's. His amusement fled as he realised he could just as well end up the woman's target. Kyle eyed the woman and dismissed her for the time being. He had no doubt there was more at play than the Imperial Princess showing up despite clear instructions for them to wait. If they thought a female envoy would make things easier with William, or indeed Alex or himself, they were sadly mistaken. Kyle had no doubt they had been informed that Alex was, along with his sister Elizabeth, at the heart of decisions being made here in Vallantia since the death of their father.

While he kept a careful eye on the delegation, he was aware that more than one member of the party below eyed him over and tested his barrier discreetly. With the increase in his own powers, he detected easily that most of the party below had access to power, particularly the princess. To his knowledge that circumstance had never been revealed in any negotiations. Then again, the outside realms viewed those who filled the ranks of the Kin differently to how they had here. Kyle assessed the power of those below and decided there was no way they were getting anywhere near William without Alex, Jess or himself being present.

"You are welcome in my kingdom even though your arrival at this time is unexpected." William turned his attention to Carl, who sat to one side. "See that they are housed and schedule a meeting with them. Some names might be nice as well."

The last was intended as a rebuke to Sylanna's envoy, who'd failed to introduce herself or the members of her party. Kyle gazed at the woman coolly and noted her blush at her blunder. The woman was intelligent enough to realise that she'd made an error, or rather another one. Arriving unannounced this way, forcing a meeting with William, was a clear breach of protocol.

William waved a hand to dismiss them, Kyle almost held his breath as he felt William pause, certain he was about to call an end to the Petitioners' Court. Yet finally he nodded, not even waiting as his people ushered the Sylanna delegation out of his presence before turning his attention back to the merchant who'd been pushed aside by their entrance. The man looked a little wide-eyed but retook his place and briefly recapped on his previous points before continuing.

Kyle could feel the anger rolling off William at the rudeness of the unexpected arrival and, he had no doubt, at finally setting eyes on the woman who was to be his consort. Kyle concentrated on sending soothing emotions at William, not even bothering trying to hide what he was doing. William knew enough to know what he was doing now but didn't rebuke him. Instead, he allowed himself to relax and listen to the merchant's concerns.

32

ANGER

William was seething, his anger bubbling below the surface. He knew Kyle was sending calming thoughts at him, trying to calm him, and he let him. An analytical part of his mind recognised that he was overreacting. It had been rude of them to show up uninvited when they'd been expressly told not to, yet he could recognise the political play for what it was. The princess showing up was the Emperor's way to send a message: as far as Sylanna was concerned, the negotiations held with his father still stood. Or rather, held with Lord Strafford as the go-between, or so he'd discovered. His father hadn't trusted the details to anyone else.

Even after becoming king, William still felt like he was being boxed into a corner.

That they had one of the Kin with them—not just one of them, but the whole party including his soon-to-be consort—made him wonder if they had gained access to things they shouldn't have. For Kyle to only now be aware of the power they all held meant they held considerable power to call on. He didn't want to think about the possibility of them being Elder. Although he didn't know how many of the Kin developed enough power to become Elder, he had the impression it wasn't many. It was something he needed to check with Edward or possibly Damien and Isabella when next he saw them.

His first instinct was to declare an end to the Petitioners' Court and retreat back to his rooms. Then seeing the disappointment on the merchant's face he'd reconsidered. He knew that some waited for months, others travelled from one side of the realm to the other just to get their moment to speak with him. Then his mind had flicked back to the time in the bar with Alex where he'd realised that part of his brother's appeal to people was that they found him approachable. He'd throttled down his anger; it wasn't appropriate to direct it at his people. They'd made the effort to appear before him for his judgement, he owed it to them to listen, not just push them aside because he thought his issues with the arrival of his future consort were more important. So he'd sat and he'd heard every single one of his people that were on the list for the Petitioners' Court. He put them before his personal temper tantrum.

William swept into his suite, hands going to the ties on his official robes. Shaun appeared as if by magic and batted his hands away before undoing the ties and removing his state robes, carefully taking them and hanging them up. He then came back and removed the crown, gathering correctly that William wanted it off as well. Shaun exchanged it for his simpler gold circlet. He could get away with it most times except when he was holding court.

He returned to his outer rooms without saying a word with Kyle simply trailing after him, seemingly knowing without prompting where he was going.

"Relax, William, you know these political games. Everyone is always trying to gain an advantage, particularly right now."

"Yes, I recognise the attempt to force my hand. Well it won't work, she can go back to her damn father!" William paced the length of his outer rooms, not even bothering to hide his anger now that he was in private.

"No William, she won't." Kyle's voice was clipped.

William spun to face it. "I'm the king! I say who will and will not be my consort, not my father from beyond the grave."

Kyle's eyes widened, then his lips thinned. "Yes William, you are the king. So start behaving like one!"

"What's that supposed to mean?" William snarled before he spun from him and slumped in one of the chairs.

"Think this through, you've read the security assessment as well as I have. You know your father consented to this match to hold back the Empire. Would you have us go to war on two fronts, William?" Kyle snapped, his eyes flashing in anger.

"No, damn it you know me better than that, you know I don't." William stared at his friend caught between anger and hurt that he of all people would think that of him.

"William, believe me if we could give you more time we would. We don't have it. We need that crown prince, the one we knew with absolute certainty would be a good king. We need that king."

William ducked his head, he hadn't meant to take out his temper on Kyle. He'd promised he was going to grow up and stop behaving like a sulky child and making everyone's life difficult. Yet here he was regressing to old behaviour at the first opportunity. The fact that Kyle had come with him into his rooms, gave him an indication of how agitated he really was. He also guessed it was due to the number of Kin that had been in the Sylannian party.

He sighed and finally allowed the emanations coming from Kyle to chase away his anger. If anything, it was an eye-opener for him. He'd always tried to understand Alex's fast, hot anger. He now realised he really hadn't understood. Not really, not until he was subject to it himself. It was hard to maintain your temper when other people's thoughts were being shoved into your head.

"Is this why you all ran off so much?" William whispered.

Kyle cocked his head to one side. "What do you mean?"

"I got angry and my shield faltered a little. I could hear them whispering in my head. Not just them, some of the others out there as well." William swallowed and was sure he'd just gone red. "The speculation about Jess, me, the princess."

"Ah. That speculation has always been there from the very first moment you and Jess were linked together. The gossip that ran the halls of the palace and the idle thoughts they didn't verbalise." Kyle's voice was as quiet as his own and he shrugged. "Sometimes, we'd run off to escape such things."

William smiled. "Other times?"

"It helped to escape the palace. Away from the court of Vallantia, they don't judge so readily." Kyle turned and walked towards the courtyard gardens, opening the ornately framed glass double doors, and he led him outside.

William considered Kyle's words, not sure it was quite right. People did judge out there, it was just a different type of judgement. Most would have been wary of the trio. That in itself was a form of judgement. Still, he took his friends meaning. In the court they had been protected by the rank they bore. Born to a lower family, more than likely they would have been killed at birth, or by the villagers once they discovered the depth of the powers they all bore.

In the court, the fact that they all bore the Taint at dangerous levels had been the worst-kept secret, at least in the inner circles of the courtiers. Of course the Taint ran strong in many of the families that made up the peers of the realm, so it was hard for them to cast stones, yet the judgement had been there all the same. That was a circumstance he'd been unaware of until he'd gone through the transition himself.

"Alex never told me he could hear what they thought. None

of you did." William felt himself relax as they walked through the private garden.

He was sure it was probably his imagination, but somehow, even though he'd always found the gardens peaceful, he found them even more so now.

Kyle glanced at him and ducked his head. "What could you have done? Tell them not to think?"

William looked at Kyle, startled for a moment, then laughed at the absurdity. Finally he looked around, frowning.

"Where's Jess? I haven't seen her around."

"She is out searching for the Order's new hideout. Do you want me to recall her?" Kyle cocked his head to one side regarding him.

William nearly groaned, trust Jess to be away from the palace at this time. Although under the circumstances with the Imperial Princess arriving it was probably just as well. It probably wouldn't go down well with his former lover at his side at functions to welcome his future consort.

"No, no that's more important. Let the Sylanna Delegation cool their heals." William sighed. "I'd hoped to give Alex more time but this seems to be right up his alley, particularly since you said they all have power. Can you go and ask him to come back please? I'm sure Edward will agree to babysit me." At that last comment he smiled wirily at Kyle, rewarded as he chuckled.

It didn't take long for Edward to show up and William watched with interest, aware of a tight communication between them. He gathered Kyle was filling Edward in on what had happened, they both turned to stare at him, Edwards eyebrow rising in obvious astonishment at something. William decided he didn't want to know what Kyle had told him but felt heat rise on his cheeks as he gathered it was something personal about him.

33

NEW RECRUIT

Kevin looked up again towards the door, although he wasn't taken by surprise. He knew exactly who was entering the room. He'd been waiting impatiently for her to get back and report how the attack had gone. He noted with interest that even Clements smiled at the sight of Amelia. He knew the worth of his slaves to the Order. Unlike many, Clements didn't cringe away even though he knew full well that Amelia was one of his new breed of Sundered.

"How did your mission go?" Kevin smiled, confident that he already knew the answer.

"It went well, Master." Amelia paused, her eyes lighting up.

"All of it? You have her?" Kevin stood up, unable to contain himself.

Amelia nodded. "It went exactly as planned, Master. Lady Jessalan is chained up in the cell you set aside for her in the caverns below and the message left for my former lover."

Kevin laughed and turned to look at Clements. "Care to come and look at our latest recruit?"

Clements' eyes lit with anticipation and nodded. "I wouldn't miss it. Well done, Amelia!"

"As soon as we've greeted our newest recruit, we can decide who will go on the next attack and reel in Lord Kyle." Kevin clapped Clements on the shoulder.

Amelia glanced at him. "I'm certain I can bring down my dear brother as well Master, it's not necessary to send one of the others."

"I'm certain you could Amelia, however I think you'll be of better use helping me to break Jessalan." Kevin glanced at her and saw a satisfied smile replacing her frown.

Kevin turned with Clements away from the map they'd been studying, making their plans for conquest. This moment was far more important. The Rathadon's stripped of one of their most dangerous weapons. A weapon that was about to be reforged into his own to use against them, Kevin laughed as they walked out the glow of victory was intoxicating.

JESS ROSE BIT BY BIT, not sure of the precise moment she was conscious. She was confused, feeling her muscles spasm, pain shooting through her. Slowly she became aware that she was restrained. If she could have sat bolt upright at that realisation she would have. Then her memories came flooding back. The ambush by Amelia. The dual poisons. She stilled as she remembered that detail, trying to assess her own state only to hear laughter.

"Ah Jess, you needn't worry. Soon you'll be my willing slave like Amelia."

A face appeared between her and the rock ceiling above her. It was a face she recognised. Kevin. The former member of the Companion's Cohort in Edward's day. The man that had joined the Healers' Guild and corrupted their members, then over the years drugged those born with the power of the veil. Jess struggled, or she tried to yet whatever she'd been given still ran in her system. Her captor's eyes glittered. Jess recognised the malice laced through with a strong dose of anticipation emanating from the man.

Kevin leant into her, cupping her face with one hand. Jess shuddered as the man's cheek pressed close to hers as he whispered in her ear. "Oh yes, that's it, fight me. It will make breaking you even more *pleasurable*."

"You might as well give in Jess. You've lost." Amelia's face replaced Kevin's and she felt her lips brush her forehead.

She stiffened and screamed as pain suddenly shot through her as Amelia used the contact between them to channel power into her. She felt her body react, arching against the restraints, her mind desperately trying to find a way out. Scrabbling at the nothing that seemed to stand between her and the power she knew was there, she could still sense it yet somehow she couldn't quite reach it.

She heard Kevin laugh. "Breaking you is going to be exquisite, Companion of the Fourth. When I'm done, I'll turn you on your precious Fourth, on your king, on your people."

This was Kyle's nightmare, one she hadn't truly understood until right this moment. Now she did, fear and horror hammered through her at the prospect that she'd be taken and used against all that she loved. Jess lunged, or tried to; the chains they bound her with didn't allow her to get very far. Kevin sat next to her, his eyes glittering with something that Jess couldn't quite place. His hand rose up and she felt Kevin's hands lightly stroke her temples.

"You will be my most devoted pet by the time I'm done with you, but the very first step will be to break you." A smile curved her captor's lips.

"I won't ever truly be yours. Not willingly." Jess spat the words at Kevin. She tried to push aside her sinking fear that it wasn't true; Kevin had plenty of practice breaking those born with the power of the veil.

"So you think now. I do hope you prove to be strong, it will prolong your torture and make it sweeter when you beg me to make you my slave." As Kevin licked his lips, Jess shuddered.

The man was repulsive and she vowed that somehow she would find a way to resist him. Jess stiffened as Kevin's hands clamped onto her temples; she found herself staring into the man's cruel eyes then her mind and body exploded with pain. Her resolve not to scream didn't even last long enough to complete the thought.

34

RETURN

Kyle found Alex without any trouble at all. He could tell his friend was curious about his sudden appearance, and the rest of the bar seemed so as well. Kyle paid them no mind and walked across, sliding onto the bench seat on the opposite side of the booth to Alex. He made no effort to hide it as he swept his powers over Alex, assessing his mood and stability.

Alex ducked his head, although it didn't hide what looked suspiciously like a smile, and while Kyle didn't hear the communication, he had no doubt that Alex had apprised another that he'd shown up. Alex had to know what his presence here meant even though he hadn't told him yet.

It wasn't long at all before Kyle sensed a stir in the bar. He glanced over to see the cloaked figure in the doorway that had drawn the attention of the guests within, definitely female and not a local. The most striking thing anyone could see of her was the deep blue cloak with silver concentric designs patterned around the edges, the voluminous hood hiding her face well.

Even so disguised, Kyle knew instantly who she was, even

without Alex's instant reaction to her appearance. She was someone Kyle had met before.

Isabella. The woman could only be Isabella.

Fascinated, Kyle watched as she turned unerringly towards their table and made her way through the bar. If anything Alex seemed even calmer at her appearance. The woman was a good influence on his friend.

Alex looked up, seemingly hesitant. He held out his hand and she took it without comment, allowing him to pull her into his arms.

"Not worried about rumour anymore, Alex?" Isabella's voice was light and teasing as she glanced around the bar at all the guards.

Alex glanced at Kyle before shaking his head.

"No, if anything, when word gets back to court my brother will probably be relieved." Alex closed his eyes briefly before opening them to gaze across at his friends. "Although I take it William wants me back at the palace?"

Isabella turned her head on his shoulder to gaze at Alex, hand rising up to cup the side of his face. Her kiss left no mistake at all about how the couple felt about each other.

Kyle grinned at the pair. "He does. You may wish to request Isabella come with you. I think you might need a human shield."

Alex swung his gaze to him, wincing in anticipation while Isabella simply looked confused.

"What's happened now?" Alex's voice was remarkably calm.

"The Sylanna Delegation turned up unexpectedly. William did not handled the surprise well." Kyle kept his voice low. With the music playing in the corner and the general hum of noise in the bar hopefully their conversation wouldn't travel so far.

"Ah. So why does that mean I need Isabella to shove in front of me for protection?" Alex's eyes narrowed, clearly suspicious.

"The Envoy is a woman and not as polished as I'd expect. I'm thinking the Emperor of Sylanna might just have more than one Rathadon in his sights." He left unsaid that he was certain that word of Amelia being stripped of her rank and being declared a traitor would have reached the Emperor.

"Obviously. It's to be expected, I'd be more surprised if they hadn't. What else?" Alex shook his head, an irritated look flicking across his face.

Kyle smiled. "They all have power and a few of them are Kin. Including the Imperial Princess."

At that little piece of information, Alex's eyes widened.

Kyle turned his head to look at the barman and gestured for another carafe and a goblet for Isabella. The proprietor acknowledged him with a nod and sent his serving staff scurrying in short order not only with more wine but a platter of finger food for the table. Isabella stirred.

"Well it's not really a surprise. The Sylannian always need men." Isabella sipped her wine only then noticing they were both staring at her.

"What do you mean?" Alex looked as confused as Kyle felt.

"It's an oddity of their people. They birth far more females than males. It's what sparked their expansion generations ago and something they understandably go to great lengths to hide. It's a weak point should others care to exploit it." Isabella looked from one to the other amused by their astonishment.

"I definitely do not need that kind of attachment." Alex grimaced.

Isabella smiled at him and patted his cheek. "It's ok, it wouldn't just be one, you'd end up with a dozen at least."

Alex nearly spat his drink out, looking at Isabella in horror while her laughter caused more than one person nearby to glance at them. Kyle smiled at Alex's discomfort and waited while he pulled himself together.

"So William needs me back in my role as Fourth and to act

on his behalf rather than Elizabeth due to the high number of veil users?" Alex clearly decided to ignore the idea that not only the envoy but several more might be after him.

"He does." Kyle kept his eyes on Alex and was relieved that he seemed ready to accept the recall to duty.

"Jess?"

Kyle smiled at the hopeful tone in Alex's voice. "No such luck, she's out searching for the Order."

"Of course she is. How did she manage to get that lucky?" Alex smiled, showing he wasn't really all that upset.

"I know, but to be fair it is her turn. Otherwise she would have been guarding William and I would have been out searching. Meaning she would be stuck going to all the official functions that will happen because of this." Kyle rolled his eyes.

Alex chuckled and turned to look at Isabella.

"Will you come back with me?" Alex looked at her, a pleading look in his eyes.

"To be the shield between you and the evil Sylannian women?" Isabella's eyes sparkled as she teased him.

Alex's lips twitched. "Yes please. If they realise I'm running scared from them I probably won't be so useful to William."

Kyle cleared his throat and they both returned their attention to him.

"You should also be warned that Ed, Cal and Kat have been invited back to the palace." Kyle gazed at Alex, judging his reaction.

Alex groaned. "Mother?"

"Your mother as well. They are housed in the royal wing. William asked them to stay and help out." Kyle watched Alex carefully; his mother was a sore point.

A look of sadness flickered across Alex's face before he finally nodded. He breathed a sigh of relief as Alex took the news far better than he expected his friend would. It would have been a little awkward otherwise.

Then again, Kyle didn't know why he'd been concerned. William was one of the few people that Alex had always listened to, and despite everything Alex had shown more compassion towards his mother than anyone had thought he ever would.

35

ASSISTANCE

Matthew trailed after Ryan, something the newly acknowledged member of the Companion's Cohort was apparently finding a little disconcerting. When he'd first started with Personal Service, he'd always been with Marcus, James or Megan, learning on the job from the more senior members. Now he was trusted one up with a handful of Elite under his command. Admittedly it was Ryan he was following around at the moment, but he'd been assured he would be swapped in to pull duty stints on all of their charges. They all had different mannerisms and responses. It was a part of his job to know how they were going to respond and hopefully put things in place in advance rather than being surprised and left flat-footed.

Of course, the job of guarding Alex and his friends was a lot more difficult than that of their counterparts who pulled duty on Princess Elizabeth or the king. Now that the king was also numbered amongst the Kin, Matthew wondered if that would change as he grew more sure of himself with his powers. He'd already accompanied Alex once on an excursion to an inn. Matthew grinned in the memory of his horror when they'd realised that the king was accompanying their charges. His happiness at being included for once so they could do their jobs had turned in a heartbeat into a sinking feeling of dread. If anything had happened to the king, their careers would have been over. The others, he'd found out later, had been just as horrified as he'd been, they were just all better at hiding it and they knew Alex, Kyle and Jess much better. They hadn't seen fit to let the Elite, who normally guarded the king, know about their charges' night-time excursion.

Ryan glanced at him with a frown. "You know, I'm not going anywhere, just back to the Complex now that Kyle has taken over watching the king."

"I gathered as much. It's still my duty to follow you around today." Matthew kept his amusement at Ryan's frustration to himself.

"I'm not exactly Alex. Next to no one knows who I am, so I doubt I'd be anyone's target." Ryan was clearly trying to work out a way around the restriction of having guards trail him around everywhere.

"Sir, you've been standing at the king's shoulder and have intervened several times now on different attacks involving the Order's people. If they didn't know who you were, I'm sure they are getting the picture now."

Ryan took a moment to mull it over.

"I think I know why Alex, Jess and Kyle have the habit of running away all the time." Ryan grinned at him, taking the sting out of his complaint.

Matthew groaned. "Please don't develop that habit."

He carefully didn't look at the guards with him as they stifled laughter at his indiscretion. It certainly hadn't taken him long to become frustrated by the disappearing act. It was amusing only when it wasn't your responsibility to make sure nothing went wrong.

"Well, I can't guarantee it. If I'm needed, I'll go." Ryan looked at him, one eyebrow rising.

Matthew sighed. "Just take us with you if you do."

Ryan paused to look at him, then at the cluster of guards that followed him in surprise. Thankfully they had all managed to stop in time without running into him. "I... you know, I haven't ever tried to take someone with me through the veiled paths. I can take myself there, travel from point to point and back again. I know Alex, Jess and Kyle have all dragged everyone around with them. I've just never done it." Ryan frowned.

Matthew saw his opportunity and jumped at it.

"Well, we could always go to the practice grounds and you could try if you wanted." Matthew kept his excitement at the prospect out of his voice.

Ryan's eyes narrowed as he caught onto some of what Matthew was hiding. He cocked his head to one side. "What are you up to?"

Matthew grinned at him disarmingly. "Nothing, honestly. You can practice on me first, if you'd like. You know I have more power than the average guard, enough to hold a shield, so any risk to me should be minimal. You can always holler for one of the others if something goes wrong."

"All right, let's go. You will tell me precisely what you are up to before we commence, though."

Matthew cursed under his breath. Ryan had been hanging around with Alex, Kyle and Jess too much. Not that Ryan had ever been naive growing up how he had, but their scepticism was clearly rubbing off on him. That he was correct on this occasion didn't mollify Matthew at all.

Ryan changed his course and headed to the Elite training grounds, obviously content to let the matter drop until they got there.

Matthew wasn't sure exactly how he would respond to his

suggestion. Regardless, the first stage was for Ryan to see if he could take Matthew with him into the veil. If he could do that, then he would suggest that Ryan try to leave him there to test his theory that he would be fine.

Ryan entered the training grounds, which at this time of day were empty. The bulk of the Elite's training sessions happened in the mornings with a few in the late afternoons depending on the shifts the guards were working. He had no doubt the regular grounds were a hive of activity, as usual.

Ryan turned and, folding his arms, gazed at Matthew steadily.

"What are you up to?"

Matthew sighed. "Well, you really do need to know whether you can drag us with you through the veil. That would be the first part, honestly. I'm willing to volunteer as your test subject. You know I have more power than the others and can shield."

Ryan considered him and nodded. "What else?"

Matthew barely stopped himself from squirming as Ryan seemed to be channelling Kyle's ability to extract information. It was something in that flat, uncompromising stare that did it.

"All right. I had an idea. It's risky but might help with the situation of Alex, Kyle and Jess running off without us. We are meant to protect them, but we can't do it when we aren't with them." Matthew let some of his frustration show. "Things are getting increasingly dangerous. The hit-and-run tactics favour the Order, not us."

Ryan frowned, carefully considering his words. That was at least something. "So what is your idea?"

"First you test your ability to take me to the veil with you. I'll hold my own shields the entire time. Then if that works, you leave me there. Come back here, then see if you can locate me and pull me back out." Matthew held up his hand when Ryan looked like he was about to explode. "Alex found the king when he accidentally transported himself to the veil and His

Majesty had no idea what he was doing. He couldn't even hold a shield back then."

Ryan closed his eyes, clearly thinking, then groaned. "Alex is going to kill me for this when he finds out."

Matthew resisted the urge to cheer. "Well, Kyle might. Hopefully His Highness is too busy to notice."

Ryan glared at him. "He might be busy, but you'd be surprised what he finds out when he wants to. Besides that, if this works I'm going to have to tell them what I've done regardless."

Matthew grinned at him. "It will work and everything will be fine."

Ryan groaned once more. "All right, let's try this before I change my mind."

Matthew pushed down his sudden nervousness at the test. He knew it wouldn't help matters at all. Ryan reached out with his powers and Matthew felt them wrap around him, tentative at first, and then with increasing confidence. Before he could even utter a word of encouragement, he felt himself being hauled into the veiled world.

Ryan faced him, grinning in triumph, his relieved laughter ringing in his mind.

Well, that worked, and you are clearly not dead, so that is a good first step.

Matthew glanced around, admitting to himself that even he had been nervous about this part. Taking a breath, he looked around him, seeing the familiar road that led off into the grey mist. He knew, or guessed, that Ryan hadn't taken them too far away from the training grounds at the palace, since he fancied he could see the faint, indistinct outline of the grounds around him. That, or his overactive imagination was playing tricks on him, which was probably more likely. His brain always wanted to grab onto some sort of reference when he travelled in the veiled world, so he wouldn't put it past his own subconscious mind to create something that wasn't there in the first place.

Right. Should we try the next step?

Matthew swallowed, pushing down his own nerves. Concentrating, he wrapped his own personal barrier around himself as he spoke.

How about a baby step? I'll withdraw my shield. If you don't suddenly drop dead, I'll move a distance away and we'll see if you manage on your own.

Matthew conceded that prospect calmed his nerves down just a little, and he nodded.

Good idea. Let's get this over and done with before I hyperventilate.

Matthew grinned tightly, seeing no point in hiding his fear. He'd be a fool not to be feeling hesitant and he got the distinct impression that Ryan knew full well what he was feeling.

Hold your shield, don't forget to breathe.

Matthew felt it as Ryan slowly removed his shield until he was left, standing there in the veil under his own power. It was his own personal shield wrapped tightly around him. They both stared at each other, then Matthew let his breath out explosively as he remembered the injunction to breathe. Laughing at himself, and a little surprised that he was still here, Matthew looked at Ryan and nodded, taking a breath. Slowly, bit by bit, Ryan drew himself farther away, leaving him standing there in the veil by himself.

Matthew looked around the grey featureless expanse of the veil. The pathway that had been there moments before had disappeared with Ryan's withdrawal. The thickening fog closed in on him and hid even the vague outline of the training grounds he'd thought he'd seen before. He shuddered as bitter cold penetrated his clothing, soaking into his skin and through to his very bones.

Matthew swallowed, pushing down his panic. He didn't

understand how Alex and the others navigated their way through this mess since there wasn't a single feature for him to use as a focus point. He closed his eyes and concentrated on keeping his shield up and breathing, trying to ignore the bitter cold and push it away. Matthew jumped as Ryan's voice sounded in his head, somehow more eerie in the all-encompassing thrum of power.

Breathe, Matthew, you are doing well. I think this will do for today. We'll practice again tomorrow.

Matthew opened his eyes to see Ryan next to him again. The cold and fog pulled back, and he was relieved to see he was standing on a pathway again. He felt Ryan's power surround him as Ryan squeezed his shoulder. Matthew didn't even try to hide his relief. It was one thing to think about doing this, it was another matter doing it and knowing you didn't have the power to get yourself out of it.

Still, he felt a small thrill of pleasure. He had been right. With practice it would get easier. He hoped.

He breathed out and felt his nervousness settle, and he nodded at Ryan, grateful that he'd waited long enough for him to get control of himself once more. He hadn't fooled Ryan one little bit; the lad was sharp. Given he'd been hand-picked by Alex, Matthew shouldn't have been surprised at all.

Matthew's smile faltered as Ryan stopped suddenly, looking at something he couldn't see and groaned.

What?

Matthew was more than a little alarmed by Ryan's response and the dread on his face when he turned to look at him didn't help one little bit.

Lord Kyle is waiting for us down in the training yard with Marcus and James.

Matthew swore; everything had been going so well. Sort of.

36

POLITICAL DANCE

Alex looked up as Joshua came into his waiting room.

"According to the staff, the envoy and her people are starting to squirm, Fourth." Joshua didn't even allow a hit of what he was thinking to show on his face. He was far too adept at his job for that.

Alex nodded and stood waiting as Joshua fussed with his formal jacket, making sure everything was in place. He nodded his thanks and walked out, with Marcus, James and a few more of their men falling in behind him. Alex had noted of late that the number of guards he had following him had multiplied, although on this occasion he had a sneaking suspicion the number of guards was due to the unexpected arrival of the envoy and the knowledge that many in their party were numbered amongst the Kin.

Alex wondered idly if the envoy had brought the Imperial Princess along with her to this meeting. From what Kyle said, the woman was Kin and quite powerful. There was all sorts of politics at play with that one. Alex had no doubt at all that when his brother calmed down, he'd start seeing the implications of the manoeuvre, particularly since when their father had negotiated this contract, the Emperor had omitted the fact that the princess was Kin, and at the time William hadn't been. There was no way they could have predicted his forced transition.

The walk down the corridor was short since the envoy and her people had been shown to a meeting room just off the royal wing, nice enough to host a foreign delegation without causing an incident while still showing the king's displeasure, since it was not the main conference room contained within the royal wing. It was a subtle message that he was sure the envoy would understand.

As he approached the entrance, the guards on duty stood to attention and the staff swung the doors open. Both Marcus and James adroitly slipped past him, surveying all in the room before moving to take up positions behind his own chair. Alex bit back a smile; everyone was being terribly official today.

Those in the room stood abruptly as he entered. One of the women at the head of the party suddenly paused halfway through a bow before straightening back up again looking flustered to see him. She had obviously been expecting the king. Alex took his own seat and waved the rather plainly dressed woman who he gathered from the description he'd been given was the envoy and her people back into their own.

"Please, sit. You bow before the king as a sign of respect. I am the Fourth, bowing is not necessary and I doubt you would be aware of the obeisance shown out of respect to my rank." Alex eyed the delegate coolly.

The elegant woman in the Emperor's colours of crimson and cream sat. That and the fact that the others in the Sylanna Delegation hesitated, just a fraction of a second, so that she could take her seat before them gave away who she was. That and Kyle's description.

"My apologies, Your Highness, Fourth. I was expecting the

king." The envoy looked at the woman sitting next to her who smiled, her dimples showing.

"Ah, well, we weren't expecting you at all, and still there is the discourtesy of not introducing yourself." Alex kept his eyes firmly on the envoy, who turned a most interesting shade of red.

The envoy stood, inclining her head to Alex. "Fourth, our apologies. If I may introduce Her Imperial Highness Princess Rosalinda Laura Spencer, daughter of His Imperial Majesty Christopher Thomas Spencer—your future queen."

"I believe *consort* has been negotiated in the contract, Envoy, not queen. I'm also the Fourth and her Imperial Highness is Kin, so under a peculiarity of Vallantian custom she falls under my authority, as do you all while in the confines of this realm." Alex made no attempt to keep the bite out of his tone and was rewarded as the colour drained from the envoy's face.

She sprang from her chair and Alex felt her drawing in her power. Waving off his guards, who were moving to intercept the envoy, Alex stared at her until she remembered where she was and sat down. Alex allowed an uneasy silence to settle on the room until the woman broke eye contact and glanced away. Finally he dismissed the envoy and focused on his brother's future consort.

"Princess Rosalinda, you and your people were asked to delay your attendance at our court. Why has your father seen fit to send you here at this time?" Alex smiled, although he was perfectly aware that it didn't soften his words.

"With the death of the prior king and His Majesty ascending the throne my father thought we should pay our respects, Fourth." The princess stumbled a little over his title but otherwise seemed unaffected by the verbal sparring. That didn't surprise Alex in the slightest.

He could see her eyes dart around as if she was desperately trying to find a graceful way to retreat. Alex let the silence stretch between them, taking a sip of water that his staff had placed on the table at his setting.

"You mean that while he'd heard of our father's death, he didn't know I was back at court and was unaware of William's forced transition, so he thought to send you and your people to take advantage of a period of instability?" Alex knew his expression was cynical and had no doubt that she interpreted it as that.

The envoy flushed again and opened her mouth to reply but stopped as the princess placed her hand on the other's shoulder.

"My father meant no disrespect, Fourth. However, you are correct that he is used to getting his own way. He did not want to give another a chance to convince His Majesty to take another as his consort."

Alex found that he respected the bluntness of her admission. His lips nearly gave him away, twitching in amusement as the envoy forgot herself again and stared at the princess. Alex wondered what possessed the woman. He doubted the Emperor would send anyone incompetent, so something in particular had obviously unsettled her.

He dismissed the woman. If she had been sent here by the Emperor with a secondary goal of snaring him, she was going to be sadly disappointed. He would lay odds that she would then set her sights on Kyle. Alex knew she would have no more luck on that score. He spread out the fingers of his own power, assessing one member of their group after the other. As Kyle had briefed him he found the princess was the strongest, with the envoy close in power. The others had power but nothing to be concerned about, at least not for Jess, Kyle or himself. While they were certainly Kin, they did not rank amongst the Elder.

"That was not our intent in asking you to delay. We are in the middle of a civil uprising from some discontent rebels. My father didn't just die unexpectedly, he was assassinated, as I'm sure your own intelligence has told you. We would not want you or your people put at risk. My brother has other things on his mind right now." Alex kept his eyes on Rosalinda, his tone dry.

"I'm sorry about the manner of your father's death." The princess relaxed incrementally, allowing her power to show briefly.

Alex was learning it was a courtesy between Kin, at least those who were friendly, to lower their shields, even if only for a brief moment, so another of their own kind could get a sense of each other's power. A slow smile spread on his lips and, while keeping his mental barriers firmly in place—he'd learnt that lesson too—Alex relaxed his control, allowing the power that was within him to shine.

The envoy gasped and recoiled in reaction before regaining control over herself. She swallowed convulsively. "Elder." Her tone held a note of awed disbelief.

Alex was glad that the years of court training meant nothing showed on his face. He knew he had power—a lot of it and more than others of his own kind he'd encountered—and that he was one of the so called Elder Born, yet he thought it would be years before he'd rise to be an actual Elder. Alex doubted the woman would have used that honorific if she didn't mean it. Then again, if the envoy believed he had access to that kind of power, all the better. She'd be less likely to do something stupid and would pass the warning back to her Emperor. They had enough of their own home-bred problems to deal with without importing more of them.

"I should warn you those who rise against the Crown have Kin under their control. If they come to the palace again, it will probably be against the king or myself. Still, show caution while you remain here in Vallantia." While they'd been foolish in coming here against William's express wishes, he believed they still deserved the warning.

Princess Rosalinda recovered herself enough that the redness in her cheeks receded. Her eyes widened slightly at his words. She glanced at the woman sitting next to her. Alex stopped thinking of her as an Envoy, despite the woman being given that title. She'd quite clearly had little if any training in that role.

"Forgive me Fourth but Vallantia has had troubles for generations. My father thought it to be the same issues. What do you mean, your rebels have Kin under their control?"

Alex settled back into his chair and indicated for one of his servants to serve drinks. He waited patiently as they offered a tray with a variety of fine selections to their guests while Joshua poured him a drink, placing the goblet close to hand. He contemplated the party opposite him.

When they had appeared suddenly in court, all of them had assumed the Emperor—and by extension his people—knew the circumstances they faced. Alex took a long sip of his drink, considering his next words. He drew his brother into his mind, admitting it was much easier now than it had been in the past.

Brother, it seems they didn't know the circumstances of what we face in dealing with the Order when they ignored the request that they not attend the court. It is just politics, William. You know how this game works.

Alex caught an image from William; he was in his courtyard garden and had calmed down considerably. Still Alex caught some of his internal struggle before he conceded.

Fill them in as you think is appropriate.

There was an evident sigh in William's tone and much of his tension at the implied discourtesy of the Sylannian delegation's arrival receded.

Alex looked at those opposite him, his eyes narrowing as he considered them. He decided a little bluntness was needed. "So who are you really? Forgive me but you are not a trained envoy and not someone I'd expect the Empire to put in this position."

The woman who'd been filling the role of envoy flushed. She opened her mouth but then closed it abruptly again as the princess laid her hand on her shoulder.

"There was trouble in our homeland, a little infighting amongst ruling families. It can be a deadly dance of daggers and so it proved for the Kortrain family line. Annabella went from the youngest daughter in a long family line to Lady Annabella Kortrain. I felt a break from the Dagger Courts prudent in case the Kortrain line became extinct. The First Wife backed me so my Emperor-Father agreed. I thought this would be good training for one who wasn't raised to rule and somewhat safer." Rosalinda looked at him calmly.

Alex processed what he'd been told and gathered that a little infighting was an understatement. If he understood correctly, an entire family line except one person was wiped out in one night of bloody fighting. "If you will accept some advice Lady Annabella, from one youngest child to another, stop trying to pretend to be what you are not. It just gives rise to confusion and misunderstanding. Just be who you are."

Annabella blushed and her shoulders relaxed as if a weight had just been lifted from her. "Forgive me for the deception Prince Alexander."

"There is nothing to forgive. If her Imperial Highness calls you Envoy, then Envoy you are." Alex allowed himself to relax even more. Despite himself he was starting to like these Sylannians. Probably just as well since one of them was to become his brother's consort.

"Thank you, Your Highness." Rosalinda's dimples showed again as she grinned at him.

Alex stood, carrying his drink over to the windows to gaze out.

"A group called the Killiam Order was responsible for assassinating my father. It was established just before the time we call the Sundered War."

"They have been around for some time." Annabella spoke carefully.

"It has only just come to light that the Order has possession of a drug, a toxin that affects those of us who become Kin, sending most spiralling down into madness." Alex heard a gasp behind him but didn't turn around.

"They are responsible for your Sundered Ones?" The princess sounded genuinely shocked.

"Yes. They have been conducting experiments for generations. Those they haven't killed outright or sent mad, they have control over. They used such a one to assassinate my father." Alex said the last quietly, deliberately leaving out any further details about Amelia.

"I am sorry, Fourth. You intend to deal with this group?" Annabella sounded matter-of-fact; it seemed she was on more secure ground while discussing assassination.

"We do, and it is why your arrival is badly timed. We are outnumbered, they have been building up for years, but we will fight them. We have no choice. Your presence here at this time complicates the issue and my king does not want any harm to come to you and yours." Alex turned to gaze at them solemnly.

"This conflict is imminent?" The princess glanced to her advisors, then back at him, biting at her lip.

Alex smiled sadly. "It is. We have a few more things to set into place if we have time. Then, for good or ill, we will fight them. We cannot allow this plague to spread beyond our borders and infect other realms, if it has not already done so."

Rosalinda stood and ducked her head politely.

"With your permission and your king's, I believe my father, the Emperor needs to know about this toxin."

Alex nodded. "I will speak with the king and have something drawn up to explain as best we can what has occurred here. Get settled in the suite you have been assigned." Alex allowed a smile to show. "There will likely be a function to welcome you all to court."

Annabella relaxed now that the conversation seemed to be on track, and she smiled. "Thank you, Fourth, that is more than we could have expected given the suddenness of our arrival."

Alex nodded to the delegation, handing his goblet to a hovering servant. He walked towards the doors, which swept open on his approach, his guards falling in behind him as he retraced his path back towards his brother's rooms.

37

FALL OUT

Ryan hesitated staring at small gathering of people waiting in the training grounds. He nearly swore since he'd been hoping they might have had a few moments before having to confess what they'd been up to. Or rather what he'd been doing since Matthew didn't have the power to do it by himself.

Ryan groaned as Kyle looked straight at him.

Are you going to come out or am I going to get irritated and pull you out?

Ryan really did groan and glanced at Matthew who obviously had no idea what was waiting for them.

Are you ready? Try to pull it together.

Ryan waited a brief moment as Matthew looked at him startled and groaned before nodding his head. Ryan knew there was nothing he could do about his guards pale complexion through his tan.

Not trusting Kyle's patients much longer although he seemed more amused right now than angry despite his firm expression Ryan dispelled the concealing veil. Kyle, having known exactly where he was standing was looking straight at him. Ryan hoped that was a trick that he would learn himself one day. The others swung around as he appeared near them with Matthew. Ryan looked from one to the other before settling his gaze back on Kyle who hadn't said a word. Just continued to stare at him. Finally Kyle's eyebrow raised, inviting an explanation.

"Well good news is I can transport another person in the veil with me now." Ryan smiled trying to appear calm. He wasn't sure if it was a good thing to be facing off against Kyle alone or if Alex would have been worse.

"Well that is a good start." Kyle's tone was dry.

"It also appears Matthew can pull his own shield around himself and stay in place without my assistance." Ryan stayed calm. Only his firm knowledge that Kyle wasn't actually angry helped him in his endeavour.

Kyle turned his gaze on Matthew, who was still looking pale but stood there stoically not even flinching under the Fourth Blade's regard.

"I can see why that experiment might be a little disconcerting. You didn't think it might be prudent to involve me in this?" Kyle turned his glance back to Ryan.

Ryan opened his mouth then shut it again, thinking about what the correct answer should be. He saw Kyle's eyes starting to sparkle as he noticed the delay.

"Now that you mention it, well it probably would have been a good idea. The result wouldn't have been different though, even if things went wrong. Given it depended on if Matthew could hold his own shield in the veil." Ryan swallowed, realising that what he'd said didn't quite come out the way he meant it.

Kyle glanced at Matthew. "Matthew, it's a good idea even if risking your own life to test it was extremely foolish. In case you hadn't noticed you are one of only four of you with sufficient power level in the Elite. Go get some sleep, you'll need it. You've just volunteered to be our test subject."

At a gesture from Kyle, Ryan fell into step as he turned to walk from the grounds towards the doors that lead to the Complex of the Fourth. Ryan noticed absently that James gathered some of the clustered guards and trailed after them. Matthew was led towards the other door that led around to the back of their own quarters by Marcus and the remaining guards.

~

KYLE WAITED until they were safely behind closed doors in their own world, removed from the rest of the palace except for their own people. He placed his hand on Ryan's back as he attempted to head off to his own rooms and guided him into one of their sitting rooms.

"Not so fast, Ryan." Kyle looked at the worried expression on the young man's face and suppressed a grin.

Kyle guided Ryan into the sitting room where Alex was waiting for them. A brief look of exasperation flashed across his face at seeing Ryan, which told Kyle that someone had also run straight to Alex to let him know about Ryan's little experiment. Kyle shook his head. He should not have been surprised. There was always someone hoping to further their own station in life by trying to bring down another. They must have cornered Alex after he'd met with the Sylanna Delegation. Either the walk between there and William's Suite or there and the Complex after he'd briefed the king. That was fast work.

Ryan stopped in his tracks at seeing Alex sitting on the couch waiting for them and looked faintly alarmed. Kyle chuckled and pushed the lad forward towards one of the seats.

"So, Ryan, you've been on an adventure, I hear." Despite trying to appear serious, Alex was clearly in a good mood.

"No, Fourth— I mean, yes, but it wasn't like that..." Ryan stumbled to a halt and looked at Kyle a little desperately.

"Don't look at me, I have an idea of what you were up to but it's yours to explain." Kyle sat down in one of the chairs near Alex and watched as Ryan wrestled with himself, apparently not knowing whether he should sit or not.

Kyle hid a smile and Alex finally took a little pity on him.

"Sit down, Ryan, or I'll get a stiff neck looking up at you." Alex's voice didn't give away what he was thinking.

Ryan swallowed, his tongue darting out to lick his lips and, looking around, he perched on the very edge of the seat. He looked earnestly at Alex.

"Sorry. I felt it would be good to know if I can transport others safely through the veiled world. Matthew wanted to see if he could maintain his own shield and stay where I left him under his own power. It seemed like a useful thing to know." Ryan spoke rapidly through his explanation, trailing off weakly at the end.

"I take it Matthew came out of this experiment alive." Alex glanced at Kyle.

"He appeared to be a little shaken by the experience but otherwise fine. The other guards informed me that it was actually Matthew's idea, not Ryan's." Kyle saw Ryan breathing a sigh of relief.

It stood him in good stead that he was willing to take all the fallout from this little experiment, even though Matthew had clearly instigated it.

"I was keeping a close watch, ready to grab him if needed." Ryan slid his glance over to Kyle. "I think the Elite are getting sick of you guys leaving them behind when you go off hunting."

Kyle frowned. He was aware that none of their guards liked

being left behind. He could even sympathise with them. It was a little difficult for them to perform their duty when they were continually left behind.

“I understand their frustration; given the way we hunt, they would get in the way.” Kyle held up his hand as Ryan went to argue with him. “If they can learn to hold themselves in the veil without us, perhaps. They’d still be too much of a target if another of the Kin showed up, though.”

“The idea has merit if it can be made to work. They would at least be closer to hand if any of us did need them.” Alex glanced from Ryan to Kyle before shrugging.

Kyle looked over to Ryan. “Do we know why Matthew was shaken up by the experience? It’s not like it is the first time he’s been in the veiled world.”

Ryan squirmed in his seat. “I didn’t get a chance to ask.”

“We’ll check on the details tomorrow. Perhaps with another trial, once we discover what the issues were for Matthew, if he is willing to give it another go.” Kyle looked at Alex with his eyebrow raised in an unspoken question.

Alex nodded his approval as he stood. “Fair enough, it’s worth trying. Although I don’t think it will quite work the way Matthew believes. Please try not to break him in this experimenting and keep me updated. If the guards can be trained to do this, it could prove to be a tactical advantage in attack planning.”

With the grilling finally over, Alex stood walking towards the doors that lead to his private domain unbuttoning his formal vest as he went. Kyle saw Ryan go bright red as he realised that Alex had obviously just come from an important meeting.

“It’s alright Ryan, given the meeting Alex was in no one would have interrupted him. Someone would have tattled on you in-between the meeting room and here.”

Kyle finally took pity on the lad and waved dismissal as he stood, watching as Ryan scrambled to his feet and retreated. His relief evident. Kyle shook his head and followed in Alex's wake towards his own suite, like him he had the function tonight he had to prepare for and was running out of time.

38

WELCOME PARTY

Kyle tried his best to conceal his irritation at being at yet another formal function, even though this one was a smaller, more intimate gathering. Now that William was king, if he wasn't in the court then he was dining with others at small gatherings—relativity speaking—like this one. On this occasion it was to host the delegation from Sylanna, in honour of his future consort. Kyle could still feel William's ambivalent feelings towards the woman he would be stuck with, and if *he* could, that likely meant that the princess could as well. Still, Rosalinda stood by his side, not even flinching. Everyone present was ignoring the future consorts' reaction to each other, or rather pretending they were. It was widely known William in particular hadn't much time at all to get used to the idea, since his father had kept him out of the negotiations.

Kyle found he was stuck entertaining the envoy, otherwise known as the Lady Annabella Kortrain. Kyle pulled himself up. He was irritated, but that was not the Lady Kortrain's fault. Being in the woman's shoes would be extremely difficult. It appeared the Imperial Court of the Emperor of Sylanna was an extremely dangerous place to be and that was just the political intrigue. Annabella was doing much better now that she wasn't trying to be something she wasn't. With all the negotiations already worked out in the match between William and Rosalinda, there was certainly no harm with an inexperienced envoy either.

Kyle noticed that his companion's gaze had wandered, and he smiled. Lady Kortrain was staring across at Alex, who stood near to William, along with Elizabeth, who acted as a chaperone of sorts. William hadn't signed the contract making Princess Rosalinda his consort yet, but it was understood he would do so. Until he did, the pair wouldn't be in each other's company alone. It was an old anachronism that Kyle found amusing. The speculation on Lady Kortrain's face was clear. There were obviously a few more things the lady hadn't caught up with yet. Lady Kortrain glanced back at him and blushed.

"Sorry, Kyle. They are both handsome." Lady Kortrain sipped her drink delicately.

"Yes, they both have extremely good genetics and their pedigree is impeccable." Kyle was careful to keep his tone neutral.

Kyle smiled pleasantly, noting that some of the clustered ladies and lords were laughing softly, hiding smiles behind raised hands.

"I believe Prince Alexander is now separated from his Consort Elect?" Annabella didn't take her eyes off Alex as she spoke.

"Yes, he is." Kyle felt that was a safe enough response.

"Before my family's troubles." Annabella's smile faltered slightly before she ploughed on. "Well, they had thought to make an arrangement with His Highness. That was to be with my elder sister of course."

"It must be difficult."

"Oh, I'm sure you must know what the game is like, Kyle.

Your family must be busily plotting and scheming as well." A shadow passed over Annabella's face before she smiled and rested a hand on Kyle's arm lightly as if they were the best of friends.

"Thankfully not as much as you'd expect. I'm not too fond of the idea given I had a member of the Order drug me with a toxin, which sent me into a murderous spiral and nearly put me under their control. Then the former Queen Joanna, who we all thought was dead took me as her thrall, turning me on Alex and forcing me to stab my best friend. I think I'd rather steer clear of entanglements right now." Kyle sipped his drink, watching as the colour drained out of Annabella's face, nearly wincing at his bluntness.

Kyle? Alex didn't look in his direction, but the concern in his tone was clear.

Kyle sighed. He was obviously leaking again, he often did when he thought about the mess he'd made of things.

I'm fine. Thankfully Annabella has her sights on you Alex, not me. Kyle nearly laughed at the wave of exasperation he felt from his lifelong friend.

"I didn't know. We seem to be saying that a lot on this ill-fated trip. My apologies." Lady Kortrain laid her hand on Kyle's arm again.

Kyle noticed that the courtiers clustered around them had gone silent, their shock apparent. He nearly swore as he realised he'd let his mouth run away from him. The knowledge that he'd nearly shared his sister's fate in being taken by the Order and that he'd been enslaved by the former Queen and technically committed treason had not been widely known. No more than Daniel's involvement had been broadcast or Jessalan's mother.

"It's me who should apologise for my short temper, Lady Kortrain. There is no way you could have known. It wasn't widely advertised." Only years of practice in the court allowed Kyle to smile and have it be somewhat convincing.

"Ah, but you cannot have been above the political manoeuvring of your family given your close association with members of the royal family." She grimaced and turned her gaze back to William and Alex.

Kyle glanced across as the doors opened and Isabella strolled in, exquisite in a burgundy gown that hugged her figure with a trail of fine lace dragging behind her. The instant attention she attracted nearly made Kyle laugh. Isabella walked unerringly to Alex. Each of them always seemed to know where the other was located in a room regardless of how many other people where between them. Isabella paused as she approached Alex. Without a word he grabbed her hand in his own and drew her into his arms. Kyle would lay odds that Alex knew Lady Kortrain was on the hunt to land a suitable husband and he was in the firing line. That would explain Isabella suddenly showing up.

"Well, that would be one reason why your quarry is off the list. It is unlikely there will be anything official, but Alex will not take another as consort." Kyle looked at Lady Kortrain, who seemed to have come upon the same conclusion by herself.

"So I see." Annabella's eyes narrowed as she gazed at Isabella and Alex.

Kyle saw the woman shake herself, then turn her gaze back to William and then flick back to Alex again. Then she turned back to him and she smiled. Kyle could almost hear the gears turning in her head as she regarded him.

"Still if there is nothing official between them? I've heard he is a remarkable man." Anabella's eyes sparkled as she obviously thought of some of the things she'd been told.

"I have known Alex my whole life. There isn't much I wouldn't do to defend him. Saying that I must warn you, if you want to leave political upheaval behind you, well to put it politely he is no more a good choice than I am." Kyle heard the women around him chuckle and a muttered comment about it being a fun time while it lasted. Kyle tried not to sigh out loud. It wasn't like he could refute the comment and if recent events hadn't interrupted he would probably be in a bar along with Alex and Jess parting the night away.

"Well it might be fun to have a liaison while I'm here." Annabella glanced at Kyle and chuckled softly, her eyes dancing in amusement.

The woman's attention was grabbed instantly as William held out his arm to Rosalinda. The princess blushed and accepted his arm, walking gracefully at his side as he led her to the garden. Kyle caught Annabella's arm when she made to follow the pair, and shook his head.

"There is no need. That is an internal private garden, they won't be totally alone." Kyle nodded as Alex and Isabella followed a discreet distance behind their king, with more of the Elite trailing them and taking up station around the garden.

Annabella looked concerned and breathed a flustered sigh. "I guess I can still see them from here."

Kyle nearly laughed. The floor-to-ceiling windows ran the length of the function room. The lamps sent pools of light across the manicured gardens. There was nowhere William could take Rosalinda where they couldn't be observed. At best they had the illusion of privacy.

As he watched Rosalinda and William walk out arm in arm, Kyle hoped his friend would behave as a king for the good of their realm, rather than the stubborn fool who wanted to cling to the past relationship he'd had with Jess. Despite his irritation at being here he was glad that at least Jess was spared this engagement.

39

UNDERSTANDING

William sighed as he walked out into the courtyard gardens and the doors shut behind him, giving at least some privacy. He could ignore the Elite—they were always present—and he knew Alex and Isabella would stand discreetly out of earshot. He knew the princess's own people would be disgruntled to be kept inside. The Elite had adroitly stood in their path when some of them had moved to follow.

He settled Rosalinda on a bench in a small grotto off to one side of the garden. It at least gave them a sense of privacy even if the reality was that everyone within the function room was watching them both avidly.

William contemplated the woman who was to be his consort. He had been advised that if he didn't go through with this, it would give the Empire cause to beat the drums of war and roll over Vallantia. If he did go through with it, he suspected it would only be a matter of time before there was conflict anyhow. At best this was a delaying tactic and Jess had been correct in her assessment. They couldn't afford a war with both the Order and the Empire. So in the age-old tradition, a contracted union between him and the daughter of the Emperor had been arranged.

"Your father didn't know I had suffered and survived a forced transition when he sent you here." It was a simple statement of fact, one of which he didn't need an answer to.

"He did not." Rosalinda looked at him calmly.

"He thought he could take Vallantia without a fight. That as Kin you would outlive me, stay young while I aged and died as a normal human." Again it wasn't something he needed an answer to.

Rosalinda smiled unexpectedly. "The thought may have crossed his mind."

"Were you meant to expedite that eventuality? I'll warn you, the title of Consort does not confer the same privileges as that of Queen." William found it strange that he remained calm.

"He thought it would be prudent to wait to dispose of you until we had produced several children first." Rosalinda looked up at him calmly, not even showing the slightest discomfort at the conversation.

"Did he even intend to allow our children to live?" William smiled, although he was aware it held no warmth.

Rosalinda paused. "That isn't a practice the Empire has engaged in throughout our history. At best they would be put aside and Vallanita would become newly acquired territory of the Empire."

William couldn't help but smile. This Imperial Princess was certainly even-headed, even though she was in a precarious position and just as likely to share his fate. He saw her glance flicker over towards the doors, her body tensing as it hadn't done all through their conversation. William glanced over to see what held her attention and saw some of her own guards had entered the garden. He noted almost absently that they were mostly women, as indeed most of her party was. He shrugged, dismissing the oddity as a peculiarity of Sylanna.

Even though her people were stopped by his own men, the fact that Kyle had joined Alex at some point wasn't lost on him. Her guards—or rather, he suspected her father's guards—were in for a rude shock if they thought they could intervene, although what they thought he would do to the princess in full sight of everyone was beyond him.

"What do you fear?"

Rosalinda's eyes darted over to the guards at the other end of the garden, then back to him. Her tongue darted out to lick her lips, and it was clear that she was suddenly tense as she hadn't been before. "You don't understand. I am the property of the Imperial Court. Even if you sign the contract, I will still be considered Imperial property. The value of my life is in this contract with you. Should you reject me, I fear I will not survive the Dagger Court on my return."

William looked at her evenly, mulling over her words —both what she had said and what she hadn't.

"What do you want from me?"

"Don't send me away. Put me aside, if you wish. Lock me away. Have children with another, I'll not dispute anything, and I'll swear they are mine if asked. Just don't send me back."

Her voice was low, trembling. While William knew that she could likely display any emotion on queue as needed, in this he believed her.

"You know as well as I do that at best this is a delaying tactic. If you attach your fate to mine you'll face a potential war with the Empire right alongside of me." William's eyes narrowed as he watched her carefully.

Rosalinda shook her head. "I would face a certain death if I returned to the Empire. I'll take the possibility of a future over that." She looked up at him and suddenly blurted out desperately, "I can help. With this problem you have right now. My brother, his dagger wives and their entire household are at the tri-border. They all have power. They will come, they will fight if I ask it."

William lifted his eyebrow. "Your brother, a Prince of the Empire and your father's son, will fight for you?"

Rosalinda looked at him, a flicker of confusion crossing her face before it cleared.

"Dashel is the son of my birth mother. He has had much success, and others were starting to see him as a threat. He will not survive the dance of daggers, no more than I would. Not even the First Wife could stop the blades flashing and blood flowing if Dashel and his house returned right now."

William considered her words and finally nodded.

"I'll not send you away. As I'm sure you are aware, I don't have a lot of choice. I cannot guarantee you won't end up under guard for the rest of your life." William held out his arm to her. She ducked her head, then straightened her shoulders. Accepting his arm, she stood up, her head high.

"That is all I ask. As a daughter of the Dagger Court, I do understand the position you are in."

William considered her. Kyle's warnings about war with the empire in their future and Vallantia's need for a king replayed in his mind. He closed his eyes briefly. It seemed duty was always in play, in every aspect of his life. He knew that he, that Vallantia would be better off in that possible future if he could bring Rosalinda closer to their side than that of her Emperor-Father.

"Understand that when I sign the contract tomorrow, you will be my consort, but you will be no one's property, not even mine, despite what the Empire thinks. The decisions you make from then are your own."

William heard her soft gasp of shock, but did not turn to look at her, he was sure she would regain her composure before they returned to the party.

40

UNWELCOME NEWS

William's head jerked up in startlement as the doors to the court opened with Commander Janson of the King's Guard entering. It was unusual for the man to intrude on a court session, unusual enough that Alex stiffened next to him. William sensed the sudden barrier that his brother had thrown up between him and the rest of the court, though he doubted Alex really thought that the commander meant him any harm. It was perhaps in response to the grim expression on the commander's face and his rushed pace—not quite a run, but only just under and certainly faster than his usual measured stride.

He stopped and bowed just in time, since William could see his own Elite were uneasy, their hands straying to the hilts of their swords. They relaxed marginally when the commander stopped two paces away from the bottom stair of the dais, as protocol dictated. William braced himself, knowing that he wasn't going to like whatever news warranted interrupting the court.

William waved away the rather confused merchant who'd

been halfway through his petition. One of the court staff stepped forward to draw the man to one side.

"What is it, Commander Janson?" William tried to exude calm as the whispers sprang up around the court.

"Your Majesty, we've just received word the village of Medford in the central lands has been attacked." You would be forgiven for thinking the commander was talking about the weather, so casual was his voice, yet William could see a tick jump in the man's face. William's eyes narrowed at the uncommon display of nerves then dismissed his concern; the commander was clearly just rattled by the report. As the whispers intensified around the court with an undertone of fear William suppressed his irritation at the man. Losing his own temper right now would only fuel the fear, potentially turning it to panic.

Feeling the veil surge, William turned his head to look at Alex.

"Hold, Alex." William's tone was firm. Alex was rebellious and wouldn't want to waste any time in getting to the village and checking out what had happened. "You will not go alone, Alex. We'll retire to the conference room. Clear the court."

William stood and motioned at the commander to accompany them as he retreated to the antechamber out the back of the grand hall. Alex said nothing but turned promptly, following on his shoulder. He could feel his brother pulsing with agitation but caught the edges of his communication with others. William was unsurprised to feel the incoming surges and see Kyle appear in the conference room closely followed by Edward, Cal and Kat. Alex nodded at them all and clearly said something else to them in that tight-knit communication they were all capable of.

He also gathered that Alex had taken his injunction about not going alone seriously. William guessed Alex thought Edward and his friends might have valuable input for him since they had experience of the Sundered War. He had no doubt his brother intended the trio to watch over him while he went to investigate with Kyle.

William settled in his chair, closely followed by the others. He waited, looking around expectantly then frowned. "Where is Jess? I would have thought you'd call her in as well."

Alex shrugged, his face calm. "I can't seem to reach her right now. She must be busy concentrating on something else."

William felt his brother's growing unease and grimaced. "Whatever she is up to it had better be important."

"I understand the importance of the news, Commander, but open court was not the place for that announcement. Were you deliberately trying to cause panic?" Alex's tone displayed his irritation.

"My apologies Fourth, of course I wouldn't want anyone to panic. I didn't consider that, just that I had to get news to His Majesty of this atrocity as soon as possible."

William held his hand up forestalling Alex's reply. That would get them nowhere, although it freed him from having to chastise the commander.

"Just keep it in mind in future, Commander. Do you have anything else that might be relevant?" William kept his gaze steady on the man, who suddenly looked nervous.

"I'm sorry, Your Majesty, but you mentioned Lady Jessalan being missing?" The commander's gaze flicked around the group who were all staring at him.

"Well, more unavailable right now. Why?" William's eyes narrowed, wishing his commander would get to the point.

"I didn't think about it until now, Your Majesty, but, well, Medford..."

"It was Medford that was attacked?"

William swung his gaze to Kyle who suddenly looked pale. He stared at Alex whose face suddenly wiped of all expression.

“I'm sorry My Lord, I'm sure it's nothing...” Janson looked down breaking away from his intense stare.

“Will someone tell me what's wrong?” William kept his tone calm although from the reactions of everyone around him, he knew he wouldn't like the response.

“Medford was one of the villages Lady Jessalan was going to check for the rebels Your Majesty.” Commander Janson gazed at him steadily.

William felt his face drain and looked over at Alex. "Will you go to investigate? Take some Elite with you and some of the commander's men. I believe there is only a small garrison of the guard in that area and they may need reinforcements."

Alex clearly bit back his frustration at the delay, yet nodded his agreement. "Get your men to the Elite training ground within the hour, Commander, and have them ready to go. Marcus, get a squad ready." Alex looked satisfied that his orders were being followed as Marcus nodded at James, and the latter departed with the commander to ready their own people. "Edward, can you, Cal or Kat suspend your search for the Order's new stronghold and keep guard over William in our absence?"

Edward nodded. "Of course, Alex. Under the circumstances it wouldn't be prudent to leave William unguarded.”

Alex looked faintly relieved, then looked at William as he stood up. "With your permission, brother?"

William nodded, waving dismissal so they could go and make their own preparations. William had to bite back his own impatience. He wanted to go with them and see first-hand what had happened in the village, yet as always his place was here. For the first time he hoped that Jess was just drunk in a bar somewhere, not fallen to the Order.

41

MESSAGES

The veil thinned and parted and the guards on point strode forward, moving through the veil one moment and striding along the dirt road leading into the village the next. Alex and Kyle followed with their guards spreading out around them. All of them were too professional to show any of the shock they felt at the devastation they walked into. One and all they fell back on duty.

Alex's eyes swept around as he walked down the road leading through the village, taking in the blackened shells of what had been homes, most of them now burnt to the ground. The bodies of villagers lay scattered in the streets, left to rot. Large birds of prey circled above.

Alex saw the signs that meant this attack was far from something commonplace, the hole in the side of what had been the local meeting place being one of them. It had been a solid enough building constructed of rock, not lumber. Only someone with a great deal of power could have blasted a hole in that—someone with the power of the veil. The elemental blue flames that licked up its walls was a testament to what had really occurred here. Alex waved his hand, willing the flames to stop. He understood the message all too clearly.

The Elite had spread out in a searching pattern, although Alex knew in the pit of his stomach what they would report. He'd sensed no sign of life when he'd scanned it on arrival, yet a part of him was hoping that someone—anyone—was still alive. Alex saw Kyle pause and crouch over the small body of a child.

"Damn them. The Order was supposedly founded to protect people. Why this cowardly attack on ordinary people who can't fight back?" Kyle stood and continued his slow walk through the village.

Alex nodded and kept walking even though he knew what he was going to find. That sinking feeling had lodged in the pit of his stomach from the minute the report had hit the palace. If William hadn't ordered him to take the Elite, he would have charged straight in by himself. Particularly as soon as he'd realised Jess was missing and that this was one of the villages she'd been meaning to clear.

The images of the dead, the putrid smell of rotting flesh mingling with that of charred flesh and smoke wafting through the village—it all would stay with him and haunt his dreams.

Alex looked at Kyle. "Given all the death's they have caused, the lives they have corrupted and destroyed, I doubt they were ever peaceful in intent. Kevin definitely isn't."

No matter how slowly he'd walked Alex finally made his way to the destroyed meeting place, and stopped, squeezing his eyes shut from what he saw. It didn't help. The image of Jess's vest pinned to the solid rock wall of the meeting house by one of her emblazoned daggers seemed to be burnt into his mind.

He looked at Kyle who'd come to stand next to him, seeing a bleakness in his eyes that matched his own. Jess had been taken by the Order. Alex didn't want to imagine what their enemy would do to Jess now that they had her in their hands. Just the thought of it made Alex felt like someone had driven a fist powered by the veil into his stomach. He imagined his uncle was still haunted by the death and destruction of his own era. Now, it was beginning again.

~

EVEN THOUGH ALEX felt like he'd been functioning on automatic since finding Jess's vest and knife, the search of the ruins didn't take them long. It hadn't been a large village, but that didn't make the pointless loss of life any less painful.

"Your Highness." Marcus's warning drew Alex's attention to an approaching delegation of villagers.

They had been waiting respectfully in the shade of a group of trees at the edge of the village while a couple of his guards had kept an eye on them; none had moved to intervene. The group paused a respectful distance away, although under the circumstances he could tell his guard still didn't like it. Alex raised his hand to wave off the extra guards. He was fairly confident he could handle the villagers. Besides that, both Marcus and James were at his shoulder, with Megan and Matthew not far off.

Alex pushed down his grief; these people deserved his attention. He pulled his attention to the group as they bowed their heads, pressing their hands to heart, then forehead. Interestingly it was a middle-aged woman who stepped forward to act as speaker for the group. Traditionally she seemed much too young for the role, yet she obviously held the respect of the others.

"Fourth, I'm Anna, Speaker for Bainefield, the next village over." She looked up at him with a confidence that gave some insight as to how she had become Speaker.

"Speaker, did any of your villagers see what occurred here?" Alex already knew the answer. His own guard would have already questioned them and reported to him straight away if they had any important information to share.

"No, Fourth. My boy felt and heard the explosions. When he saw the smoke, he ran straight to me and raised the alarm. We came as soon as we could but it was over when we got here. I sent Paul's boy, a good rider, off to Vinestead to pass word back of what happened as soon as we saw this." Her expression was grim as she glanced beyond him to the destruction and death.

"I thank you. Your king thanks you." Alex was genuinely grateful they had tried to come and help. Many would have barricaded themselves in their own dwellings and left their fellows to face their own troubles rather than risk their own lives to help.

The Speaker nodded, her eyes sad. "They would have come our way if it had been us. Fourth, it's not right to leave them like this, but we know the guard likes to see troubles themselves before anyone cleans up."

Alex looked over to the nearby captain of the guard they'd brought with them. "Captain, do you have what you need?"

The man stepped forward, nodding. "Yes, Fourth. With your permission I'll coordinate with the Speaker and her people. The guard will assist in the clean-up. I'd also like permission to leave some of my men in these parts."

The captain left it unsaid that if the attackers came back, there wasn't much his men could do except die right alongside of the villagers, yet seeing the relief on the faces of some of the villagers, Alex realised they would appreciate it.

"With your permission, Fourth?" the Speaker interjected, looking at him earnestly.

Surprised, he glanced at her. "Go ahead."

"I've been in communication with the Speaker of Vinestead and some of the other nearby villagers. It's a bigger village with more resources, and we've decided to move there for the time being. We'll take as much of our stock and provisions with us as we can. It might be easier for the guard, since there is already a unit stationed there."

Alex nodded his permission and went to turn, only to halt at a muttered conversation amongst the villagers. He glanced back to see them prodding the Speaker, who sighed and looked at him apologetically.

"My apologies, Fourth. We sent word to the Healers' Guild, but we don't know if you would have heard." She grimaced and waved one of her own men to silence.

Alex glanced at the captain and Marcus, both of whom shook their heads. Having found out about the involvement of the Healers' Guild in this evolving mess, Alex's interest was piqued.

"What is your concern, Speaker?"

"Our journeyman healer is normally based in Vinestead and travels in rotation around the surrounding villages. She's missing, Fourth. No one has seen her for a month, as best we can work out."

Although he gathered that she at least didn't expect that he could magically find their missing healer, he also doubted word about the events that had unravelled at the Healers' Guild had reached here yet. If it had, she would probably be more concerned than she appeared to be. Alex traded a glance with Kyle, wondering how many journeymen healers had suddenly gone missing. It was a detail he would have to check with Aaron. He knew the Grand Guild Master of the Healers' Guild had issued a recall for all his healers so they could have their bonds checked. The last he'd heard was a report that not all the healers were compromised. Still, it was unlikely those that were would have obeyed the recall in the first place.

"Thank you for the information, Speaker. If you will give the details to the guard, I'll make sure the Healers' Guild hears that this region does not have access to a healer." Alex kept the wince from his face. He knew exactly what that would mean for the locals, although to his shame he wouldn't have known any of it before his run-in with Ryan. The memory of the thin piece of metal being poked through the boy's skin, with the twine being pulled through by the metal to seal the wound, still made him shudder.

Alex dismissed them and issued orders for his own people to gather. It was time they went back to the palace to report. After a bit of consultation with the captain of the guard, he assured them that one of his men possessed a reasonable mind-speaking gift. The man couldn't do much else, not even warm his own drink, but he could call out back to his twin brother regardless of the distance between them. It was one of the reasons the brothers often pulled duty with the Elite. Satisfied they had a viable method of communication, Alex waved dismissal at them and gathered those coming back with him for their return to Vallantia.

42

AMBUSH REPORT

William watched with a steady gaze as Alex reported on what they'd found at Medford. At least the burning anger he felt had a legitimate cause. He'd known it would be bad when he'd heard Alex advise the guards outside his doors that they weren't to be disturbed. He almost wished a polite request for him to come to the Complex of the Fourth had arrived instead. Some of his councillors grumbled that he kept going to the Complex of the Fourth rather than having Alex, Jess and Kyle come to him, all indignant outrage —he was the king, after all.

William didn't disclose that he grasped every opportunity that came to him to disappear into the confines of the Fourth's sanctuary. It was absurd, but somehow he had more freedom there than in his own space. It was ridiculously easy for the assorted lords and ladies to concoct a reason to gain access to him in his own suite in the royal wing.

Or it was, now that he had recovered and Alex wasn't using his authority as Fourth to ban them all from his suite. William had grinned at that. His lords had grumbled over that injunction as well, not quite sure how to take Alex's sudden assertion of his authority. Not that they admitted it, but he could tell they were a little afraid of Alex's sudden open display of power in William's defence when their father had been cut down. None of them quite knew how to deal with this new self-assured Fourth, one who had power they couldn't counter. So while William hadn't quite worked out how to keep everyone out of the Royal Suite, now that Alex had ordered it be done the order would be followed explicitly.

"You're sure?" William looked from Alex to Kyle to see equally blank faces, which did not disguise the waves of distress that rolled off the pair.

"We're sure." Alex's voice was soft as he handed a bundle of cloth to him.

Feeling the weight of the bundle William looked down, unwrapping the fine cloth, realising it was a vest. One of Jess's and her dagger. He'd recognise that crest anywhere and there was no way Jess would leave one of her daggers behind if she'd had a choice about it. He already knew the answer, but he had to ask.

"You can't sense her?"

"No and trust me I've tried." Pain flickered on Alex's face.

William was reminded that while Jess had been his lover off and on and someone that he thought of as his friend as well, Alex and Kyle had practically grown up in the nursery together with her. The firmest of friends. Where there was one, you'd find the others and more often than not, trouble. They'd all been fiercely loyal to each other, excluding everyone outside close family. It had been an exclusive friendship that none had been able to breach.

"We both have. If she heard and was able to respond, she would have." Kyle's voice was rough, reflecting the pain he was feeling, an echo of Alex's.

William stood and began to pace, running his hand through his hair trying to distract himself. At least when he showed signs of agitation in front of Alex and Kyle, neither of them panicked. Coming to a decision, William turned and pinned the pair with his gaze.

"No more going anywhere by yourselves on these investigative forays."

"William—" Alex broke off at his glare.

"No, Alex. Alone you are at risk." William kept his gaze on Alex until his brother held his hand up and nodded.

Satisfied, William turned and made his way over to the large windows, from where he looked out over the garden. He could always trust Alex once he'd conceded something. Even if Alex often disregarded what other people asked of him, it was rare for his brother to directly go against William's will, particularly when Alex knew that he was right. No matter how much Alex might dislike the idea of taking someone with him, he would do it if commanded.

"All right, but it will slow the search for the Order considerably." There was a hard edge to Alex's voice.

William nodded. "It may but Jess is already lost. I won't lose the pair of you as well because I failed to enforce sensible precautions. Damn it, this is my fault."

"William, no this could have happened to any of us." Alex shook his head.

William ducked his head, guilt and grief flooding him. He turned away not wanting to face either of them.

"It is, if I hadn't wasted so much time behaving like a fool. Do you think it was Amelia?" William looked up at Kyle.

"It's likely. She is a Weaponsmaster and we know now she has power that was obviously being suppressed." Kyle closed his eyes and took a steadying breath.

"I'm sorry I didn't believe you. Your judgement."

Kyle shook his head.

"Jess is not dead. I'd know, we'd know if she was dead. We would have felt it." Alex's lips compressed into a thin line.

William opened his mouth to respond, then closed it again. He wished that Alex would at least yell at him, something. Alex didn't have to be told that Jess might just be better off dead given what the Order did to those with powers. Alex knew it already.

"You're not going to like this, either of you, but I have an idea." Kyle looked at Alex who paled as communication passed between them.

William didn't think it was possible for his brother to go even paler, but he did. Alex turned his back and walked over to the drink cabinet to pour drinks, three of them. He didn't have to ask. William took a breath and sat down on the couch, he figured if Alex went pale at this idea then he would need to sit down. As Alex turned, his face now under control William gestured to the chair. Both Kyle and Alex complied, the pair of them sitting together on the long couch facing him. Alex but a moment after Kyle, pausing he leaned over to hand him a drink. William took a sip then finally fixed his gaze on Kyle.

"What idea am I not going to like?" William steeled himself, he knew if Alex didn't like it, then he certainly wouldn't. The fact that Alex wasn't protesting told him that while his brother may not like it, he obviously agreed with whatever it was.

"The Order was obviously waiting, watching our movements." Kyle kept his unflinching gaze on him.

William nodded. "To take Jess, they must have used overwhelming numbers. That would take planning."

"So I keep searching, make a target of myself. When they try to take me, we take them. Or at least one of them." Kyle's gaze didn't flinch. "You asked us yourself why we hadn't captured one of them."

William took a breath to calm himself. Yelling right now would not help in the slightest. There was obviously more to this plan. Or he hoped there was or he was going to order the healers to drug the pair of them insensible to stop them doing something foolish.

"Tell me the rest of it." William knew his eyes flashed, showing a little of his irritation at the part of the plan revealed so far. Then again since he'd been the one foolish enough to put the idea of capturing one of the Sundered into their heads this was, in part, his own fault.

43

CONFINEMENT

Jess lay back, sucking in breath, ignoring the tears that streamed from her eyes as agony ripped through her body. It wasn't just Kevin that tortured her, it was Amelia or the one who wore her body that did as well, while Kevin looked on elated in the background. Amelia had been Kyle's little sister, Alex's Consort Elect. It made Jess shudder to think that she could be turned, that she would inflict this pain on Kyle or Alex.

It wasn't just the power of the veil that Amelia used to inflict pain on her. This time she cut her flesh with knives.

The poison prevents you from escaping.

Jess screamed as Amelia's blade plunged into her side.

But don't worry, sister, you'll heal without even a scar to show and we can play again.

She tried to retreat as Amelia's whispered words entered her head, shuddering with fear over what nightmare they would come up with to inflict on her next. Some of them were simple really, yet no less painful.

The other day, yesterday? Jess was losing track of the days, it was difficult to tell in the cavern without the sun to keep track of and the lamps in her cell burning constantly. Amelia had her strung up by chains tethered to the ceiling and big brutes, Sundered, beat her mercilessly on command. It seemed meaningless at first other than Kevin's apparent need to cause pain.

The torture will break down your barriers Jess. Don't worry, the next stage will begin shortly. My master will enter your mind. You will beg him for release. Then, you will really know pain. Amelia's cruel laughter rang in her head.

She lay there in that moment in-between pain trying desperately to get around the limitations placed on her. She knew she needed to escape, yet she was well and truly trapped.

Amelia sat in her cell, her arms wrapped around herself, rocking slowly back and forth. She knew the other was torturing another poor soul. Her master Kevin used her to great effect that way. She glanced up at the windows that would grant her a view to the outside world and shuddered. She didn't want to see what she, what the other was doing yet something about those ragged screams called to her. Nagged at her that the person that her other self was hurting was someone she knew. Someone she should recognise.

Increasingly of late she was finding it hard to remember. To remember who she was, who she had been. To remember the life she'd had. This reality, sitting in a cold cell in the fading light, sitting here in a dirty, ripped silk shift, was fast becoming the only thing she knew.

Amelia glanced up at the windows, again. Squeezing her eyes shut she stood, trembling. Taking a deep breath she opened her eyes, wincing at the cry of agony she heard. Taking one slow step after the other, she went over to the windows and before she could change her mind she grabbed the bars and stared out into the world. Her body was in the caverns below where she now lived. As she'd thought a woman was being tortured, being turned into someone like herself.

As she screamed again Amelia finally let herself look at the other woman's face and froze, stepping back from the window, horrified.

No.

Anger bubbled up in her and she ran back to the windows forcing herself to look at her Jess. They were trying to break down her barriers, just like Kevin had done to her. Assessing Jessalan's condition, a whimper escaped her. She was nearly lost, she could see Jess was almost at her breaking point. That is when Kevin would start to take her mind, chipping away until Jess herself begged for it to stop. Begged for Kevin to take the pain away. She would do anything to make it stop, she would call Kevin master. Once she did that, Jess would be lost. She knew. It had happened to her.

Fight Jess! Lock yourself away, do not give in to them!

Amelia yelled at Jess, forgetting she was trying not to bring attention to herself. She didn't want her other self to realise she was still here, let alone Kevin. She looked down at the woman who'd tried her best to make her feel welcome when she'd become Alex's Consort Elect. She realised Jess had slipped into unconsciousness. She knew the torture would stop for now. She had to be awake for them to take her. She had to willingly give herself to her new master, Amelia knew that was how they achieved their best results. She could also see they'd resorted to physical abuse. They'd want Jess's body to heal, to heal just enough so they could begin again.

JESS SUNK into despair and retreated into darkness willingly as her only escape from her reality. Just as darkness claimed her she heard a voice, yelling at her.

Fight Jess! Lock yourself away, do not give in to them!

She moaned as she slipped further into unconsciousness, aware she was going mad. The voice had been Amelia's voice, as she'd been before she'd been taken and warped by the Order. She wondered why of all people she would dream that Amelia was trying to help her. The former Consort Elect of the Fourth was one of the ones taking great delight at torturing her.

Amelia wasn't the one trying to save her.

44

SLIPUP

Kyle walked through the town, the third he'd been assigned. A thin slice of the veil hung between him and the village, keeping him from the sight of prying eyes. He walked past the small orderly wooden houses that looked like shadows, not quite substantial. The path he walked on was smooth even though the street he walked down was cobbled. He was here, yet not here. Not quite.

This place was small and remote and he couldn't see why the Order would be here. It would have been a bad tactical move, with no way to hide their presence. The commander had a point, he guessed: a thorough approach to the search was a good idea, even if it was proving to be just as frustrating.

Kyle opened his mind up, letting his powers range out, tendrils stretching out from him in all directions around the sleepy village. Seeking ones like him. Seeking those that didn't fit in a place like this—or a large mass of people that didn't fit. Not here, where everyone would know each other. The village was that small.

As Kyle concentrated, questing out with his powers, he felt a sharp pain in his mind, followed up by searing heat in his side. He stiffened, breath catching in his throat as pain lanced through him. He suddenly caught the appearance of bright surges of power around him that hadn't been there moments before. Feeling a burning intensifying on his back, his training kicked in.

Acting on instinct, he rolled to one side as a blast of power rolled past him. Intense pain shot up his side as he stood up. He drew his weapons and cast around with his powers to find who was attacking him.

Oh, poor confused one.

The voice echoed in his mind. Realising his mistake in opening his mind up in the way he had, Kyle tried to block out and suppress anything that wasn't him. The words splintered, turning nonsensical, bouncing around in his head. He fell to one knee, head clutched in his hands. Laughter sounded in his mind, multiplying and colliding as if split into many parts.

He doubled over as a sharp pain assailed him, dropping his sword and curling in on himself. He heard laughter echo in his head once more and while he didn't recognise his adversary, he did recognise his mind signature. The controlled madness, the emptiness of a Sundered yet more in control. This was one of the Order's captured, controlled Kin.

He rolled over onto his back, looking up, eyes widening to see the Sundered swim into his vision. Kyle felt himself stiffen and spasm, screaming in pain as power ran its course, uncontrolled, through his body. Kyle remembered Alex telling him about the power surges he'd suffered through. He'd wondered if he'd made a miscalculation, this was something he hadn't factored in. How could he? The timing was appalling, but a small part of his mind assessed that was probably what was happening, triggered in part by his stupidity in opening his mind up and the perfectly timed assault by the Sundered and others. The fact that it had been necessary was beside the point.

With pain wracking every part of his mind and body, Kyle wasn't sure if the laughter was his own or belonged to the other. He was aware that he fought on some level, but he had little control.

Kyle looked up to see the Sundered standing over him, yet the expression on his face was unrecognisable.

Kyle flinched as the man's blade, wreathed in power, flashed down towards him.

DEVON SMILED at seeing Kyle walking through the village just as he'd been told his adversary would. He nearly laughed to see the man had foolishly opened up his mind. Devon conceded it would make searching this place and the people surrounding it easier, yet it also made this attack almost too easy. He and a few of other Sundered Ones had waited in place, carefully not drawing any power at all so as not to draw attention to themselves. Kyle would have to be paying attention and be almost on top of them before he would notice their presence. As it was, they likely looked no different to the man's inner eye than any of the villagers.

Not believing his luck, Devon launched his attack on Kyle, throwing one bolt of power after the other at the man. Seeing Kyle buckle and fall to one knee, Devon smiled in triumph and closed the distance between them. He was about to capture another of the Companions to join his master's ranks. Devon laughed, this one had been too easy. He almost paused at seeing Kyle's body spasm in response to another attack, one that he couldn't perceive. Then he shook himself. He could ask his master about the oddity later.

Devon closed the distance between them and stood over his fallen victim, relishing in his obvious pain. Grinning, Devon drew in his power to deliver one more blow to his victim which should deliver him to unconsciousness.

His eyes widened as ghostly tendrils of power swirled around, a power that did yet did not exist to his second sight. It seemed as if time slowed around him. As he flung his power at Kyle the world seemed to slow down, everything seemed at a painfully slow speed, he saw Kyle's face turn up to look at him. Instead of fear, flames danced in his eyes.

With no telltale surge of power to give away what the other man was doing, Devon felt a giant fist of ethereal power that he couldn't see slam into him and he was flung back. His eyes widened in shock as in a move too fast for him to track, Kyle, who was on the ground, defeated one moment, stood upright the next with no perceptible sign of movement.

Devon scrambled back, drawing the power to him, trying to put as much distance between himself and what Kyle had become. He didn't understand it; somehow the man had gone from victim to predator. Kyle blurred as he closed the distance between them, his whole being seeming to glow. As Devon propelled himself desperately backwards not wanting to take his eyes from whatever Kyle had become, he gasped in shock as he hit a solid barrier behind him. Screaming as he felt power, a power not his and far grater than his own wrap around him and hold him in place.

ALEX WINCED as Kyle's power wrapped around the Sundered One, he had that brief moment, thinking he would just contain his attacker. Then he lashed out with his power and blades until the last of his attackers fell at his feet. They had half-thought they had enough of them to take a couple of the Sundered. As it turned out the one Kyle had just dispatched had been the only one left alive, since Kyle had rather effectively killed off the others as well. Despite their plans failing miserably in achieving their objective it had been a spectacular display. Veil charge lightning cracking down all around, seemingly at random until you realised all of Kyle's attackers were being fried in the process.

He watched Kyle, fascinated to see the play of power run through him. He'd experienced this, but not actually witnessed it before. He winced this time in sympathy, recognising the incredible, pure power his friend was channelling. He knew the pain Kyle must be going through as well. The flickering power in his eyes indicated it was likely that Kyle himself was absent from decision-making right now. That and the rather abrupt detour from the plan to capture at least one of their enemies.

"Well, this was something we didn't count on." Edwards dry voice spoke from his side.

"Do we really want to be standing here, right where he can see us?" Kat was on his other side, her thought echoing what was going through all of their minds.

Alex couldn't dispute either of their sentiments and it seemed neither did the veil. He could see and feel the waves of power rolling ever outwards, power sparking and striking all around. Personally he paid it no mind, he knew it wouldn't hurt him. Even out of his mind, Kyle would not hurt him. It might be Kyle's unconscious mind in control right now, but it was still his friend.

While the veil rumbled with the disturbance that was Kyle coming to his powers Alex saw Kyle's eyes, dancing with flames of power, as he looked up from the dead body of his attacker to focus his gaze on them.

Alex looked over, seeing Damien and Isabella approaching, carefully. The five of them had taken up points to give them coverage no matter which direction the Sundered came from or tried to run. Damien and Isabella had been on the far side of Kyle's position. As the brother and sister drew closer, they added their own power to the shield they had between them and Kyle...though Alex had the suspicion that right now Kyle would have no trouble blasting through their shields. His body, mind and powers were on automatic right now.

Remembering what you'd been able to do or repeating any of those feats while not in that state was another matter entirely. It was something that Alex found frustrating. It wasn't like the healers with their school, there wasn't a veil academy. Alex pushed that thought aside, he'd give it consideration when they had time. Right now they were all a little busy dealing with the various crises. Of course the current little problem was Kyle, who was a little out of control.

"Withdraw back to the palace, I'll stay with Kyle." Alex didn't take his eyes off his friend, who stood there, his gaze unwavering as he continued to stare at them.

"Alex, he's not exactly in his own head right now." Isabella dragged her eyes away from Kyle to him.

"Kyle won't hurt me. I think, if it's just me, he will snap out of it." Alex realised he sounded far more confident than he felt.

He also didn't add, Kyle was displaying a power level like his own, higher than what they possessed. Of course, they all knew how to use their powers better having had much more practice, but he didn't feel pointing that out would be helpful.

"Granted I don't think Kyle would knowingly hurt you, but right now? That's a big gamble Alex." Edward shook his head.

"From my own memories I tended to attack and kill those who attacked me. I... just trust me on this one. Go, I'll deal with Kyle." Alex swept his gaze over the four of them. He was relieved as he sensed their agreement.

After a brief pause as they consulted how best to coordinate their withdrawal, they simply disappeared, pulling themselves away as rapidly as they could.

Kyle surged forward suddenly, power writhing around him, eyes wild only to stop in his tracks as Alex interposed himself between him and the direction his prey had disappeared. Alex swallowed, hoping he'd been correct in his assessment. Alex knew from going through his own transition, when he was numbered amongst the ranks of the Broken with blackouts and killing. What Kyle was now, his mind overwhelmed, was not the same as the Sundered ones. The Sundered would kill any they encountered. Kyle, in his current state, would only kill those who were a threat to him.

Kyle, it's me, Alex. You're going to be alright.

Alex kept his mind voice soft and light, knowing that Kyle's mind and body felt like they'd been burnt raw with the power that had suddenly started channelling through. It took some time to realise that it wasn't hurting anymore as that same power helped to heal what it had damaged.

The threat's gone now. You're safe.

Kyle's power flared around him as he ducked into a fighting crouch, eyes glowing even brighter. Alex was about to throw his own barriers up when he took a shuddering breath, power draining from him to more normal levels. His eyes when he looked up simply reflected confusion rather than power.

Alex? What did I do?

Kyle was trembling as his body and mind which had been preparing to fight reacted from the sudden withdrawal of anything to attack. Alex closed the distance between them and caught Kyle as he slumped, Alex controlling their descent down. Kyle groaned accepting it as Alex helped soothe away the remaining pain that shot through him.

Transition. The Sundered who attacked you are dead, no one else.

Kyle pushed back looking at him; as understanding dawned on his face he groaned.

I killed all of them? The idea was to get one alive.

Alex held up his hand. *It's ok, it was a long shot and it's not like you were in control.*

You stayed. Damn it Alex, I could have killed you. Outrage flashed in Kyle's eyes as he contemplated the thought of what he might have done.

I've been through this remember. I was fairly confident you wouldn't. Alex started drawing them both through the veil back towards the palace.

Kyle looked at him, his eyebrow rising. *Fairly?*

Alex laughed and was relieved when Kyle's humour returned as he laughed with him. He could feel the exhaustion that was claiming Kyle so he directed them back to his suite. Alex remembered he'd slept for days with only a few brief moments of being awake after his last bout of transition. Of course he'd also had to rip out the hooks and bonds Amelia had left in him but he knew Kyle would feel far better after he'd slept.

45

VOICES

Joanna woke, staring up into the darkness, a solitary tear tracing down her cheek, his voice whispering in her head as it had since the day he'd tried to kill her.

You're mine.

They can't shelter you forever.

It only gave her marginal solace that he'd failed not only in killing her, but also in killing Alex. She knew her mind had broken under the combined onslaught of one of the Sundered trying to take her life and the burden of turning Kin. The trauma of knowing Alex was left to fight alone without her aid. Waking up in her own cold, dark tomb.

I will kill your son.

You will be mine.

Joanna turned her head, seeing Edward asleep beside her. He'd tried to protect her. To protect Alex. She knew there were times she hadn't made it easy. She eased herself out of bed and transitioned into the veil, one thought on her mind.

Alex.

~

ALEX FELT the press of the mattress into his side, aware in a part of his mind he'd obviously been lying on it for too long. He turned over carefully, not wanting to wake Isabella. He kept his eyes closed, hoping he might be able to convince himself he was still asleep. Not acknowledging he was actually awake worked. Sometimes.

He didn't have to open his eyes and draw the drapes of his room to know it was way too early for him to be awake. He hadn't had anywhere near enough sleep; the dragging weight of exhaustion still settled on him. As it occurred to him that something must have disturbed his sleep, he realised that it wasn't just Isabella's breathing he could hear next to him. His eyes snapped open to see a figure standing beside his bed.

Despite himself, Alex gasped and lurched upright in bed before he recognised the woman staring down at him. He heard Isabella wake and sit bolt upright, the lights in the room suddenly flaring to life. Alex glanced at her, then lay a hand on her shoulder with an apologetic smile.

"Mother, what are you doing here?" Alex tried to keep the exasperation out of his tone, but feared he'd failed. He really did need to speak to his uncle about keeping a closer watch on her.

"Be careful, Alex. He wants you. He said he was going to kill you." Her voice was soft, catching on the end in a sob. The tears flowed unchecked down her cheek.

Alex stopped himself from groaning, but it was a close thing. He could sense the prickly edges of her mind. She wasn't entirely consumed by madness, yet she wasn't all in her own mind-space either. Alex sighed and climbed out of bed, pulling on the robe that he'd flung over the back of the bedside table. He turned and gathered her into his arms as she began to sob.

He'll kill you, he said he'll kill you.

Alex closed his eyes against the wave of fear and pain he felt emanating from her.

Sshh, Mother, I'm fine. I'm alive. He didn't kill me.

He kept whispering to her, reassuring her that he was alive and fine. Feeling the incoming signature, his eyes flicked up over her head to see Edward materialise in his rooms. At least Edward had the grace to look apologetic.

46

ALLIES

Kyle almost hummed as he walked back into the Complex of the Fourth, crossing to their private living areas. Instead of going to his own suite, he turned and walked into Alex's. He grinned at Joshua who stared at him, and raised his fingers to his lips. Alex's servant grinned back at him and shook his head.

Kyle reached his bedroom door and opened it, quietly easing himself inside the still dark room. Looking over to Alex's bed he saw, as he'd guessed, that his friend was alone, thankfully; he would have had to beat a rather hasty retreat if he'd had company.

Grinning impudently, Kyle ran across the intervening distance, the soft rugs muffling his progress across the room, and leapt onto the bed. He laughed as Alex snapped awake and he found himself flipped onto his back with Alex holding his wrists and glaring down at him. Alex rolled off to one side a moment later, his snarl turning into a weak grin.

"Damn it, Kyle, I could have killed you." He chuckled in amusement despite his words. This was a game they had played as children, always trying to sneak up on each other.

"No, I was *fairly* certain you wouldn't." Kyle's eyes danced. "Come on, get up. William has tasked us to go and fetch his consort's brother and his people. I am ordered that this is official and we are not to go alone."

"What, he couldn't get one of his other minions to go fetch them? Surely my brother realises by now he has a palace full of them."

Kyle ignored Alex's complaint and lunged over suddenly, unceremoniously pushing his friend out of bed. Alex swore as he hit the floor with a thump, then laughed, unable to keep up the facade of being irritated. Kyle's good mood and the return to childish behaviour, even if it was just for a moment in these dangerous times, was too infectious.

ALEX AND KYLE kept their hoods up as they arrived in Amberbreak, although given they materialised in the village square with their guards in tow and they were all wearing clothing bearing the crest of the Fourth, he knew no one would be fooled. Word would undoubtedly travel fast through this bustling trader town that the Fourth and Fourth's Companion were here.

"The docks are this way." Alex took the lead in directing them, he knew this town.

They turned and walked off down the street, taking a main road that led directly to the docks. While he was usually inclined to use the side streets, he didn't see any point right now. They were hardly being discreet with the guards following them, so there was no point. Marcus and James were on duty, with a team of Elite arrayed around them.

Alex dismissed the thoughts of the upcoming battle, pushing them aside as they approached the docks. There were several of what appeared to be barge trader families docked, as usual. He smiled as he sensed them note his approach. That was another reason for the more formal approach. They would soon know exactly who they were and understand, even though they were outsiders, that they spoke for the Crown.

Alex scanned the docked barges as he approached, noting the slightly smaller one closer to the dockside office. One glance at Kyle told him he'd picked it as well. It didn't seem to be built to hold much cargo and at least on outward appearances looked more comfortable, the wooden benches with cushions and tables under awnings on the deck being one giveaway. They both made their way towards it without comment.

Alex noted the appearance of what seemed to be soldiers dressed as sailors at the edge of the walkway up to the boat. He frowned as he noticed that most of the guards on the deck were female, with only a handful of men. The men that were there were young and wore silver collars. Alex shook his head and pushed the oddity aside to investigate later. At least they didn't pull up the plank between the dock and the boat. Not that Alex or Kyle needed the walkway to get on the boat, but it was a good sign. Alex stopped as Marcus and half of the other guards slipped in front of them on the narrow walkway and they made their way up to the deck of the ship. Marcus paused before stepping onto the deck, looking to the guards at the top.

"The Fourth and the Fourth's Companion are here on business of the Crown to speak with your masters. Step back and keep your hands away from your swords. We don't want any misunderstandings to occur." Marcus stared at the guards coolly, he wore his authority like a well-worn cloak. It suited him impeccably and he was in his comfort zone, with not a hint of hesitation showing.

The door to the main cabin opened and a woman appeared in the doorway, speaking in a rapid-fire clipped language that Alex didn't understand, yet the results spoke for themselves as the guards on the deck backed up. When Marcus was satisfied with the distance between them, he boarded, placing himself between the unknown entity of the woman and cabin. His squad streamed after him and took up their positions.

Alex waited patiently with Kyle until Marcus was happy with the other guards in position and waved them up. Appearing officially as the Fourth was so much more tedious than showing up unannounced.

~

KYLE LOOKED at Alex and couldn't help rolling his eyes, which caused Alex to grin at him. All this posturing. It was so much simpler for them to move around without all the pretence.

He tried to keep his amusement from showing on his face at the stand-off between Marcus and James and the guards on the barge as they insisted on entering the cabin with them. Their Elite won that particular contest and took positions on either side of the door. Kyle entered and saw the woman who'd intervened standing behind a chair with two other women. They all gave off the appearance of softness, wrapped in silks that draped around their bodies and showed off their figures. The long curved daggers strapped to their waists gave the lie to that softness. His gaze focused on the occupant of that chair. The male had long dark hair held back by a strip of leather. His eyes were an intense dark brown. Kyle had no doubt this was Rosalinda's brother. He was wearing soft lounging clothes but Kyle didn't miss the set of fighting leathers on a stand in the corner of the cabin.

"You are welcome, Prince Alexander, Lord Kyle. You may call me Dashel." Kyle noticed that he didn't introduce the women, which left him wondering whether they were guards or servants. Although it was odd: he hadn't missed the fact that the women far outnumbered the men on the barge. He'd gotten the distinct impression that in Sylanna, children belonged to their father. Women became the property of their husbands once an agreement had been made between the interested parties—agreements in which the women had little say.

Kyle glanced at Alex as they took the proffered seats and realised that his friend was content to sit back and let him handle the conversation.

"Thank you, Dashel. We bring an invitation from our king and his future consort, your sister Rosalinda, to attend the court. With your people." Kyle smiled, nodding thanks to one of the women who handed him and Alex each a tall glass that frosted as the woman chilled it. Kyle took a cautious sip, pleasantly surprised by the tart flavour of what he guessed was some kind of fruit juice. He looked curiously at the women.

The woman who'd intervened and gained them admission to this inner sanctum swatted Dashel on the shoulder.

"You are being rude to our guests, Dashel. They are desperately trying not to cause offence and to work out who we are." The woman looked up at them and smiled, dusky eyes smouldering above dark makeup.

Dashel sighed. "My first and prime dagger wives. This rather annoying outspoken one is my first, Raquel. Next to her are my primes Natasha and Kaitlyn." A look of suffering crossed his face and he whispered at them, "Do yourself a favour and do not get married. They become insufferable."

Kyle spluttered, hastily pressing a napkin to his lips while Alex nearly spat out his drink.

"Wives?" Alex's eyes widened as he took in the three women arrayed behind Dashel; he'd thought Isabella had been kidding about Sylannians having multiple consorts.

"Well I only have two—prime wives, that is. We left to come here before Raquel could finish bickering for a third prime wife. I think two prime wives alongside my first wife is enough for now." Dashel glanced up at Raquel, who patted him on the shoulder, smiling down at him.

"Never mind, husband. Perhaps I'll find a third while we are here to help your sister settle her own household." Raquel looked up at them and smiled.

"My brothers in the Imperial Court were starting to think I was one of the Emperor's favourites. They began to see me as a threat and I'm certain a dance of daggers was about to be unleashed within the Imperial House. The First Dagger Wife and the Emperor, my father, were becoming a little concerned. So, here I am, my whole household including my wives, servants and guards exiled to Vallantia with my sister." Dashel sighed again, but there was a hard edge to his eyes and he didn't look all that upset.

"Rosalinda indicated that her father still viewed her as his property." Kyle frowned, trying to put in perspective what he was seeing here and what Rosalinda had said.

Dashel grimaced and unlaced the top of his shirt to reveal a red and cream collar around his neck. "We are all the property of the Imperial House. Rosalinda may have had her collar cut off, been elevated from a daughter of the Imperial House to the rank of Imperial Princess for this match with your crown prince, but do not mistake it. She is as much Imperial property as I am."

Raquel squeezed his shoulder and he looked up at her and smiled. "We are grateful to be here. Otherwise I fear our household would have been overrun by now."

Kyle stared at the woven red and cream collar as Dashel did up the ties to his shirt once more, hiding it from sight.

"Will you come to the court?" Kyle didn't know what to make of the conversation, and so fell back on the duty imposed on them by William.

"My king warns you that we are about to embark on a war. You may wish you were back in the Empire taking your chances with unrest in the Imperial Court." Alex's expression was solemn, his tone blunt.

“We will come as your king and Rosalinda commands. We’ll take our chances with your troubles over the dance of daggers.” Raquel made the announcement and Dashel nodded his acceptance. Kaitlyn excused herself and the door had only just closed before they could hear the rapid-fire orders she issued to those out on deck.

Kyle made sure to hide his surprise well. Despite everything he’d thought he’d known about Sylanna, it appeared that Raquel and her fellow wives had far more say than what he’d imagined.

Kyle had to stop the very inappropriate laughter that nearly burst from his lips. William was going to have his hands full with one Imperial Princess once she’d grown accustomed to her new surroundings.

47

UNEXPECTED ASSISTANCE

Brian looked down at the long bench and picked up the tray of food. They had given up trying to get him to kill innocents. It was a shame really, he'd liked seeing the frustration on their faces. Instead they ordered him to feed some of the others they kept down here, he guessed they thought this way he was at least useful. He followed these instructions, not that he really had a choice since they didn't go against the boy's instructions not to kill.

Brian turned, carrying the tray of food out, crossing the floor and down a tunnel to a side cavern. This one housed those that were too young for the Order to corrupt; he had fed all of them except the smallest boy, the one they referred to as Jimmy. A sweat broke out on his forehead as he struggled with himself, yet despair filled him as he learnt once more that which bound him was too strong. Every day he struggled with that which bound him, wanting to take the boy, to disappear from this place and take him to safety. Degree by degree he was getting a little better, yet he was bound here in the caverns, unable to flee to freedom, let alone free the boy.

He turned into the alcove carved out of the rock, big

enough to contain a sleeping cot and not much else to see the boy Jimmy sitting on the cot's edge. He looked up at Brian as he entered and reached out to grab the tray he held out. Then he heard a moan, the moan of the one further down the next tunnel that ran off this one. Even the thick rock was not enough to keep her screams of agony from reaching this place.

Jimmy looked up, his eyes sad. *They're hurting her.*

Brian stood for a moment, astounded. The boy had never said a word to him before, he'd never heard the lad speak at all. Not one word. Until now.

Yes lad.

They're hurting her like they did Ty. He's funny in the head now. The boy's lips trembled.

Brian struggled for a moment then caught the image from Jimmy's mind. Tyson was his older brother, he now ranked among the Sundered.

Yes Jimmy, they are trying to hurt her like they hurt your brother. Brian refrained from mentioning that they would do the same thing to the lad as well when he grew up enough. It would scare the child. Brian turned to make·his way back to his own sleeping area now that his task was done but halted when the boy spoke again.

Are you going to get food for her now?

No. I'm forbidden to give her food. Brian looked at the boy seeing his face screw up in concentration as he thought that through. He looked down at his own tray then back up.

But why? Everyone needs food.

They want her weak, so they can hurt her. Like your brother. Brain looked at Jimmy, wondering if he truly understood.

I got sick once and I didn't eat for a long time. When I started to feel better Mommy told me I had to eat so I could get strong again. At a moan from the one they were torturing, Jimmy shifted on his cot, looking sad again.

Your mother was right. Food helps us all stay strong. Brian turned and walked back down the tunnel, a smile on his lips.

He could hear as the boy thought it through, just as he heard the soft footsteps that walked in the direction of the far tunnel. He couldn't help their current victim, he was forbidden, but Jimmy might be able to.

~

JESS WATCHED as Kevin pulled the stopper off one of the flasks. He poured a careful measure of the clear liquid from the flask before turning back to her, a pleasant smile on his face.

"Now, Jess it's time for your dose." Kevin's voice dripped with false concern as he leant over and pinched Jess's nose shut.

Jess tried to keep her mouth shut but as she failed and her mouth opened gasping for breath Kevin expertly poured the first of the poisons into her mouth. She choked, unable to help it as the liquid ran down her throat.

"Now my pet, relax, trust me ingesting it this way is much faster. Although I thought your first dosing was quite ingenious." Kevin smiled, laying his hand lightly on her temple and Jess felt the muscles of her neck relax as healing power soothed her throat. "You see the power bubble around the knife held the correct dose of poison; my minion released the power bubble after she'd stabbed you with it. We just had to give it time to work through your system."

Kevin nodded satisfied and turned back to the small table, placing the stopper back on the flask. Then he grasped the second one and taking a small spoon, he poured some into it.

Now my pet open your mouth for me and take your medicine. Kevin's voice held concern.

Jess felt herself trembling and her mouth opened. Kevin smiled and poured it into her mouth.

Very good my pet, I'm pleased with you. You see, I don't have to hurt you when you do as I command.

Jess felt tears track down her cheek and fear ran though her as she realised she'd complied with Kevin's order. She hadn't meant to, it was like her body and mind were betraying her.

"The second dose as you saw is much smaller than the first, which is why the Sundered one just had to slice you with his blade." Kevin caressed her cheek. "This way we can get this unpleasantness over with sooner. Don't fret, as soon as the medication settles on you we can continue your treatment."

Kevin's eyes glittered as Jess moaned as the dual medications raced through her system. He turned and placed the stopper in the second bottle and stood, smiling down at her.

"Now I'll leave you to rest and finish healing from your last session." Kevin smiled, a possessive light in his eyes. "You will belong to me Jess. Before I'm done you will call me master." Jess squeezed her eyes shut as Kevin turned with that last parting shot and left her cell.

Jess was unable to help the moan that escaped her lips. The drugs Kevin had administered combined, burning through her system, locking her up, making it impossible somehow for her to use her powers. She could see it, it ran through her but every time she tried to grasp it, the energy slipped away as if part of her brain was no longer functioning properly. Since she was awake, she knew they would be back soon. They would start up again, Jess felt the tear trace from her eyes down her cheek to the cot she was chained to. She wasn't sure how much more she could take, how much longer she was capable of resisting Kevin. There was a part of her that desperately wanted the constant pain to go away.

Hearing someone walking into her cell, Jess whimpered.

Please no more. Jess froze inside, she hadn't meant to utter those words. She knew that was what Kevin wanted, he wanted her to give in to him.

Feeling something touch her lips, Jess opened her eyes, stunned to see a pair of grey eyes staring back at her. Jess wondered if she was dreaming or hallucinating since the eyes belonged to a small boy. As liquid touched her lips, spilling into her mouth she swallowed convulsively.

You need this more than me. You need to stay strong.

Jess stared at the boy and swallowed another mouthful of the water, wondering who he was. If he was real. Jess would have laughed if she didn't think it would hurt. The water had certainly felt real. She almost protested as the lad took the mug away, it was only now that she'd had some that she desperately craved more.

Jess watched the boy as he smiled, then held a segment of fruit to her lips. Jess chewed slowly, closing her eyes. It seemed like a lifetime ago that she'd last eaten food. She knew she shouldn't have much, it had been long enough she'd be sick if she overate now. The boy watched her closely and held another segment to her when she finished the first.

Thank you. That will be plenty.

The boy looked at her, concern emanating from him. *Are you sure? I don't mind sharing my food.*

If I eat too much, too fast, I'll be sick. Thank you for helping me. Don't let them catch you lad. Jess was concerned, although by the looks of the child he was too young for him to be anywhere near transition. He was only a little boy.

I won't, I'll bring you more later. The lad nodded, picking up his mug and tray before disappearing out of her cell.

My name's Jess, what's yours? Jess figured she couldn't keep thinking of him as boy or lad.

There was a pause as the lad thought about it, then replied. *I'm Jimmy.*

Jess smiled as the mind voice floated back to her and felt unaccountably better. Only a short moment ago she'd been about to give up, to give in to her captors. Yet now she wouldn't, or she'd try not to. She had to stay strong and find a way to beat them. If not for herself, for the boy, Jimmy. Jess shuddered at the thought of what horrors the boy must be seeing and hearing down here. Someone had to get the child out of this place.

48

DISORIENTATION

Joanna looked around her rooms, a vague unease settling on her. Things didn't quite seem right but she couldn't quite put her finger on what exactly was wrong. The servants had obviously been busy moving things around and redecorating. It was odd, since she didn't remember asking them to do so.

Looking at the rumpled sheets on the bed, she guessed Michael must have spent the night in her room. She swung around at hearing a noise behind her, hand rising to her chest. A slow breath escaped her as she saw a serving girl curtsey.

"Do you need anything else, m'lady?"

The serving maid kept her eyes on the ground, seemingly a little flustered. Joanna frowned; she didn't remember having ever seen the girl before. It was unusual for new servants to be assigned to her.

"No, thank you, that will be all."

Joanna kept her eyes on the serving girl as she bobbed again before retreating. She couldn't work out why she was so unsettled and jumpy today. She took a deep breath trying to expel the disquiet that weighed her down. Perhaps it was time to find Michael and drag him away from the tedious affairs of state, even if only for a brief time. A smile curved her lips. Spending time with him always diverted her attention.

Decision made, she nodded to herself, smoothing down the front of her dress as she walked from her rooms. The young guards on duty suddenly snapped to attention, looking vaguely panicked as she breezed past them.

"Where is the king?"

"Um, the king, my lady?"

"I believe that is what I just asked. Where is he?"

The two guards looked at each other and swallowed before looking back at her. She pressed her lips together, eyes narrowing as she felt her irritation starting to rise.

"He's in council right now." The guard's face flushed, his eyes widening.

She repressed a sigh, turning from them and heading down the corridor towards the main council chamber. They really were too young for their duties and obviously easily flustered. That was another thing she would have to mention to Michael.

"Um, my lady, you really shouldn't..."

She ignored the attempts to stop her, not that they were trying that hard other than protesting. Her eyes narrowed again as their words sank in. She would add them thinking they had a right to tell her what she should or should not do to the list of their infractions. She smiled when, after a brief pause, the thump of their booted feet made a deeper counterpoint to the clip of her own court shoes as they hastened to trail after her.

JOANNA GLARED at the guards who tried to protest her entry into the council room.

"You forget yourself. Stand aside or the king will hear of

your behaviour." Joanna fumed as she pushed the doors open herself.

This day was beginning to feel as if she had been dropped into someone else's life. Pushing her way into the council chambers, she straightened her shoulders as heads turned to look at her, the animated conversation coming to a halt.

Joanna felt a moment of confusion as she glanced at the gathered lords and ladies in the council chamber, not recognising any of them. It gave her pause to wonder what was being discussed with what must be minor lords. The guards who'd followed her had stopped on the threshold of the room.

"Mother. Can I help you with something?"

Her back stiffened and she glanced around the room. Her eyes lingered as she stared at the young man sitting where Michael should be, wearing state robes and the crown. Outrage swelled inside of her. Michael's servants would really need a stern talking to for allowing an impostor into his private chambers. Joanna wondered if he'd managed to sneak in while Michael had been in her rooms the night before.

"I'm not sure who you are, young man, but it is treason to impersonate the king." Her eyes were wide as she glared at the Elite. "Where is Michael, what have you done with him?"

The young man leaned forward, his face in his hands, a muffled groan coming from his direction. She smiled. He was obviously contrite at having been caught out playing king with his friends. So he should be. He was going to be in serious trouble when this mess was sorted out. Joanna gathered these were the offspring of some of the lords and ladies present currently in the palace, although she didn't recognise any of them. She pushed her momentary confusion aside; it wasn't like she should be expected to know everyone.

The man pretending to be king looked up, brushing his dark hair from his eyes. Her breath stuttered as she caught sight of his intense blue eyes. Something about his eyes, and the way he pushed his hair back with his fingers, stirred a memory, yet no matter how much she teased at it, the memory just wouldn't surface. The would-be king looked at those sitting around the table with him, clearly exasperated.

"Leave us. We'll reconvene and discuss the remaining issues when this is dealt with."

Joanna felt her back stiffen again at his gall to continue to play his game.

Even worse was the way some of them looked at her as they trailed out of the room.

JOANNA LOOKED up as another young man appeared in the council room—literally appearing out of thin air. She shivered at a cold breeze washing over her and looked around. A wave of fear flooded her and she took a step back as he walked towards her. She looked over at the guards, not understanding why they didn't intervene and help her. Joanna froze in place as she was grasped in an unseen hand that prevented her from moving. Then he was on her, grasping her head, forcing her to look up into his startling blue eyes that looked vaguely familiar. She raised her own hands, laying them on his wrists, intending to try to break free, but she froze as his voice echoed in her mind.

I'm sorry for the cruelty, Mother.

Confusion flooded her as this one called her mother, just like the one pretending to be the king. Then images started to appear in her head, one after the other. A perplexing jumble, some her own, some from another mind. If she could have screamed, she would have. She recognised herself, her little boy, her son. Her apparent death at the hands of a Sundered One, as he drew his cruel hunting knife across her throat. Blood, her blood, spurting from her throat as she crumpled to the ground. Discarded. Forgotten.

"Alex!" She sobbed as she recognised the danger her perfect little boy was in, with no one there to protect him from evil.

Images started to bombard her mind, one after the other, and somehow she was aware that they were her own memories, not ones forced on her by this man. Image by cruel image the picture of her life burst in her mind and understanding grew. She'd watched over her boy and his friends when she could over the intervening years, often trying to soothe his fears and nightmares when she could.

Then she saw a fight, others trying to kill her and her friends, another that she knew she had controlled.

Kyle.

The name floated up to her conscious brain. She knew this man. She'd seen him take his blade and plunge it into the other man. This man in front of her. Then Kyle's voice, angry and filled with anguish, as he rounded on her. His words echoing through her mind.

Damn you, Joanna. That was Alex! You made me stab your own son!

Joanna made no move to wipe away the tears she felt tracing their way down her face, as she remembered the time that had passed. Trembling, she sobbed as she finally recognised that it wasn't a stranger who held her in his vice-like grip. It was Alex.

A final image flashed into her mind, breaking her heart as she remembered. Michael, lying in state.

Dead.

She glanced at the one she'd thought moments before was pretending to be king. It was William, she recognised him now, and he wasn't pretending to be king. He now shouldered that burden in truth.

"I'm sorry, I was confused." Joanna felt Alex relax, his power releasing her, and she sobbed as he gently wrapped his arms around her. "What have I become?"

Coming back to reality, this reality, hurt.

Every, single, time.

ALEX RELAXED as his mother came back to herself. If it wasn't so dangerous, it might have been kinder to let her remain in that world, where her life had been easier.

As her trembling subsided, he glanced at Ryan. The duty of watching over William today had fallen to him, while the rest of them had been out looking for signs of the Order's new hiding place.

"Ryan, if you could take my mother back to her rooms, please? I'll be there as soon as we've sorted out some issues." He left unsaid the *watch over her* part of the order, although he was certain he caught that part without it being said. "Mother, go with Ryan please, I'll drop in and we'll have tea."

"But you drink coffee." His mother looked up at him, her lips trembling.

Alex felt his lips twitch but managed to keep a straight face. "I'll drink some coffee and you can have tea or something stronger if you wish."

He shook his head as she turned to leave with Ryan as her escort. The two junior Elite who'd been trying to make themselves inconspicuous turned to follow.

"I don't suppose you two would care to explain how Joanna got all the way here in the first place?"

They looked at each other, then the more senior one spoke up, looking embarrassed.

"My apologies, Fourth, she just came barging out of her suite. We sent for assistance but well, she is His Majesty's mother." The unfortunate guard swallowed nervously.

Alex glanced at the door as Marcus, James, Megan and Matthew entered. He shook his head as amusement replaced his irritation, gathering the backup had just arrived. He waved dismissal at the guardsman and nodded at Ryan.

"Go, I'll be there when I can."

Alex walked over to the table and pulled out one of the chairs, looked at William and sighed.

"Sorry, we'll leave someone behind to keep an eye on her. She seems all right most of the time, but other times..."

William shook his head. "Other times she's completely mad or regresses to the past with no understanding of the time that has lapsed."

Alex waved Marcus into the room.

"Can you assign someone a little more senior on the doors, particularly when we aren't there?" Alex frowned. "Perhaps a mind-speaker, if you have one who's strong enough to at least yell for help if Joanna goes wandering like that again?"

Marcus nodded. "Of course, Your Highness, we'll get it sorted."

Alex nodded, then turned his attention back to William. "So, shall we get this meeting you were in the middle of finished? Or will you defer it to another time? They are all waiting on your pleasure in the anteroom."

William raised an eyebrow at him. "So you're going to stay and be my keeper, Alex? You hate these meetings."

Alex plastered a woeful expression on his face. "Well, someone has to."

William laughed. "I'm sure I can manage to keep my own mind shield up now, and I know I can yell for you if I need something."

Alex stood up and walked across to the windowsill where he took up position, leaning against one edge with his booted foot resting on the other.

"In normal times, yes. With Amelia on the loose I'll not risk you. She's already killed Father while I was wallowing in self-doubt. I'd never forgive myself if I failed you as well." Alex turned his head to gaze out the window as his brother gave instructions for the councillors to be allowed back into the room.

"It wasn't your fault, Alex. None of us predicted what Amelia was capable of. What she would do." Alex looked back to see William's expression was clouded. Then his brother's expression cleared as he turned his attention back to the councillors who filed back into the room to take their accustomed place around the table.

A few of them threw curious glances at him although most of them ignored his presence. They were used to one of them being present, even if it was in the background, while his brother held court, regardless of whether it was a full court session or one of the smaller court sessions. They were all getting used to the addition and when they thought of the not-so-distant events, Alex was sure they all understood the necessity. Most of them were smart enough to realise what he, Jess and Kyle were capable of. Ryan was more of an unknown to them, but they'd had the security reports from the incident at the Healers' Guild and knew that Ryan was credited with saving the lives of the Guild Masters. That was good enough for them, even if they didn't quite understand what he'd done.

49

CELLS WITHIN

Jess felt her back arch, Kevin's fingers biting into her skull, eyes boring into her own. She gasped for breath as her throat seemed to close up as Kevin's power poured into her.

Please....

Jess heard Kevin laugh and yet more power poured into her, she tried to twist away in pain yet had nowhere to go. The pain just amplified.

Hide Jess!

Jess tried to pull her head from her tormentor's grip, her body stiffening as her brain felt like it was exploding, Kevin hammering blow after blow at her. Then she felt herself shoved aside, pushed back in her own head. Her body still writhed in pain, she still screamed yet somehow she felt removed from it.

Don't say it Jess, don't give yourself to him. You'll be lost if you do!

Jess spun, it looked like she was standing in the veil, surrounded by grey mist, yet she couldn't be since she knew her body was still chained up being tortured.

It's that place in your mind where you go when you dream, at least that is where I think it is.

Jess spun around and stepped back as she saw Amelia appear although insubstantial as if she wasn't really here at all. Her hair was matted, her shift was ripped and stained. Jess swallowed, wondering if all the punishment that she was being inflicted with, had finally snapped her mind.

Amelia?

Yes Jess, build a wall around yourself here in your mind. He's pushing you to the point where you will willingly give yourself to him, anything to make the punishment stop. You will be lost when you do. It's how it works. The ghost Amelia looked over her shoulder, fear running across her face.

You're still you? Jess took a step towards her. *You're hiding in your own mind?*

No. I gave in. I'm her. I think my master kept this small piece of me locked up in my own head so I'd know what I've become. Amelia looked at her, tears glittering in her eyes.

Then you can be saved...

No Jess, I'm his. He has his hooks into every part of me. But he doesn't have you. Damn it Jessalan, fight him. Don't give up! Amelia's eyes glittered at her, flashing in anger.

I don't know if I can.

You can. Lock yourself away, don't say it. Don't beg him, don't invite him in willingly just to make the pain go away. Amelia had closed the gap between them, speaking rapidly, her voice fierce. *Fight!*

With one last look over her shoulder Amelia's presence vanished, disappearing without a trace. Jess looked around, swallowing nervously. She was certain she must have gone mad but she was much happier hiding within her insanity than waking up to feel the pain again.

She looked around and following Amelia's advice, if the other woman had been real, she built up a wall around herself.

A couch appeared and she slumped back into it. She knew it wasn't real, it was a dream, yet it was far more comfortable than waking up would be right now.

It was strange, she could feel her body writhing so she knew that there was a part of her that was still there, still suffering. Yet she wasn't. She concentrated and with a start she realised that she was staring out of her own eyes again. Fear shot through her for a moment as she wondered if she'd accidentally woken herself up.

She calmed a little as she realised she was still feeling a little detached from herself. Even if she was looking out of her own eyes. She felt her face sting as Kevin slapped her, frustration on her tormentor's face.

"Damn it! I thought I had her for a moment there." Kevin slapped Jess again then turned away.

"She will break, Master. They all do eventually, she's just stronger than most."

Jess couldn't see her but the voice was Amelia's, the sadistic Amelia who belonged to Kevin. Not the sweet Amelia who unaccountably was still locked up inside her own head. Who had done her best to try and save her. Problem was, she still didn't know how to free herself. Jess retreated back to her chair, rebuilding her wall around herself absently as she thought through the problem.

JESS SAT, with her eyes squeezed shut, beads of perspiration springing up on her forehead. Yelling in frustration she sprung up from her chair. This refuge of hers might give her a certain amount of safety from giving herself to Kevin, a place to hide from the punishment being inflicted on her body. Unfortunately other than being able to look out of her eyes she didn't seem to have any control over her body anymore.

Oh, certain reflexes worked. Her body convulsed when Kevin used her to play out his torture fetishes. She breathed and screamed. Swallowed the poison when Kevin fed it to her but it was like her body was on automatic while she was absent. Hearing footsteps Jess moved forward to peer out of her eyes. It was the lad, Jimmy. While she couldn't do much else she could talk with him.

The mug was held to her lips and she swallowed the water, grateful as it slid down her parched throat, grateful for the sweet undertone. The lad didn't try to feed her, they'd worked out after the first visit the boy had made after she'd retreated that she couldn't chew. Instead Jimmy had compromised, he squeezed the juice from the fruit into the water.

I wish I could do more. Jimmy's mind voice trembled, as if he was trying not to cry.

You've done more for me than anyone else here Jimmy. This isn't your fault. Jess swore, wishing she could get up and hug the boy.

I should go.

Jess heard Jimmy stand and turn. Jess's eyes widened as she had a sudden thought; although it was probably a crazy one it was the only thing she could think of.

Wait! Jess called out, nearly breathing a sigh of relief as she heard Jimmy turn and walk back to her.

Is there something else I can do? Jimmy's tone was hopeful.

Jimmy, tell me, are there two flasks on the table near my cot? Jess hoped they were still sitting right where she'd last seen them.

Yes.

Can you carefully pour the liquid of one of the flasks into your mug? Jess smiled, or at least she did inside her own head.

She waited, hearing the stopper come off one of the flasks and liquid being poured into what she assumed was Jimmy's mug.

Alright. What now? Jimmy's voice held a hushed note of curiosity as if they were conspiring.

Jess nearly chuckled. *Take the other flask and careful not to spill any pour it into the one you just emptied.*

Jess could feel Jimmy was intrigued as he followed the instructions, even if he didn't understand why.

I didn't spill any. Jimmy was terribly proud of his accomplishment.

Jess conceded she was as well. *Well done. Now the last thing, pour the contents of your flask into the empty flask.*

Jess could sense Jimmy's confusion about the set of tasks he'd been given. They made no sense to the boy but he followed them anyway. Jess heard the trickle of the liquid into the flask.

Alright, now what?

Make sure the stoppers are on the flasks and put them back where you found them. Jess listened carefully and heard the scrape of the flasks across the wood of the table. *Thank you Jimmy. You've been a big help.*

If you say so. A clear note of confusion was in Jimmy's tone.

Make sure not to drink from that mug Jimmy and go to the bathing area to wash your hands. The poisons they give me are in those flasks. Jess explained carefully, hoping Jimmy would follow his instructions.

Now she just had to wait. It was a risk, a big risk but Kevin had been so careful about the quantities. She hoped that when she was dosed with the wrong quantities of the dual poisons that it wouldn't have the same effect of stopping that part of her brain that controlled the veil. Of course being given the wrong quantities of each medication could kill her as well, but she knew she was remarkably hard to kill. As they'd proven with the punishment they'd inflicted on her, she healed well.

She hoped she'd either be able to use her powers again or that between the torture and the overdose of the different medications, it would be enough to tip her over the edge and she'd function without conscious control. She just hoped Alex was correct in his guess about how he'd functioned when he'd had his blackouts. That he'd only kill those who tried to hurt him, not those that didn't.

50

FACADE

Simon froze, drawing his shields tighter around himself as he looked at the scene below, increasing his protection but desperately trying not to draw attention while he did it.

He'd intended to give one final warning to Kevin that he needed to move. Now. Yet what he saw chilled him all the way through and left him grateful that he maintained the habit of checking not only where he wanted to appear but the immediate surrounds before he materialised anywhere.

There was what he'd expected to see—the dull glow from the normal humans, clumped together outside the castle walls, and scattered throughout the estate house. Then the fitful, stuttering glow that he recognised as the Sundered Ones off to one side, the ones his spies had told him were in the underground caverns accessed by a network of natural tunnels running beneath the estate. There were a couple of dead places that on closer inspection proved to be Kevin, of course, and the former Lady Amelia, now of the new breed of Sundered and a few others like her, all shielding. Unless you were looking for the signs of it, no one would notice them.

Except for the one void he'd checked, the one that had frozen him to his core. The one that on closer inspection had proven to be the Scholar Clements. Normal humans didn't produce the carefully shielded dead spots. They weren't capable of it. That meant Scholar Clements was not human.

At first he thought the man was trying to take advantage of Amelia; he was certainly using up most of his focus on her to the exclusion of all else. Whatever he was doing with her, it made other things slip—like his shield.

The so-called Scholar Clements shifted in his mind's eye as he watched, flickering from the elderly scholar to a much younger man. It took everything in him not to draw the veil to him and flee. He wasn't sure what Kevin was thinking, but that man, the so-called leader of the Order, was Kin.

Or perhaps Elder.

Simon bit his lip, wondering whether his friend really hadn't seen it. For the apparent scholar to do what he was doing, it had to mean he was Elder. An Elder who'd been going to extreme lengths to hide what he was. There would be no need to hide that with Lord Kastler; the man was only a human and wouldn't notice anyway. That meant he was hiding what he was from Kevin. What Simon couldn't work out was how his friend, after all this time, did not know. Or if he did, what he was thinking.

Simon edged back into the veil, degree by degree, desperate not to draw the attention of the other. It was one thing for a human to dispose of the current ruling family and try to place himself as the ruler of Vallantia. It was clear even to him that despite what the fool Kastler thought, it was never going to be him on the throne. Kevin he could have dealt with as the power behind the throne. This Clements, or whatever his name was, was an entirely different matter. He doubted an Elder who'd gone to these lengths would be content to allow another, even a puppet, to take the throne.

Simon paused his retreat, frowning. He just couldn't work out why an Elder would go to these lengths, hiding behind the facade of being human and behind the Order...

He shook himself. Why didn't matter. This situation had changed.

Simon swore and pushed indecision aside. He carefully scanned the Kastler estate and discovered Kevin in a room down the other end of the hall from the one the so-called leader of the Order was in. Carefully, keeping his personal shield wrapped tightly around him, he edged into Kevin's rooms. As he dismissed the veil, appearing in Kevin's room, his friend jumped with a curse, only to relax a moment later when recognition dawned on his face.

"Simon, you gave me a heart attack. What are you doing here?" Kevin slumped back into his chair, putting aside a map he'd been studying.

"Kevin, it's not too late. Leave this madness, let the Order fend for itself."

Simon saw contempt spread on his friend's face.

"You always did lack ambition, Simon."

"Damn it, Kevin, listen for once in your life! That man who calls himself Clements is Elder!" Simon hissed at his long-time friend, keeping his voice low.

Kevin's eyes widened in shock, before he threw his head back in a hearty laugh.

"Really, Simon, I know you are a coward and terrified of Edward's wrath should he discover our treachery, but this is ridiculous. That old man is not Elder. I think after all this time I would have noticed if he was."

"I know what I saw. You need to back away from this madness."

Simon felt his stomach sink as he saw the condescending expression on Kevin's face.

"Go back and cower in you den of thieves, Simon. You were never meant to rule."

Simon slowly drew the veil to him, withdrawing as gradually as he'd come here. It had been a risk to try to warn Kevin. He should have known better, but at least he'd tried. He knew what he needed to do next. That was something he faced with even more trepidation than that with which he had faced the man he'd thought of as a friend.

51

LEARNING

Kyle turned to look at the lady he was talking to, and smiled an apology that he hoped wasn't too brittle.

"Excuse me, my lady, I think I'll take a seat, it's been tiring of late." Kyle glanced across at Joanna, then back to the lady.

As he'd hoped, a look of understanding crossed her face. As he'd hoped his unfortunate slip where he'd mentioned that Joanna had kept him enslaved had swept the court.

"Of course, my lord." Moisture welled in the ladies eyes as she looked across the garden where Joanna sat, calmly and back at him. He turned to walk to a small sheltered grotto.

He gestured discreetly to James, who took up position with his fellow Elite at the entrance of the grotto without comment. As he relaxed back onto the lounging chair in the garden, he had no doubt even this small a withdrawal would cause gossip, but right now he didn't really care. After all, his unfortunate slip-up from the other night where he'd mentioned his enslavement was doing the rounds already. He had no doubt the gossips would attribute his current withdrawal to the fact that Joanna was present at the garden party.

He contemplated disappearing to his rooms but knew that would be unacceptable. As he'd promised, William had signed the contract between himself and Rosalinda. It had been a small affair with only a handful of the highest-ranking lords and ladies of the court invited along with Dashel and his wives. Even while planning for a major conflict with rebels, when your king takes a Consort Elect, there needed to be some fuss over it. Rosalinda was taking everything in her stride, including the lack of the usual pomp and ceremony that would have accompanied this occasion. As soon as arrangements could be made, she would be elevated to be his consort in truth. It was a slight delaying tactic, but given that the delegation had arrived unannounced, and the ongoing issue with the Order, it was one that they felt they would get away with. If Rosalinda was upset by a small garden party rather than a grand ball to celebrate, she certainly wasn't giving any indication of it. Not that she really expected anything else. Rosalinda was raised in the same school as they were.

Kyle glanced at William across the garden, always the centre of attention, with Rosalinda on his arm, playing the perfect host. Yet there was still that stiffness. Granted, apart from Alex, he was probably one of the few who noticed it. Still at least William was trying to come to terms with all the changes in his life. With actually being the king and his new consort.

Kyle, are you all right? Alex's enquiry came just a moment later.

Kyle could see Alex standing not far from William, although he carefully did not look in his direction. He smiled. Alex knew that if he looked at him then everyone would notice.

I'll be fine, just tired. You were just correct I should have stayed in bed. Still it would have caused more gossip if I had.

Which gossip? About Jess or you and Mother? Alex's tone held sympathy even though as always he was subject to his own set of rumours.

Both. Kyle sipped his drink, not allowing the frustration he felt to show.

Kyle was about to emerge from the relative privacy of the grotto when he heard a stir as the courtiers moved and a buzz of conversation. Kyle looked over and smiled. Isabella had made her appearance at the lunch and was making her way across the garden towards him. Isabella had been at the palace after returning with Alex, but hadn't made many appearances. Just because she hadn't officially appeared in the court yet didn't mean that rumours weren't swirling around about Alex's mystery woman. Alex and his exploits were always a hot topic in the court. He always had been, more so than his siblings. Of course, that was likely because he gave the gossips in court a lot more to talk about. Seeing the flare of jealously in some of the ladies of the court made Kyle smile. Now speculation about Isabella and Alex might replace all the speculation about him. He waved the guards off as Isabella passed between them and sat down next to him.

"Isabella, it's good to see you again." Kyle grinned at the woman, who was fast becoming a friend. He could see why Alex liked her.

Kyle grasped her hand and brushed his lips on her fingers.

"William made a point of issuing the invite, so I thought it would be rude not to attend." Isabella sat back, her eyes tracking over towards where the brothers stood.

"Well, an invitation from a king could be considered a command, even if you aren't technically one of his subjects." Kyle laughed, glad to have a distraction from the direction his thoughts had been going.

"True, not that I've spent much time consorting with kings."

Kyle glanced at Isabella and saw the woman's eyes were

drawn across the garden towards Alex. Kyle flicked her gaze between the two, then chuckled.

"Alex is dying inside that you are over here and he is cornered over there." Kyle gestured to one of the circulating servants and appropriated a drink for the two of them.

"He'll survive a few moments." Isabella smiled. "You should still be resting, how are you?"

"I want to just curl up and sleep but, with the Order, Jess going missing, William taking a consort, I don't have the luxury." Kyle heard the exhaustion in his own voice, and mentally kicked himself. "I'll be fine. This function won't go on forever and I can go crash, sink into oblivion again."

Isabella looked at him for a long moment. "I know it may not seem like it right now, but all these things will resolve, eventually all of this will be but a moment in time."

"What do you mean?" Kyle looked at Isabella, startled at that last comment.

"I grew up in a time when warlords roamed this place, each scrambling for territory over the top of all those that looked to them. As hard as it was, that time passed." Isabella's head tilted to one side, her eyebrow rising.

"I'm not sure that really helps right now but I get your point. I think it's time we joined the others, before we start yet another rumour."

As Kyle stood, he offered his arm to Isabella who stood and linked her arm with his walking with him. As they walked from the grotto across the garden, the eyes of those in attendance tracked their progress, filled with speculation. Kyle smiled as he walked straight to William and Rosalinda, both of whom had noticed his approach.

The lord that had been speaking to them turned his head to see his approach and stepped aside. Isabella greeted both William and Rosalinda, congratulating the couple before joining Alex. Alex wrapped his arm around her waist.

"I'm sorry William but can I test your patience by stealing your Consort Elect from your side?" Kyle kept his face calm.

"Rosalinda?" William turned his head to her but didn't release her arm until she nodded.

Kyle what are you up to? Alex's mind voice was suspicious.

"Of course Kyle, I think a chat is long overdue." Rosalinda smiled and fell into step with him as he turned and led the way back across the garden.

It's fine Alex, I'm not going to get into a fight or anything. Kyle chuckled. *Although it might be fun!*

"This must be difficult for you, regardless of being something you were trained for from birth." Kyle commented lightly, aware that every eye in the garden was watching them avidly.

"It's not so bad, there were worse prospects my Emperor-father was considering than William." Rosalinda glanced at him and smiled. "You are not just the Fourth's Blade, you are the King's Blade. So have you decided I am too big a threat to your king?"

Kyle nearly blinked, Rosalinda was blunt and obviously not concerned with polite chatter, perhaps a smile or two and laughter as they strolled through the garden to put some of the rumours to bed.

"I am, just as my father was before me. Should I put an end to your existence?" Kyle glanced at her.

"I am my father's daughter but I will fight for the survival of this small piece of life that I now possess." Rosalinda looked back at him solemnly.

Kyle considered her and suddenly chuckled. "It would certainly prove to be a challenge, taking your life here in the middle of a garden party. Particularly to not have everyone know it was me."

"Surely everyone would already suspect you anyway, Kyle?" Her tone was light, despite the fact they were talking about death.

"The thing about being the Blade is while sometimes I am expected to be the very visible threat, at other times a little subtlety is called for."

"Ah, so if you were tasked with taking my life you think it would be as the unseen blade of the king?" Her eyebrow arched.

"Given the reaction your father would have I think it would be best to make it look like an accident." Kyle smiled, finding himself relaxing in her presence. "However that is not why I wanted to talk with you."

"Ah, so not in your capacity as Blade, so which duty compels you? Are you Lord Kyle right now or just Kyle?"

Kyle gave it consideration. "Just Kyle I think. Give William time Rosalinda, he only found out about all of this the night his father died." The memory of that horrible night in the court was still burned into his brain.

"So it is William's friend who speaks. Your concern is not necessary Kyle; unlike William I knew almost from the outset about the negotiations for this union. After all this is a contract arrangement between myself and William, it is not necessary for it to be anything more. Although I admit it would be easier if we could at least become friends."

Kyle knew that everyone was watching their progress around the garden avidly, although what they expected from him he didn't know right now.

"I know William, I think you will have that friendship and more." Kyle hoped Rosalinda believed him since in this respect he was being absolutely truthful. They walked in silence through the garden, Kyle carefully navigating their path to make sure they stayed in sight of the main party at all times.

"It is a rare thing for the children of emperors and kings to have a friend that they know and trust implicitly. Rarer still when they go on to become the king. It would be good if we could be friends as well."

"I think you will find you will have more than one friend in this court." Kyle glanced at her and smiled, surprising himself when he realised it was genuine.

"So, should we have a fight or something? I hear it's a hot topic amongst the courtiers." Rosalinda's dimples showed as she grinned.

Kyle threw his head back and laughed. "Oh, now that might be fun. I'd love to see you fight with your knives."

"We could make a real show of it." Rosalinda's eyes sparkled with mischief. "We could wait until we were halfway back to William then start hurling insults at each other."

"Then after that, hmm... rip a sleeve or two, then draw weapons on each other."

"We'd need to throw up a shield, to stop the guards from interfering and spoiling our fun." Rosalinda whispered, glancing over her shoulder at the Elite that trailed behind them.

Kyle joined her and looked over at Meghan, James and their fellow guards. They were all too professional to look alarmed or laugh.

"It might be wise. I think they'd feel it was their duty to intervene." Kyle grinned and they walked in silence for a few moments.

Rosalinda glanced at him. "So tell me, is there a trick to keeping the various lords and ladies, who all insist they have vital business with the king, out of William's rooms?"

Kyle chuckled at the unexpected question. "Be firm with the Elite and William's staff, insist said lords and ladies make an appointment unless it is a genuine emergency. Of course you could also threaten to turn the first lord that talks his way in, who in fact doesn't have an emergency to discuss, to ash. It worked a treat when Alex did it."

Rosalinda's eyes widened. "They believed he would follow through with such a threat?"

Kyle grinned. "Oh, they couldn't be certain he wouldn't do it, particularly while William was recovering. Alex wasn't taking anyone's nonsense and he has a reputation."

"The irresponsible younger prince, with power enough to be regarded as dangerous. Who rebelled against authority and frequented all the wrong parts of town with his two best friends." Rosalinda's eyes widened in fake shock as she glanced at him.

"Yes, that would be the one." Kyle smiled although he felt a stab of pain at the reference to Jess. It was like a piece of himself was missing.

Sympathy shone in Rosalinda's eyes and she turned to him, stopping their progress back to the party momentarily.

"I'm sorry for the loss of Lady Jessalan, I didn't mean to cause you such pain."

"She's alive; we'd know if she died." Kyle looked across at Alex who stared back at him, the pain of that loss passing between them. The acknowledgment that they both realised that she was alive and being tormented by the Order.

Kyle was shocked as Rosalinda drew him in and hugged him, pushing back to look him in the eye.

"This fight will end, Jess will be restored to you both and you can all run off to frequent all the wrong bars." Rosalinda's tone was firm as she nodded. Almost as if in her own head just because she ordered fate so, it would happen.

Kyle glanced across at William where he stood chatting with Alex and Isabella and he smiled. Sensing their regard William looked over at their approach, Kyle could tell he was more than a little relieved that he and Rosalinda hadn't resorted to sticking knives in each other.

"One more thing, even though William was born and raised to be king, he needs something, just a small piece of life that is his own separate from duty. He always has."

Rosalinda looked at him then over to William, speculation

in her eyes then a smile spread on her lips. “Thank you for your advice. I think, Kyle, we shall be friends you and I.”

Kyle laughed despite himself and determined that when that future happened, perhaps on occasion William’s consort may like to join them in frequenting some of those bars.

52

LONG SHOT

Jess paced in her little dream cell in her mind, if Amelia had been correct and that was where she'd stashed her. She knew it didn't help at all but it gave her something to do. She didn't have long to wait, or at least it didn't seem to. It was hard for her to tell the time in the cell where her body was chained up, let alone the one here in her mind.

Kevin came to gloat and dose her with the poisons. Thankfully Kevin seemed to take her withdrawal as a sign that she was right on the edge and about to break down. Jess could almost feel sorry for the man, he was correct but not in the way he hoped.

Right on cue Jess felt her body stiffen in reaction to the drugs she'd been fed and Kevin, satisfied, walked from the room. Jess felt the poisons rushing through her body, yet there was no immediate response. She sighed, gathering she was left with the option, the hope that because the quantities were off she'd be able to manipulate the veil again. Turning she slid down the wall of her hideout to wait. A dagger materialised in her hand and she flipped it absently, tossing it up into the air, feeling and hearing its slap into the palm of her hand. She had to admit this dream world of hers was awfully realistic. She considered it for a moment then realised that it probably wasn't that surprising. After all nightmares could feel absolutely real, even moments after you'd woken up from them. Some people even said their daydreams were just as vivid.

Jess heard a faint crackling noise and looked up, her dagger disappearing mid-toss as she stood. The walls of her refuge had turned black and she was plunged into darkness. She realised her eyes must have closed.

Ah, I guess it's the overdose option after all...Jess commented to herself almost absently.

Hearing a faint crackling noise Jess spun around squinting, saw faint pinpricks start to flare, then silver white power bled through the darkness forming glowing lines. She swallowed and was just coming to the conclusion she may have miscalculated when she sunk into oblivion, her consciousness fled.

POWER CRACKED IN THE VEIL, pure bolts of power cracking down, crossing between the veil and the real world. Those close by with power had time to surge up, wondering what was happening only to be knocked into unconscious by a wave of energy.

Deep down below the ground in her cell Jess screamed, her muscles straining against her restraints. The timber the cot was made of splintered, the rock wall cracked and Jess was up off the bed. The manacles that had bound her were still around her wrists and ankles, chains dangling yet she paid them no mind. Power writhed around her and her eyes glowed.

Jess?

She looked down, hearing that soft voice to see a small boy. There was a small part of her that recognised that this one,

Jimmy the name seemed to pop up into her head, had helped her. She held out her hand and after a brief hesitation the boy took it. Pulling the child into her arms, ignoring the pain that wracked her she fled this place. Instinct in the absence of reason propelled her back to another place, a person that another part of her equated with safety.

ALEX SAT NEXT to William at yet another council meeting, restraining a sigh. William's fate of seemingly unending meetings and court sessions as the king, was far worse than his own role of being the Fourth. He was impatient wanting to get out and search for the home of the Order. To find his friend. William had cancelled the majority of the meetings he normally had to suffer through but unfortunately, even in a wartime setting he couldn't cancel all of them. He would have preferred if William had cancelled the regular Petitioners' Court as well yet his brother or rather, his king wouldn't hear of it. He'd simply commented that people had come a long way to talk with him, the least he could do was listen. William had reasoned, the war effort wasn't going very far at all until they located the Order's new hiding place and the rest of the realm didn't stop in the meantime. Alex grimaced. It wasn't a statement that he could refute.

Alex felt the veil shudder, he threw a barrier around William reflexively. His face paled as the power pealed and cracked in the veil. His eyes widened as he felt the incoming rush of power, recognising instantly who that power belonged to. The conversation stopped and councillors looked at him uneasily at his reaction and the Elite closed up ranks in front of William facing towards the threat that suddenly appeared in front of them.

"Hold!" Alex threw the weight of his power behind the order willing everyone to stop.

He walked forward slowly, one careful step in front of the other never taking his eyes off the person who'd appeared in the council chamber, slumping to the ground.

"Your Highness...." James put out a hand only to stop as Alex shook his head and pushed the Elite aside with his powers.

He could see the shackles binding the wrists of the woman who knelt swaying, her head bowed. Her arms loosened and the child she'd been clutching to her chest toppled to the ground. Alex saw the play of power and without taking his eyes off the person in front of him he spoke.

"James, clear the council chamber. Someone get Master Healer Aaron. Now." He spoke softly so as not to startle the broken one who still hadn't looked up.

Please don't hurt her.

Alex dismissed the scrambling of those in the chamber to exit, it seemed none of them were inclined to argue.

I won't hurt her. Jess is my friend.

The young boy looked at him, then back at Jess who still knelt, swaying from side to side. She finally looked up and Alex could see her eyes were still blank even though they didn't dance with power anymore.

The boy looked at Jess then back at him.

She locked herself away and now she doesn't know how to get out.

Alex nodded as if that made sense, hoping it would reassure the lad. He hoped that Aaron would know what it meant since he certainly didn't. He was about to yell for the healer once more when the doors to the council room were opened and Aaron was ushered through. To give the healer credit he barely paused as he took in the sight of Jess kneeling on the floor, clearly in need of assistance before he picked up his pace.

Aaron observed Jess and looked at the small boy who still stood between them and Jess. The child showed no inclination to move as he looked at them all, distrust clear in every line of his body.

This is Master Healer Aaron, he can help Jess. Alex saw the boy look from him to Aaron, yet he didn't look convinced.

Alex would have cursed if he'd thought it would do any good. He would have just yanked the child out of the way but since Jess had clearly been protecting him, even while out of her mind he didn't think it would go down well. It was funny really. He could charm a whole bunch of strangers in a bar if he put his mind to it. Or at least convince them to move aside and leave him be. Yet he was stumped in how to deal with the boy. A throat cleared from behind him and Alex nearly swore as he realised that William was still here, or had returned when they'd worked out that Jess hadn't done anything.

My name is William. His brother knelt and smiled, holding out his hand.

The boy looked at William, his lips trembling. *I'm Jimmy. Can you help Jess? They hurt her.*

William nodded. *We are certainly going to do our best. Let Aaron tend to her, Jimmy.*

Jimmy reached out a trembling hand and William gathered him into his arms. Jess tracked the movement, tensing but otherwise didn't move.

"Don't take Jimmy out of her sight William. Jess is reacting on automatic, she's not really conscious right now." Alex looked over and saw the lad was tucked into William's arms and wondered how his brother did it.

Then he shook his head. William had always had a knack to calm frightened children who possessed more power than they should. His brother had successfully dealt with him his whole life after all. He still remembered William soothing him from all those nightmares he had woken up from when he was younger.

Alex put his hand on Aaron's chest as he went to move forward.

"Not yet Aaron, give me a moment."

Alex closed the distance between himself and Jess, reaching out to his friend, or at least the shell of his friend. He was terrified that her mind had been destroyed by whatever the Order had done to her. Jess's body trembled as he touched her; her eyes closed and she slumped. Alex staggered, catching Jess and lowering her to the ground, cradling her in his arms. He looked up as the doors to the room opened again and Kyle walked in, closely followed by Edward, Kat and Cal. The fact that they had just walked in quietly meant they had assessed the situation before barging in, not that he would have expected anything else.

"Aaron, the lad said Jess locked herself away, and doesn't know how to get out." Alex looked at Aaron, hoping the statement made sense to the healer.

Aaron nodded then looked at the child who still rested in William's arms although tears streaked down his face as he looked at Jess.

Can you show me Jimmy? I don't want to hurt Jess more than she already is. Aaron smiled and sent soothing thoughts at the boy.

Jimmy looked up at William who nodded. *You can trust Aaron. Jess trusts him, he's saved her life before.*

The child looked back at Aaron, his eyes still distrustful. *Chelsie took us to them. She helped them hurt Ty!*

Alex swallowed, closing his eyes briefly as the wave of anguish from Jimmy rolled over him. He caught the image that appeared in the boy's mind of a woman, a healer, tied to a strong sense of hurt. All Jimmy knew was that his parents had sent him and his brother away, given him to the healer. He'd heard his brother scream in the caverns, seen the dead being taken out. Healers had hurt his brother. A healer had hurt Jess, tried to make her wrong in the head like the others that lived, like his brother was now.

Jess trusts Aaron, she wouldn't have come here otherwise. William's mind voice was calm and soothing.

Please, help us to heal Jess from the hurt that has been done to her. She's my friend, it pains me to see her hurting. Alex looked at the lad and sent images into his mind, images of him, Kyle and Jess growing up and getting into mischief. Jimmy relaxed, then giggled, covering his mouth at some of the memories Alex shared with him. *Shhh... don't tell on us, we'll get in trouble.*

Jimmy looked up at William then back at Alex and giggled once more then nodded and looked at Aaron as the healer spoke.

Can you tell me what happened?

Jimmy shook his head, his head drooping. Then he looked at Jess's unconscious form and back at Aaron.

I can show you where she is.

Aaron's eyes widened and he nodded. *That will be helpful Jimmy. The more I know the better the treatment I can offer.*

Jimmy stared at Aaron who stiffened as the boy bombarded his mind with images and feelings, all of them forming a picture. As they broke communication Aaron staggered, only to be steadied by Kyle.

Ah, I see. Thank you Jimmy. I can help Jess now. He smiled at the lad and moved to Kyle's other side.

Alex looked at Aaron noting that while he laid his hands on Jess's chest he didn't place them on her temples, the usual favoured placement from every experience he'd had with a healer.

Aaron looked at him and spoke softly. "Jess was tortured by one who was healer trained. If I place my hands on her temples she may retreat further."

Alex nodded. "Do you need anything from me?"

Aaron smiled. "No, just being here is enough."

Alex watched fascinated as Aaron sank into a trance state, which he didn't normally do. Alex tried not to worry yet the longer it took the more he thought the worst. Seeing the state of his friend, shackles on her wrists and ankles, he could feel Jess's ribs close to her skin. She'd lost way too much weight.

"Somebody get those things off her." Alex jerked his chin at the manacles that still bound Jess.

He glanced around at the others and realised he wasn't the only one who was worried. Kyle sank to his knees and grasped one of Jess's hands in his own, the nightmare of his own experiences reflecting in his eyes.

"Don't you dare die on us Jess." His heartbroken whisper sounded overly loud in the mostly-empty courtroom.

Alex closed his eyes, echoing the sentiment in his head, throwing vengeance out into the world.

When I find you, you will pay for what you've done!

"Brother, can I at least sleep and eat first?"

Alex opened his eyes to see Jess looking up at him and started laughing weakly, relief flooding him. Kyle threw himself onto Jess hugging her fiercely.

53

THE LAST THING

Alex tried to keep his attention focused on the discussion being held at the security council, but the session had gone on longer than usual and he found he was getting irritated. Not that it was an unusual circumstance for him but he seriously had better things to do right now than pander to the whims of a bunch of lords and ladies. The bulk of the responsibility for the coming conflict rested on his shoulders, not theirs. Most of their valuable input had occurred weeks ago. Lately it was just a rehash of what they had already discussed. He was spinning his wheels until they could find the Order's hideout, which was the cause for the majority of his frustration.

"All of the men that can be spared across the realm have been recalled, Your Majesty. I think you'll find that in combination with the Elite and the personal guard units the lords are providing, you will have an overwhelming force at your disposal." Commander Janson glanced down at his notes then back up, his face grave.

"Thank you Commander, I'm sure your men will come in

useful." William looked around the table. "Now if there is no more business?"

"Fourth, how is Lady Jessalan?" Alex nearly groaned. With the arrival of William's consort, Lord Stanton wasn't the first of their peers to decide to make a play for Jess.

"Recovering, I'm sure she will appreciate your enquiry after her welfare." Any hope the matter was dealt with was in vain as the lord continued.

"I'm sure it was a mistake, but I tried to see Lady Jessalan today, to offer comfort while she recovers, only to be refused admission." Lord Stanton smiled at him.

Alex had to admit it was it looked genuine enough but, with this particular topic it was wasted.

"No mistake, those were my orders. Until I and the Master Healer," Alex nodded at Aaron who sat halfway down the table "have assured ourselves that Lady Jessalan has fully recovered she is not to be disturbed."

"Does she remember where she was imprisoned? It would be a big help if she could just give us a few details." Lady Cain's tone was condescending.

Alex stared at the pretentious lady, who'd only recently assumed her house's seat, down the far end of the table. He felt his temper start to rise at the implied insult, that Jess was deliberately withholding information but with effort restrained himself. Alex was almost grateful when Commander Janson cleared his throat into the silence that followed.

"Fourth, I know we discussed Sir Ryan and a squad of Elite staying here in the palace, to protect the king, once the campaign is launched against the rebels." Janson glanced up, his gaze sweeping around the table.

"We did discuss that contingency, more as a courtesy than a need." Alex kept his gaze steady on the commander. He had no desire to rehash this conversation given he knew William's opinion on the matter. Which was, he was going to participate in any battle when it happened.

"Of course Fourth. I just thought I'd mention, going over our numbers, well if you think Sir Ryan, with his skills and the extra squad of Elite will be of more use to you during the battle? Well, I'm sure the King's Guard will have sufficient numbers here, in order to maintain the security of the palace and guard His Majesty."

Alex stared at the commander for a moment before answering, endeavouring to keep his tone even. "I'll take that under consideration Commander, thank you for the offer."

William looked around the table. "If there's nothing else?"

It was a throwaway question, which he made obvious this time since he stood as he said it. Alex stood just a moment behind him. The scrape of chairs on the floor intruded on the silence that followed that question as the other members of the security council caught up and stood. Alex walked out of the security council meeting on William's shoulder, both of them turning to walk down the corridor towards the Complex of the Fourth.

ALEX COULD BARELY STOP himself from pacing. He knew his frustration was born of the necessity of planning this battle, the need to make sure everything went off exactly as planned. It didn't help that he was trying to at least appear calm for William's sake.

William had always been a calming influence, at least until he had undergone a forced transition. Now he battled with himself, as many did going through transition, but it was worse for William in some ways since his was forced. He had never been meant to be numbered amongst the Kin and the fear he would go mad because of it like their mother had been very real.

Added to that was pressure of being elevated to king well before anyone expected, their father having still been fit and healthy and expected to rule for years yet if Amelia hadn't cut him down. There was also the wrinkle of a Consort that he didn't want being thrust upon him. With all of that William, had been struggling with his composure.

Giving up, Alex growled in the back of his throat, standing from the chair he'd been pretending to lounge in and he began to pace the length of the sitting room. All their actual attack planning was now being done within the confines of the Complex of the Fourth.

"How is Jess? Really?" Regardless of all his issues it was William who was calm right now.

Alex smiled grimly. "She's cooperating with the healers."

William turned to stare at him. "I already get that official line. They used Amelia to help torture her, that will take time to recover from. Now I hear she seems to be convinced Amelia's still trapped in her head as well. What do you think?"

"I think we can't do anything about Amelia until we find the Order. When we do, she will try and kill us." Alex had to admit the idea troubled him, more than he cared to think about.

Before William could respond the doors opened and both of them turned to look. Jess trailed in, still in her sleepwear. Kyle held out his hand to her and she walked across to the lounge he was on and slumped into it without ceremony.

"Jess is fine, just a little exhausted, thanks for asking though." Jess looked at them both, troubled. "Amelia is still in there. If she'd hadn't risked what little of herself that remains, I'd be their creature right now. "

"Which is why you are still having nightmares, which is understandable." Energy flowed from Kyle, soothing and restful.

"Fine friend you are, giving away all my secrets." Jess's tone was playful, yet with an edge of fragility. She didn't rebuff Kyle's efforts though, which she was perfectly capable of doing.

Kyle wrapped his arms around her, kissing her cheek. "With sleep and rest you really will be fine. In the meantime, we will be there to chase away the nightmares."

"It's only fair, you helped chase away mine all these years." Alex sent his own reassurance to his childhood friend.

He and Kyle traded glances. They were both on the same page on this one. When they found the Order they were going to do their level best to destroy them. This was one organisation that was not going to rear its ugly head again if they had anything to say about it. Which right now, thankfully, they did.

"Alex is right, Amelia will try to kill us, but I have to try now that I know we were wrong. Damn it Alex, I'm sorry. I should have trusted your instincts, but against everything I thought I knew, there is a part of her still there." Jess closed her eyes as she took a shaky breath not bothering to even try to hide her distress.

Alex looked up as Isabella and Damien appeared in the sitting room without ceremony, followed closely by Edward. He looked at Jess, having the sinking feeling if he didn't come up with something, Jess would go after Amelia alone. They may not be so lucky for her to escape a second time.

"If the others are willing to take the risk, well we already had a plan in place to capture one of the Sundered." Alex looked around the small group.

"Admittedly that didn't work all that well last time." Kyle look embarrassed.

"Well, that wasn't entirely your fault, it's not like you planned to take a break from your own mind." Edward smiled at Kyle, then his expression turned grave. "I take it, when we find her we are going to try and capture rather than kill Amelia?"

Alex nodded. “Then Aaron can hopefully assess her.”

They all nodded agreement, although Alex could tell that most of those present didn’t actually believe Amelia was still locked inside her own head. They were trying to break Jess’s mind, but he had no doubt it had just been one of the tools in their arsenal. Still for Jess’s sake and his own if he had to admit, everyone was willing to try.

“How did your meeting with Olivia go? Do you think she will help in the conflict with the Order?” Alex pushed his mind away from the matter of Amelia, going back to why they were meeting in the first place.

“Not sure yet. She might, she tells me every day their numbers dwindle as the Order tracks them down and takes them.” Kyle shrugged. “I’ll keep up the contact.”

Alex nodded and turned his mind back to the problem of containing the Order as a whole. It was one thing to safely trap one Sundered, rather than kill it outright. If the Order had the numbers that they feared it would be impossible to stop them all. Once they launched their attack, there was nothing to stop them from fleeing, which meant this madness could and probably would spring up again.

“Damien, Isabella, the barrier that surrounds Ilarith, could you raise such a thing again?”

Alex spun to see Jess staring intently at the brother and sister. It seemed he and Jess were both considering the same problem. The pair looked at each other and shrugged before looking around the room.

“We could, but…”

Isabella’s eyes tracked over to his own. “It only takes a higher level of power to perceive the barrier.”

“There are some who would work out its properties as soon as they saw it.” Damien shifted in his seat and looked almost apologetically at them all.

Alex crossed the room back towards them all. “Show me.”

He was aware his tone was short but didn't care. He knew that not only Isabella but Damien as well knew him well enough to know what he meant.

It happened like this.

Isabella's voice filled his mind, with Damien's presence, the pair of them showing him a series of fleeting images that burst into his mind one after the other in quick succession.

Alex chewed his lip and slumped back into his chair, aware of the eyes of everyone in the room being on him as small little discs of power materialised in front of him, one after the other moulding briefly into different shapes before bursting as he thought through the problem. Playing with the power, he concentrated, weaving the different strands together to form different types of barriers and shields, dismissing them almost before he'd finished.

"Those who can't detect it won't be able to pass through, but..." Damien shrugged.

The bubble of power Alex had been playing with burst as he finally focused on Damien. Slowly he turned his gaze on Isabella.

When you found me, after Kyle stabbed me, how did you penetrate the white nothingness?

Isabella looked at him, startled. *I didn't, I felt you and called you. You broke your own barrier and came to me.*

Alex stood up. Closing his eyes, he thought back to that time, the awful white nothingness. The lack of power that had surrounded him. Trying not to think about what he was doing too much, Alex wove the power around all of them in the room, both calling power and repelling it at the same time, using the power within to fuel the bubble that surrounded them. It wasn't any one type of power but a combination of all the power that surrounded them, threaded through with that shining white power. A sense of stillness descended, of the world around them being dead.

Edward stood and looked around, then shuddered.

"Alex, what have you done?"

"Can you see it? Feel the barrier around us?" Alex looked at his uncle intently, grinning as he shook his head.

"No, I know you've done something, I felt you start to manipulate the veil, but I can't see it." Edward shuddered again and ran his hand through his hair as he looked around.

Damien stared, wide-eyed. Standing up, he paced one cautious step after the other, raising his hand. Alex saw the moment Damien's hand hit the barrier, and the fleeting shock that flickered on his face only to be replaced by curiosity a moment later.

"How have you done this? *What* have you done?"

Alex looked to Kyle and then Jess, who both came to him slowly, but unlike the others they looked around curiously. Alex's eyebrow rose.

Kyle grinned. "I see it, but I'm not sure I caught what you did."

Jess nodded in agreement. "Show us?"

Alex shared the memory of what he'd done with his friends and the others as well—not that he fully understood it himself. He saw a look of understanding dawn on their faces. Their eyes started to glow as they reached out with their own power, contributing to his own, proving at least that they could not only see what he'd done, but recreate it.

Equally obvious was that the others, while they seemed to understand what he'd just shown them, they still couldn't counter it.

Isabella shifted uncomfortably in her chair. "Alex, could you take it down now?"

Alex walked over to her and pulled her up from her chair.

Breathe. I couldn't work out how to get through it the first time either. Like this.

Embracing Isabella in his own power, he guided her mind

through the nothingness to reach the power on the other side of the barrier. He felt her gasp and relief flood her as she suddenly broke through.

Damien, who'd been following along with his own mind, echoed her, sighing as he too worked a way through the barrier. Interestingly William seemed the least affected of all of them. While he too tested the barrier, he didn't seem at all uneasy, unlike those of them with more power.

Jess's eyes glittered. "I think we've found out how to contain our rebels."

54

MADNESS

Joanna flashed through the veil, following that whispering voice that she despised and feared. The world around her rumbled, dark and menacing masses forming as she passed, grey, black and red. What looked like lightning struck around her, yet she knew it wasn't lightning. It was easy to ignore the surging energy. She knew it wouldn't hurt her. One word ran though her head, over and over on repeat.

Kill.

Her goal was clear. She had to track down and kill the monster before it hurt Alex. A thrill of fear ran though her, thinking of harm coming to her little boy. She *had* to protect him from harm. Sensing movement from another in the veil, she thrust out her hand, throwing power, shunting the stranger away. She didn't dwell on how she knew about manipulating the power. Everything she did was running on instinct. Right now, she had one goal.

Joanna paused, her head swinging around as she cast around trying to pinpoint where that whispering voice lived.

Fear me, I am your death.

Joanna spun around snarling, the veil around her rumbling and roiling as she accelerated through it, certain now exactly where her enemy was.

~

RYAN GROANED, looking at the empty chair in the garden where he'd left Joanna. He'd only been distracted for a moment—a moment long enough for her to disappear. Alex had given him one job, and it was a job he apparently sucked at. Quickly scanning the palace and surrounds confirmed what he'd dreaded: she hadn't just moved to another part of the gardens here at the palace.

She was gone.

Alex was going to kill him when he found out.

He looked around, and seeing the Elite on guard made him feel slightly guilty. He knew they hated it when they were left behind. Even though he figured that looking after him was the least of their duties, member of the Companion's Cohort or not, he didn't reckon he was all that important. At least it wasn't Matthew on duty; that would have made him feel even more guilty after everything that had been done for him. Ryan shook his head. Delaying was not getting him any closer to finding Joanna and getting her back to the palace where she belonged, preferably before Alex showed up and worked out she was missing.

Or the king.

Ryan knew the colour must have drained out of his face at that thought.

Without giving it another thought, he transitioned into the veil, stretching out his senses to locate Joanna. He swore. She'd managed to cover quite a distance while he'd been dithering. She wasn't hard to detect since she wasn't shielding her presence at all. He could tell from the churning energy surrounding her that the sweet, reasonable Joanna had disappeared. In her place it seemed a murderous Joanna had appeared. While her many personalities were endlessly fascinating, he was horrified that death was on her mind. Muttering another fervent curse, he sped after her.

His eyes widened in shock as he was hammered with a physical blow. It flung him back and he hit the ground, rolling a distance before he stopped. Ryan looked up and found himself on the side of the road. The force of her blow had flung him from the veil back to the real world.

Ryan looked up at the startled travellers on the road who'd backed away in fear. Two of them drew swords and stood before the others, their intent to protect them clear. Ryan nearly laughed. He may not be as good as the Elite, let alone Lord Kyle, but even he found the way they waved their swords around funny. He assumed they thought it was menacing.

He picked himself up from the ground and dusted himself off. He raised his hands in a placating gesture. They stared at him and lowered their swords. He was rather startled as they placed their hands first on heart, then forehead, a sign of respect often given to the Fourth. He guessed the villagers recognised the Fourth's crest on his vest.

"My apologies for startling you." Ryan tried his best to look reassuring. "I'm sorry, there is a matter I need to attend to."

He paid the group of travellers no further mind and re-entered the veil, careful this time to tighten his shields. Joanna was a law unto herself when she went off in a spiral of madness. He wasn't quite sure how she was able to do some of the things she could do. It was probably because she didn't know she wasn't meant to be able to do it in the first place. Of course, Alex wasn't much better, so it shouldn't surprise him.

Locating her wasn't all that difficult.

~

JOANNA FROZE in place at seeing the dark, malevolent presence of her tormentor, the one who'd broken his oath in his sworn duty to protect her and her son. She could see others, many of them. She paused and snarled in frustration. If she appeared in the middle of that room, the others would intervene and he would live. That would leave the traitor free to go after Alex. That wasn't something she could allow.

Traitor, I'll not let you hurt my boy.

Deep in her own mind, she wept. She'd failed Alex once, but not again. The one who promised further pain and suffering for her and her son would die. Joanna stilled as he became aware of her presence. Frustrated at his lack of response, she snarled and drew her own power.

BRIAN'S EYES OPENED, and he stared up at the rough rock ceiling above him as he had done so many times before. She was nearby. He could feel her, hear her chant in his head. A smile stretched his lips; she'd come to kill him. None of the controllers were nearby. Normally he would be unable to take this opportunity, but they hadn't chained him since they'd changed his medication. Of late they had begun to reduce the amount they dosed him with so he could feel the veil. However, they'd also commanded him to stay here, so he did. He was incapable of disobeying that order, he'd been their creature for too long. He wrestled within his own mind against the compulsions on him. He hoped that with the recent change he could break free, even for just a moment.

He felt power surge around him as he heard her scream with rage. He laughed. Eyes throughout the cavern flashed open, yet like him they had no free will to do anything except lie there. All of the thousands of enslaved, aware there was one of power nearby yet incapable of doing anything. There was no way he could have gone to her to meet the death he wanted, longed for. That didn't stop her from grabbing him. He'd been terribly afraid she'd come for him in the camp. That would mean her death or worse. The former queen may have been driven out of her mind with madness but even so, she wasn't stupid.

Finding himself in the veil, he faced her. She burned so brightly with power that if he'd been capable of it, he would have knelt before her to accept his fate. What seemed like a lifetime ago, the time in-between a living hell, she'd been his queen. It had been his duty to protect her.

Until the Order had taken him. That had been the ultimate, soul-destroying betrayal of everything he'd been. Or at least it was when he had the presence of mind to realise what a monster he'd become.

Brian saw her eyes flare as she drew both her dagger and power. Without a controller compelling him to fight and kill, he didn't even try to resist. He bowed his head as she struck. Knowing his release was imminent, he smiled as his body crumpled at her feet.

Thank you for your mercy, my Queen. I'm sorry I failed you.

RYAN SHOWED a little more caution in his approach, not wanting her to fling him out of the veil this time. Not that he was certain how she'd managed it the first time. Ryan paused, frowning as he noticed that Joanna had come to a halt. She stared at something, although he couldn't tell what it was that had attracted her attention.

He felt the colour drain from his face as she gathered her power, drawing someone to her. As Joanna faced off against one of the Sundered that she had inexplicably drawn to her, Ryan drew his own weapons and power. Closing the distance between them, he had the sinking feeling he would not make it to her in time. He saw her strike and to his shock her opponent made no move to defend himself. The Sundered just allowed her to kill him, his last words to her echoing through the veil.

Ryan walked up to her carefully as she sank to her knees next to the Sundered. As she looked down at the creature, her face was blank, and the fire died from her eyes. He knelt carefully at her side and eased her dagger from her hand. She made no effort to resist him. He placed the dagger, safely contained by a spare loop of leather, on his belt. Her voice sounded in his head, perfectly calm, as if she hadn't just killed one of the Sundered Ones.

He said he would kill Alex.

Ryan looked from the crumpled form of the Sundered back to Joanna and urged her up to her feet.

He's dead, Joanna. He can't hurt Alex now.

He kept his own tone light, not wanting to startle her. He felt nothing but compassion for this woman who had once been queen. She'd led a life of torment and madness at the hands of the Order and the Sundered who'd plagued her nightmares. Ryan finally looked towards what looked like a village nestled at the base of the mountain and froze, his breath catching in his throat. Throwing as tight a shield around them both as he could manage, he pulled them both away from the village, the estate that towered over it and the field of tents that spread out beyond them both. Ryan was grateful that Joanna seemed to have returned to one of her more compliant personas and did not resist.

He wracked his brain, wanting to get Joanna back to the relative safety of the palace, but he didn't want to let this place and its occupants out of his sight. It would be easy for the Order to up and move camp. They had more than proven they could move around at will in large numbers.

Ryan sighed and hoped Alex wouldn't rush in trying to take

the encampment by himself. He'd learned Alex could be a little impulsive and he didn't really know how the Fourth was going to react. He'd picked up enough from Joanna to know that she believed the Sundered she'd just killed was the same one that had tried to take her life all those years ago. Ryan had no doubt at all that Alex would also pick up those details from his mother just as easily. How he would react to the death of the monster from his own nightmares as a child was anyone's guess. He bit his lip before taking a breath and reaching out with his mind.

Alex, I've found the Order's encampment. Or rather, your mother did.

55

DISPUTE

Ryan waited with Joanna for what seemed like a lifetime. For once she was calm and compliant, although she kept throwing distrustful looks over towards the Sundered she had killed, almost like she was checking that he wasn't healing and about to come back to life and try to attack her. He had to admit he was keeping an eye on him as well. The Sundered had a nasty habit of not being dead when they should. Still, he was certain this one actually was dead, even if he didn't know how he'd come to that belief.

Ryan looked up startled as Alex appeared with Kyle and Jess. He felt certain he must be staring at them bug-eyed. There wasn't the usual surge that he associated with Kin arriving through the veil. Then again, he'd noticed that Alex tended to be a law to himself where using the power was concerned, much like his mother. At least Alex wasn't crazy. Heeding his warning, all of them were tightly shielded. Joanna, who'd been at his side one moment, was suddenly in Alex's arms. Ryan nearly swore. She shouldn't have been able to do that either. He should have seen her move.

I'm sorry. I'm sorry. He said he was going to kill you. I couldn't let him kill you.

Ryan saw Alex stiffen as he caught the other information Joanna unwittingly sent—that 'he' was the Sundered who'd tried to kill her all those years ago, the one responsible for the shared nightmares they'd suffered over the years.

Shhh, Mother. It's all right, I'm not angry with you.

Kyle closed the distance to the body of the fallen Sundered and with a quick, expert thrust of his long knife he plunged it up from the abdomen towards the heart. Ryan knew he'd gone red in embarrassment. He hadn't even thought to make certain he wasn't getting up again. The Kin could heal a lot of things, but not a strike to the heart or the loss of a head. The heart was the easier kill shot. Kyle wiped his blade on the fallen Sundered's shirt before standing to look at the village.

Jess moved to stand near him.

You are right, this is where they are hiding, Ryan. Well done.

Alex pushed his mother back and looked at her. Ryan could sense that he was sending soothing emotions at her.

Go with Ryan back to the palace, Mother. After we've checked this place out, I'll come back and we'll have that tea.

Ryan watched fascinated as the burning power that flickered in her eyes and ran along her body melted away from Joanna. Now she looked unremarkable. Kin, but unremarkable. Even more telling was that Alex didn't pay the elemental fire any consideration at all.

Come, my lady, let's go back to the palace and let Alex do his work.

Ryan paused momentarily when Joanna held out her hand before he stepped forward to offer his arm. He felt slightly foolish, since it was an old courtly gesture and despite the king's pronouncement he didn't actually feel like a peer of the realm. Either way, she seemed cooperative right now so he wasn't going to complain. He pulled her with him as they made their way back to the palace, only this time he swore one of the servants could go fetch the tea. He wasn't letting Joanna out of his sight again.

~

ALEX WAITED as Ryan left with his mother, then closed the distance between him and Jess who stood staring at the castle below. Placing his hand on his friend's shoulder he felt the tremors that shuddered through her.

Jess are you alright?

Jess wiped a tear away, not bothering to even try to hide the equal parts of pain and fear on her face.

It's not just the army camped out front. This is where they kept me, below in the caverns. See them?

Alex turned to look back at the village and castle. He could see the fires of the army out front, that was bad enough. There were more men camped here than he liked. But under the surface, in vast caverns below the castle he could see the bright fitful glows of the Sundered, most of them muted. The sight made him pale. There were thousands of them.

I see them.

He returned his gaze to the castle itself and the flag flying prominently from the battlements. His eyes narrowed.

Unless I am very much mistaken, this is Lord Kastler's estate.

Kyle looked at him and nodded.

You are not mistaken.

He is a little weasel of a lord, although he stayed away from me for the most part. Jess's tone was empty of emotion.

William is not going to be happy.

Jess and Kyle snorted in amusement at the understatement.

We should get back and report. Before he manages to convince someone to bring him here.

Kyle groaned at the thought but did not dispute the fact

that William might do exactly that if he didn't find out what was going on soon. Unfortunately with Rosalinda and the other Sylannians in the Palace he might just be able to do it.

ALEX REALISED that his prediction about William not being happy with this particular report had been an understatement. Alex could sense the cold waves of anger that rolled off him and Alex hastily extended his own personal shield to encompass his brother's suite, smiling tightly as both Kyle and Jess did the same. They didn't need every sensitive soul in the palace aware that their king was suffering a bout of white hot rage. While they had known they'd find the Order holed up somewhere, it was unexpected for them to be not only at a lords house but in the very home of one of the great houses.

"Kastler is harbouring the Order?" William spun and glared at him.

"It does appear that way." Alex didn't take his brothers glare personally, he knew it wasn't him that his brother was mad at.

"You know he tried to convince Elizabeth to dispose of me?"

Alex spun to stare at his brother, only realising his own anger had surged to match William's when Jess and Kyle threw him equally alarmed looks.

He shuddered, feeling his brother seethe as he once again turned his mind to the betrayal of one of his sworn lords. Alex tried hard to suppress his own anger at finding this petty little lord had threatened his sister and his brother's life.

"I'm going with you all during the attack on the estate."

"No, you are not." Alex stared at his brother and his lips compressed into a thin line.

"I'm the king damn it Alex and I say I'm going!" William's face grew stubborn, his eyes narrowing as he snapped.

This time Alex knew the anger was directed at him and he

stood, coming face to face with William. "Yes you are the king, so start acting like it. Damn it William think!"

"It's my duty...."

"It's your duty as king to stay here, to stay safe. Do you want more of our people dead because they are throwing themselves in front of you?" Alex knew that was a cruel accusation to throw in William's face. He'd seen his brother's nightmares from the assassination of their father.

William's eyes widened in shock and he stepped back. "How is it any different with you being there? You think your men won't put themselves between you and harm?"

"I'm the Fourth, William. It is my job to risk my life, just as it is yours to stay safe and lead our people."

Alex glared at his brother as he opened his mouth to argue, noting the uneasy silence from all the witnesses but ignoring it. On this occasion he was right. It was his duty to protect the people. To protect his king. On this occasion he would not just give in to William's will. Alex's lips thinned, but he kept his own roiling anger carefully behind his shields.

"Damn it Alex, I have a right to face them."

"You do, when the battle is over. Trust me William, I'll have the Elite lock you in one of your own cells if I have to. You will not be at the battle, I will send someone when the battle is over, judgment over your lords will lay with you." Alex spun and walked out of his brother's suite before he could raise any more arguments, aware that Kyle and Jess followed him silently.

The guards who'd been on the doors carefully kept their eyes straight ahead, but Alex knew they would have heard the yelling match between him and the king. It was also likely all the servants in this section of the palace had been party to it as well. Alex nearly groaned at the thought of the rumours that were bound to fly through the serving staff in the palace. Once they all started to gossip then it was only a matter of time before the other residents of the palace knew as well.

The doors to his own domain opened promptly as he stormed through them and when they closed behind him Alex turned back to see both Kyle and Jess staring at him. His eyes narrowed.

What?

Jess raised her eyebrow at him. *Perhaps just a little harsh?*

I know but I'm also right. I won't have him put himself or others at risk on the battlefield.

Alex spun and retreated to his own rooms, leaving the arguments behind. This was one occasion where he would not be moved. His brother would not put his life at risk and unfortunately for his brother. King or not, as the Fourth, in this particular battle it was him that had the last word. Whether his brother liked that or not was immaterial, as long as he stayed safe.

56

CONFESSION

Simon ran his fingers through his hair and paced the length of his sitting room. His own people stayed well clear, knowing how agitated he was. He paused, looking out the windows over the city; he could just see the outline of palace in the distance. Normally the view over the city calmed him, but tonight it had no effect. It hadn't since he'd discovered the truth about the so-called Scholar Clements.

He stared at the distant palace, and with a frustrated growl he pulled the veil to him, moving along the veiled paths in that direction. He swore explosively, aware there was no one around to hear him.

Damn you, Kevin!

He'd spent the intervening years building up a life for himself. He was no one's saviour—he was self-aware enough to know he never had been—but he wasn't evil about to rise and inflict itself on the world, either. There was just no clean way he could see out of this particular problem.

Simon groaned. He knew what he had to do, but to take that path he would be betraying the one man who'd been his friend, or what passed for one, for a very long time. He wasn't sure if that would make him a worse person or a better one.

He didn't have to look for the people he needed. He knew where they were; his people sent him daily reports on their whereabouts. He'd spent so many years keeping track, and old habits died hard.

It didn't take him long to get to the palace and find those he sought. They were all conveniently congregated in the Complex of the Fourth. Simon groaned again. He knew he had to decide one way or another, and fast, or it would likely be taken out of his hands. Unlike Kevin, those below were not sloppy—well, not since the death of the king they weren't, anyway. He knew from what his own spies told him that one of them regularly checked for intruders, sending their powers out in a sweeping scan to detect someone like him hiding in the veil. Of course, they shouldn't be able to spot him if he was carefully shielded. Looking for the 'dead' patch only worked in the real world, not if someone was in the veil, yet somehow the rules didn't seem to apply to them the way they did to him. He'd always thought Edward along with Kat and Cal were scarily powerful, but they paled compared to Alex, Kyle and Jess. The only thing the younger three were missing was time to grow and learn.

Simon shuddered as he felt a wave of power roll over him. He blanched as the power paused and he had the distinct impression of a pair of green eyes narrowing, and that power gathering around him. Simon swallowed. This is what some of his talented men had reported, and why he now resorted to using some of his normal human spies in the kitchens. Simon stepped through the curtain in the veil, without undue haste, his hands in clear sight, aware that all gazes in the room swung to him. The power that started gathering in response was breathtaking, if also frightening.

He waited patiently while they all relaxed—marginally

—although he noted all of them kept their personal shields up. Simon almost smiled, not sure if he should feel flattered or not that this lot thought they needed them against him.

"Simon, this is a rather unexpected visit." Edward appraised him, his expression guarded.

"I have a confession to make. If you could all hear me out before you kill me, it would probably be worth your time." Simon swallowed as the eyes of all those present in the room narrowed.

It was Alex whose face cleared first, and he gestured to a spare seat before sitting back down in the comfortable lounge. Kyle and Jess looked at Alex, and Simon could tell something passed between them before they followed his lead and sat as well.

"So, confess."

Simon couldn't tell anything from Alex's expression. He noted that Edward, Kat and Cal all sat as well. Normally he'd be more relieved, but he could see that none of them had relaxed at all. The six sets of eyes that stared at him intently were more than a little unnerving.

"The Order is at Lord Kastler's estate. I've known for some time." Simon took a breath trying to settle his nerves.

"We've recently become aware of their location. Is there more?"

Simon looked over at Kyle and swallowed. In a way, the fact that they knew where the Order was made him feel marginally better, even if he now burned with curiosity as to how they'd found out. He looked over to Edward.

"Kevin, you remember him from the Cohort?" Simon paused as Edward, Kat and Cal all nodded. "Well, he's involved. He's the one that helped refine the drug the Order has been using on those with the power of the veil."

"We know that too. There was that little fuss at the Healers'

Guild a few months back prior to the king's death." This from Kyle, whose voice was cold.

The only thing that kept Simon from fleeing was that Kyle hadn't drawn his weapons and still looked in control. He'd come a long way from the man who'd nearly lost himself to permanent thraldom. Simon looked down, breaking the eye contact.

"There is another. The leader of the Killian Order, Scholar Clements. He's not human, and I doubt he was ever really a scholar. He's of the Elder, I'm certain of it, and taking great pains to hide who and what he is. I tried to warn Kevin, but he didn't believe me." That last he got out in a rush before any of them could interrupt him and rob him of his will to confess everything. Somehow it was important to him for them to know that he had tried to warn Kevin.

Simon looked around the group and frowned. There wasn't even a hint of the shock he'd expected to see. He hadn't expected panic, not from this lot, but he'd really expected *some* sort of reaction from them.

"Is that what made you come forward? An Elder pretending to be human with a toxin able to control or kill the majority of those of us who are of the Kin?" Alex picked up the drink next to him that he hadn't touched the entire time Simon had been here and took a sip.

Simon swallowed and nodded. "I'm no one's hero, I've killed—"

"So have I. I've even uttered similar words. I'm no hero. Yet people persist in thinking I am one." Alex smiled, although it didn't reach his eyes. It was the first flicker of emotion Simon had seen.

"Kevin is one thing. He's not really as powerful as he thinks, and his ambition exceeds his capability. I figured Edward would find out and deal with him sooner or later. I even told him that back before you all hit the Healers' Guild. This other one, though, Clements—if that is his real name. I wouldn't want someone like me or Kevin who, unlike us, has access to *real* power, in control with no-one around with the power or the ability to counter him." Simon swallowed.

"That is an awfully blunt assessment of yourself, Simon." Jess was regarding him steadily.

Simon almost wished they would yell and scream. Condemn him. Something. Anything other than this stillness.

"I'm the Skull Lord, I rule over the thieves and scoundrels in this world, yet I'm still constrained by a higher authority." Simon dipped his head towards William. He hadn't failed to notice the king had been sitting quietly listening just as intently as the others. "I have still tried my best. My people all have a roof to sleep under, food, clothing, and those with the power of the veil that might have been killed by their own ignorant relatives have found shelter and training in my ranks. I still don't fool myself that I should be ruler over all. I'm just not that nice a person."

Simon relaxed at that last; on this he had sure footing. He knew his world and made no apologies for the life he led. In some ways he found it suited him much better than pretending to be something he wasn't. Yes, he was a killer, but other than that rather regrettable time back during the Sundered War, he'd lived by his own set of ethics. If anything, that incident, on reflection, had taught him why someone like him should not rule. He'd worked in his own way all this time to set up his own boundaries and morality.

"Does our foreknowledge of it make it easier that you just betrayed your friend?" Kat was looking at him intently. She had that look on her face, a look he recognised from old. A look that said she knew far more than she was saying.

Simon laughed, hearing the bitterness in it. "No. By coming to you with this, I just broke one of the few rules I'd managed to keep in my life: never betray my own."

William stirred in his chair, drawing Simon's attention. That was rightfully his king even if he'd never personally pledged allegiance.

"Yet you were a member of the Companion's Cohort. We are your own."

Alex looked at his brother and then relaxed. "You simply got lost on the way a little longer than some of us."

"I am told you gave shelter and protection on occasion over the years for our mother when she showed up." William was looking at him intently, causing Simon to squirm in his chair.

"I... Well, she's... forgive me, but she is mad, driven mad by the nature of her transition. It could have happened to any of us. She was the queen. I simply watched over her until Ed came to take her back to the safety of his estate."

"You owed her nothing, yet you sheltered her anyway. You have our thanks for that." William smiled at him as Simon swallowed convulsively.

"If you'd come to me when you first knew what Kevin was up to, so many things could have been averted." Edward's voice was harsh and grating.

Simon was about to answer when Alex intervened.

"Yes, it might have. Yet I can't help but feel Clements, whoever he is, would have gotten away." Alex and Edward stared at each other. Simon was struck by how similar they were. Both the Fourth, generations apart, yet bound in duty.

They sat in silence and Simon finally stood up, figuring they had no more questions for him, at least for now. William stirred again, looking up at him.

"Do not think to cross the Fourth again, Simon." The king waved his hand in clear dismissal.

Simon looked at the king, confused. "Don't cross the Fourth? What about you?"

William smiled. "I'm the king, Simon. You are the Skull Lord, just by breathing you cross the crown. The Fourth, however, has an entirely different role and rules. He has jurisdiction over the Kin. You are his problem."

He shuddered as he retreated into the veil. This king was dangerous. He couldn't help but wonder which set of Fourth and Companions the king would send after him if he did manage to displease the Crown again.

"Simon, wait."

"Yes, Fourth?" Letting go of the veil, Simon glanced at Alex.

"Could you get the local farmers and dependants from around the Kastler estate to safety, under the cover of night?"

Simon frowned and chuckled weakly. "Saving people is generally not a line of work the League of Skulls participates in, but yes, I think we could."

"What about the servants in the estate itself?" Simon swung his gaze to Kyle, who was looking at him intently.

"Some, yes. It probably won't surprise you to know that Kastler isn't very popular with his servants or the people on his lands. They battle to survive with what they have left after the tithe. Even Kastler will know something is wrong if he wakes up to an empty estate house."

Simon jumped as a throat cleared near him. He found himself looking at Kyle's manservant, who'd been adroitly filling everyone's glasses and seeing the snack trays were kept stocked up without really being noticed. If Simon's information was correct, the man was a relative of sorts, a bastard child of one of Lord Kyle's uncles, totally loyal to the Strafford family and, rumour had it, excellent with a blade.

"You could take me in." Bennett transferred his steady gaze from him to Lord Kyle.

"Bennett, I know you think you can do this..."

Bennett cut Kyle off. "I can. Well, for as long as it takes you all to attack. The Skull Lord here is correct. Even Kastler is going to know something is up if all his servants are missing when he wakes."

Simon shook his head at the servant. “What if Kastler recognises you?”

“Not likely. Joshua maybe, but me? He wouldn’t have had much cause to notice me.” Bennett shrugged. “If he does, I’ll gladly stick a dagger between his ribs.”

Simon felt his eyes widen and he swallowed. He’d almost forgotten how obscenely loyal people were to the Rathadons and Straffords.

Almost.

“Let me know when and I’ll do what I can.”

Seeing no objection, Simon nodded and gathered the veil to himself, fleeing to the somewhat dubious safety of his own lair.

57

IDENTITY

Alex stirred as the discussion started going around in circles again, this time about Clements—his identity and motivation. Kevin was a known entity thanks to the input from Cal and Kat, whose opinions had been scathing. Clements had turned into another matter entirely since it was discovered his entire backstory had been a lie, largely due to Jess's efforts. Even she had reached a wall in her investigation, with no loose threads that any of them could think of to follow up on. Simon's information had shone a little more light on the issue, yet still left them wondering who the man, or rather Kin, was. The image that had flashed into Alex's mind from Amelia when she'd thought of her master occurred to him.

"So according to Simon, Clements must be Kin, and likely powerful enough to be Elder," Alex mused.

Jess shook her head. "He is also an elderly man. I haven't seen a Kin yet of any power who ages. It's that self-healing thing."

"Don't jump down my throat, but during one of those regrettable liaisons with Amelia..." Alex held up his hand as his friends started to protest. "When she spoke of her master, an image of Clements and another younger man that I didn't recognise flashed in her mind, along with a strong sense of fear."

"Are you sure the younger one wasn't Kevin?"

"I'm certain." Alex recalled the dual image, showing his friends what he'd seen.

Kyle and Jess both shook their heads. Neither of them recognised the younger man.

Kyle shrugged. "Show him to Edward. After all, they recognised Kevin, and if that other is Kin or Elder, he might know."

"Also Damien and Isabella, perhaps. They've been around longer. For that matter, have we even shown them the image of Clements?" Jess looked at him with her eyebrow raised.

Alex groaned, embarrassed that he hadn't thought of checking with Isabella sooner. Of course he'd rather not have to explain to her the part about the images of the other man coming from Amelia's mind while he had been sleeping with her.

Lady Cain shrugged. "Does it ultimately matter who he really is? We know where they are now."

Alex turned to stare at the lady. "It will matter a great deal when we engage with the Order."

"None of us desire to get ambushed unexpectedly by an Elder we didn't know about if we can avoid it." The condescension in Kyle's tone was clear.

Alex shook himself, recognising in himself a delaying tactic. It was best to get this over and done with.

Isabella, do you have a moment to spare? Alex smiled at her immediate acceptance despite the circumstances.

It didn't take long before the door to the conference room opened and, in a rarity for Isabella, she actually walked in.

Alex stood up and crossed the room to greet her, kissing her on the cheek even though they'd only been apart for a few hours.

"What do you need, Alex?" Isabella kept her eyes on him, choosing to ignore the others in the room.

Alex ducked his head and took a breath before looking back up at her.

"You remember we are looking for the Order? That its leader is a man who was my old tutor?" Alex didn't look at his friends or the others in the room.

Isabella nodded. "Of course."

"Can I show you his image and that of another man, a younger one? We thought if either of them was Elder, you might recognise them." Alex swallowed as he looked at her.

Isabella's eyes narrowed, her head cocking to one side. "That isn't something you need permission for, Alex. What aren't you telling me?"

Alex felt his cheeks heat. "The image of Clements and the younger man flashed in Amelia's mind when she was thinking about her master."

The silence stretched between them for a moment. Alex didn't realise that he was holding his breath until she nodded in understanding. He was relieved to see no anger evident in her expression.

"Show me what you perceived from her mind, Alex. All of it."

Alex smiled, but knew it didn't reach his eyes. There was nothing about this that made him happy. Indeed, Isabella seemed to be coping with Amelia being thrown in her face again better than he was. Shaking himself, Alex thought back to that time with Amelia, replaying the incident. He didn't try to hide any of it; there was no point in trying to spare himself. Isabella was already fully aware of what he'd done, probably better than any other in this room.

As calmly as she'd handled his infidelity being brought up again, her reaction at the image that flickered between that of the old scholar and the younger man was unexpected. Alex cut off the memory as the colour drained from Isabella's face. She trembled and backed up, bumping into the wall behind her. The veil reacted with her, the air around cracking with power in response.

No!

Alex closed the distance between them, or tried to. She erected a barrier around herself, her emotions swirling with fear. She shook her head, hands rising to her face she sank down the wall to sit on the floor, a sob escaping her lips.

"Clear the room. Now."

Alex heard Kyle's order to the councillors and heard their chairs scraping, rustling clothing and footsteps as they left the room, but didn't turn to watch their exit.

He stiffened as he felt an incoming signature, relaxing as he recognised Damien. He knew full well that Damien could have shielded his arrival from normal detection, which suggested he'd meant Alex to know it was him.

Damien materialised in the room a moment later. He nodded briefly at Alex, his eyes going to his sister who seemed locked in her own world and not even aware that he'd come.

"Alex, what happened? What caused this?" Damien kneeled next to his sister, gingerly touching her shoulder to no effect.

Alex swallowed and threw the memory at Damien. The other man paled, stepping back as the breath exploding from his lips. He closed his eyes, pain etched in his features, clearly shaken.

Alex glanced at Jess and Kyle, both looking equally as bewildered and concerned as he was.

Isabella, let me in. You're safe, he does not have you now. That time was long ago.

Waves of reassurance emanated from Damien as Isabella finally looked up, lost, tears streaming down her cheeks. Recognising her brother, she sobbed. One moment she'd been crumpled on the cold stone floor, the next she was in Damien's arms.

It's him, he's not dead. He'll try to take me again.

Isabella's mind voice shook with emotion. Damien continued to soothe her, his own eyes flashing in anger as he glanced over her head at the three of them.

ALEX STROKED Isabella's hair gently as she slipped into exhausted sleep. He waited, reinforcing her normal sleep with a compulsion of his own, a reassurance that she was safe and should sleep. Finally certain that she would rest, at least for the time being, he eased himself off the bed, pulling the blankets up tenderly before kissing her gently on the forehead and slipping out of his rooms. He entered the lounge, and seeing the concern written on the face of his friends and Damien, he smiled sadly.

"She's asleep for now." Alex nodded at William, who'd shown up as well. He sighed as he sank down into one of the remaining leather chairs. "All right, who was that, Damien?"

Alex was almost certain that part of him didn't want to know the answer, yet the other half of him knew that he most certainly did. Seeing the fear struck into Isabella that way brought out a strong protective feeling in him.

Damien shook his head, his face still pale and obviously still shaken, even with the anger still lighting his eyes.

"Aiden. He was my warlord before I came into my full powers. I was his creature, and he owned me. He owned us." Damien glanced up as Kyle handed him a drink. He closed his eyes as the nightmares from the past played in his mind, sharing them with the group.

Alex remembered the story Isabella had told him of her past and he blanched, sucking in a shocked breath. William looked ashen as the memories from Damien flooded his mind and he finally understood, as they all did, why both Isabella and Damien had reacted so badly.

"This man, Aiden, the one Amelia fears. He is this warlord from the past?" William sounded grim.

Damien nodded. "His likeness is burned into my mind. I'm never likely to forget."

Jess looked horrified. "He's the one who took Isabella as his bed slave to punish you?"

"Yes. After we fled during the uprising... well, it took years before I felt strong enough to go back and check. There was no sign of him, and I thought him dead. By then Vallantia had risen from the ashes of his old domain. Your family has ruled this realm since those days."

William wore a small frown creasing his forehead. "You believe that Scholar Clements works for this ancient warlord?"

Damien laughed bitterly. "No. I think your so-called Scholar Clements *is* Aiden."

Alex was drawn back to the conversation from his brooding. "Scholar Clements is an old man."

Damien looked at him. "You can make others see what you want them to. That flickering between the old man and Aiden, that was Amelia seeing through his projection."

Alex watched in fascination as Damien's appearance changed in front of his eyes. Instead of the Elder he was familiar with, there was suddenly an old grey-haired woman sitting in the chair, smiling kindly at him. Alex heard the others gasp in shock but ignored them. His eyes narrowing, he opened himself to the veil a little more, allowing more power to flow through him. He wielded it, tightening the barriers around his own mind, and used it to focus in on Damien, who now appeared to be someone else entirely. Finally he saw it—the woman flickered, replaced by Damien, switching back and forth between the two. Alex let out his breath and relaxed back in his chair.

Kyle shook his head in disbelief as Damien dropped his ruse. "That is a little disturbing, Damien."

"If this is true, if Clements really is this old warlord come back, then why didn't he just kill us all when he was in the palace and had the chance?" William for his part looked fascinated.

"Aiden was always a coward. He had power that was rare, very rare, in those days. He used it to cow and intimidate others. He took and used people like me to do the dirty work. He hid behind our strength, using the threat of destroying our families, our villages, if we didn't do as he wanted. He would have taken great delight in trying to corrupt you all. It is what he is, what he does."

"He took your sister and you finally snapped, rising against him?" Kyle nodded as if things were starting to make sense.

"The villagers did, yes." Damien shook himself and took another sip of his drink.

"So he is building an army that can't turn against him? Taking innocent children who can't fight back, warping them to create his Sundered army to hide behind? Using Kevin to do his dirty work?" Jess's eyes glittered with anger.

"At least we know what we face. Now we just need to eradicate them. This time we'll make sure Aiden does not survive."

Damien shook his head, glancing at them all earnestly. "It is good you know who and what he is, but I'd keep the focus on Kevin. He is the blade that Aiden is hiding behind. I doubt time has cured Aiden of his cowardice."

Alex frowned. "You don't think he is the real threat?"

"No. In my day, I and the others in the warband—your own ancestors—were the dangerous ones. Without us fighting for him, he could not have wrought the devastation he did." The pain of that memory reflected on Damien's face.

Alex nodded, put his drink aside and stood, every line of his body determined as he thought of the coming battle. He looked over as Kyle stood without hesitation, a fire in his eyes. Jess smiled coldly, nodding as she stood. The veil surged around the three of them, reflecting their bond, determination and warning. It rolled out across the veil, warning all with power that the Elder Born had risen with intent.

58

DISTRACTION

Kevin frowned at the Sundered One lying on his cot. He was totally unresponsive. Neither he nor his other healers could work out why their new mind control technique along with the toxin worked to bring back some of the original Sundered but did nothing for others. Not that it mattered, he supposed. They could still use the mad ones, they were just as effective in their own way.

He straightened and turned as he felt the shimmer of power, relaxing as Amelia appeared from the veil walking across the cavern towards him. He shook his head. He was grateful he'd taken the time to make Amelia his thrall, she was proving to be so useful.

Kevin's eyes narrowed. "You've met with Lord Kastler's pet commander, I take it?"

"Yes, Master. He thinks there is an opportunity to strike at the Fourth through his new woman." There wasn't even a hint of emotion in Amelia's voice as she relayed the meeting, including the images of the woman that she'd caught from the commander's mind.

Kevin relaxed with effort when he realised he was grinding

his teeth. The woman Amelia showed him was stunning. He didn't know how the Rathadon prince did it, how the man attracted such exotic creatures to his side. Then he smiled, glancing at Amelia. The commander did have a point, though. He was certain it would crush Alex to lose yet another of his women to Kevin.

He had given it some thought. Even though Simon was a coward, he did have a point. The longer they delayed here, the more likely they would be discovered. He glanced back down at the unresponsive Sundered he'd been working on with Jenny and sighed. This one was lost to them.

He looked up as Clements stirred and spoke. "The Fourth's new woman, did the commander say who she is?"

Amelia turned her head to look at the leader of the Order, not a hint of expression on his face.

"Yes sir. He told me it is a woman called Isabella."

Kevin almost laughed out loud at the look of desire flickered across the old man's features. Not that he could blame him.

It was time for action. It was time that the Order came under his full control and their assault began. He just had to think of a way to get rid of Clements discreetly; it wouldn't do for them to succeed in this endeavour only to have Clements end up being the king of Vallantia.

AMELIA STARED out of eyes that were no longer hers, knowing she shouldn't be taking such a big risk while her other self was awake. She almost recoiled in fear as she saw Clements, the one that she knew was actually one of the Elder called Aiden. He'd plagued what little peace she'd had left trying to wrest her away from her master. He terrified her.

She cringed as his head swung around taking a step back in

sudden fear. She saw the flash of desire cross his face at the mention of Isabella. Her other self watched dispassionately as he turned to leave.

Amelia dared to hope.

If he was foolish enough to go after Alex's new consort, he would die. The brief run-in she'd had with Isabella had told her the woman was powerful. Not only that, but Alex would react badly to any attack, so even if Isabella didn't kill him, Alex would.

Amelia didn't even notice the satisfied smile that curved the lips on her real body, in response to her satisfaction.

CLOSING the door of his bedroom carefully behind him, Aiden scowled and allowed the seeming of the tottering old man, the Clements identity he'd assumed, to drop off him. It had seemed like such a good idea when he'd started on this endeavour, yet now he found it restrictive. Aiden walked over to the window. He couldn't really call it a suite fitting of a ruler, yet he knew he had some of the best rooms in the estate with the exception of Kastler's own.

Grinding his teeth, he seethed at being stalled at every turn. He had a veritable army spread out below awaiting the order to attack. Frustratingly, the fool Kastler controlled the guards his nephew brought them, as well as the house guards that looked to his lords. Kevin controlled the Sundered through his corrupted healers.

Even wresting control of Amelia away from Kevin had been beyond him. For a thrall trapped behind the layers of an imposed personality, that small grain of herself that remained was incredibly elusive.

Aiden smiled coldly, his eyes glittering with malice. It was all he could do to sit through the discussion, pretending to be unconcerned when they'd received the briefing from Amelia after her meeting with the spy. The daily goings-on of the Rathadons didn't concern him.

There was one detail that had held his attention to the point it had been hard for him to conceal his interest: Isabella, his Isa, had moved into the palace and was linked to Alexander Rathadon. That the ungrateful wretch had lived and never sought him out all these years deserved punishment. That she believed she could give herself to another when she already belonged to him, no matter how many years had passed, showed the traits and influence of her traitorous brother.

Aiden reached out, pulling the veil around him, no longer caring if Kevin sensed the power draw. There were enough other Kin, not to mention the Sundered below in the caverns, that he doubted the man would attribute the use of the veil to him. It was time that he took back his personal property.

Then he would reveal himself and the dithering would stop. The assault to take back his land would commence.

59

ASSISTANCE

Isabella walked through the suite, not having to pause as the doors were opened promptly by attentive servants. Smiling her thanks, she walked out into the private garden. She knew Alex would join her when he was free from his latest meeting. Her brother had tried to warn her how restrictive linking herself with Alex, with the Fourth, would be, yet she had dismissed his worrying. As it turned out, he'd been correct. Her every move, sigh and expression was watched and speculated and gossiped about.

Isabella smiled. Jess and Elizabeth had proven themselves to be the sisters she'd never had, guiding her through the political intrigue of the court and showing her that she didn't have to behave like a trophy in this world she found herself in. Indeed, Alex liked the fact that she was independent, strong-willed, and sought shelter with her when he needed it, trusting she would protect him when he did, just as he would her.

Isabella breathed in the perfume from the flowers in the garden bed, and it calmed her mind. Let the other simpering women of the court bat their eyes and lean all over Alex.

Isabella chuckled. She knew now that such behaviour didn't interest Alex in the slightest.

She froze, her inner eye switching, the garden fading around her with the veiled world coming sharply into focus. She had a moment of fear coursing through her as she recognised the incoming signature in that moment before he arrived.

As Aiden appeared from the veil in front of her, Isabella stepped back, eyes wide, body trembling as her mind screamed. All the intervening years that put a considerable amount of experience and distance between her and her childhood suddenly meant nothing. She was instantly transported back to the scared little girl she'd been all those years ago.

You are mine, Isa, you have always belonged to me.

His mind voice was just as seductive as she remembered, and it caused her to shiver and gasp. She felt his feather-like touch run over her body, almost caressing her with his power.

That's right. Stop fighting me. You know you can't fight me.

Isabella looked up and saw his eyes—greedy, possessive eyes—taking in all of her from top to bottom. He was just as attractive as she remembered, and he could still pin her in place with a smouldering gaze. As he closed the distance between them, she felt a tear track its way down her cheek. For all that he seemed like the perfect companion—tall, strong, good-looking—he was flawed. His insides did not match the outside package. She knew inside the man was cruel, sadistic and possessive. Lurking behind the hazel eyes was the malevolent man she remembered.

As a part of her mind shrieked, and then the feel of the hilt of the ceremonial dagger that Alex had given her as a gift pulled her back to the present. She was no longer that scared, helpless little girl, the one that couldn't fight back.

Isabella ducked her head, letting her shoulders slump and a tremble wrack her body, feigning a defeat she no longer felt. She knew she'd succeeded when she felt his surge of triumph.

Isabella glanced through her hair and saw Aiden was nearly upon her, licking his lips and laughing as he snatched at her arm.

~

AMELIA STARED STRAIGHT AHEAD, waiting, hoping the other would sleep in time. As she started to rock back and forth, her cell growing even smaller, she stared at the door—the door that Aiden always tried to get through to get her. Fear surged in her and threatened to overwhelm her.

Don't let madness come. Not yet.

Her own mind voice rattled around in her head as she battled to stay. Battled with her own madness, tried to hold it at bay long enough. Amelia wept. Her hair was matted and fell in front of her eyes, and she was suddenly a scared little girl with a ripped dirty shift that was too big and pooled around her.

Fight.

She screamed, and her hair straightened and suddenly she was standing, herself again. She ran at the door before she could think about what she was doing. Her hands trembling, she pulled back the bolts and shoved it open. She'd managed to help Jess somehow, when the other woman had been held by her master. Her lips thinned. She may not be able to control her own body, but she could obviously affect the world around her in some ways.

Amelia ran, the walls, bars and chains that had kept her safe melting away in front of her. She pulled power to her as she ran, but this time she didn't run away from that malevolent presence that was Aiden. She ran towards that evil. She could sense him, his being pulsing like a beacon.

She paused when she saw him, a faded ghostly version of him, reach out to grab the woman. To grab the woman she'd only ever met once, but she knew this woman was Isabella. The one that Aiden desperately wanted to possess. As his hands closed around Isabella's arm and started to pull her towards him, Amelia shrieked.

No!

She pulled in power sharply, not stopping to wonder how she was doing it, and slammed it into Aiden. She had a brief moment of triumph as she saw him stagger. Then he turned to gaze right at her through the veil. Amelia froze and despite her earlier resolve, started to back up in fear.

ALEX SHOOK HIS HEAD, hoping that this meeting, one of a seemingly endless stream of meetings, would be over soon. Still, it potentially resolved one problem they'd been grappling with, which was getting as many innocents out of harm's way as possible before battle commenced. Just because their lord was a traitor didn't mean that they were.

"Alex, I know you disagree but I insist on participating in this attack." William's expression looked stubborn.

Alex was about to reply when he felt a surge of power accompanied by a thrust of fear.

"Stay here." He spat at William, then stood abruptly while pulling the veil around him, aware that Jess and Kyle came with him, and together they covered the short distance to the courtyard garden in the blink of an eye. The blast of power and fear had been Isabella's.

Alex appeared there to see Isabella blast a man in front of her, as her mind screamed in fear and anger. He only had a moment to recognise that the man was Aiden. Before he could do anything himself, the old warlord stumbling, a look of shock on his face, fled into the veil.

Alex swore and glanced at both Kyle and Jess before he

closed the distance to Isabella. He gently pulled her into his arms.

"Isabella, it's alright, he's gone." Alex could feel the tremors running through her body.

It was all he could do to remain calm himself, but the threat was gone and it wouldn't help Isabella at all if he allowed himself to be lost in anger.

As sanity returned to Isabella's eyes, Alex allowed them both to sink to the ground as she sobbed. He didn't say anything. He knew he didn't have to. He just sat with her as she wept.

Looking up to Kyle and Jess, who stood nearby, he could see the protective barrier the pair had thrown up around them all.

"We need to push forward with the plan. Attack before they can come at us again." Alex was surprised that his voice was calm.

"I'm coming on the attack." Isabella's voice was soft but firm.

"Isabella, no, you've had a big shock." Alex stilled as Isabella stared up at him.

"I am coming, that man will die this time. He will not escape again." Isabella's eyes were cold, her voice containing a quiet fury.

Kyle and Jess looked between them both and nodded and disappeared without a word to follow up on their own instructions.

60

TRAITOR'S MOVE

Only pausing long enough to scan the palace, Jess and Kyle appeared before Bennett, who stepped back, startled at their sudden arrival.

"Are you sure you want to do this? Go into the Kastler estate?"

Bennett finished placing one of Kyle's formal jackets back on a hanger before turning.

"Yes, my lord."

Nodding at Jess, Kyle swept his long-term servant up with them, dragging him along as they jumped back into the veil, to the meeting room. Kyle watched with interest as Jess reached out and scanned the veil for recent trails. They both knew Simon's path would be one of them. As Jess shared what she was seeing in her mind's eye Kyle could see the paths taken by those who had left this place by disappearing into the veil. Some were faded, a hint as to how long ago they had occurred. It gave them both pause that they could still detect those trails, and they could both tell they weren't from someone weak in the use of the veil. Some of these departures seemed ancient.

Concentrating, Jess brought Simon to the forefront of her

mind. Kyle watched, fascinated as he felt her power spinning out and a couple of paths, the footprints of their user, came into focus. His eyes narrowed as he realised how many there were, yet there was one set of prints that glowed more brightly than any of the others.

Kyle wasn't conscious of either of them making the decision, yet found they were speeding through the veil together. The world around them blurred even if it was only for a moment, and it was less time than a couple of heartbeats before their progress halted. Kyle found himself staring through the veil at the room around him that came sharply into focus. He stared at Jess, while they didn't think this task really needed the both of them, after all that had happened this wasn't the moment to get sloppy.

Looking at the scene below it seemed Simon hadn't wasted any time and was in conference with some of his people—his most trusted, she gathered, since a quick assessment told her they were all Kin.

"Damn it, don't be fools! The current Fourth and his Companions are dangerous." Simon's expression was clouded by anger.

"So now we are conscripted, doing the bidding of the king?" This from a young-looking man.

"The new king is like none that Vallantia has had before. He's one of the forced Kin. You've seen what his mother is like even out of her mind." Simon's gaze swept around the others in the room. Kyle was rather impressed when they all ducked their heads, conceding his point, proving he had more power over them than what his first impression was showing him.

"Mad. Unpredictable. Wild."

Kyle turned to see the young man who'd spoken, leaning on the windowsill. He looked neither angry nor upset.

Simon nodded. "Except Alex and his Companions got to

the king in time. They shielded him, protected him from descending into madness."

The man turned and looked at Simon, a knowing smile on his lips that didn't reach his eyes. "We chose a side. If we side against the Rathadons, any that survive will track us down."

Kyle looked at Jess, his eyebrow raising, and she nodded. Agreeing they'd heard enough they dispelled the veil so she stood in the room with them. He traded glances with Jess, curious how Simon's den of Kin thieves would react.

They focused on the intruders that appeared in their midst, their shock evident as they drew their power and lashed out. Kyle and Jess stood, allowing their outburst to roll over them, although Kyle made sure to keep Bennett within his shields. The fact that Bennett had his dagger in one hand and sword in the other facing towards the threat he perceived at their back made him smile. Their shock as neither he nor Jess suffered any harm from their outburst caused him even more amusement.

"You don't have time for this foolishness and yes, if you betray the king, he will track you down and kill you." Jess allowed herself to smile although her eyes were dead. "The Fourth, Fourth's Blade and I will serve him well in this cause."

Kyle held his breath, watching them as they considered Jess's words, his eyes narrowing as Simon stepped forward and placed his hand on his heart then forehead, and bowed his head.

"Companions, we will do as the Fourth requests, given that it lies within our abilities." Simon's tone showed no sign of deception, and his people stared, wide-eyed, at this turn of events.

Kyle closed his eyes briefly, taking a calming breath. "We don't ask that you fight, only that you clear the surrounding villages and estate of the innocent, or as many as you can before dawn."

Simon's eyes widened. "Tonight?"

Jess pushed back that feeling that would overwhelm her if she let it.

"Tonight. The old threat you were concerned about showed his hand. The attack will happen at dawn." Jess didn't elaborate.

Kyle smiled, she didn't need to. Simon, with his background and training if he was as smart as he thought he was, could fill in the blanks.

"We'll do what we can, Lady Jessalan, Lord Kyle."

Kyle reached into his pocket and drew out the ring he'd grabbed from the Complex before leaving. He looked down at it, then back up at Simon. Kyle hoped that Alex would forgive him for this but William did effectively throw Simon back under Alex's authority. None of them were innocents. They weren't the shining examples of what people typically thought heroes should be, not Alex nor Jess and certainly not himself.

"You were once a member of the Companion's Cohort. You left in dishonour. Take this opportunity to redeem yourself." He ignored the startled muttering from Simon's men as he held out the ring to him. "The Fourth needs you. Your king needs you."

Simon's eyes widened, and Kyle thought he saw a fleeting expression of pain flicker across his face as he gazed back at him. He took the ring with a shaking hand and slipped it onto his finger.

"I failed the honour of the Cohort once. I won't again. I and mine will do as you command, Companion." Simon dropped to his knee, his sword quickly withdrawn from its scabbard in a smooth motion and held with its hilt pressed to his forehead in that ancient symbol of contrition.

61

HELP

Simon closed his eyes as conflicting feelings he couldn't quite put a name to crashed over him. He pushed them all aside to deal with them later if he chose. Right now they didn't have time. A rueful smile spread on his lips. He had no doubt the Fourth would track him down and kill him if he failed. His Companions had just proven how easily it could be done should the Elder Born have cause to focus on him.

Aware of the silence that had settled on the room since the Lady Jessalan and Lord Kyle had revealed his secret before they left he stood, turning to face his people. They looked at him astounded, all except his most trusted. Keith still leant against the windowsill, he may have looked relaxed to the casual observer but he was ready to leap to his defence if needed. Blake on the other side of the room made no pretence of being relaxed, his hand was on his blade as he watched everyone else for a sign of dissent.

"So now you know my past. A past I'm certain you've all speculated about long before now." Simon smiled as a bark of laughter sounded in the room.

"You could say that my Lord Skull." A grumbling voice muttered from the back of the group.

"I see those two don't look surprised by the news at all!" The strident complaint set off muttering of agreement amongst those here.

"Blake and I, well let's just say we've known Simon for a very long time. You fools should be grateful the Fourth's Companions left us alive after you all tried to attack them." There was heavy sarcasm in Keith's tone at the last point.

"You can't have failed to notice even with your combined might the Companions didn't even break out a sweat." The others swung to look from Keith to Blake as his voice rumbled across the room.

"You've never come face to face with the previous Fourth, let alone the current holder of the title. If you had you wouldn't be standing here grumbling at me." Simon intervened, they didn't have time for this discussion. "Blake you will be with me helping to clear out Lord Kastler's estate. Keith and Lain you will clear out as many of the farm workers as you can. I trust the three of you to select suitable teams to get the job done. We leave within the hour."

Simon turned his back on them all not waiting for acknowledgement. They would obey. They knew what he would do to them if they didn't. After the Lady Jessalan's and Lord Kyle's display they undoubtedly knew what she could and would do if they failed to follow the orders they'd been given.

Gesturing at the Fourth Blade's manservant to follow him he left the room. He didn't bother to check that the man followed him. He was too well trained not to. Simon needed to change if they were to complete the task they had been given, his current attire wasn't fit for the purpose. Even though neither of the Fourth's Companions said anything, he'd not failed to notice they'd brought Bennett with them.

Simon had to admit a grudging respect. There was a huge

risk to the man to be left there in the heart of enemy territory, just to hide the fact they'd smuggled out innocent servants and given more time to his Lord, before the attack. Although thankfully he hadn't been lying when he'd said the commoners looking to Lord Kastler held little to no loyalty to the man. That would make that part of this task somewhat easier.

LAIN RESISTED the urge to swear as a dog growled deep in its throat off to his left before breaking into full-throated barks. The warning carried across the farmstead. He looked over to the looming Kastler estate settled into the mountain and relaxed marginally. It looked close, he could even see the glow of the campfires from the armed rebels they'd amassed. He knew though that they were far enough away that even if the men heard the dog, they wouldn't think too much of it. He hoped. The bigger problem was if the lights of those who lived out here started to flare. That might draw attention.

"Let's move, get these people out of here. Someone shut that dog up, don't kill it." Lain really did groan, being a do-gooder made his life so much harder.

Like all those who led these parties Lain was capable of pulling the veil around himself and his small party. To move through areas undetected. Mostly. Animals could sometimes be a little problematic.

He couldn't travel through the veil himself, Blake, one of the Skull Lord's seconds had dropped him and his men off here on his way to his own assignment. He had clear instructions. Get the farmers and labourers out. His path had been clearly laid out for him right down to how much ground they had to cover before dawn. He didn't quite understand what the Fourth and his Companions were going to do. Or why it was dangerous for commoners to remain in close proximity. After the Companions' display, apparently impervious to their combined best efforts, he didn't argue.

Lain didn't waste time with further instructions. It was the beauty of working for the Skull Lord. Everyone knew what their leader would do to them if they failed him. Lain gathered the veil around him almost reflexively, sighing as the dog yelped once then was silent. He picked up his pace heading to the main house, hearing the footfalls of his assigned group heading to their own targets.

Lain eased open the door to the main hut, relieved when the hinges didn't groan in protest. Even though he'd never been in this particular residence he knew exactly how it was laid out. The Lord Kastler owned everything and all the labourers on his land paid him dearly to live here. Not that they had enough left after they paid tribute to even attempt to go elsewhere. They were effectively stuck with nowhere to escape to. Until now. All of these farming communes on the Kastler estate were built exactly the same. He could have found his way to the sleeping areas blindfolded.

Even though he was confident about his surroundings he walked across the small living area cautiously; he hadn't survived this long by being sloppy. That was how one in his profession died very quickly. Easing back the curtain that hid the sleeping alcove Lain wasted no time, closing the distance between him and the man sleeping on the bed with his woman. Drawing his blade, he laid it on the woman's throat, clamping his hand on her mouth. Her sudden squeak of alarm and thrashing was enough to wake the man sleeping next to her. He lurched up then froze as he saw the predicament his partner was in.

"Hush, both of you. In the Fourth's name, by order of the King you are to leave this place." Lain glanced down at the woman who'd stilled at his words, although still tense. Not that he blamed her. "Unless you both wish to share your lord's fate when justice is dispensed."

Lain withdrew his hand and blade from the woman, cautious yet relieved when neither did anything immediately stupid.

"Since when did your kind do the bidding of the Fourth and the King?" The woman's voice was harsh but barely above a whisper.

Lain couldn't help but smile, this woman had a spine still, despite her lord doing his best to beat it out of the people who looked to him.

"Since the Fourth's Companions, tracked us down in my master's lair and ordered us to. The Skull Lord isn't stupid, your lord's wrath is nothing compared to the Fourth. Besides I have no doubt the man's head will be separated from his body before the sun clears his estate."

"This is some kind of trick, you just want us to leave so you can take everything." The man's voice growled at him.

"Don't be stupid, the likes of us don't have anything. Not for the likes of the Skull Lord's men anyhow." The woman's tone was scathing as she rose from the bed herself and looked at him. "Where should we go?"

Lain almost forgot himself and laughed. She was correct of course the bulk of people beholden to Lord Kastler had very little to call their own. Certainly not enough in normal circumstances to draw the attention of the League of Skulls.

"Just dress, quickly and follow me and my men. We'll lead you and the others out. We don't have much time, I'm told we don't want to be here come dawn or we'll be trapped and potentially share your lord's fate." Lain shook his head holding his laughter back as the woman bullied her man in harsh whispers into dressing and berated him until he complied, meekly leaving the house as ordered.

Lain glanced around seeing the rest of his people appearing

not long after with the others that lived in this farming commune. Gesturing to his men, they rounded up their charges and headed them up into the surrounding hills and safety.

~

SIMON SWALLOWED the curse he'd been about to use as the woman screamed. Half his men froze, Blake got to her first, clamping his hand on her mouth.

"Hush woman unless you want to join your lord in death!" Blake hissed at her.

Blake's face went red as she bit down on his hand, struggling like a hellion in his arms. A couple of the other men went to his assistance. Simon heard the doors to the kitchen, where the woman they'd discovered was preparing for the morning, crash open. Two of Kastler's guards came charging through the doors. They skidded to a halt, their eyes wide in shock, before they grasped for their swords and charged towards them. This time Simon swore, as one of his men went down, clutching his stomach unlucky enough to be sliced open by the backswing of the sword of one of the guards.

Reinforcing his shields, throwing them wider than he'd had them previously to give as many of his people coverage as he could he drew his own sword. Throwing caution to the wind, trusting most on the estate were still asleep since the kitchens were located in the bowels of the estate house. One of the advantages of the place being built into the mountain were the thick rock walls in this section that were part of the mountain itself.

Despite the years it had been since he'd had to defend himself with a sword, it seemed he was still better with it than Kastler's guard. He cut the man down without a hint of guilt. The guard was just doing his job, unfortunately for that guard so was he. Hearing a grunt and the clatter of a blade on the stone floor Simon spun, fearing another of his men had gone down. He froze, stunned. Bennett stood, looking down at the fallen guardsman, who lay at his feet dead on the ground, neck snapped.

Bennett finally looked up, his eyes glinting with amusement as he saw them all gaping at him.

"What? You thought I was placed with Lord Kyle just to look after his clothing?"

Simon eyed the man with a new appreciation of his skills. "I knew your function. It's just given the Fourth's Blade's own skills your own have rarely been seen."

Bennett looked over toward the woman being restrained and sighed. He walked over to the her and he squatted down in front of her, just staring. He didn't do anything else that Simon could observe but the woman stilled. Simon could see the blood running through Blake's fingers, but still his hand remained firmly clamped on the woman's mouth.

"Listen to me woman. You can either get clear of this place before the Fourth's people arrive or stay and tie your chances with your lord." Bennett nodded at Blake as the woman stirred and he removed his hand cautiously from the woman's mouth.

"You'd have me believe you speak for the Fourth? You lot are nothing but cutthroats," the woman hissed at Bennett, her eyes sparking with outrage.

Bennett kept his eyes on her and eased the black glove off one of his hands, revealing a signet ring. Simon didn't have to see it up close to know it bore the Strafford crest. Only the most loyal of their people were awarded them, it had been a practice for generations stretching back even beyond his time in the Companion's Cohort. Those who bore them tended to be in roles where they might have to take another's life to protect the one they served. It didn't surprise him at all that Bennett bore one. The woman's eyes widened in shock, indicating even she recognised it. It was a rarity for a commoner to have such protection, so it was the stuff of legend amongst those who served.

"I serve the Fourth's Blade. Choose woman, we can not guarantee you will live if your choice is to stay." Bennett slowly pulled his black leather glove on as the shocked servant nodded.

"Please. I'm sorry, tell me what to do."

Bennett looked over at Simon then back at the quiet woman who, now that she'd stopped struggling, the men let go.

"Show us to where your fellow serving staff are bedded down. Then you'll all be taken to safety." As she nodded scrambling to her feet Bennett backed off.

"WAIT HERE, while I get Bennett into position." Simon glanced at Blake who nodded his face calm.

The servants clustered close clutching small bundles with only the few items they could gather in the time that they had. Although it wasn't like they had to leave much behind. He'd known how little these people had, he'd read the reports, yet it was pitiful to see that most of what they had could be contained in one small bundle clutched to their chests.

Simon gestured to Bennett who moved closer to him, thickening the veil around them he pulled them through the estate. This was the dangerous part. The manservant to Lord Kastler had his own room on the upper floors close to his lord. Simon knew that there were more guards on the upper levels and the most powerful of the Kin, including Kevin and the Elder were up there. He just hoped they were still asleep.

Not wasting any time, knowing every second pushed them closer to dawn and the time those sleeping above were more likely to wake if disturbed he ghosted them through the estate. It was worth the risk to save the time. Thankfully due to his previous visits he had a basic idea of the layout of the upper floors and the woman from the kitchen had been most accommodating once Bennett had calmed her down. She'd described how to get to the manservant's small closet-like room tucked down a corridor that ran off the servants stairs.

Simon didn't pause as they reached the upper floors. Keeping the veil wrapped around him like a comforting blanket he stalked up the hallway, drawing Bennett with him. Ducking down the corridor which was right where the cook had said it would be, he spied the wooden door tucked into the far corner of the corridor that didn't lead anywhere else except some stairs to the level below. Without pause he pulsed them towards the door, easing though it without opening it.

The room on the other side of the door really was about the size of a closet. In fact looking around he was sure his own dressing area was bigger. Realising there wasn't much option anyway he motioned for Bennett to stay put. Bennett shrugged and leaned up against the door to wait.

Simon took one step towards the figure lying on the cot, placing one gloved hand on the man's mouth, while the other lay on his chest, with a small burst of power to strengthen his arm and keep him pressed to the bed. A startled, terrified squeak made its way past his hand.

"Hush, I'm not here to kill you. You've seen me before."

Lord Kastler's manservant's eyes were wide as saucers as he looked up at him. He replied with a muffled response that Simon interpreted as.

"Yes."

"Your lord will answer for all that he has done to the king come dawn. You will come with me to a place of safety." Simon gently removed his hand as the manservant nodded.

After a brief pause, relieved that the servant didn't scream to wake the whole upper floor up, Simon stepped back, his back against the wall behind him to give room for the manservant to get up.

The man scrambled out from the cot, his head swinging from him to Bennett still pressed against the door. His face crumpled and he shook his head.

"My Lord will know something is up if I don't tend to him when he wakes." His voice trembled.

"It's alright. We have a replacement for you." Simon jerked his head to Bennett.

The manservant turned his gaze on Bennett, his expression clouding. "You don't understand, My Lord has exacting standards. He'll know you aren't trained to serve as a lord's personal servant."

Simon couldn't help the soft snort of amusement that statement caused him. Bennett for his part simply bowed his head in acknowledgement to the man.

"It's alright, I think he'll manage." Simon grabbed hold of the manservant, not trusting him to stay close and looked at Bennett. "Are you sure of this? I can take you out with me now."

Bennett shook his head. "I'm sure Simon. Go, get them all to safety, I'll be fine and my Lord Kyle will be here in no time I'm sure."

Simon nodded at Bennett and pulling the veil to him once more disappeared into its folds retracing his way back to the room where he'd left the rest of his men and the servants. Barely pausing he swept them up with him, drawing them through the veil to retreat beyond the borders of the Kastler family estate. They'd done their part. Now it was up to the Fourth and his people.

62

MISSION

Kevin folded the veil around him and went to the caverns below the castle. The time for hiding was nearly over. Today they would make their presence felt, word had gone to the commander to kick off the battle by launching an attack on the king with his men inside the palace. That action was sure to cause a distraction and with everyone's eyes and focus on the attack from within they would launch their own attack. If they were lucky Janson might even succeed in killing the king.

The loss of Jess had been a blow to their cause, he'd been so close to breaking the woman. Kevin frowned; he'd been so certain the poison would work but it seemed it had failed allowing Jess to escape. He'd set some of his healers to work on the dual poison and to refine it more. Or at least they would if he could find out what went wrong. Jess's escape had forced their hand though, they couldn't risk holding off on their attack. When Jess recovered, she might have enough knowledge to lead the king and his men here. So, they'd been faced with the choices, attack or run. They were so close to their objective that running away had been unpalatable to them all.

Moving through the underground levels he came to the large cavern where the Sundered slept. As he'd known she would be Jenny was tending her patients, Chelsie assisting her. Even though Jenny had proven to be useful she was becoming problematic. She was growing too powerful as a healer, her own healing abilities working at trying to undo the compulsions he placed on her. He was constantly having to reinforce them to keep her in check.

Both of the healers looked up at his approach. Chelsie looked awed to see him. She was a good enough healer at a basic level but wasn't yet capable of fighting him off.

"Chelsie, why don't you go and rouse Tyson and a handful of the other Sundered." Simon smiled and gave her a nudge.

"Of course, Master Healer." Chelsie turned and walked through the ranks of cots heading off to do as he requested without question.

He turned his gaze on Jenny who stepped back, confusion on her face.

"Master Healer, what...."

She froze as he grasped her head, inserting himself into her mind, compelling her to freeze.

You will take the Sundered and go to the Summer Palace. You will assist with the attack on the king.

Kevin grimaced as he felt her mind try to shy away from his orders and reinforced the bonds he held her with. She stiffened as his power ran through her then slumped as he overcame her. She staggered as he released her, looking around momentarily disorientated before she smiled.

"Of course Master Healer. We'll go straight away."

Jenny nodded to him then turned and walked over to Chelsie, helping the other healer to rouse some more of the Sundered so that she could go off to do as she'd been compelled to. Kevin smiled, at least that was one potential problem out of the way.

63

A BETTER KING

Kastler stood motionless, allowing his people to fuss over the final touches to his attire. He frowned at the worn look of his best tunic as his manservant cut off a loose thread at the shoulder. He squared his shoulders. When he was king, he'd finally be provided with clothes appropriate to his standing.

Nodding his thanks, he turned and walked from his rooms, practicing his stately walk. Kings did not run. Others ran to serve the king. He frowned, pausing to look at the servant who helped him.

"I haven't noticed you before. Where is, um... my usual servant?" Kastler cursed internally at being unable to remember the servant's name. Then again, there were so many of them, it wasn't like he could possibly be expected to remember all of them.

The servant gazed up at him. "Colin had an emergency and had to leave, my lord. He asked me to assist you in his place."

Kastler's frown deepened. There was something about the servant that was tugging at his mind, but he couldn't place it.

Shrugging, he dismissed the problem and continued down the cold stone hallway, careful not to appear to be in a hurry.

Not that he'd spent much time in his life running, but he had found it somewhat irritating that his own people weren't quite as prompt at serving him at times, not like the servants fawned and jumped at the slightest whim of the current members of the royal family. Kastler smiled. Soon that would all be his. The servants would then be showing him the respect that he was due.

Kastler frowned and looked around. "Where is everyone this morning?"

"It's early, my lord. I think they are all still at breakfast. I sent a runner to alert them when you rang for me." The servant's tone was smooth and unruffled.

Kastler considered the man's words and sighed. It was so hard to get good help.

As he walked along the bare stone corridor towards the front sitting room, he thought through all the things he would have to do as soon as the Rathadons were gone. He would of course have to take over the royal palaces. It was only appropriate, since they were the symbol of the royal family. He would have to give careful thought as to which of his other relatives would take over these old family estates.

He glanced at the servant walking with him, suddenly uncomfortable with the echo of his booted feet in the empty hallway.

"William, the false king, will have to be disposed of when I ascend the throne." Kastler glanced at his servant to see his bland expression.

"Well, it will be hard for you take it if the king is still sitting on it, my lord."

Kastler thought he heard a hit of mockery in the servant's tone, but that couldn't be right. The man wouldn't dare.

"A public execution would probably be best. It wouldn't do

to leave him alive to foster rebellion in the less enlightened of our people." This time the servant wisely kept silent. He wasn't sure why he suddenly felt the need to discuss his plans with a servant anyway.

Turning his mind back to his current train of thought, he realised Alexander would have to join his brother in that public display, there was no question in that. The boy was too dangerous and had proven to be resistant to the medication developed by the Order.

The scion of the Strafford line, Kyle, would also have to die. While it had been proven in the past he could be controlled with the medication, he was too close to the current ruling family. Such a pity, in a way, since his rumoured skillset sounded intriguing. Having a trained assassin at his beck and call would probably be essential.

He made a note to check into others who might fill such a role for him. There was bound to be upheaval with this change and some lords who would decide to support the Rathadons no matter how far they had drifted from what they should be.

The Lady Jessalan.

Kastler only realised he'd sighed out loud when he noticed a darting glance from his man. He smiled. At least his servant was starting to be more attentive already.

Lady Jessalan was such a beautiful creature. It would be a shame to waste one such as her, but he'd been informed she was too dangerous and would not abandon her allegiance to William, Alexander and Kyle.

Kastler stumbled as the floors and walls started shaking, his man adroitly steadying him with a strong grasp on his arm. A deep rumbling filled the air and Kastler swallowed, aware the servant was looking at him.

He straightened, trying to appear as if the building shaking hadn't scared him. He reached the door to the sitting room and here he waved his hand—it only shook a little. It was a gesture he'd seen William and Alexander use and he was gratified to see his guards at the door step forward and push them open.

He sniffed at the fact that the door didn't open quite fast enough for him to sweep in, leaving him standing for a moment. He would need some new doormen; the king had staff whose sole job seemed to be opening doors. Guards were for, well, guarding him, so they shouldn't get distracted by opening doors. He was about to be king. He shouldn't have to wait for the doors to open.

He glared at the men on guard, letting them see his displeasure before sweeping into the room. He'd deal with them later. This was a momentous day and he wouldn't let his servants' incompetence ruin it.

The doors thumped closed behind him.

"I've decided the attack will—" Kastler stopped, frozen in place.

Kevin was standing at the large windows looking down at the grounds below with a steady stream of curse words. Kastler's jaw nearly dropped. He'd never heard the healer swear before. He continued his way across the room to see what it was that held the attention of the healer to the extent that Kevin hadn't even acknowledged his entrance.

As the floor shook again, with a deep rumbling coming from outside, Kastler grasped the back of a long leather lounge. He gasped in shock as Amelia appeared out of the air, right there in the room between him and Kevin. He'd known she was Tainted, but still, she'd never done that before in his presence and it unnerved him. Her drawn sword made him swallow nervously.

He looked up towards the windows, unwilling to move closer to the pair, and he saw cracks of lightning running across the otherwise blue skies outside the windows.

Kevin's steady stream of expletives ceased, and he swung around, a look of contempt on his face.

"You fool! The attack has already begun. That out there is the Fourth and his people."

Kastler took a step back from the healer, unaccustomed to being treated like he was nothing but a servant. He knew he'd gone suddenly pale as the words sank in, and he hadn't marshalled a single indignant word in his defence when the healer along with Amelia suddenly disappeared from the room.

Trying to steady his breathing, Kastler made his way to the large windows, where he looked out to see an army on the grounds below—rank upon rank of guards all emblazoned with the king's crest, banners of other lords in prominent display, with more and more guards arriving seemingly from nowhere. They just appeared.

The yelling and screaming started as Kastler stared at the scene unfolding below. A day that had started with such promise was suddenly looking a fair bit bleaker.

64

BARRIER

Alex took a deep breath as he strode through the veil, Jess on one side, Kyle on the other, as they had for so many years of their lives. A path formed before them as they walked—not that he found it necessary to feign walking anymore, or for a path to appear, but the old familiar method felt soothing. The blank mist of the veil remained shapeless around them rather than taking form as they wished it. Unlike in the past, that was taking conscious effort. He'd noticed of late that wherever he trod in the veil, a wild forest would ripple out around him. He'd come to realise it was his own mind forcing the shape on the veil around him.

The veil was power, vast and seemingly endless. Impressionable, almost waiting to be moulded and used in any fashion he wanted. The veil reflected those of power that strode its paths. Today, none of them wanted to tip off to their quarry that they were coming for them.

Simon and his people, who were also Kin, had begun the evacuation of as many of the villagers and servants from the Kastler estate as they could under the cover of darkness. From their position high above the surface where they normally trod,

Alex could see the small trail of people as they were ushered away towards the relative safety of the Summer Palace and Callenhain.

Edward, Cal, Kat, Damien and Isabella stood in the veil, each heading units of the Elite and Guard still loyal to the Crown. While Damien and Isabella weren't as proficient at fighting in combination with the Elite, both were more than capable of protecting the units assigned to them from those with power, leaving the Elite to deal with the traitors camped around Kastler's estate. He'd tried to convince Isabella to stay behind but she wouldn't hear of it. He resolutely pushed that concern out of his mind. Isabella had proven more than once that she could look after herself.

Alex shook his head and turned his mind to their own units of Elite who stood in the veil, waiting for the three of them. Matthew and Ryan's experiment had prompted testing with the Elite and a small group within their ranks had proven to be strong enough at holding their fellow Elite in the veil. It had taken a great deal of practice and none of them really liked being cut adrift in the veil this way, but none of them panicked. All of the Elite stood in formation, just as they'd practiced, waiting for Kyle, Jess and himself to go and fetch them.

All good, Marcus? Alex kept his mind voice controlled in a tight communication for Marcus alone. The rest of the Kin didn't need to hear the conversation, even if it was unlikely they would understand its meaning if they caught it amid the constant chatter in the veil.

Yes, Your Highness. We're waiting right where Damien dropped us off.

Alex smiled. Marcus had practiced enough; his mind voice was calm and he exuded confidence. Then again, he'd come to the disturbing conclusion that his Elite would run straight into certain death for him. It was a level of loyalty he had no doubt of. He still didn't know what he'd ever done to earn it.

Hearing movement in the veil, the undercurrent thrumming with an unfamiliar signature, Alex frowned and looked in the direction of the incoming people.

It's Olivia and some of her people. Kyle informed him.

The wild Kin that Kyle had run into, Olivia had shown up with a handful of others of their kind. Just as she'd promised she would. Alex traded surprised glances with Kyle who shrugged. Edward took charge of the new arrivals, sorting them into details.

When he felt Jess nudge at his mind, Alex took the hint and drew his attention back to their own immediate role. Even though he wasn't aware of using much power, the scene below them came sharply into focus as soon as he thought of their destination. While he had been preoccupied checking on everyone, they had arrived. From their position high above, they had a view of not only the old manor house, but the entire Kastler estate.

He'd seen it before, but it still gave him pause, the rows upon rows of tents filled with guards. Still, it wasn't that sight that concerned him. They'd brought in enough guards from all over the realm to more than compensate for that. It was the glowing life force, the one that screamed of the Kin—lots and lots of Kin. Those would be his problem. His, Kyle and Jess's problem, that was, while the others dealt with the guards. Once the enemy troops were contained, some of the others would be free to help, or so they hoped.

Alex closed his eyes and took a deep, calming breath, then turned to face his friends. They both looked back at him steadily, neither of them showing the combination of nerves and anticipation that he had no doubt they felt just as he did.

Ready?

Both Jess and Kyle nodded gravely at him, and he heard the affirmative replies from the others, each of them heading a unit of the Elite and King's Guard, waiting for the signal to appear at the Kastler estate and begin the attack.

Ready, my friend. Kyle's eyes started to glow with power as he gradually increased his draw on the power of the veil.

Jess drew her attention back to him as she finished her own final checks. Alex could see not only her eyes glowing with power, but the bands of power tracking their way across her entire body. Alex knew he probably looked the same to their eyes.

Let's settle this. Jess's grin answered his own and Kyle's as she lightened the tense mood they were all feeling with a subtle wash of reassurance.

Tensing, Alex took one final breath, then spoke one word.

Now!

The reaction from his two friends was as immediate as his own. All three of them went from a slow, low level draw of power to opening themselves fully to the veil and hauling power from all around as fast as they could.

There was a pause in the veil, as if the realm around them hadn't quite caught up with the change. All three of them acted in concert, wielding the power they were channelling to take the form they wished. As they threw the power out from themselves, a dome of white, sparkling energy began to form, each of the thirds they produced snapping and merging together seamlessly. Alex knew he was glowing all over, power seeping from every pore of his body as were Kyle and Jess.

Then the veil outside the barrier that had formed around the Kastler estate reacted to their outpouring of power. The world darkened and roiled around them, power cracked and rumbled throughout the world. Alex could see the impact of what they'd done rain down, crossing the barrier between the veiled world and the real world. Alex ignored the crackling all around him and through him. Unlike when he was going through transition, it didn't hurt anymore. It made him feel alive.

Alex allowed the power to flow through him, washing away the fatigue that hammered into him as soon as they were done. He knew the three of them were all on borrowed time. There was only so long they could continue before passing out to sleep off their exertions, even with the power level they had all attained. Alex only hoped none of them would collapse until after they were done. Even if they did collapse early, hopefully the others, in conjunction with William's guards, could finish the job. Alex chuckled under his breath. Of course, since the barrier was self-sustaining, everyone would probably be stuck in here until the three of them woke up.

Now! Alex sent the command to Edward, Cal, Damien and Isabella.

At once they parted the veil that until that moment had hidden them from view, each of their units moving to surround the enemy. All of them had been briefed on what was going to happen, and barked orders from their commanders kept the men and women focused as they ignored the reaction of the elements around them, trusting those with power at their heart to protect them all from those things they couldn't control. True to their training, the guard swept forward, engaging with their surprised enemy. Panicked men and women yelled and screamed as the king's people appeared out of nowhere and they found themselves surrounded.

Alex didn't pause to watch the drama unfold below him. He moved, with Kyle and Jess by his side. They each collected their own units of Elite, who had stood waiting in the veil, held in position by Marcus, James and Meghan.

They moved in perfect sync with each other, their skin sparking with power as the energy they held glowed. They weren't making any efforts to conceal what they were anymore. As those below would deal with the mundane guard units below, while the three of them would start on the Sundered and Kin who had flocked to the Order's banner.

Alex felt awareness flare in the Kin below as they recognised a source of great power near them. Hardly aware of the movement, Alex launched into action, his sword sweeping free of its scabbard as the Sundered started popping into view from where they'd been hidden in the caverns below.

65

LEFT BEHIND

Matthew laughed at the expressions of the Elite that had relieved the night shift—that startled look they had when briefed that their charge was actually still in residence and had not managed to get himself taken to the battle. He'd been disappointed when he'd been told he was being left behind, on detail to protect the king. Of course he'd been briefed of the argument between King William and the Fourth and the idea of locking the king up in the cells if he tried to go to the Kastler estate was alarming. The fact that he could ride there should he take it into his mind to do so even more so. He hadn't, yet, so that was a relief. At least he was in good company in his misery at being left behind. Ryan had not been happy either, but one look from the Fourth before he made the mistake of uttering an objection had prevented any arguments. As the doors closed behind him, he waved at the guards outside and was halfway down the hallway before he stopped and turned, looking back at them.

Keeping a carefully neutral expression, he walked back towards the two men loitering outside the doorway.

"Is there something in particular either of you needed?"

Matthew looked from one to the other of the King's Guard. The silence stretched for a time before they looked at each other, then back at him. The younger of the two shifted his weight from one foot to the other before tugging on his tunic.

"We're fine, but thanks for checking. You Elite types are always so courteous." The smile plastered over the older guardsman's face was far from sincere.

"We try. What are you doing here?" Matthew thought bluntness was in order; he was tired and needed his rest, so being civil wasn't his top priority right now.

"We were put on guard detail here." The younger member of the King's Guard swallowed convulsively, looking faintly alarmed.

"Ah, very well then. Have a good evening." Matthew nodded and turned, walking away as if he didn't have a care in the world.

What the guards couldn't know, since none of them would have seen beyond the doors they were standing outside of, is that it was simply a long corridor with another set of doors at the other end that members of the Elite stood guard over. Beyond that was the King's Suite. The only people who should be in this particular corridor were members of the Elite. It was a private access way used by the Elite and not public. The only other way the two guards could have ended up at those particular doors was to use the servants' access corridors, and they shouldn't have been using those either since in this particular part of the court it was only the personal servants to the Royal Family that utilised them. He couldn't even remember using the servants' corridors himself except when they'd been scouring the palace when Lady Amelia had gone missing.

Harry?

Other than a slight pause, the response was quick.

Matthew, what's up?

You have some uninvited guests standing outside the Elite

entrance. Don't alarm them, but it might be prudent to reinforce the men on the inner doors.

When you say uninvited guests, you mean...?

Two members of the King's Guard who claim they have been stationed there.

That isn't likely. Matthew could feel the sudden spike of alertness from his fellow member of the Elite.

Correct. Keep things low-key, but make sure to double our guard without them knowing it, and be aware that they might be in other locations they shouldn't be.

Trying his best not to speed up—if he started to run the guards on the corridor would be alerted that something was up —Matthew continued on his way back to the Elite barracks. He passed through the doors and it took all the self control he could muster to keep walking casually. As if he didn't have a care in the world. There were members of the King's Guard here as well. The King's Guard were responsible for the perimeter of the palace and the realm in general. They also had their own barracks and common areas, he'd never seen them here either.

Once he passed through the doors assigned to Personal Service area he took a moment to check their quarters. He almost felt foolish when he didn't discover anyone here, other than himself. He shook his head, something was off. He'd rather be proven wrong and have everyone tell tales of his imagination for years to come than risk being the one responsible for the king being killed. Coming to a decision he ran down a side corridor, crashing his way through the door at the end. Finally, he understood the part of training that involved running as he pelted down the access corridor to the Fourth's Complex. He knew Ryan was in residence since he'd checked in earlier before adding the Royal Suite to his rounds.

The Elite on duty outside the doors to the Complex of the Fourth tensed, then relaxed marginally as they identified him.

Matthew had to admit, he was relieved to see them and not members of the King's Guard. Their eyes widened slightly as they realised he wasn't stopping and swung open the doors.

"Matthew?"

The voice of the senior member floated after him as he ran through.

I'm probably crazy, but be alert, I'll explain after I've briefed Ryan. Just let me know if you see any of the King's Guard heading this way.

Reaching the common area he skidded to a halt then ran toward the Cohort wing. While Ryan had been up when everyone had left, he guessed he'd decided to go back to bed, it was still early. As he burst through the bedroom door, Ryan sat bolt upright, a burst of energy lighting up the room. Matthew froze, looking up at the ball of light and wondered if Alex had taught him that particular trick or if he'd just learnt it because he was around Alex, Kyle and Jess so much.

"Matthew?" Ryan looked like he was swallowing down the panic of being abruptly woken up.

"Ryan, I think we have a problem. You can call me crazy, I'm probably an idiot but I'd rather be a laughingstock than ignore this."

That got Ryan's attention and he sat up frowning.

"What's wrong? Don't tell me the king snuck out of the palace." Ryan paled at the thought.

Matthew couldn't help the smile, despite the circumstances. At least they had similar concerns.

"No. I'm probably just overreacting, but well, what the hell are the King's Guard doing on the doors to the Royal Suite and in the Elite barracks?" Matthew wished he could have explained better what it was that had all his alarm bells ringing. He knew that just saying it that way it sounded stupid. He felt like he'd been reduced to a junior recruit again, jumping at shadows and imagining things going wrong.

Ryan slid off his bed, reaching for his weapons belt and strapping it on.

"Just as well I didn't bother changing. Let's go and make sure we are both laughingstocks." Ryan finished strapping on his belt.

Matthew nodded and stepped forward, assisting Ryan with equipping his weapons, relieved that Ryan had taken him seriously.

~

RYAN LOOKED out the windows that lined the side corridor they walked down, noting the dawn spreading across the sky and ducked his head. The battle at the Kastler estate would have started by now.

"The king is on the move, he's heading to the planning room."

Ryan looked at Matthew and nodded, he should have guessed the king wouldn't be able to sleep and would be up and moving early. The planning room was actually one of the smaller function rooms that had been turned into a war planning room with maps and enough space for all the interested parties that had a say during the planning phase.

"Who's with him?" Ryan knew they only had a handful of them that had been left behind.

"Harry" Matthew held up his hand as Ryan went to comment. "Yes I know, that's why he called me, as soon as the king left his rooms. I gave instructions to get more men on the door, but it didn't happen in time. I'd be going to join his detail now anyhow."

Ryan shook his head, there had been a plan. Of course William was the king and could change the plans whenever he wanted. It was up to them to scramble and catch up. Ryan snorted, suddenly amused, and caught Matthews startled glance.

"Well at least he's still here and not running into the wrong part of town to party in a bar."

Ryan traded grins with Matthew, but as they came out of the access doors that would put them in the corridor the king would be using to get to the planning room, his breath nearly froze in his heart.

Ryan saw that the commander of the King's Guard was blocking the corridor William was walking down. Even more alarming were the King's Guard coming up from behind, in between his own position and the king. The fact that his fellow Elite who'd been on the king's doors walked on William's shoulder and was moving to place himself between William and the commander only relieved his anxiety by a little.

"Commander, you forget yourself." William's voice was clipped.

Ryan felt the world around him slow down. He saw the commander and his men start to draw blades from their scabbards. A move that killed any hope that Matthew had been wrong in his suspicions.

Ryan could feel the undercurrent from William change. His expression moved from irritation at his path being blocked by the King's Guard, to alarm as he realised they were drawing their swords. The king and the two members of the Elite with him turned side on, seeing the team of King's Guard cutting their retreat from behind as well.

While the action in front of him seemed to play out in slow motion, Ryan drew his own blade in a smooth practiced move. He was aware that Matthew did the same at his side. As the king started to draw his own weapons, he saw one of the Elite closest to their own position slump to the ground as he was cut down before he could finish drawing his own blade. Ryan drew his own power, desperately afraid he was too late.

66

CLOSE QUARTERS

A triumphant grin split Kyle's lips and he bit back a bark of laughter as he saw Kin try to flee through the veiled world only to bounce back from the barrier that enclosed them. They would have felt it snap into place even if they hadn't known what had happened. Without pause, Kyle nodded at Kat and they both gathered their own men, wrapping them in power. He was aware that both Alex and Jess did the same; each of them knew their own roles. As much as he hated to leave Alex and Jess to fight the Kin and Sundered—who, once they worked out they couldn't escape, were turning to fight—he knew his own role.

Turning his mind's eye to the bright sparks of light that shone in the caverns below the Kastler estate, he surged to that place. In that fleeting moment, he knew the slumbering ranks of the Sundered below were being roused by the healers with them. As each was woken from their healer-induced slumber, they fled the caverns to join in the battle above.

Get ready.

At his warning, he heard the scrape of blades from his

combined Elite and Guard, all of them carefully chosen as some of the best close-quarters fighters in Vallantia.

With a cursory check that took just a split-second, Kyle pulled them all into the vast cavern. His men, well-practiced and still in their fighting formations, lashed out at those around them with barely a pause. Kyle looked up, meeting Kat's gaze briefly as she appeared on the other side of the cavern with her own guard unit. Their goal was simple: kill as many of the Sundered who lay in drugged slumber in the cots before the corrupted healers could rouse them and send them above to fight. The more of them they could kill here, as they slept, the safer their friends who fought above would be.

Kyle allowed himself to fall into the flow and patterns of the fight, losing himself in the battle. A Sundered One's eyes flashed open and he surged up in the cot only to slump, his light dying as Kyle's blades flashed, flickering with the power that danced down their length. Keeping in formation, they dispatched one Sundered after the other as they made their way methodically across the cavern, the floor where they'd passed becoming slick with blood.

"My lord!" The terse warning drew Kyle's attention to the far side of the cavern where some of the healers had managed to wake their charges.

As some of the healers worked fervently to flush enough of the toxin in the Sundered so more would stir to join their ranks, some of their brethren stood in a file behind the Sundered Ones who charged forward. Kyle smiled tightly as he turned with his unit to face this new threat. These Sundered weren't simply waking and lashing out. They moved in coordination with each other in some semblance of a unit. Kyle guessed that these were some of the ones that had been used to sack the villages of Vallantia, leaving death and destruction in their wake.

Kyle pulled more power into himself, refusing to acknowledge the fatigue nipping at his edges. He knew that if he was starting to feel tired then his guards must be in a worse state. While he knew his Elite could use the veil, albeit not much, the regular guards would be unlikely to have the ability to draw on the veil to refresh themselves. In a twist, without pausing to think about it, he sent energy into his guards around him, both Elite and regular alike. He only knew it had worked when James threw him a startled glance. The guards wouldn't know what had happened, but Kyle could see from their suddenly sharp movements that their growing exhaustion had been washed away. He had no doubt they probably thought it a second wind at seeing this new threat. His Elite had enough ability to not only sense what he did, but understand it.

Kyle bit back a curse. While they had managed to wade through many of the Sundered before the healers could rouse them, they'd still only managed to get through a small fraction of those who slept down here. The healers, now working in concert with each other, were waking their charges faster than he and his group could cut them down. The group under the control of the healers that faced off against them was managing to slow their progress down while more and more of the Sundered woke and disappeared, no doubt joining the battle that raged on above.

Lashing out with his blades, he cut down another of the Sundered who'd confronted him. Kyle lunged at another opponent, grimacing as others rose to take the places of the ones they'd killed.

"My lord!"

Kyle turned his head and saw James and the rest of his guard unit that he'd dragged with him battling against the Sundered. He only hoped that Alex and Jess were able to deal with those that had woken and joined the battle above.

Drawing himself back to his own part, he launched himself at the handful of Sundered that had his guards backing up. He threw yet more of his power towards his people, setting their blades flaring with an elemental fire much like his own, making every strike they made against their enemy more effective.

Kyle lost himself in battle once again—just him, his blades, and his guards who depended on him to keep them safe from the Sundered's power and the next enemy. His world slowed down as it often did when he fought, or perhaps he sped up. He'd never been able to work out what caused the phenomenon. He was aware when a couple of his men fell but didn't allow it to distract him from the task at hand.

Cal!

Kyle staggered as Kat's desperate cry rang in his head, a cry echoed by Edward. Tears sprang in his eyes as a wave of pain and loss washed over him. He knew what had happened and that caused another bout of intense desolation to hit him. Kyle spun to see Kat on her knees, staring sightlessly straight ahead of her, tears streaming down her eyes.

Kat. Kyle nearly doubled over, fighting to increase his mental shields as he tried to reach her.

Kat, behind you!

Kyle lunged forward as a Sundered reared up from behind Kat to grab his mentor and friend. As the hands clamped on her head Kyle screamed a denial.

No!

ALEX'S BLADE SWEPT OUT, and took the head of the Sundered who'd appeared before him. Not quite satisfied, he followed through with a controlled burst of power that incinerated the body before it crashed to the ground. Instead the ashes floated down on those below. Alex grinned, aware it was ruthless of him and entirely inappropriate, but he was sure Isabella would be proud of him. For once he'd been perfectly controlled in his action. If he hadn't, everyone would likely be ash right now.

Alex staggered as the image of a cavern, with a multitude of Sundered rising from their beds and the sudden spray of blood, interposed itself on the reality in front of him. He took a steadying breath, realising it was Kyle and his battle deep in the bowels of the castle. Taking a moment, he sent a burst of energy to his friend who battled below before wrenching his attention back to his own task. Kyle and Kat might be battling alone, with only their guards around them, but they were the best suited to that particular task. Given how many of the Sundered Kyle and Kat's party were managing to take out before they could be roused to fight, it was a gamble that had paid off.

Drawing his attention back to the fight occurring above ground, he noted with a critical eye that the ground assault had gone to plan, mostly. The ground forces protected by Edward, Cal, Damien and Isabella had taken the forces amassed by the Order and Lord Kastler by surprise and had them contained, or would shortly.

His own party and Jess's were dealing with the Sundered and Kin who rose to fight. While he had to admit they were a little outnumbered, they were aided by the fact that the first thing most of them did was to try to flee, only to rebound off the barrier. If the situation hadn't been so dire, their stunned and panicked reactions would have made him laugh. Their realisation of their containment caused more than one group to throw their weapons down and hand themselves over to face the king's mercy. Alex felt a momentarily sympathy for some of these men and women, handed over by their commanders and lords to a traitor's battle for a cause not necessarily their own.

As soon as the ground assault was in hand, both Isabella and Damien would join them in cleaning up those of their brethren who were mad, or just plain bad.

Alex spun when despite the interference of all those using

the power of the veil, he felt a signature that he would recognise anywhere.

Amelia.

He sensed that she wasn't alone, although that wasn't unexpected. There was one other signature with her.

Alex wrapped his own party in his power and surged forward. He resisted the urge to laugh outright as Amelia and her party slammed right into the barrier he, Kyle and Jess had constructed. Even if in the back corner of his mind he admitted it was partly relief, he hadn't been quite convinced that their barrier would contain them, even with the trials they'd conducted.

The shock of hitting the barrier that they plainly hadn't seen threw his targets out of the veil, slamming hard into the damp ground. Alex crossed the distance to the far side of the battle in an instant and hit the ground running, Marcus on his side with the rest of his men in formation around them. He dispelled the veil and blocked out the rest of the battle raging around him as he moved to engage with his own targets. He had no trouble identifying Amelia as she shook herself and stood up, drawing her blades and spinning to face him. The man to the rear he knew was Kevin, formerly a member of the Companion's Cohort when Edward had been the Fourth.

Kevin had his own sword drawn but seemed to be making a great deal of effort to keep Amelia between him and Alex. Alex's eyes narrowed as he saw the rippling barrier Kevin had thrown around himself, keeping others at bay. He seemed to be unconcerned about the Sundered who were being cut down. Alex gathered it wasn't Kevin's mind that was directing the others since he seemed wholly focused on him right now.

The healers, contain the healers, they are controlling the Sundered!

Alex heard Ryan's warning but he didn't let it distract him.

Other than being aware of them and the deadly dance taking place around him, he was leaving the Sundered to the others.

Alex stumbled as a combined blow from Amelia hammered into his shields. He kept his own personal shields in place as he countered thrusts both physical and mental from his two opponents. Alex sucked in more energy, allowing it to flow through him before he lunged at Amelia. The shock of the blast distracted Amelia briefly but she twisted and avoided his power-sheathed blade as it cut through her shields, heading for her neck. Alex nearly cursed as his blade caressed her skin, close enough to draw a thin line of blood.

He lashed out with one of his blades and parried Amelia's own strike. Alex was keenly aware that while he was stronger, unlike him they hadn't just expended a great deal of energy putting a barrier around the Kastler estate. That, and Kevin had continued to carefully keep behind Amelia, not engaging directly in the fight. If he had, Alex had to admit even if it was only to himself, he might have been in way more trouble right now.

Alex had to keep pushing the fact that it was Amelia he was fighting aside. It was one thing to argue that she was a traitor, she'd killed his father. She'd inserted herself into his mind, convincing him he loved her. Tried to trick him into the ranks of the Order.

All of those things were true but, in his heart, he saw that girl. His best friend's little sister that he'd defended from the drunken fool in the court all those years ago. He saw the woman she'd become, and it broke his heart that he'd failed, failed in his duty to protect her.

Oh how sweet, lover, you still care. Amelia's mocking voice entered his mind, her eyes dancing as she stared at him.

Cal!

Alex reared back under the pain and loss that rolled over him from Edward and Kat as they sensed the death of one of their closest friends. In that moment of distraction he felt the air explode from his lungs and he stumbled under the onslaught of multiple blows, this time from both of them. Drawing his attention back to his own part of the battle, he caught a flash of blade, he rolled aside and jumped back to his feet but not before he felt the stabbing pain of a small knife plunge into his side.

That's one, lover.

Alex looked at Amelia, shocked as her laughter rang in his mind.

Isabella fought with the guards around her, she let them do what they were good at, fighting the rebels. She did what she was best suited for in this fight. She, like the others within their ranks with power, took on the Sundered as they appeared from the depths of the caverns below to fall on those that fought above ground. The difference in some of the Sundered was astounding. Some were the mad ones that they were all used to, the ones the tales were about with no intelligence in them at all, they lashed out in pain and anger at all around them. Then there were the newer breed that had started appearing in recent times. The ones who seemed to have a little more control, yet bound in madness all the same. There were very few like the former Consort Elect of the Fourth. That was a relief. Regardless of that they were still badly outnumbered.

As she fought Isabella kept a part of her mind scanning the ones with power as they appeared. There was one signature that she was looking for, one that she would know anywhere.

Sensing a Sundered appear Isabella launched herself at her, before she could even orientate herself, her blade sliding into the woman's chest and into her heart. Her enraged scream died as did the light in her eyes and she crumpled to the ground.

"My Lady!"

Isabella spun and saw the cause for concern, their group had encountered someone with a little power that fought on the other side. As she jumped herself and those assigned to her protection detail forward, blinking in and out of the veil she assessed the one who fought on the other side. He wasn't strong enough to be Kin, but he was strong enough to be a problem for the units that she was here to protect.

Isabella's eyes narrowed and she propelled herself forward, regardless of her assessment of the individual she reinforced her personal shield, extending it to cover her protection detail and those in the front line of the battle. Her blades flashed as she took on her opponent, his grin of victory faded to be replaced by panic as it dawned on him, he was severely outmatched. Pulling in power she blasted it at the man whose eyes glazed as her power rolled over him and he toppled over, unconscious, as did those closest to him. She didn't understand the orders to preserve as many lives as they could herself. These men and women were trying to kill them. Why let them live to try again. Yet she did her best to abide by them.

Assuring herself this threat was down and not getting back up in a hurry, Isabella folded the veil around herself and her detail and moved them back into position towards the centre. From here she could get to any position she needed to quickly. Not that they really needed her skills all that much against these members of the Order they were fighting. The skill of the men and women who fought around her for the king were a level far above that of those who fought for the Order. She suspected that Alex had placed her here with this crew to protect her as best he could. The fact that she had Cal with his group on one side of her and Edward with his on the other confirmed it for her.

Suddenly she felt it, that signature in the veil that a part of her brain had been scanning for. Isabella spun rising above her battle group, her eyes narrowing as she saw movement through the battle.

Aiden.

Her eyes narrowed. He'd abandoned his old man persona to take his actual form. There was a formation of Sundered in front of him, cutting down any opposition they encountered and a curious couple of people clustered around him that he kept close.

Go Isabella, this part is nearly over I can cover my group and yours as the mop up concludes. Cal was looking at her from his own position nodding at her.

Go, we've got this. Edward's head jerked towards Aiden and his group as he jumped them closer to the barrier.

Isabella smiled, noting neither of them seemed terribly concerned. None had managed to pass the barrier Alex, Kyle and Jess had set in place. She doubted that Aiden would prove any different. Particularly the way he was jumping towards it. He was either terribly out of practice or trying not to draw the attention of those he feared were more powerful than him. Then again, he could just be trying to sneak out without being noticed, that was within his character as well.

Isabella's smile turned hard, her eyes narrowing. Not this time. He would not survive, sneaking away from the misery he'd created again. Sending her thanks to Cal and Edward, Isabella wrapped the veil around her and pushed herself towards Aiden's position.

Jess swept through the battle, merging from the veiled world to the real world from one moment to the next. Megan and the rest of the guards took the blinking from one place to the other with a practiced ease, holding their defensive positions around her, lashing out with their blades and power to take on the lesser adversaries that rose before them.

Unlike the units of their counterparts who were mostly mopping up the rank upon rank of traitorous guards and members of the Killiam Order, they were going after the Sundered. Jess was aware of Kyle and Kat battling in the caverns below in an attempt to take out as many as they could before they rose. Still, given the numbers they faced, even both of them together couldn't kill them all. It hadn't taken long at all for the Sundered to start popping into the midst of the battle. Most turned unerringly towards her or the others with power. Some, a very few, just fell almost ravenously on whomever they landed in the middle of regardless of whose side they were on. Those were the Sundered she was used to. It showed they'd still managed to catch the Order before they were completely ready.

The bulk of the ones who shed the veil and launched to attack her or Damien, Isabella, Edward and Cal seemed to be guided by another hand. There was some purpose in their attack and some glimmer of intelligence reflected in their eyes. These were the new breed of Sundered, and way more dangerous, although their powers and sanity—if it could be called that—varied greatly. Thankfully the Order hadn't managed to create as many like Amelia as they'd obviously hoped.

Jess lost track of time, lost in the depths of the fight, with one Sundered falling only to have another take its place, one after the other. In a rare pool of calm, Jess spun as she felt Amelia's signature and saw her hit the barrier around the Kastler estate with such force that it threw her and her companion out of the veil into the real world. Jess couldn't help the chuckle that escaped her lips at that.

The surge of power as Alex responded first would have taken her breath away if she hadn't been so used to it by now. Hauling her attention back to her current position, she swung her blade with the weight of the veil behind it, taking off the head of one of the Sundered before he'd had time to even scream at her. Jess went to move in Alex's direction, to help even up the odds in his favour, only to be set upon by multiple Sundered that seemed to be piling up in their haste to get to her.

Dismissing Alex for now, she concentrated on her own task, even though her first instinct was to go and fight at Alex's side. Growling in frustration, she cut down yet another of the Sundered, who was immediately replaced by another.

Cal!

Jess spun, feeling like she'd taken a physical blow as the pain and loss in that one word screamed by two mind voices hit her. Jess's vision blurred as tears sprung in her eyes, she knew that Cal was dead, even if she didn't know how it had happened. She pushed aside her own grief, now was not the time to fall apart, war didn't wait politely to allow mourning. She turned looking towards where she knew Cal's group had been, off to the side of the estate. When she'd last checked on them earlier they had things in hand. Now she saw mayhem. Jess's mind went blank for a moment as she struggled with what she was seeing. Members of the King's Guard had turned and were now fighting, cutting down men and women that they'd been fighting alongside just moments before. A small group of fighters still stood fighting desperately as their battle had turned and they found themselves surrounded on all sides.

AS KYLE SURGED FORWARD, Kat finally rose back up from the instant depression she'd slumped into. She tensed and her eyes widened as she realised the Sundered behind her had his hands clamped around her head. As he began to snap her head around Kat's blade flashed and she spun in the same direction.

Her blade flashed up with a precision born from an extremely long lifetime of practice, slamming up and into the Sundered's heart. She stood staring, eyes wild with pain as she stared down at the Sundered who collapsed at her feet.

Kyle made it to her side and pulled her into his arms.

I'm sorry. I know it hurts to lose someone you've been so close to for so long. Kat didn't reply immediately, but he felt her tears soaking into his shirt.

It feels like a part of myself has been torn out. She pulled away, wiping the tears that streamed from her eyes.

Cal wanted this madness put to an end. He wouldn't want you to die as well. Edward needs you. Alex needs you. I need you. We can mourn his death later, when this is over.

Kyle pulled her back in and kissed her forehead, giving both of them another few moments to pull themselves together.

The healers, contain the healers, they are controlling the Sundered!

His eyes narrowed as he contemplated the healers at Ryan's warning. They'd known it was the healers breaking the Kin, turning them into the Sundered, but controlling them? He wondered briefly how Ryan had come by this information; if the lad had managed to sneak here with the attack group, he was going to be in trouble. Kyle shook himself, that was an issue he could deal with later.

He knew he didn't have the power left to enclose the whole cavern in a barrier. He'd discussed the option with Alex and Jess but they'd discarded it as being too risky. If they put the barrier around the cavern alone, that would have left those above the freedom to escape. He did, however, judge he had enough to deal with the healers. The instant fatigue he felt —and pushed aside—let him know that he couldn't keep drawing power the way he was without payment.

Kyle reinforced his shield around his guards, then jumped, merging into the veil and passing over the line of Sundered. Without pausing to think about it, he shoved the healers back with a blast of power into a small alcove in the cavern wall. Gritting his teeth, he drew even more power, batting away their feeble attempts to breach his personal shields to control his mind. Kyle threw up a smaller version of the barrier they'd thrown over the whole estate at the entrance of the alcove to stop them physically, and a second to stop them reaching his, or anyone else's mind.

Kyle stumbled as the onslaught on his mind, no matter how feeble, suddenly ceased. He caught himself on the rough rock wall as his knees buckled from exhaustion. Finally Kyle looked around the cavern, silent now except for the ragged breathing of the king's men. The floor of the cavern, worn smooth over generations of use, was now slick with blood. Under the direction of James the guards began to methodically check that the Sundered Ones they'd dealt with were dispatched properly—a grizzly task, yet they couldn't risk that any of these ones would heal and rise to attack again.

James moved over to one of the Sundered who was still bound to his cot with shackles. He glanced back at Kyle.

"What of these ones, my lord?"

Kyle shook himself back into action and moved over to the one James was inspecting. Kat moved to inspect one of the others, looking down on the wreck of a human chained to the cot.

He shook his head. This one was young, hair unkempt, bones showing clearly as if he'd been sick and lost weight recently. Kyle pushed the anger that rose in him down, making a quick assessment of the handful of Sundered who still lay unmoving. Each of them looked like they were just this side of death and Kyle judged them unlikely to wake or survive without healer intervention.

"Leave these ones. I suspect the Order hadn't finished with their so-called treatment."

James nodded and stood. "Yes, my lord."

"We'll get the healers to check on them when we're done with this mess."

With one final sweeping look around the large underground cavern, Kyle gathered his remaining men to him. Pushing weariness aside once more, he dragged them all with him into the veil and moved them the short distance up to the old estate house itself.

It was time for the second of his tasks during this fight.

67

ENGAGEMENT

Jess wrapped herself and her group in the veil, jumping the short distance to the small embattled group that were now fighting for their own survival. Sensing a turn in the battle more and more Sundered were popping into the middle of the fight. They fell on those who were defenceless from above and without Cal there to pick them off it was turning into a slaughter.

Without thinking about what she was about to do Jess appeared in the middle of the cluster of Sundered who'd appeared. Throwing her head back Jess drew in power from all around her, to the point she could feel it lick up her arms and body, knew her eyes glowed with power. Jess spun and as she did so, she spun the power from her. In her mind's eye she could see the Sundered as they appeared around her and she directed that power as it left her moulding it into daggers that tracked towards the Sundered. The daggers of pure power flew out from her one after the other with deadly accuracy, taking out the Sundered who'd turned to her like they were attracted to her burning bright power, like insects to light.

Other daggers spun further to the rear of this small group

fighting for their survival, unsuspecting enemies to the rear collapsed as the dagger that they couldn't see or defend against slammed into them.

As the Sundered and the ranks of the enemy around her thinned, Jess felt darkness close in on her. Here in the middle of the embattled group surrounded by enemies she felt herself slump even as she battled to stay conscious.

ALEX WAS aware of a shift in the battle ranging around him yet tried to concentrate on his part of it. He had to trust his people to all do their parts. His task in this battle was right here in front of him.

Alex went on the offensive, forcing Amelia and Kevin on the back foot as they retreated. He ignored the others around him, trusting Marcus and his guards to either deal with any problems or alert him if they couldn't.

Feeling an explosion of power Alex gritted his teeth, not looking although he desperately wanted to. It had been Jess, he knew it, then where Jess had been, there was a sudden blankness.

Oh Alex, you're being awfully careless with your Companions. Amelia smirked at him.

Don't worry, I'll make a point of taking care of the rest. Kevin's eyes glittered at him as he threw his taunts.

As Alex stared at Kevin, Amelia darted forward, her blade slashing, he felt it draw blood on his arm as he backed up, throwing a blast of power to push them both back.

Amelia backed up, staring at him in anticipation

That's number two....

Amelia's eyes widened as she heard her other self talking to the man she'd been fighting.

That's number two....

She'd known she was fighting at her master's side but hadn't wanted to know, except as those words filtered past her guard she paled. She knew what that meant, the last time her other self had uttered those words Jess had fallen into the Order's hands. Scrambling to her feet Amelia ran to the windows, looking out she saw Alex looking back at her as if confused. She saw the signs of the fight he'd been in with blood from a slash to his upper arm and the indications he'd been stabbed in the side.

No, no, no....

Amelia's head shook in denial then she froze.

She remembered she'd been able to help Jess. Then there was the smile that had curved the lips on her body when she'd thought of Aiden dying. She'd helped distract Aiden when he went after Isabella. She looked around her cell, she realised Brian had been correct. It was her cell, where she'd put herself. Not where her master had stashed her as some form of torture. If he'd had that in mind he would be paying her visits to gloat.

Her resolve firmed, he wouldn't take Alex. She wouldn't let him. She'd already been used to hurt him enough.

Amelia screamed, pushing back the paralysing fear as it threatened to overwhelm her. She started to run, but this time instead of retreating with cell doors slamming behind her, the doors to her cell blasted open. The layers of locks and chains that had kept her bound, safe, shattered exploding outward. The darkness that had surrounded her receded as she ran, the light increasing. She felt the sudden confusion of her other self and not pausing to consider the consequences she wrested power for herself, blasting it out at the other. The darkness shattered under her assault and she felt her body stagger. Amelia pushed the sudden pain she felt aside. Far from being cowered by it, the feeling spurred her on. She felt it herself. Felt pain from her own body, not just as the other.

Amelia came out into the light, a gasp of breath coming from her mouth as her body drew in air. Alex stood not far away, a shield between him and where she currently stood.

Amelia spun, her swords flashing as she launched herself at her master. She knew she didn't have long, the other might be gone or banished for now but her master still had his hooks in her. She could no more block him out of her mind now than she could for even a single moment since she'd given herself to him, begged him to take the pain away. She didn't need long though, she just needed to delay her master long enough so that Alex could clear the poison from his system. If anyone could, she had faith he could. Particularly since Jess had somehow managed it. She had no doubt Jess would have told Alex.

As Kevin reared back in shock, Amelia screamed and launched herself at him, drawing power as she did so. She wondered if her eyes glowed with flames, as she'd seen others do and hit out at Kevin with her mind and sword. She felt clumsy, sluggish, not used to commanding her own body anymore but her limbs still responded. Kevin may have been shocked by her turning on him but he recovered, deflecting her efforts with his own. Then his eyes narrowed and she felt it, that roaring blast of power that hit her mind.

Amelia had an instant to hope she'd given Alex enough time, she screamed although this time in pain, as she felt like her mind was splintering. Fire raced through her, as if Kevin was trying to cleanse her body of her presence.

Amelia felt her body slumping, the world around her receding. She wondered if she really was herself, how many of her had existed before now. She gasped as cracks began to fracture the world and splinter then as darkness claimed her, she smiled as she realised it wasn't the world that splintered.

It was her.

~

KYLE SEARCHED the estate house for the one signature that he knew he'd recognise. He hadn't realised how much he wanted her to still be here until disappointment surged in him when he couldn't detect her presence here in the house.

Amelia?

Kyle immediately felt foolish, the sensible part of his brain knew that he wouldn't receive a response. Wherever Amelia was he was certain that Kevin was. She wouldn't leave without her master. He held onto the hope she would be contained safely and the healers could help her, release her from the prison of her mind as they had him. He dismissed her from his mind with effort, he still had a job to do. There were enough outside who he had no doubt would recognise Amelia and deal with her.

Kyle made sure to grab hold of the guards closest to him and hauled them with him, appearing within the confines of the castle walls, although this time above the ground.

He ran down the stone hallway, Kat running at his side with the drumming of booted feet behind them assuring him that they hadn't lost any of the guards during the short jump in the veil.

A door opened suddenly to his right, causing Kyle to draw his power in reaction. A couple of guards got halfway into the corridor and froze, their hands straying to their sword hilts. Time seemed to slow for Kyle and he could see their fingers wrap around the hilts, the protracted scrape of metal as they started to draw their weapons, their eyes wide with fear. Kyle withheld the strike he'd been about to perform. Instead he shoved the obviously terrified household guards back into the room behind them. The men went flying through the air disappearing through the door, and Kyle heard the thump and grunt of pain as they landed.

Two of James's men shot past him, following the men through the door.

Kyle paused, taking a breath as adrenaline and power surged through him. He closed the distance to the end of the hallway. Matthew and his men opened the door, and he followed close on their heels.

His eyes settled on Lord Kastler who sat, gagged and tied unceremoniously to one of his large leather chairs. Bennett stood close behind with his blades in his hands.

A smile graced Kyle's lips as he stalked forward, his guards fanning around the room. He felt the waves of coldness roll out not only from him but Kat as well. Kyle nodded to Bennett, who took his knife and cut the gag from Kastler, pulling out the wad of fabric that had been stuffed into his mouth.

The lord sat quivering. He reeked of fear.

"I… I'm a lord… The king will hear of this!"

Kyle chuckled, feeling genuinely amused. "Oh, you fool. You don't know your king at all."

"You dare! I'm one of His Majesty's lords." Kastler's bluster was ruined by his quivering lips.

"Exactly, Lord Kastler. You are one of his lords and you raised your banner in rebellion." Kyle gestured to James, who issued orders to his men.

Lord Kastler started to scream and hurl threats at the men who formed up around him, one on each of his arms grabbing him in a vice-like grip.

That dealt with Kyle glanced out the window and saw the rather uneven battle unfolding, with Jess unconscious at the centre. A small group of defenders ringed her, fighting off the Order's units that seemed to surround their position. His eyes widened as he saw it was Olivia and the wild Kin she'd brought with her that were maintaining cover over the small group, combining to pick off the Sundered that seemed to keep appearing, at their position.

Kyle glanced back at Kat. “Can I leave the rest of the mop-up in here with you?”

“Go, Kyle. I and these guards can handle those who remain.”

Kyle didn’t wait any longer, hauling himself into the veil.

68

ASSISTANCE

As Harry, badly outnumbered, fell to the blades of the commander and his men Ryan threw his power around William.

"It's time for the Rathadon line to die. Lord Kastler will be a more fitting king than you ever could have hoped to be."

Ryan could see the deadly glint in the commander's eyes. As the commander lunged, William's own blade rose to counter it.

"Ryan...." Matthew's blade rose and his own shield sprung up.

The traitors that stood between him and his king turned and with a yell charged at him. Making a snap decision Ryan wrapped the veil around William even more tightly, and grabbing Matthew as well he hauled them all into the veiled world. William staggered as the blade he was in the middle of defending against was no longer there and spun around to see Ryan and Matthew.

What's happening down there?

As William glanced around him Ryan was reminded that neither the king nor Matthew were strong enough to part the veil enough to see what was happening in the palace. As Ryan drew his attention back to the palace, he heard the screams and clash of blades. The fighting hadn't stopped because he'd pulled the king out of their reach. Looking at the Elite barracks he paled, seeing most of those remaining in the common room had fallen to the blades of the King's Guard who'd outnumbered them and attacked without warning.

The fighting continues Your Majesty. It's spreading all over the palace. Ryan concentrated and pulled the handful of Elite battling in the Elite common room to him.

Matthew and William both started to see more of the Elite appear; to their credit the men lowered their blades after spinning to face the new threat. Ryan saw the relief evident on their faces as they spotted the king.

Ryan, we need to get back there and fight. Take me back to the palace. William's tone held the note of command.

Ryan looked at his king and remembered the Fourth's injunctions to keep the king safe.

No Your Majesty. Our job, my job is to keep you safe.

Feeling an incoming surge and hearing terrified screaming Ryan spun, his eyes widening as he saw a group of Sundered appear in the court. They were cutting down everyone in their path. Hearing the wailing of a child, Ryan closed his eyes. It would only be a matter of time, if they looked up here he had no doubt they'd come after the king.

What's happened? William had conflicting emotions playing out on his face.

It's not just the King's Guard anymore, there are some of the Sundered down there. Don't inform Alex, if he takes down the barrier around the Kastler estate before they have dealt with the rebels, everyone will suffer.

Ryan's mouth firmed. Perhaps he could keep them occupied, concentrating on him rather than others.

Ryan spun to look at Matthew. *Can you hold the king and the others here? Just as you practiced?*

Matthew nodded. *I can.*

Ryan, you can't fight alone, they'll kill you. William's voice grated.

I ran on the streets before Alex found me, remember? Fighting and moving in confined places is something I know. Stay here. Ryan stared at Matthew who nodded and expanded his own shields around the small group.

Ryan turned from them, stepping back to the fight in the palace, towards the Sundered who cut down those they encountered. He didn't feel the need to remind the king or Matthew that he hadn't been a very good thief, that seemed beside the point.

Ryan looked around and spotted the wailing child who was standing next to his fallen mother. At his arrival the Sundered looked up at him, diverted from their immediate prey. Repeating the trick he'd performed on the king, Ryan reached out grabbing the child and flung her into the veil towards Matthew.

With a scream the Sundered charged through the ranks of the King's Guard who stood to one side. They grinned as the Sundered ran straight at him. Ryan staggered back under the combined attack from multiple Sundered on his shields. Then suddenly he wasn't alone anymore.

Dashel grinned at him as his Dagger Wives parted, taking him into the centre of their protective detail. Ryan's eyes widened seeing their flashing daggers take out members of the King's Guard who backed away from the sudden onslaught. He could feel their burst of power as they repelled the Sundered. He finally understood and appreciated what the term Dagger Wives meant.

"Come Ryan let us help you. The dance of daggers in the halls of a palace, this is our kind of fight."

Ryan nodded, daring to hope for the first time since the traitors sprung their attack that maybe he might survive. As they fought their way through the palace there were signs that others had joined the fight against the attackers. Ryan tried to block out the screams and just concentrate on the job at hand. He wanted the Sundered concentrating on him, not on where the king might be. As they attacked, a man in a servant's uniform came out of a side corridor, with a cluster of children around him, looking over his shoulder. He skidded to a halt, panic on his face as he saw the fighting in the open hall he'd ran into and then looked behind him again, frozen in panic.

Ryan spotted more Sundered and guards coming down the corridor the servant and children had run from. Sparing a moment of attention, trusting those around him to defend him if needed, he grabbed the servant and children, flinging them into the veil to the king.

"Ryan, the one behind the Sundered ranks, if we continue to distract them from the front, can you take her out?" Raquel who'd been fighting on his other side directed his attention to a woman standing behind the Sundered.

Ryan gritted his teeth in effort as he deflected more strikes against his shields and glanced at the women Raquel meant.

"I think so, why?" From what he could see her eyes were oddly blank and she wasn't even carrying a weapon.

"There is a strangeness between her and the ones you call Sundered, I think she is directing them."

Ryan nodded his agreement, when he saw the ones from the corridor behind had made it into the hall, their eyes glowering at him as their victims had disappeared. One of them in the centre looked up, then back at the woman who grinned then disappeared into the veil.

Ryan blanched. "They're going after the king!"

Before he could respond he felt Rosalinda expand her power as she gathered half the dagger wives to her.

"Deal with these ones, I'll not let them harm William." Rosalinda disappeared from sight.

Ryan swore. "Damn it!"

He wanted to go but he couldn't leave this threat here either. In a quick move he pulled the veil around him and ran, lifting himself up and over the ranks in front of him to the woman to the rear. Gritting his teeth, he swung his sword and dropped the veil just as it cut through her neck. The woman didn't even have time to scream as she crumpled to the ground. Ryan looked up to see if Dashel needed any help with the Sundered, only to stare in astonishment to see the Sundered slump to the ground.

WILLIAM MUTTERED a curse and stopped trying to get himself out of the veil by himself. His rudimentary powers just didn't want to cooperate. While he'd transported himself into the veil while he'd been sick, it had taken Alex to get him out. He'd also never been able to duplicate the feat. He glared at Matthew, who simply stood, concentrating holding the grey mist of the veil a short distance from them, so they stood in a clustered group in a sea of fog. Finally he sighed. There was no point in blaming Matthew, while he could hold them here safely, Matthew couldn't get them out of the veil any more than he could himself. They were stuck until Ryan or someone else came and collected them.

William jumped, startled as a child suddenly appeared in the veil, landing not far away from where they stood in a pool of grey mist. William took one step only to have Matthew place a hand on his chest.

It's alright, I'm not going far, I'll just get the child. Like you, I can survive in the veil until we're rescued. I take it those others can't?

No, they have even less power than you do, Your Majesty. Matthew shook his head.

You hold this position, trust me I'm not going far but I won't leave the child to be lost. William edged his way out, keeping his eyes on the child.

He shuddered at the sudden chill as he stepped just outside of Matthew's protective shield and picked the small boy up. Turning he kept his eye on Matthew and walked quickly back into the circle, not bothering to hide his sigh of relief.

Random people from the palace appeared without any fanfare, were flung into the veil by Ryan. As their little group grew in size, after they got over their shock, he obtained at least some information of the battle in the palace.

William spun as he heard someone arrive in the veil, his smile faded as he saw some Sundered appear a short distance from them. A clear emotionless voice instructed them.

Tyson, kill the king, kill them all.

The Sundered in front turned his eyes unerringly on him. *Yes, Healer Jenny.*

William drew his sword as the Sundered launched straight at them, several of the other Sundered descending on them through the veil. William shoved the children behind him as his handful of Elite battled against the Sundered. His relief as a number of the Sundered fell to their blades was short-lived as three of his Elite fell as well. As bad as these Sundered seemed to be at fighting, they still managed to take some with them due to numbers. William could see sweat break out on Matthew's forehead as he battled to keep them here, tethered safely in the veil and fight off Sundered at the same time. As he fought, William spared a moment of thanks that Alex had insisted on running him around the practice field to brush up his sword work.

Hearing a gasp, William looked aside and saw Matthew go down, a sword protruding from his chest. The one that had been called Tyson pulled his blade free then looked up to meet William's eyes and smiled.

Your turn, Your Majesty.

Tyson blurred, then suddenly appeared in front of him blade sweeping down. William stumbled as he felt hands trying to drag him back as he desperately raised his sword. He'd forgotten about the collection of servants and children behind him. He fell back and without Matthew to hold it at bay the grey mist swept over him. A dagger flared to life in the veil, taking Tyson's head off his shoulders before he could finish his sword stroke. Tyson's body toppled on top of him and he rolled it aside in time to see the veil being pushed back and the woman who'd directed the Sundered go down, dead at the hands of Annabella. After checking her adversary really was dead, Annabella made her way back towards him, taking a position with other members of their party leaving him at the centre of their protective circle. Their blades all drawn, looking fierce they faced out towards any threat that may appear.

Rosalinda sheathed her daggers to kneel beside him, her hands checking him.

Were you hurt, husband? Her dark eyes, filled with concern, stared into his before she drew herself back to the task of patting his body gently. William realised she was looking for signs that he'd been stabbed, looking for blood.

He captured her hands in his. *No, thanks to your timely arrival I'm in one piece.*

Taking a deep breath William stood, Rosalinda by his side. He stared at her more than a little stunned that she'd come to his rescue.

You said to me in the garden that I didn't belong to anyone, not even you. Rosalinda's hand rose, touching him gently on the arm as if she was still trying to reassure herself that he was unharmed.

I did. William smiled, despite the circumstances.

You said my choices were my own. Her eyes continued to stare into his own.

I meant it.

I've made my decision husband. I'll not stand by and see you slaughtered. We stand and fight together, it is our way and if we fall, we will fall together. It won't be from cowardice or inaction.

William took a breath contemplating Rosalinda and nodded acknowledgment. He smiled and wished they'd met under different circumstances and she hadn't come here while they were in the middle of a war. Then again, if she hadn't been here and been perfectly capable of fighting in his defence, he'd be dead right now.

"ALRIGHT BOY, game's over, where have you hidden the king?"

Ryan spun, his shields and sword rising automatically as Janson's voice grated behind him. He froze as he saw Janson held Princess Elizabeth in his arms, a blade at her throat. He stepped forward only to have Janson press the blade deeper against her throat. Ryan stepped back as he saw the evidence of blood trickling down Elizabeth's throat, staining the white lace collar of her gown bright red.

Elizabeth's eyes locked onto his. "Don't give him the king."

Ryan winced as Janson shook her. "Shut up woman, or despite Kastler wanting you as his consort you'll die here where you stand."

As three of Dashel's wives silently appeared behind Janson, Ryan gathered more of his power to him. Concentrating on the knife at Elizabeth's throat he delicately wrapped the tendrils of his power around the blade.

"You know I can't tell you where His Majesty is Commander, it's my job to protect the king."

As Elizabeth looked relieved, Ryan looked into Janson's eyes and called out to the dagger wives approaching Janson, one quiet step after another from behind with their knives drawn.

Now!

As he yelled that one word Ryan pulled the knife to him with all his strength as Dashel, thinking fast, drew Elizabeth away from her captor into his own arms, as soon as the knife left her throat. Dashel turned shielding her from the view of her attacker with his own body, as Raquel, Natasha and Kaitlyn launched themselves at Janson barely a heartbeat later. Their deadly knives flashed, expertly ending his life before he could even utter a scream.

69

THE BATTLE

Isabella blocked out the battle raging around her, the screams and clash of blades, none of it mattered. Reinforcing her shields she drew her blades focusing on her nemesis.

I am not a child, not his slave, he is not my master anymore.

The words were like a litany in her mind, reminding her not to be afraid of this man. She'd come a long way from the scared little girl she had been. The terrified girl who was taken as a bed slave, who was used as punishment and leverage to ensure her brothers obedience. Making a quick assessment Isabella launched herself through the veil, sweeping in on the Sundered that were clearing Aiden's path for him as he headed in a straight line to the barrier. The way they were behaving she had no doubt that Aiden was directing them somehow. She either dealt with them now or she guessed they would hamper her efforts to destroy her former master.

Isabella cleared her mind and launched herself into the midst of the Sundered, her power shunting them aside, sending them tumbling from the unexpected attack. They rose, screaming in anger as they spun to face her. Isabella ran straight at the one in front of her, blinking at the last moment as she plunged her blades and power into the Sundered one, then drawing them out sideways. She spun around, not waiting to see the top half of the former Kin's body fall separate from the bottom half. Her blades slashed down, flaring with her power slicing through the neck of the next Sundered that closed in on her. She ignored the spray of blood, blinking back into the veil as the third of the Sundered charged at her, screaming in rage as she suddenly wasn't there. She blinked back into the real world, behind the Sundered and before he could spin and face her again she jumped up, her blades clearing his head and she drew them across his neck as she used her power to both pull her back and push him forward.

Isabella assured herself they were dead then looked up scanning for Aiden. He'd fled while she took on the Sundered, as she'd expected. She spotted his trail, he wasn't even trying to hide it now, just making a straight line as fast as he could towards the barrier. Isabella's eyes glinted as she watched the one she'd once been terrified of, flee her. She watched, sucking in air not concerned at all as she watched him run straight at Alex's barrier. She felt a surge of relief and triumph from him as he drew close. She watched as he ran straight into it, she felt it as he registered his pain and shock as he bounced right off.

Isabella drew more power into herself, she was aware she was starting to glow with energy, which would attract attention of the Sundered but she didn't care. She had one goal in her mind. As Aiden spun she knew the moment he spotted her, she saw the fear and panic in his eyes. As she jumped herself across the intervening distance after him, he folded the veil, moving himself back towards the estate house. His own power lashing out at her as he blasted past her caused her to hit the barrier herself. The air exploded from her lungs and she felt the charge of power from the barrier jolt her as she hit it. As she crumpled to the ground, she had a new appreciation for the confining barrier that the Elder Born had spun.

His laughter floated back to her along with his voice. *I will reclaim you. You are mine girl never forget it.*

Isabella shook her head Taking a breath she pushed aside her inner demons that rose in her head as soon as she heard his words. She took a deep breath, feeling the tremors that raced through her, that ancient fear the sound of his voice invoked.

No! I'm not yours any longer.

Isabella flung her own words at him and gathering the veil propelled herself towards him. Feeling her approach he spun, pulling in power himself, thrusting it at her. Isabella paused, allowing his blast to wash over her, unresisting. She heard Aiden's crow of victory as he closed in on her. Allowing herself to be one with the power around her as she'd observed Alex seemed to be able to do. She used that moment and opened herself fully to the power around her, drawing it into her, draining all the power she could from their immediate vicinity.

As Aiden laid hands on her and hauled her into his arms, as she knew he would, she channelled the veil through herself, through the blades that she shoved up under his breastbone towards his heart. His eyes widened and he stiffened as she followed through, channelling the power she pulled from all around her into the man that had possessed her as a child.

That power passed through him and he threw his head back and screamed.

She felt it as her blade pierced his heart and in that moment she felt herself blasted by the combined power they had both channelled. Isabella found herself flung from the veil to crash into the real world on the cobbled courtyard out in front of the Kastler estate. She hit the stones hard, sinking down as pain crashed down on her. Ignoring her screaming muscles, they'd heal, she gritted her teeth and looked up, dark flecks rained down, covering the cobblestones and everyone standing in the courtyard in a black ash, it was all that remained of her adversary.

KYLE CROUCHED over Jess as soon as he made it to her side, the fear he'd felt as soon as he'd known she was in trouble receding. He could see she was breathing and encased in a white shimmering barrier. It was as if a small part of her brain, the self-preservation part was still functioning while the rest of her slept. He stood, drawing his swords and took a quick assessment of the mess around him. His own protection detail had merged seamlessly with Jess's.

He saw Olivia, with two of her people combine efforts to dispatch yet another Sundered almost as soon as it appeared.

Kyle beware the King's Guard, things were in hand and they turned on us. Kyle pulled the veil to himself rising slightly above and joined his efforts to those of Edward and the wild Kin.

Cal? Kyle knew there was a part of him that didn't want to know but knew he had to.

The fight was nearly done when the King's Guard turned on us, they cut him down from behind, while he was shielding the front line. There was raw grief in Edward's mind voice, yet he battled on regardless.

Kyle swore as yet another Sundered popped in above them, as if they all knew Jess was unconscious and vulnerable. He lashed out with his power-fuelled sword, not even waiting to watch it drop before he turned scanning his surroundings.

Spying a group of healers off to one side near the estate house, Kyle called out.

Olivia?

The woman turned her head to look at him. *Yes Fourth's Blade?*

Can you and your people take out the healers? They control the Sundered.

Olivia looked over where he indicated the cluster of healers over to one side of the main courtyard. A chilling smile lit Olivia's face.

It would be our pleasure Fourth's Blade!

Kyle's eyes widened. *Try not to kill them if you don't have to.*

Olivia looked back at him, her mouth downturned as if he'd just taken all the fun out of her day. Olivia gathered her small band of wild Kin and they all made a straight line towards the healers. With a rather effective blast of power, the unsuspecting healers were knocked unconscious.

Kyle spun, seeing some of the Sundered Ones slump to the ground, stopping right where they were and not heeding any danger to themselves. Others screamed in mindless rage and started lashing out indiscriminately around them. Damien and Edward both drew the veil, popping around the battlefield with their own group of guards containing and taking down the Sundered that remained dangerous.

They gave barely a cursory glance at those that had slumped to the ground with vacant faces. They'd deal with those who seemed to be a threat first. Those others could wait.

Kyle added his own efforts to the others, helping to clean out the last of the Sundered that were fighting. Once that was done they should be able to help their men fight against the threat the members of the King's Guard had become.

Alex stared at Amelia and Kevin, trying to understand why they were both gloating. Why they were both staring at him as if they were waiting for something momentous to happen. Then he remembered Jess's warning, about the dual poisons they'd used on her to prevent her reaching her powers and his face paled. A look of confusion crossed Amelia's face and she seemed to stumble. Throwing up a shield Alex dismissed the pair for now and turned his attention inward. He traced that which was not a part of him as it raced through his system. His current exertions weren't helping to keep the two poisons apart.

Drawing on his power Alex focused on the poisons in his body, and in a twist of the method he'd used to cleanse himself of the bonds Amelia had placed in him, he sent that white, silvery power inside himself, using it to flush the poison out of his body. As the power raced through him. Alex became aware of another battle that raged nearby. Alex looked at his enemies only to see Amelia had turned on Kevin. The smirk had faded from Kevin's face as the man fought against her.

Alex could barely contain his shock but continued working leeching the poisons from his system. He smiled in triumph as the poison formed, droplet by droplet into small balls suspended in front of his face, held there, encased by a white glowing ball. Alex felt a blast of energy from Kevin and winced, yet it didn't hit his own shields. Alex looked up and saw Amelia stiffen and collapse to the ground. Kevin turned to him.

You'll make a fine replacement for the loss of my slave, Fourth!

Alex looked up, catching Kevin's eyes and saw the triumph fade to be replaced by panic as he realised what the two balls of fiery liquid were that floated in front of Alex. Alex's eyes narrowed and the balls of power containing their cargo hurtled across the intervening space and speared into Kevin, piercing his skin with ease. When the balls were in Kevin's body the fiery spheres of power joined and then burst. Alex's power then sped, spreading combined poison throughout Kevin's body.

"You think you've won Fourth? It will be a hollow victory. What a shame you left your brother all alone in the palace." Kevin spat the words at him, although it would have been more effective if he wasn't looking panicked, mind desperately trying to grasp at power that he couldn't use, finally trapped in his own mind.

"Marcus, keep a guard on Kevin, although he shouldn't be able to use his powers for a little bit. His own poison should keep him contained." Alex waited until Marcus nodded and detailed two of his men to stand over Kevin.

Alex frowned and then he paled, turning around he saw the battle still raged on around him even though most of the Sundered appeared to have slumped where they stood. Yet still people were fighting, dying.

Alex scanned the battlefield, spotting who he wanted over the far side near the estate house and called out.

Olivia, I need your assistance!

It didn't take long before Olivia appeared before him, her eyes taking in Amelia slumped on the ground, her eyes vacant. Then her eyes narrowed as she spotted Kevin under the watchful gaze of the Elite.

"He can't access his powers right now, but can you assist my Elite in keeping watch over him?"

"You aren't planning that he stay alive after all he's done I hope Fourth?" The woman's dark eyes turned to Kevin then back to him.

"No, but I feel another has more right to pass judgement on him." Alex gazed at her calmly.

"Very well Fourth, but if he even looks like being able to use his powers he will die." Olivia's eyes narrowed.

Alex nodded, then his gaze rested on Amelia his smile fading. "Can you keep watch over Amelia as well. Ensure no one else harms her. If they do or even look like they might, you have my permission to kill them."

Olivia glanced at Amelia where she sat, staring vacantly and her expression sobered.

"As you command Fourth. There are many here, our Kin, who did not deserve their fates."

Alex nodded his thanks then turned back to the battle, without even having to think about it he jumped between where he was and where he knew Kyle and Jess were. He'd think about exactly how he'd known where his friends were later. As the screams and clash of blades rang out all around him Alex grimaced, throwing up a barrier between him and those that battled.

He knelt down beside Jess where she lay, a shimmering bubble of power around her.

"She's alive." Kyle knelt down on the other side.

Alex looked up at Kyle and nodded before returning his gaze back to Jess. Alex closed his eyes and called the veil to him, then pushed it down into Jess.

Jess, my friend, wake up. We can all sleep later.

Alex watched as the breath caught and her chest heaved, before settling back down.

We need you. Alex breathed more energy into her.

She gasped as the power he'd gathered rushed into her, sitting upright her eyes flaring silver. Finally they stood. Alex was aware they were all channelling the veil, power flaring from them. They didn't have to think about it, or consult as their power arched out connecting with Edward on one side of them and Kat on the other. The power flowed out from them to Damien and Isabella, linking them all together. As they rose up above the battle the sky darkened and lightning cracked and ran across the dome of the barrier above the Kastler estate.

As the battle lines paused, the enemy flinching back at the display above them Alex took control of their combined energy and thrust it out. As the power rolled out over those who fought like a wave, lightning cracked down, the ground exploding, chunks of grass, earth and rock flew into the air. Tendrils of power flooded out over the fighting force. Men and women slumped with gasps of pain as energy hammered into them and they collapsed into the ground.

Alex had a moment, a very brief one, to feel satisfied before his eyes widened. A wave of power splashed up the barrier before crashing back down and rolling back towards them. Throwing up his hands in an instinctive reaction, his protective barrier strengthened and expanded to cover himself and their people. He breathed a sigh of relief as he saw his friends do the same. The very air around them thrummed, the veil sparking and flaring as it rolled back over them all to the far side.

Taking a breath Alex exerted himself, urging the veil to settle, drawing as much as he could of it back into himself. There was that moment, the moment where the silence was deafening. Then the moaning of the injured started. Their day wasn't finished yet.

Alex looked at Jess and Kyle; they flung their arms around each other, taking a moment to share their mutual grief. Over not only the loss of life but their relief that they had survived it, the screams of those around them receding into the background.

Once they'd freed their own people from their fiery cages Alex turned his gaze to the dome above them that still contained the Kastler estate. He grimaced and jerked his head up at it.

"Feel up to helping me deal with that? Otherwise none of us will be going anywhere." Alex smiled despite himself as Kyle and Jess nodded.

Alex transported himself into the veiled world with Kyle and Jess appearing next to him. Not that any of them really needed to; they could have taken it down while still in the real world. Power flowed to him a lot easier from the veil, and he felt it was an advantage they could all use.

Kyle and Jess both grinned back at him and, opening themselves up further to the veil, they drew in more power.

Let's get this done, Alex. I have a feeling none of us are too far off having to collapse in a bed. The fatigue was evident in Kyle's mind voice.

With the three of them drawing in energy, the veil around them began to surge and rumble in response once more. Alex opened himself up further, this time pulling more of that pure white power that had terrified him the first time he'd encountered it. It rushed into him, spreading comforting warmth through him. Alex knew that to another's eyes he'd be glowing with the power filling him, as it burst through and ran along his skin. Bolts of power rained down all around them, striking with loud booms. Alex paid it no mind, knowing none of it would hurt like it used to—not any more.

He glanced from Kyle to Jess, noting they both glowed, their forms blending in and becoming indistinct from the power they both channelled.

All right, my friends, let's bring this barrier down.

On his command, the three of them unleashed their combined power on the barrier, seizing it in their mental grip and pounding away at it. At first the shield, being a thing of living power, tried to resist the change they were willing on it. Then it started to buckle. With a groan, the wall started to undulate, running the length and breadth of it. Alex, seeing the tiny points of light shimmering through the wall, narrowed his eyes. He thrust the power he held at the small pinpricks of light. As he hammered at it, the holes became bigger, with large rents looking like they were peeling back.

With a final ear-splitting shriek, the wall gave way, bursting outwards under their combined assault. Alex fell to his knees as the shockwave hit him, the vibrations rushing out over the world. He looked at the wave of power rolling out over the land and looked at his friends a little wide-eyed. Sensing another explosion, he threw up a hasty shield covering them all as a shockwave rebounded in their direction.

Alex looked up and grinned weakly.

Oops.

Kyle and Jess chuckled under their breath.

70

JUDGEMENT

William appeared in the courtyard where Lord Kastler had been dragged along with the identified minor lords that had joined in his rebellion against the Crown. He thanked Ryan who'd transported him here once Alex had given the all clear. Rosalinda and the Dagger Wives that had defended him in the veil spread out in an arc behind him. Rosalinda had flatly refused to be left behind given the treachery of the King's Guard. He looked around, his eyes settling on the lords who'd turned traitor, they were all bound awaiting his judgement. Lord Kastler's mouth popped open and colour drained from his face. Then he started struggling, looking around trying to gain support from those watching.

"See? He's unfit to rule, he's one of the monsters!" Lord Kastler swayed as one of the guards holding him cuffed him on the back of the head.

On William's approach the guard on the other side of the traitor struck the back of his legs, causing his knees to buckle. They pushed him down onto his knees.

William stopped, looking down at the man who only months earlier had pledged his fealty to him at his coronation.

"Is there any compelling reason why I should spare your life, Alfred?" William heard the bite in his own tone, making no effort to hide his anger.

"I denounce you. You're no king of mine, just a monster," Kastler spat.

The guards behind him reacted promptly, one cuffing him over the back of the head. With his hands tied behind his back, Kastler screamed as he went face first onto the paved courtyard. The other guard leaned forward and grabbed him by his hair and hauled him back up. He moaned, blood running freely from his nose.

William shook his head. "There is a monster, there has been since before the Sundered War, and it is the Killiam Order."

"You'd say anything to cover your perfidy, false king!" Alfred's eyes were wide and bulging.

"Lord Alfred Kastler, you are guilty of treason. I hereby strip you of your rank, lands and holdings, which revert to the Crown. You will pay for your crimes with your life." William waved off the guard who stepped forward to carry out the sentence.

As far as he was concerned, if he was going to order the death of one of his own lords, then he needed to be willing to kill the man himself. William put his hand on his hilt and realised it was his ceremonial blade. It was fully functional, but not really designed with this grisly work in mind.

Alex drew his own sword and took a knee, offering it up. William gravely took Alex's blade, noting almost absently his brother had made time to clean it off. Alex stood and backed up a step.

Use the veil, channel the energy to reinforce the blade and increase your own strength, just as you've practiced in training.

William acknowledged Alex's guidance with a nod of his head. Taking a breath, he drew energy into himself, allowing the intoxicating feeling to fill him. The blade sprang to life as he willed power into it.

He drew his arm back and swung with all his strength. Kastler's scream was cut off abruptly the blade sliced through the traitor's neck without even a hint of resistance. William didn't flinch as the blood spurt; he'd somehow forgotten about the blood. Alex and Kyle hadn't, as they threw up hasty shields to protect him and the guards. The headless body toppled to the pavement with a dull thud. William glanced down at the blood trailing down the blade in his hand, a drop forming on the tip and dripping down to join the growing pool on the ground.

He looked up from the body to those who looked on. Silence had settled on the other captives, fear weighing heavily on the courtyard as they realised their coming fate. Three of the lord minors had survived the fight.

The guards yanked their head back as William walked towards them, sword in hand.

ALEX WATCHED as his brother passed judgement on his lords and they paid for their acts with their lives. The last person left shackled and kneeling on the cobbles of the courtyard, watched over by members of the Elite was Kevin. William looked back at him holding out the sword.

"Fourth, I cede this one to you for all the harm he has caused, should you wish to pass final judgment." William's face was calm, the pulse of his anger not as heated yet still simmering in the background.

"Thank you, Your Majesty." Alex walked forward and reclaimed his sword without ceremony, then glanced across at Edward, the other's grief at the loss of one of his long-term companions still evident. “I think there is another who has a greater claim, should he wish it and you permit?”

Alex looked over to Edward who looked to William.

“Edward Jonathan Rathadon, former Fourth, during the time of the Sundered War. Do you claim right to pass judgement over this one, who once rode in your Companion’s Cohort?” William’s voice carried across the courtyard and all eyes turned to Edward.

Edward swallowed and walked slowly forward and bowed. “Thank you my King, I will.”

Edward drew his own sword and closed the distance between him and Kevin. The blade shone with power as it sliced through his neck. The only sound in the courtyard was the thump of Kevin’s head on the ground.

“King William, Fourth I’m sorry that I did not see what he was capable of, the harm he would do.”

Edward looked at both of them, regret showing clearly in his eyes, before he nodded and walked back to his place at Kat’s side.

MASTER HEALER AARON watched with a heavy heart as the king dispensed his judgement on the rebel lords, all of them paying with their lives. As a healer he found the loss of life distressing, but he steeled his heart. These men had committed treason and had led others in the same. Lives, both human and Kin, had been destroyed for generations due to the atrocities committed by the Killiam Order. William could have sat back and others could have carried out his sentence, but he took the burden on himself. If you held another's fate in your hands, you should at least have the decency to face them with valour.

“Try to reach for my mind again and you won’t live long enough to face the king’s judgment,” Kyle growled, his eyes still glowing with power as he looked at one of the prisoners he held.

The Guild Master inspected the other prisoners being watched over by Alex and Kyle.

"Does anyone speak up for these ones?" William's voice was cool, like he was discussing the weather rather than determining whether someone should live or die.

Aaron stirred, walking forward and taking his cue from the Fourth's attitude earlier. If anything, that had flagged William's mood. He sank to his knee, a clear supplicant.

"My liege, on behalf of the Healers' Guild I beg mercy for these ones and ask that they be transferred to our care."

William turned to pin him with a cool gaze. "On what grounds do they deserve our mercy?"

"Their healer bonds were corrupted by one in the position of power over them when they were but junior trainees, my king. They had no choice after what he did to their minds." Aaron fought the urge to explain; he was aware William knew all of these details.

"What do you propose to do with them?" William glanced over at the former healers and back at him.

"Put them in care. Reset their bonds. When we are certain of their rehabilitation, they will be put to work under the guidance of a senior healer. They will make amends for the damage done, even though it was at the will of another." Aaron didn't take his eyes off William.

The Master Healers had debated long and hard over what should be done if any of the suborned healers survived. They'd come to the heartrending conclusion that even though their actions were not of their choosing, the former healers could not be trusted again. They had helped destroy the lives of thousands of Kin from across Vallantia who'd done nothing but be born with power. There had been very little reprieve for the Sundered kind, for the most part driven to death in this battle by those controlling them. After everything the healers had done, if the king spared them, they would be closely supervised and spend the remainder of their lives in service to the people of Vallantia.

William glanced at the Master Healers arrayed behind him. "Are you ready to take them into the custody of the Healers' Guild now?"

"Yes, my liege."

"I haven't forgotten the Healers' Guild's role in this mess. Those acts may be buried in our history, but you will advise your Guild Master never to act against the Crown or the people of Vallantia again, even by omission." William's tone brooked no resistance.

"You have our pledge, my liege. We regret deeply that research by the Healers' Guild wrought so much pain and death." Aaron remembered his horror when he'd discovered in the old sealed reports that the Healers' Guild was ultimately responsible for the Sundered and the Killiam Order both.

Aaron knew the Head Guild Master had pored over the reports himself, hoping the results were wrong, only to come to the sickening conclusion that it really had been the old healing guild research that had unleashed the Sundered plague on them all. The Head Guild Master in that day should have come clean about what they'd done and certainly should have kept a closer eye on Gail Killiam. The list of symptoms in the reports had pointed clearly to their medication being used, yet the Guild in that day had hidden their own involvement in releasing that madness-inflicted horde out of fear.

The king regarded him for such a long time that Aaron began to worry despite knowing that William was a reasonable man. He shifted uncomfortably as the stones of the courtyard started biting into his knees, yet he knew as a supplicant begging a favour he couldn't stand until the king gave him his response and permission to stand.

"They are victims as well, although that does not pardon their guilt. Take them, rehabilitate them if you can. If any of them harm another again, their lives will be forfeit." William indicated he could rise.

Aaron sighed in relief, accepting the assistance of one of his Master Healers to stand. It was at least a little more graceful than he feared it would have been if he'd try to stand by himself. He bowed, and the king dismissed him, so he gathered his Master Healers to him and went to take charge of the prisoners. As they approached, he paused to raise his hands to his heart, then to his forehead, acknowledging the Fourth and his Companions.

The Healers' Guild owed them a great deal for their intervention. He shuddered thinking of the damage that would have been done to their ranks if they hadn't uncovered the traitor in their midst. That one of the Kin could infiltrate the Guild and remain hidden for all those years represented a massive failing —one that was being rectified.

Alex nodded acknowledgement and gestured to the prisoners he was assisting to contain. "They are all yours, Healer. We will release them from the shields we are maintaining once you have them under your control."

"Be warned, they are fighting the restraint we have on them even though it doesn't look like it." Kyle grimaced and stepped aside as one of his healers went to stand in front of one of the corrupted healers, placing his hands firmly on the woman's temples.

"Yes, thank you for the warning, Lord Kyle. We can see they are resisting all of you. We will get them under control and release you from this burden." Aaron nodded at his people.

They each closed the distance between them and one of their former colleagues and dove into the others' minds without question. All of them were well aware of the need to gain control quickly. If these ones escaped their care before they had the chance to repair the damage done to their minds, their lives would be forfeit.

Aaron watched on as his people completed their work, his lips a thin line. They had a heavy task ahead in making sure no one in the Guild could be taken like this again. The knowledge they had failed to protect junior trainees in the Guild's care, allowed them to sink under the control of another, weighed heavily on them all. He would ensure it never happened again.

Each of the prisoners sank into a deep sleep under the compulsion of the healers. Some of Aaron's colleagues rushed forward with stretchers, and the prisoners were moved carefully onto them and bindings secured them to their beds. There would be no chance of escape for these ones.

Aaron looked over at the even smaller group, huddled together on the ground with a few of the Elite standing guard over them: the small handful of Sundered who'd survived the death of their controllers, their masters. He could feel the emanations coming from their minds; the ability to reason and communicate had fled them. All that was left of them was the shells of their bodies that had survived. Aaron closed his eyes and took a deep breath, turning back to his king.

"Your Majesty, I beg one more boon of you, although it may test your patience."

He was about to sink to his knees again, but stopped at a gesture from William.

"What favour do you seek from the Crown, Aaron?" William's voice was steady and without a hint of emotion, his face expressionless.

"Those few broken Sundered that survived. Sanity has fled them and I fear there is nothing we can do to repair the damage to their minds. Let us take the burden of those ones into our care, for as long as they should continue to live."

William looked over to the small huddled group. None of them tried to escape. Indeed, none of them seemed capable of it. Amongst their number was Amelia, the former Consort Elect of the Fourth, rocking slowly back and forth, her eyes just as vacant as those that sat with her.

"Take them and care for them well. Like your surviving healers, these did great harm, but choice in this fight was taken from them."

Aaron bowed as William turned away, obviously dismissing him. Given the fate of the traitorous lords, he had feared the worst for these remaining few.

ALEX'S EYES settled on Amelia and he felt as if he'd been stabbed in the heart at the sight of her, sitting on the ground, staring straight ahead rocking back and forth, broken.

"Wait, healer." Alex spoke softly and with effort pushed himself off the wall he'd been leaning on.

The healer who'd been about to lead Amelia away stopped and looked at him a question in his eyes as he backed away on Alex's approach. Alex knelt in front of Amelia, brushing a strand of hair that had escaped her braid from her face. He leant forward and gently brushed his lips against her forehead.

You gave what little of you was left for me in the end. I probably would have fallen to Kevin if you hadn't fought. Thank you. He spoke softly into her mind although he knew she wasn't able to respond.

All that remained inside the shell of her body was the image flickering in her head of a crazed young girl in a dirty ripped shift that was too big for her, matted hair covering her face. She rocked back and forth in a cell, isolated, her rail-thin arms raised with her palms pressed against her eyes, locked in the madness of her own mind.

Isabella had said she'd been under the domination and mind

control of another too long to be able to survive. That coupled with the power Kevin had blasted at her during the battle had destroyed the spark of her that had survived the Order's torture and tampering. There was very little of Amelia left, with the various shells of the personas she'd worn most of her life stripped away. The only true part of her remained—just the terrified little girl who'd been betrayed and taken as a child. A child consumed by madness after being locked away from the world since childhood. He looked over at Kyle, and his friend looked haunted.

He walked forward and dropping to his knee he pulled Amelia's unresponsive form into his arms, resting his cheek against the top of her head.

I'm sorry little sister, I'm sorry I didn't try as hard to save you as you did to save us. Tears traced their way down his cheek as he grieved for her.

Isabella walked forward and placed her hands lightly on Amelia's temples. Alex watched as the cell in Amelia's mind rippled away to be replaced by a room, with rich furnishings. Instead of sitting on a cold stone floor she now sat on a fine rug, her hair was groomed and piled on her head in an intricate design. Her torn and dirty shift replace by a beautiful, deep green gown threaded with gold and silver thread. The coronet, necklace and bracelet signifying her as the Consort Elect of the Fourth once again adorned her.

"It won't last, but it's better than a cell." Isabella looked sad and backed off.

The healer moved forward and checked Isabella's handiwork.

"Ah, that is a kindness Lady Isabella. We will ensure it does last." The healer smiled and nodded.

Alex took the hint and climbed to his feet as did Kyle backing away to allow the healer to take his charge.

"Is that what would have happened to me? If I'd stayed

bound to Joanna and anything had happened to her?" Kyle swallowed and looked from Isabella to Aaron.

Isabella looked grim. "Yes, Kyle, you were almost lost as it was. Those taken as thralls lose their ability to function without a master or mistress."

Alex frowned. "Yet the healers seem fine."

Aaron shook his head. "What was done to Amelia and those like her is not the same as what we do with the healer trainees."

"How is it different, healer?" William had calmed down by now, and seemed merely curious.

"We do not enslave the minds of those with the healer's gift, Your Majesty. We simply put compulsions on them not to harm others with their gifts."

"That is why you think you can help the healers whose bonds were broken?" Alex looked over towards the corrupted healers who sat in a group together under the watchful gaze of Aaron's people and some of the Elite.

"Yes, Fourth. It's not quite the same thing."

"What will you do with her?" Kyle's voice was soft as he watched Amelia being guided to sit in the back of a carriage.

"We will settle her in a room in the Healers' Guild. She and the others will be confined but well cared for, for as long as they survive. In their current states they don't have the ability to cause any further harm."

"She's still powerful, Aaron. Should she recover enough to use the veil, she could be a risk to you all."

"With what is left of her mind, I do not believe she will ever have that capability, Your Highness. We will closely monitor all of the surviving Sundered and take steps should it prove necessary." Aaron's assessment was blunt. He turned to walk away, but paused to turn back at the last. "Be assured we will continue to seek a cure, but we are not hopeful."

71

A LIFT

Alex leaned in the shade of the wall, trying to make it look like he wasn't monitoring his brother. He figured he was failing miserably, aware that Kyle and Jess were doing the same. His brother's simmering anger that had been bubbling away below the surface since William found out about some of his lords turning traitor had started to dissipate, although he suspected William was more angry at them leading their people to death in a pointless war. All of them had tried their hardest not to kill everyone they were lined up against—not an easy task when those same people showed no similar compunctions. Still, in credit to their own forces, they had done a remarkable job.

Hearing of the events that had transpired in the palace Alex suspected he'd still be seething with anger himself at the commander and his men turning traitor both in the palace and here, if he'd had the energy to sustain it. As it turned out, all he wanted to do was get back to the palace and collapse in bed, before he collapsed out here. He suspected Kyle and Jess were in no better shape than he was.

He glanced over to where Aaron and his healers were busy

with the wounded. They had placed their charges, the ones the king's mercy had spared, in a healer-induced sleep so they could tend to the wounded.

The Acting Commander of the combined forces of the various loyal lords stepped forward and bowed smartly.

"The rest of the prisoners are all restrained, Your Majesty."

"See they are transported to the palace. Do we have space in the cells for them all?" William frowned, looking out to the grounds below with the rank upon rank of household guards who'd followed their lords into treason, and those who had been members of the King's Guard who'd turned traitor.

The Acting Commander shook his head in response. "We'll construct some temporary cells, Your Majesty."

Alex watched as William dismissed the Acting Commander, sending the man off to dispatch his own orders to his men.

"What will be done with them all?" Alex spoke quietly, for his brother's ears only.

William glanced at him. "If the healers can assist in determining the truth for those that hold with their master's viewpoint, they'll join their lords in death. If they simply followed the instructions of their command, they'll be given a choice: serve or die."

Alex considered William's assessment and in the current moment, with the heat of battle only just starting to fade, it seemed to be a fair compromise. He clapped his brother on the shoulder.

"Fair enough. How are you?"

William looked at him and smiled bitterly. "It had to be done. If I couldn't do it myself, I had no right to ask it of you or anyone else."

Alex ducked his head. "Yes you do. It's one of the perks of being the king. You have plenty of minions to do your bidding."

William gestured to the lines of shackled prisoners. "With those ones, another can carry out the judgement. For my forsworn lords? For aligning with all of this? Even with the knowledge they had of what the Order was doing and the assassination of Father? No. That is a sentence that I had to carry out myself."

Alex looked around and nodded, seeing that everything was in order.

"With your permission William, let's get back to the palace, before I create a scene and pass out here." Alex grinned tiredly at William's startled look. "If someone has the energy to transport us, at least. I fear I'll collapse if I try even such a simple thing right now."

William's startled look turned to one of concern as he nodded and after issuing his last few orders he finally indicated he was ready. After a quick conversation it was Isabella and Damien who pulled them all into the veil and transported them back to the palace.

72

NEW LIFE

William walked into the inner sanctum of his suite, sighing with relief as the heavy doors shut behind him. The weeks since the battle had been intense neither the world nor duty stopped just because you wanted a break from the turmoil.

Still, he was relieved. Reports were filtering in that Vallantia was returning to normal. Those that had fled their homes for the dubious safety of the bigger towns were going back to their communities. New lords and ladies had been acknowledged to take up the forfeited lands and titles of those forsworn.

He was even starting to come to terms with his unwanted powers. He may not have wanted that additional burden, but it was his now regardless of what he wanted. To his relief they made little difference to his life right now, it wasn't like he had much power anyway.

William walked straight through the other rooms to his bedroom, starting to take off his cloak, only to pause as another hand grabbed the heavy garment from him.

"Allow me, William." Rosalinda's dark eyes stared up at

him for a moment before she turned and placed the garment on a hook by the door.

William stood, stunned. He licked his lips as she walked gracefully forward and rose up on the balls of her feet to remove his crown, turning to place it on its pedestal. William knew that Shaun, who seemed to be missing, would appear at some point to put everything away.

"Rosalinda. I'm sorry, I haven't been trying to ignore you..." He stopped as she placed her fingers on his lips.

Smiling, she drew him deeper into the room, and pausing near the bed she looked up at him through her eyelashes.

"I know you haven't, but I'm told things are starting to calm down." Her voice was low and husky.

William found himself unaccountably nervous as he looked at her and finally noticed she was only wearing a brief shift of flowing silk that didn't leave much to his imagination. He found his face heating up as she reached up and started to unbutton his shirt, peeling it off slowly. She looked up at him again and her fingers made quick work of the fastenings on his trousers.

"It's time we conceived an heir." Her hand ran up his chest.

William swallowed. He reached with one hand and pulled at the ribbons that bound her silk gown before he could think too much about it. The silk slid smoothly from her and pooled at her feet. He picked her up, turning around and placing her on the bed.

"This could take some practice."

Rosalinda smiled and reaching up to pull his head down for a kiss. William decided that Vallantia and its worries could look after itself for a time. Rosalinda was right. He needed an heir, and he suspected that this wouldn't be the most arduous of his duties as king, and in fact might be one of the few he actually enjoyed.

~

WILLIAM NODDED his thanks to the Elite as he passed between them and entered his brother's rooms in the Complex of the Fourth. His face fell as he looked down on his brother's still sleeping form.

Alex, Jess and Kyle had all fallen into a deep sleep on their return to the palace. It seemed Alex hadn't been joking when he'd said he wanted to get back before he collapsed. He had only the assurance of the healers that they all still lived. Thankfully for his state of mind, Isabella had reassured him and hadn't seemed worried. She'd pointed out to him that Damien had fallen into such a state for weeks after putting the barrier up around Ilarith. He'd eventually woken up unharmed by his prolonged slumber.

William turned as Isabella walked into the room from the gardens beyond. She smiled and kissed him on the cheek.

"How is Rosalinda this morning?"

William grinned. "Cursing my name. It's all my fault she feels so sick, apparently. I don't know, I distinctly remember it was all her idea."

Isabella's eyes sparkled. "I'll make sure to call on her. The healers confirm everything is well?"

"Yes, the twins are growing as they should."

Isabella's eyes widened. "Twins? When did you find out?"

William nodded. "The healers informed me they detected the split from one life force to two this morning."

He had been a little shocked by the announcement and ordered the healers not to let Rosalinda out of their sight—an order that his Consort had immediately countermanded with a disgusted look in his direction. She'd informed him she was pregnant, not dying, before shooing him out of his own bedroom, which she seemed to have taken up permanent residence in. Actually she seemed to have taken it on herself to rule the entire royal wing. She bossed around the servants and guards and, not so coincidentally, William himself, when he was in his suite. When he allowed himself to think about it, he was stunned to find he didn't actually mind. She'd created a haven for him where the lords and ladies who'd previously treated his private domain as their own, coming and going as they desired, suddenly showed a little more restraint.

"Twins? How long have I been sleeping?"

William spun to see his brother curled onto his side, staring up at him with a grin on his face. William closed his eyes briefly as relief flooded him. Isabella swept past him and climbed up on the bed, throwing her arms around Alex. William smiled. It seems she had not been as blasé about the length of Alex's sleep as she'd pretended.

"Just over a month."

Alex held Isabella close and looked up at her, his eyes wide in shock. "A month? Um... sorry." He grinned, not looking apologetic at all. "Didn't mean to. Congratulations. The impending birth of your heirs lets Elizabeth and myself off the hook, and I'm sure she's as grateful as I am."

"Thank Rosalinda." William shrugged. "It was all her idea. I am king of the entire realm, but she is in charge in the royal wing." He chuckled.

The first lord Rosalinda had thrown out of their domain had been a little stunned, but had not dared to burst in again. He'd sent a messenger and made an appointment before seeing the king ever since.

"Your Majesty, Lord Kyle and Lady Jessalan are both awake as well." Aaron came hobbling into the room. "I guess there is no point in telling you to take it easy?"

Alex laughed. "Not in the slightest. I feel fine, if a little shocked at the whole slept-for-a-month thing."

Alex looked over as his doors opened again and Kyle burst into his rooms with Jess firmly in hand, followed by harried-looking healers who stopped just inside the door. Both of the healers looked shame-faced and a little alarmed that their patients had managed to escape their care.

Kyle and Jess clambered up on the bed with Alex and Isabella, all of them grinning at each other, looking for all the world like they'd regressed to childhood. William looked at them and groaned. Now that they were awake he couldn't imagine it would take much time for the three of them to find trouble. That, or trouble would find them.

~

ALEX LOOKED around the clearing he'd burnt out what seemed a lifetime ago.

"You don't do anything by halves, do you Alex?" Jess grinned at him.

The great forest was never held back for long and regrowth was spreading in a startling fashion. The previously blackened earth he'd left behind him now had trees and shrubs growing back, the patches of green startling against the black.

"Shall we?" Kyle looked at him

Smiling, Alex nodded and transferred to the veil with both Kyle and Jess, yet they stayed in this recovering devastation he'd wrought. Closing his eyes, he allowed the power to flow into him, aware that both Jess and Kyle did the same. Peace, calmness, and a sense of right descended on him—unlike previously, when he'd been blinded in pain and agony, his body and mind still in transition and unable to cope with the seemingly ever-increasing power. He knew to another's eyes they'd all be radiating power right now, more than most could hold, and he knew they weren't even trying at this stage. That was about to change.

Alex opened his eyes and drew that pure white energy into himself, then funnelled it out, willing it to take shape. Energy rumbled and cracked all around them, but they ignored it. It couldn't cause him or Kyle or Jess any harm now. Around them the veil rippled, and out of that power they spun a vast estate house. The grounds around erupted as trees grew fully formed, vines stretching between them, and grass sprouted up out of the ground in a wave covering the blackened earth. Cobbled pathways seemingly formed out of nothing, winding about manicured gardens—a replica of the gardens of the royal palace in Callenhain. The three of them spun higher in the air and looked down on their handiwork. Their very own palace glittered below, lit with the burning colours of the setting sun.

Amberbreak stood in the distance, with an impenetrable thick forest between Alex's new retreat and one of his favourite places in the realm. His eyes narrowed, and the earth groaned, the crack of splitting lumber sounded, and a paved pathway formed between this place and the outskirts of the village. He had no doubt that the villagers would discover it eventually.

Taking a deep breath, he concentrated once more, feeling power from both Kyle and Jess join his as a shield formed like a bubble around their new retreat, keyed to allow a few—a *very* few—of their kind entry. Others of lesser ability would be shut out, unless they granted passage. This place would serve as a sanctuary for those with power, especially those who needed training. It would be a refuge for those of their own kind going through transition, should they want it.

Of course, the fact that it stood out here on the tri-border was no coincidence. Rosalinda was absolutely certain that her father would have a tantrum when he worked out his carefully laid plans hadn't worked. Alex doubted her Emperor-Father would find it terribly amusing. Perhaps the Elder Born being camped out on his doorstep might just give him pause.

He looked at his lifelong friends and grinned. It would be years yet before he judged they would feel like retreating from the world, that time when they, like their relatives before them, would stand aside to allow others to pick up the burden of duty, but at least they had a place prepared for that day.

Alex knew the shockwaves from their crafting were rolling through the veiled world. He had no doubt that the shock would assault some minds and knock them into unconsciousness. Those of power would sit up and take notice, their eyes turning to assess those who caused the world to tremble.

They would know that the Elder Born had come into their own and entered the world.

ALSO BY CATHERINE M WALKER

THE BEING OF DREAMS

Shattering Dreams

Path Of The Broken

Elder Born

EMERGENCE (Available late 2021)

Unwanted (Coming)

Sacrifice (Coming)

Defiance (Coming)

NEWSLETTER

If you'd like updates of my progress, promotions and advance notice of when the next book comes out drop by my website and join my newsletter.

You'll receive a copy of the character chart that I created while I was writing the Shattering Dreams and a few other extras as well.

Visit my website to get started!

Catherine M Walker